LAETITIA RODD
AND THE CASE
OF THE WANDERING
SCHOLAR

ALSO BY KATE SAUNDERS

The Secrets of Wishtide

LAETITIA RODD AND THE CASE OF THE WANDERING SCHOLAR

KATE SAUNDERS

BLOOMSBURY PUBLISHING
NEW YORK • LONDON • OXFORD • NEW DELHI • SYDNEY

BLOOMSBURY PUBLISHING
Bloomsbury Publishing Inc
1385 Broadway, New York, NY 10018, USA

BLOOMSBURY, BLOOMSBURY PUBLISHING, and the Diana logo are
trademarks of Bloomsbury Publishing Plc

First published in 2019 in Great Britain
First published in the United States 2019

Bloomsbury Publishing Plc does not have any control over, or responsibility for, any
third-party websites referred to or in this book. All internet addresses given in this
book were correct at the time of going to press. The author and publisher regret any
inconvenience caused if addresses have changed or sites have ceased to exist, but can
accept no responsibility for any such changes.

ISBN: HB: 978-1-63286-838-1; TPB: 978-1-63286-839-8; eBook: 978-1-63286-840-4

Library of Congress Cataloging-in-Publication Data has been applied for

2 4 6 8 10 9 7 5 3 1

Typeset by Integra Software Services Pvt. Ltd.
Printed and bound in the U.S.A. by Berryville Graphics Inc., Berryville, Virginia

To find out more about our authors and books visit www.bloomsbury.com
and sign up for our newsletters.

Bloomsbury books may be purchased for business or promotional use.
For information on bulk purchases please contact Macmillan Corporate and
Premium Sales Department at specialmarkets@macmillan.com.

To the memory of my dear friend, Nick Henderson

Come, let me read the oft-read tale again!
The story of the Oxford scholar poor,
Of pregnant parts and quick inventive brain,
Who, tired of knocking at preferment's door,
One summer morn forsook
His friends, and went to learn the gipsy-lore,
And roam'd the world with that wild brotherhood.

Matthew Arnold, '*The Scholar Gipsy*'

Every door is barred with gold, and opens but to golden keys.

Alfred Tennyson, '*Locksley Hall*'

He told how murderers walk the earth
Beneath the curse of Cain –
With crimson clouds before their eyes,
And flames about their brain;
For blood has left upon their souls
Its everlasting stain!

Thomas Hood, '*The Dream of Eugene Aram*'

One

THE MORNING AIR WAS warm and tender, filled with the scents of May: the wild grasses and flowers on Hampstead Heath, and the ripening hayfields beyond. Mrs Bentley and I had taken our work out into the back garden, to bask in the sun like a pair of lizards; she was shelling peas, I was darning a stocking. It was one of those golden days when the heart simply rises up and even the greatest sorrows fall away.

I was rather proud of that little garden, though it was nothing more than a tiny strip of grass bounded by sooty brick walls. When I moved into Mrs Bentley's house in Well Walk, two or three years before the time of which I am writing, there had been no garden at all; merely a dank yard behind the wash house. Once upon a time, as wife of an archdeacon presiding over a comfortable establishment in Bloomsbury, I had employed a gardener. As an impoverished widow, I was now forced to do the work myself – but I am country-born, and knew well how to make things grow. My dear mother gave us each a patch of garden to tend; my brother's quickly turned into a blasted heath, but I loved grubbing about with my trowel – I will never forget how proud I was when Papa praised my first lettuce.

I took a cutting from the climbing rose in my brother's large garden in Highgate, and managed to persuade it to creep up our sunniest wall. I paid the youngest of Mrs B's five sons to nail up a wooden trellis, and planted a honeysuckle – a triumphant honeysuckle, now full of bees and spilling extravagantly over the wall into the garden of the retired sea captain next door.

Memory becomes more vivid with age; I was three years past my half-century, but the scent took me straight back to the summer twilight in the garden at home, when I was a romantic girl and my dearest Matt was a handsome young curate, and he asked me to marry him beside a great fountain of honeysuckle. Dear me, how happy we were – and how certain we would be happy for ever!

There is a good reason why Providence does not allow us to look into the future. I did not expect our romance to end as it did, with poor Matt's sudden death. He was a vigorous man of one-and-fifty, who had known scarcely a day's illness in his life – which explains why he never got round to making provision for his widow. It would have grieved him very much to see me in my reduced circumstances; this was what gave me the courage to make a new life from the ashes of the old one. The Lord 'tempers the wind to the shorn lamb'; though I felt utterly abandoned, I know now that my every step was guided.

For surely it was more than mere coincidence that brought me here, and matched me with Mary Bentley – my landlady and supposedly my servant, who instead became one of my dearest friends. She was small and bent and wrinkled, with faded blue eyes and sparse white hair, and when I first came to inspect the house, I took her to be in her dotage. She was younger than she appeared, however, and (apart from her rheumatism) perfectly energetic and capable. Her white hair had once been flaming red; I could see the colour for myself in the russet heads of all her five sons and their legions of children.

The late Mr Bentley had been the Hampstead postman. To make ends meet, Mrs B took in lodgers, and I was delighted to discover that she had once, more than thirty years ago, let rooms to the poet John Keats and his two brothers.

'Very nice-mannered boys, they were,' she would say sadly. 'And they died too young; my heart just about broke for them.'

Matt would have teased me, and called me 'sentimental', but I took the Keats connection as a hopeful omen for my new life in Hampstead. Certain people (my brother's wife) did not believe the house in Well Walk was sufficiently genteel for the widow of an archdeacon, and predicted that I would give up the 'experiment' after a few weeks. Certain people (see above) thought it quite outrageous of me to assert my independence, when they had been counting on me to stay in the bosom of the family as an unpaid governess – the common fate of the poor female relation, if she's not careful.

There was a brisk knocking at the kitchen door. I put my darning aside and went to answer it. I liked to spare Mrs B when I could – and I was lying in wait for the butcher's boy, to make a serious complaint about the last order of mutton (fatty and hung too long).

To my surprise it was my brother, grinning all over his face and smoking one of his horrid little black cigars.

'Fred! What are you doing here?'

'It's such a glorious morning, I couldn't resist taking a stroll across the Heath, and I knew you'd be overjoyed to see me.'

'Hmm, I suppose you can come in – but not the cigar.'

'Now, Letty, don't be a spoilsport.' He blew a smoke-ring. 'My house is filled with nurses and babies, and my chambers are enormously dull at this time of year. You're my only refuge from sober duty.'

'Thank you for that doubtful compliment. I assume everything is all right at home, or you wouldn't look so pleased with yourself.'

'Yes, of course it's all right. Everyone at home is horribly healthy.' Fred gave me one of his wicked smiles, just as he used to when he was eight years old, and trying to drag me into one of his illicit schemes; I'm afraid he usually succeeded, though I was supposed to be the 'sensible' one. 'Your latest niece is eating and screaming round the clock, and Fanny's starting to complain again – always a good sign.'

My brother, Frederick Tyson, was one of the most celebrated criminal barristers in London. The goriest murders were his delight, and the popular press loved him for the extravagance of his performances in court; the stationers' windows in the streets around the Old Bailey were crammed with cartoons of his portly and flamboyant figure, always brandishing a large white silk handkerchief (I considered the handkerchief rather vulgar, and out of keeping with the solemnity of the occasion, but when did he ever listen to me?).

As a little boy, Fred was plump, with dimples and curls; at the age of fifty, he looked like a disreputable cherub. His wife had lately been confined with their eleventh child; his children were all healthy and bonny, and had brought immeasurable joy into my childless existence – but I could not help observing that Fanny was at her most agreeable when expecting, and often wondered if my brother kept her in that condition on purpose.

'And besides,' added Fred, 'this isn't a social call.'

'You have some business for me?' This sharpened me up at once; I had a small reputation as a private investigator, and relied upon my brother to find me suitable employment. 'I do hope it's something substantial this time.'

My last paid assignment had been a handful of guineas for escorting the daughters of a Portuguese grandee around the Great Exhibition, which had just opened and was all the rage (it was a long time before I could admit how tedious I found the whole experience – hours in an oversized hot-house looking at machines, while my feet ached like fury).

'More than decent,' said Fred. 'I don't know the particulars, but the client is as rich as Croesus – and very willing to pay through the nose for your services.'

We set forth half an hour later, after I had changed my 'everyday' gown of washed-out grey cotton for my good black silk and black silk bonnet. My clients, as I knew from experience, needed to be assured of my perfect respectability – and what could be more respectable than a clerical widow in black silk? They liked me to look a little dowdy and unremarkable, but without any worrying signs of shabbiness.

'You couldn't be more proper,' Fred said, giving my silk skirt an impertinent tug. 'The Archbishop of Canterbury himself would look shifty beside you.'

'Stop it!' I snatched my skirt away from him. 'Make yourself useful and tell me about the case. You said we could walk to the house; where is it?'

'Near Preacher's Hill, and the old Spa gardens. The house belongs to a Dr Chauncey; our man lives there as a private patient.' Without any change in his genial manner, my brother was suddenly businesslike. 'His name is Jacob Welland; he made his fortune with what's politely known as "guano", and impolitely as "bird-droppings". The enquiry was delivered to my chambers yesterday afternoon, by a dashing young footman who looked like a brigand in a light opera – olive skin and black eyes; a Spaniard or Italian. He caused absolute havoc in the office. All the younger clerks were taking turns to snuffle at the keyhole trying to get a peep at him – Beamish had to drive them away with a ruler.'

'And what is the assignment?'

'That I don't know; the letter only mentioned a "family matter".'

'I daresay he wants to inspect me first.'

'Well, it's bound to be a scandal of some sort; that's what "family matter" generally means.' He blew another smoke-ring. 'Five bob says it's adultery.'

'Fred!' I knew he was teasing and I should not rise to it – but I could not allow him to speak lightly of such a serious matter.

'Oh, keep your hair on. And please don't tell me what Papa would say.'

'You shouldn't make jokes about the Commandments.' (Precisely what Papa would say; poor man, he never could overcome his innocent amazement that his son refused to follow him into the Church.)

'I have the highest respect for the Commandments; Number Six keeps me in continual employment.'

The morning was so fine, and the prospect of a new case so interesting, I decided to ignore him – and I had to pay attention to where I was walking. New buildings were biting at the edges of Hampstead Heath, including the splendid new church that was taking shape at the top of Christchurch Hill. The sunny air rang with shouts and hammerings; every pavement seemed to be blocked by planks, wheelbarrows and perilous heaps of bricks.

Rosemount, the house of Dr Chauncey, had been built in the previous century, when Hampstead enjoyed a few unlikely years as a fashionable spa. It was a long, low red-brick, surrounded by generous gardens and screened from the road by a row of elms.

6

The door was opened by a young maid in a fresh 'morning' gown of figured blue cotton, a great deal better than the old gown I had just taken off, which Mrs B was threatening to cut up into dusters.

We were shown into a drawing room, handsomely appointed and furnished. There were no signs of illness here; it was a hospital with only one patient. Before I had time to make my usual lightning assessment of the surroundings, a footman entered.

'Mrs Rodd, Mr Tyson.'

Fred grinned at me and mouthed the word 'brigand'. So this was the footman who had caused such a sensation amongst the clerks at his chambers. He was very young, a stripling barely emerged from boyhood; tall and slender of build, and as handsome as a god, with the sort of dark eyes that romantic lady novelists like to describe as 'flashing'. Despite his stagey looks, however, he wore a livery-jacket of sober grey, and his manner was quiet and respectful.

'My master expects you. Please to follow.' He spoke with a heavy accent that I could not place.

The young man led us through the dustless hush of the house, and into the sudden fug of a large conservatory with a glass roof; if not for a door open to the terrace, the thick, damp heat would have been uncomfortable. There were tall stands of potted ferns (very fashionable, though I had always considered them rather ugly plants); I first saw Mr Welland through a screen of long, crinkled, curling, dirty-green fronds.

'I cannot get up, please forgive me. Thank you for coming quickly; time is one thing I cannot buy.'

He did not need to explain why he was in a hurry. The signs were only too plain, and only too well known to me – the breathless, whispery voice, the hot, bright eyes and nervous, strumming, skeletal fingers. Jacob Welland was dying of consumption, the same pitiless disease that killed poor John Keats; 'where youth grows pale, and spectre-thin, and dies'.

(My dearest Matt once told me, after burying a young girl we had both known from infancy, that seeing such suffering made him angry with the Almighty; he could never help weeping at the funerals of children he had christened, and consumption took so many; whole families sometimes.)

My brother made the formal introductions. We sat down in two basket chairs, next to the invalid's couch and close to the open door. Looking behind the signs of his illness, I judged Mr Welland to be about forty years old. He had the sandy remnants of fair hair, and eyes of burning, fevered blue. Despite the heat, he was swaddled in a sumptuous dressing gown of quilted blue satin.

'You do not need to convince me of your discretion, Mrs Rodd,' Mr Welland said. 'You have been recommended by someone I trust to the utmost; let us save time by getting straight down to business.' He said something in a language I recognized as Spanish; the young footman bowed and backed away through the trailing fronds. 'I need you to find someone, but nobody must know that you are searching, least of all your quarry. If he thinks you're after him, he'll run for cover like a hare.'

'I can do all sorts of things without anybody knowing,' I said. 'But I don't understand; is this man a runaway, or a criminal?'

'He's my brother,' he whispered. 'Joshua Welland. My only living relative.'

'And you're leaving him everything, I suppose,' said Fred. 'Pardon my cynicism, but people who are about to inherit fortunes are usually only too easy to find. Have you tried putting a notice in *The Times*?'

'I want to see him before I die,' Mr Welland replied, faint and calm, as if addressing us through a sheet of glass. 'Chauncey can't keep me alive beyond a few more months.'

'When did you last see him?' I asked.

'Ten years ago,' said Mr Welland. 'Just before I sailed for South America. To my everlasting sorrow, we parted in anger. There are amends to be made – for our mother's sake.'

'Yes, I understand.' (I wanted very much to know the reason for the quarrel, but Mr Welland was pitifully short of breath, and there were facts I needed first.) 'Can you describe him? How old is he?'

'He'll be thirty now. Young enough for a man to start again.'

'Is he tall or short? What colour is his hair?'

'Golden, our mother used to call it.' His voice was feeble, yet his blue eyes burned with purpose; I understood that the determination to find his brother was keeping him alive. 'Money is no object to me. My lawyer, Mr Harold Mitchell in Barnard's Inn, will provide anything you need. The money that I have left with him includes your fee, Mrs Rodd.'

The sum he mentioned, so off-handedly, was enormous; it was all I could do to keep my composure (I'd been hoping the fee would run to a new 'everyday' gown, but this would buy me silk).

Fred pursed his lips, and would have whistled if he hadn't caught my eye in time. 'I know Mitchell. It's a good firm.'

'Mrs Rodd, will you take this case?'

'Most happily, Mr Welland.' I banished the money to the back of my mind to concentrate upon the poor invalid. 'While this is not my usual line of work, I have had some experience of finding people who have gone missing.' (Most notably in the Heaton business, my first successful inquiry, when I found the supposedly deceased spinster aunt living in cheerful disgrace with a half-pay captain.) 'Do you know for sure that your brother is still alive?'

'Oh yes, there have been several sightings recently.'

'I beg your pardon?'

'Joshua is something of a white stag,' Mr Welland said. 'He lives like a wild creature, in hedges and ditches. The country people know him and protect him.'

'You hinted that he doesn't wish to be discovered,' I said. 'If this is so, I cannot do more than inform you of his whereabouts.'

'He must be told that I'm dying. And that I wish for his forgiveness.'

'I'm happy to carry your message, Mr Welland, though I must admit that I don't quite understand why you need me to do this.'

One corner of his mouth hitched into a painful smile. 'Because he won't run away when he sees you.'

'Why would he run away?'

'He has turned his back upon the world.' Mr Welland stopped to catch his breath and recover his voice. 'I've written this down. My brother got himself to Oxford as the very poorest of scholars. Poverty broke his heart in the end; when his clothes were in rags, he simply walked out of his college into the countryside, and has lived there ever since.'

'Do you know where, exactly?'

'I can't be exact. Somewhere to the south and west of Oxford, around Cumnor Hill. And he's been seen as far as the Vale of the White Horse.'

'When you say he has been "seen", what do you mean? Has someone spoken to him?'

'I mean,' Mr Welland said slowly, 'that there have been sightings.'

This was intriguing; I could scarcely begin to imagine the kind of man I would be seeking; a clever, highly-educated man, who had apparently lived as a wild creature for the past ten years, and was soon to be a wild creature with an enormous fortune.

Fred irritably mopped his forehead with his handkerchief; the conservatory was humid and cabbage-smelling. 'Is your brother in his right mind? Forgive me, Welland, but my sister ought to know if she's chasing a lunatic.'

(Exactly the question I had been trying to frame myself, less bluntly.)

'My brother is not a lunatic,' Mr Welland said. 'An eccentric, an oddity, perhaps. But not "mad" in the sense you mean. He is a philosopher; he made a reasoned decision to walk away from the modern world. I'm not trying to spoil the life he has chosen. I simply want to see him again before I die.'

'I understand.' We were running out of time; he was exhausted, with two angry discs of red on his doorknob cheekbones. 'Mr Welland, it would help me very much to know why you and your brother argued all those years ago.'

'A woman?' suggested Fred, with a quickening of interest.

'Yes,' Mr Welland whispered. 'A woman – strange to think of it now. It was a woman. We both loved her. And she died.' His breath was failing; he gasped like a fish. With one of his shaking hands he gestured towards the table beside him. There was a silver bell amidst the invalid's clutter, which I rang vigorously.

The young footman appeared in a matter of seconds. He took a small brown bottle from the table and shook a few drops into a glass of water. I was touched to observe how gently, how tenderly he held the glass to his master's lips. For one moment, in the depths of Mr Welland's fearful eyes, I saw him looking at the young man with an expression of what I can only describe as love.

(As the daughter of a clergyman, I could not avoid seeing the sermon in this scene; all the gold in the world had not bought Jacob Welland a loving family; the only face he had to love was that of a servant.)

After a few minutes, he recovered just enough to clasp my hand with his bony sticks of fingers. The young man handed Fred a pile of papers, neatly bound with legal-tape, and the interview was at an end.

The air outside was deliciously fresh and cool after the stifling heat of the glasshouse. Fred groaned with relief and lit a cigar.

'Well, that was a decent morning's work, wouldn't you say?' He loosened the tape to take a rapid look at the papers. 'Hmm – yes – yes – all shipshape, as far as I can tell. I was longing to ask Welland what we should do if he died on us, and he's left instructions for precisely that.'

'He has thought of everything.' I took the papers from him. 'I do hope we find his brother in time.'

'Of course you will – a few half-crowns scattered around the villages, and you'll flush him out in a matter of days.'

'You're assuming this will be an easy matter. I'm not so sure. Mr Welland has already tried and failed to find him – or he wouldn't need my services.'

'Have you decided where you'll be staying, during your hunt for the White Stag? I don't suppose you have any connections in the area.' We both smiled when he said this, for the extent of my 'connections' amongst the clergy had become a family byword and joke, and Oxford positively swarmed with the blessed creatures.

'As a matter of fact,' I said, 'this will be the ideal opportunity to visit Arthur Somers and his wife.'

'Who?'

'Mr Somers – of course you know him.'

'Never heard of him.'

'Yes you have, he was the young curate we had in Herefordshire – the one with yellow hair, that you called The Daffodil.'

'Oh, yes,' Fred said, remembering at last (he had met Mr Somers when he visited us for a few days and ate every morsel of food I had in the house). 'He married that gloomy girl who had forty thousand pounds.'

'Rachel Garnett.' I was slightly annoyed that I couldn't think how to argue with this description; though crudely phrased it was perfectly true. Miss Garnett did indeed have forty thousand pounds, and was of an undeniably serious character. 'Mr Somers has a living just outside Oxford, and their house will make an ideal base for my enquiries.'

'She was quite pretty,' Fred said. 'Or she would've been if she hadn't dressed herself like a nun. What did she have to be gloomy about, anyway? Forty thousand pounds would cheer me up no end.'

Two

I WROTE TO RACHEL SOMERS as soon as I got home, boldly announcing my arrival the following week. This was a matter that had to be dealt with quickly; I had liked Mr Welland, and I honoured his desire to win his brother's forgiveness before he died.

'He said nobody must know that I'm searching for him,' I told Mrs Bentley later. 'I have already decided to take exactly the opposite approach; I want everyone to know, so that I can be sure my message is delivered. There's so little time.'

'You might have longer than you think,' said Mrs Bentley. 'People can put off dying for ages when they're waiting for something. I had an old aunt who hung on for weeks until her son came home from sea, and then out she went like a light.'

'Yes, I've seen the same thing, but I daren't take the risk in this case; poor Mr Welland can't last for more than a few weeks. I will see to it that Joshua gets the information, after which it will be up to him to decide what to do with it.' I was back in my old gown and we were drinking hot brandy and water beside the kitchen fire. Mrs B had run out to the nearby tavern for a half-quartern of brandy and produced sugar and a lemon from I know not where; this was how we celebrated a new case, and I always liked to hear Mary's ruminations. 'What a shame it is, when brothers fall out.'

'It's a rare thing, if my boys are anything to go by,' said Mrs B. 'They've had their fights, but nothing bad enough to cut them off completely. In my experience, there's only two things will do that – money or a woman.'

'In this case, a woman. I haven't read Mr Welland's account yet, but he said it was because they both loved the same girl, and she died.'

'I knew it!' Mrs Bentley was solemn. 'Love or money. And love's the worst.'

'The most urgent business, as far as I'm concerned, is my packing for Oxford. I can't travel in my silk, but the black marocain is too warm and the poplin is in a sorry state.'

'Oh, you can leave that with me,' Mrs B said. 'All it wants is airing and ironing and holding over a hot kettle, and I'll have a go at your gloves while I'm at it.' (Despite her rheumatism, she had a talent for dragging garments back to respectability from the very brink.)

'My brother changed one of Mr Welland's banknotes; I can put a nice sum into the Windsor Castle box, and I expect you to use it.'

'You always leave too much, ma'am,' she protested.

'You know it drives me to distraction when you're stingy on my behalf.' I was laughing softly now, for this was our eternal argument. 'Apart from anything else, it makes me look hard-hearted. Think of my reputation, and make sure you spend Mr Welland's money on coals and decent food and candles. I have my spies, dear Mary, and if I hear that you've been caught sitting in the dark again, I shall be most displeased.'

There were shouts outside in the street, and a burst of raucous singing – one of the cockney ballads that were so enormously and annoyingly popular at the time, with a howling 'Toora-loora' chorus.

'As Vilikins was walking in the garden one day,
He saw his poor Dinah as cold as the clay,
A CUP OF COLD POISON did lie by her side,
And the little ducks said that for Vilikins she died.'

It was late and our jug of brandy was empty. Mrs B went to bed and I went upstairs to my small drawing room, to study Mr Welland's papers by the light of the china lamp that had once graced my large drawing room in Bloomsbury. Above the fireplace, watching over me like a benign spirit, was the portrait of Matt by Edwin Landseer; a gift from the diocese the year before he died, and now my dearest possession.

The papers given to me by Mr Welland included banknotes, a pass for the railway and two letters of introduction to men who had seen Joshua (or claimed to have seen him) since his disappearance: a fellow of his college and a local landowner conveniently close to where I would be staying. There was also, as Fred had said, a sheet of instructions headed 'In the Event of my Death' and a sealed letter addressed to Joshua.

Most interesting to me, however, were several sheets closely written by hand.

TO WHOM IT MAY CONCERN

Herewith a full and true account of the wrong done by Jacob Welland to his brother, Joshua.

We grew up in Kent. Our father was a clergyman of the meanest rank – a poor curate, keeping someone else's living warm for a yearly pittance. Our mother was the daughter of another poor curate. I was their oldest child. My brother Joshua, born ten years later, was their youngest. There were two girls – Mary and Ruth – who lived and died between us. All Joshua knew of them was their little grave in the churchyard.

Our poor mother always said Joshua was her late blessing, sent by Heaven to heal her broken heart. He was our golden boy – healthy, handsome and sweet-natured. I had never been much of a scholar, but Joshua soon showed signs of a remarkable intelligence. By the time he was seven he had nearly exhausted our father's stock of learning and knew every book in the house (there were not many) by heart. It was clear to us all that Joshua needed an education. It was equally clear, however, that we could not afford it. Schools, books and tutors cost money, which we did not have; as the poet says, 'Every door is barred with gold, and opens but to golden keys.'

I was at that time an impatient hobbledehoy of seventeen. Thanks to the dozens of begging letters fired off by my father, I had lately joined the ranks of the civil service as a junior clerk in the Navy Pay Office at Chatham. As far as my parents were concerned, my fortune was made. But I hated the work, which mainly consisted of copying long lists of names and numbers. I hated my damp lodgings beside a brewery. Chatham was a town of sailors. The great ships at the docks loomed over the buildings, magnificently mysterious, promising all kinds of freedom and adventure.

I told my father that I could make money for Joshua's education if I left my office and joined one of the trading ships. He refused to hear of such a thing, having worked hard for his position in life as a 'gentleman'.

The immediate problem of Joshua's education was solved, for the moment, by a neighbour of ours, a Mr Thorne – an impoverished eccentric who lived amidst mountains of books. He proved himself a most excellent teacher; it was thanks to him that Joshua won his scholarship to the grammar school in our nearest town.

I had not, in the meantime, lost my desire to escape and make my fortune. This is not an account of my life and career; it is only necessary to state that I defied my father and sailed off to America. I did not make my fortune overnight; there was much struggle and hardship in the life I had chosen. The life suited me, however; I never once regretted turning my back on the civil service.

Joshua was a gangling youth of sixteen when I saw him next, with just the same modesty and sweetness of character, though he was Head Boy of his school and widely admired for his scholarship. It was largely due to Joshua's entreaties that my parents forgave me so readily for running away to sea.

Though my wealth was still in the future, I had at least saved enough for independence. I bought a small farm near to my father's parish. It was a bad investment, for which I paid too much. The farmhouse was dark and damp and the land decidedly marshy. I made something like a living. It is odd to think that I might be there now – if only she had not come.

Yes, there was a 'she'; what else could have divided two such devoted brothers?

Her name was Hannah Laurie and she was a distant cousin from my mother's side of the family. She was an orphan, sixteen years old when she came to us, with the bright golden hair that looks red in some lights and eyes of the purest blue.

Our father welcomed the poor orphan into our home, and not only from Christian duty. Our mother was failing in health and her wits had begun to wander. Hannah became her nurse, her companion, her friend – almost one of her lost daughters.

I fell in love with Hannah, but I knew in my bones that Hannah did not love me. Though nothing had been said, it was plain to all around us that she loved my brother.

I am not a jealous man by nature, and I made the best of the situation for the next few years, until our parents were both dead. Hannah was left utterly alone, without house or income, or anything more than the clothes she stood up in. Joshua had nothing and could do nothing.

I often think how different this story would have been if we'd had any money.

Hannah would never have married me.

I didn't need to force her; the poor girl was only too grateful to find a refuge with me. To put it bluntly, she had no choice. Somewhere deep down, I was fully aware that I was taking advantage of a helpless creature. *A butterfly loses its loveliness when it is trapped and pinned to a card. I believe that Hannah was fond of me, that she looked up to me – but she was not happy. I did my best to ignore the bitter fact that her heart belonged to someone else.*

I did not tell my brother of our marriage until after the event. Joshua was deeply hurt and angered by my betrayal and vowed he would never see or speak with me again. I admit now that my actions were despicable. Here were the only two people left on this earth that I loved, and I had given them nothing but pain.

That sweet girl would never have cast herself into the darkness if not for me. Shortly after Joshua left his college to commence life as a woodland hermit, I lost her. She left with only the scant belongings she had brought with her, fading out of my life like breath upon a mirror. Her note contained just two words: 'Forgive me.'

I searched for her. I sent other people to search for her across miles of countryside. I did not care that they laughed at me. I did not care that they pitied me. I was certain she had followed my brother. I never did find them, though I heard all kinds of stories – that they had joined a band of gipsies, or built a house in a tree, or run off to the Antipodes.

After nearly a year, a trusted friend sent word that Hannah had died. The news took a long time to reach me and the grass had grown over her grave by the time I saw it. She lies in the peaceful churchyard at Shotton Barrow. There was no word from my brother. I took myself and my broken heart to South America, where I made the fortune I no longer wanted. I can only hope Joshua makes better use of my money than I did. If God is merciful I will see him again before I die.

JACOB WELLAND 1851

I read this romantic story several times and sat up brooding over it until after midnight. Mr Welland had not given me much in the way of facts about his brother. It might help, I thought, to visit the grave of Hannah Laurie. I wondered how she died, and when she died – this innocent girl who had, apparently, run off with the raggle-taggle gipsies.

Hannah had committed a grave sin in deserting her lawful husband for his brother, but I could not condemn her; she had been forced to choose between a decent roof over her head, or a hedge under the stars. Mr Welland was right to admit that he had taken mean advantage of her helplessness. He knew she and Joshua could not declare their love openly because they were too poor to marry. A better man would have found a way to assist the young couple, instead of tearing them apart.

And love had won in the end, when Hannah chose the hedge after all – as the old song says, what cared she for her goose-feather bed? I found myself hoping, against all my principles, that she had found a little happiness before she died.

Three

I TRAVELLED TO OXFORD IN beautiful haymaking weather, hot and still beneath a sky of purest blue. For once, the train journey was tolerably comfortable. In my First Class carriage the windows stood open, letting in equal amounts of summer breeze and soot. In the Third Class carriage that trundled along behind us (in those days nothing more than an open wagon with wooden benches) a holiday mood prevailed; someone had a concertina and there were loud choruses of popular songs – 'Vilikins and Dinah', of course, and the equally wearisome 'I'd Rather Have a Guinea than a One-Pound Note'.

The mood was contagious. It was delightful to see real countryside again, and the fields and woods and thatched farmsteads took me straight back to my dear father's parish in Gloucestershire. I was looking forward to the long country walks I would be making in my search for the wandering scholar.

And I was greatly looking forward to seeing Rachel and Arthur again, for the first time since their marriage – more than ten years ago, now that I thought about it. Rachel and I exchanged voluminous letters every few months, but letters conceal as much as they reveal and I had wondered several times if she was truly happy.

There was a personal and somewhat ignoble reason for my concern. I had aided and abetted this marriage, and considered it my greatest triumph of matchmaking – my earnest (and wealthy) young friend and my favourite of our curates. My dearest Matt, however, did not like it, though he would never give me a proper reason for his disapproval. The unfortunate fact was that we had often argued about Arthur Somers.

He came to us fresh from Oxford, so recently ordained that (as Matt said) the paint was still wet, and I quickly became attached to him. He was sensitive and gentle, and deeply sincere in his desire to do good, and he was very easy company at a tea-table. His pale yellow hair and soulful blue eyes caused female hearts to break right and left (I am in no position to criticize, having myself fallen in love with a handsome young curate). I was sure he would be engaged to one of our local young ladies in a matter of months. That was what generally happened to our curates (the record was held by one Mr Knox, bagged by the youngest Morrison girl inside a fortnight).

This young curate, however, remained resolutely single. His lodgings in the village were bombarded with cakes, pies, blancmanges and warm socks, and these offerings were received with nothing more than ordinary courtesy. I began to wonder if he already had an understanding with some unknown lady. Or perhaps he'd had his heart broken.

In the end, my curiosity made me ask outright one evening, when the two of us were confidential beside the parlour fire.

'I'm too poor to think of marrying,' he told me.

'You'll be appointed to a good living one of these days,' I said. 'And then you will need a wife.'

Mr Somers said, very quiet and grave, 'I don't intend to marry, Mrs Rodd. I will best serve God's Holy Church as a celibate.' I had sense enough not to repeat this to my husband, already exasperated by his curate's Romish leanings – Holy Communion taken every five minutes, Latin prayers, and all the other practices brought into fashion by the so-called Oxford Movement. Of course I tried to argue him out of the 'celibacy'; as the wife of a clergyman I could hardly do otherwise. Here, however, I hit a brick wall; mild and sweet as he was, he could be surprisingly stubborn.

Miss Rachel Garnett arrived in our parish rather dramatically, as a fugitive; her family were dissenters, and they had disowned her when she joined the established Church. An aunt of her father's, exiled for similar reasons, took pity on her and offered her a home. She was a handsome young woman, with heavy-lashed eyes of dark grey in a pale oval face and smooth hair of a fine auburn. She dressed herself, as Fred had said, in plain, nun-like gowns of penitential grey, and she was intensely serious.

Once I had come to know Rachel properly, I grew very fond of her. She was intelligent, her piety was deep and sincere, and her wish to do the Lord's work entirely genuine. And she had forty thousand pounds from the family brewery, settled upon her absolutely by her late father. She fretted about the morality of this, and wondered if she should give her fortune away, until it was all I could do not to box her ears. As far as I was concerned, this sweet-natured young woman could best do the Lord's work by getting married and building a happy family. I would not have matched her with Arthur if I had not been certain the two of them were already falling in love.

'Phooey,' said Matt.

'What do you mean?' I was indignant. 'They're always together. And Rachel has positively blossomed!'

'My dear, that damp sprig of parsley doesn't have the backbone to fall in love.'

I decided he was simply too cross with Arthur to see reason. Someone had complained to the Bishop about certain Romish antics, there were rumours in the villages that Arthur was planning to turn them all into Catholics (if this sounds a little hysterical, it is only an indication of the bad feeling around at the time; it was just before Mr John Henry Newman caused national outrage by leaving his parish to join the Church of Rome), and it took Matt several stern sermons to end all the foolish tittle-tattle about Jesuit plots.

He did admit that Mr Somers's marriage would make a fine excuse to get rid of him without (in his words) 'causing a stink'. Thanks to Rachel's fortune the young curate was a man of consequence, and he landed the living of Hardinsett, five miles outside the city of Oxford.

Is there a more beautiful city in England? The towers and steeples, golden in the setting sun, rose up across the meadows as we approached, like fairy castles as old as time.

The railway stopped short of the castles and I had to concentrate upon getting off the train and finding my box. I saw Rachel before she saw me – a slight, elegant figure in a grey dress and bonnet, both of the plainest style, but of the best material and very well-made.

'Mrs Rodd – my dear Mrs Rodd!' She clasped both my hands. 'I can't express how glad I am to see you!'

She had come in a small closed carriage, again of the plainest style, but the fact remained that it was brand new. I was glad to see that her fortune was being used to buy convenience, if not luxury. We drove through prosperous farming country, and Rachel smiled to hear my exclamations over the deep green lanes, the hedges filled with wild roses and the men in smock-frocks driving their cattle home.

'You'll see that we live at least a century behind the times here,' she said. 'The modern world doesn't touch us. Just a mile or so from the railway, it is possible to slip into a world that hasn't changed since the Norman Conquest.'

'It's quite lovely,' I said. 'And I hope the weather holds – I'm here to explore the countryside.'

'Are you able to tell us anything?' Rachel knew about my work and was surprisingly keen on the most lurid details. 'Your letter was very mysterious.'

'There's not much to tell – I suspect you and Arthur will know more than I do, and I rather hope that you'll be able to assist me.'

'Most intriguing! I'll try to contain my curiosity until Arthur wakes up for dinner.' She quickly added, 'He's not ill; he spent the whole of last night sitting up with a man who was dying, and he was so exhausted when he came home this morning that I ordered him to bed.'

'Oh dear,' I said. 'It does nobody any good if he works himself into the ground.'

'Just what I'm always saying to him! He drives himself until I worry for his health. I daresay you remember his mania for self-denial.'

'Yes, indeed.' (Oh dear – a memory flashed into my mind, of the time Mr Somers 'fasted' for Lent so thoroughly that he fainted during Matins; I had seldom seen Matt so angry.)

'We've just entered our parish; you'll see the church and the rectory when we turn at the next crossroads – oh, I wish there was light enough for you to see it properly – I truly believe this to be the prettiest place on earth!'

For the rest of the drive, Rachel pointed out local landmarks, or the outlines of landmarks; bridges and barns and village taverns, all equally mysterious in the gathering twilight. When we stopped I had an impression of a square church tower in a nest of greenery, and a large house beside it with glowing windows. It was an old house, built of the soft, golden Oxfordshire stone, and so like the dear home of my childhood that the lights behind the lattices, and the great bed of lavender next to the stone porch, made me absolutely see the place, though it had been pulled down years ago.

The coachman handed me out of the carriage. I stood on the gravelled drive and took great draughts of that sweet summer air. The front door opened and a servant in a plain black gown and white apron emerged.

'Mrs Rodd.' The woman bobbed me a curtsey. 'It's a pleasure to see you again, ma'am.'

'Oh, I forgot to tell you,' Rachel said, 'Mrs Richards is our housekeeper now; she came last year when Aunt Harriet died.'

'Mrs Richards – of course! How very good to see you.' When she stepped towards me into the light I knew her at once and we shook hands. 'You're a reminder of the old village, and the happy times we had there.' She was tall and muscular, with a blunt-featured face, sharp black eyes and endless reserves of patience (which she had needed when working for Rachel's mean little wasp of an aunt; that woman drove servants away by the dozen).

'Thank you, ma'am,' said Mrs Richards. 'Will you come upstairs?'

There is always, at the end of a long journey, a moment when the whirlwind stops and you know that you have properly arrived at your destination; it suddenly dawned on me that I was almost faint with longing for a cup of tea and liberally grimed with soot.

'Yes, you must be dreadfully tired.' Rachel, seeing my fatigue, put her arms around me and kissed my cheek. 'I'm so glad you've come! Now I'll leave you alone until dinner.'

'This way, Mrs Rodd, if you please.' Mrs Richards trudged upstairs ahead of me, keeping up a friendly flow of conversation over one shoulder. 'Dear me, I don't like to think how long it's been! As Miss Rachel said, I came here last year after old Miss Garnett was gathered. The man's brought in your box and I'll send the girl up with a can of nice hot water; I'm sure you'd like some tea and a little something to eat.'

She ushered me into a most delightful bedchamber at the front of the house, with mullioned windows that looked out across a patchwork of dusky fields and meadows. In a remarkably short time I was sitting in an easy chair beside a small fire, eating triangles of bread-and-butter and slices of pound cake while Mrs Richards made my tea.

'Now that you're visiting, ma'am, they've let me serve up a decent dinner for a change.'

'I know you're a celebrated cook,' I said. 'Don't they always have a decent dinner?'

'Not them! They eat like birds, and the master's always "fasting" for some saint's day or other. I said to Miss Rachel – Mrs Somers, I mean – that I wasn't going to take any argument about tonight's dinner. I said, I'm doing a fish course and a meat course and a pudding, and that's that.'

'I'm extremely glad to hear it,' I said, relieved that I would not be condemned to hungry holiness.

'It would make you cry, to see the poor stuff they ask me for. You may call me old-fashioned, Mrs Rodd, but in my day, a clergyman was expected to keep a good table.' She added, 'As you and Mr Rodd always did, ma'am.'

'Thank you, that was mostly due to Mr Rodd being rather greedy,' I said, smiling at the memory (as far as Matt was concerned no dinner was complete without a sweet pudding). 'And we had a great many guests at our table in those days. Do Mr and Mrs Somers have many visitors here?'

'Not that sort of visitor, ma'am. They don't go into society as they should. You'll meet the curate, Mr Barton, and that's about it.'

I longed to ask Mrs Richards if she thought they were happy; while I was still framing the question, she answered it anyway. 'Between ourselves, ma'am, what this house needs is a few children. I know Miss Rachel feels it keenly.'

'She has all my sympathy; I know from experience how hard it is to accept the Lord's will when one is denied children. But has there never been a sign?'

'Not while I've been here,' said Mrs Richards. She shot me a wary look; I had a sense that there were quite a few other things she would have liked to tell me. 'I hope you'll be comfortable, ma'am.'

Four

'MY DEAR MRS RODD, this is a joy! I'm almost inclined to be thankful for the heinous crime that brought you here – and I hope it keeps you here for a good long time.'

Arthur and Rachel were waiting for me in the drawing room. Arthur was thinner and older than I remembered, otherwise just as handsome, in that white-and-gold, plaster-saint fashion. Rachel had dressed herself in a very pretty evening gown of palest blue silk. I thought what an enchanting picture they made together, against the background of this charming room, with its fine old furnishings and bright new hangings. A pair of glass doors stood open; the warm summer night was heavy with the scents of stocks, of honeysuckle and jasmine.

'There is no crime on this occasion,' I reassured them. 'Heinous or otherwise. I am here on a mission of mercy.'

'No gruesome murders?' he teased.

'I'm afraid not.'

'Never mind; I shall swallow my disappointment and seize the chance to show you the parish. I'm hoping you'll give me some advice about the work that needs to be done here.' Falling back into the old, easy manner, he added, 'And please accept my apology for being asleep when you arrived.'

'I hope you are rested now,' I said. 'Rachel told me the reason.'

'I was helping an old man into the next world,' said Arthur. 'Tom Goodly, who wanted to make his confession to me, poor man; his wits were wandering all over the place.'

There was a loud tradesman's whistle outside and a stranger stepped briskly into the room from the garden – a brawny young clergyman, so tall that his head brushed the honeysuckle over the glass doors as he crossed the threshold, and he had to shake the blossoms from his thick brush of dark hair.

He saw me, and exclaimed, 'I do beg your pardon, I had no idea there'd be anybody else here – or I certainly shouldn't have barged in from the garden—'

'Didn't Arthur tell you? Oh, my dear!' Rachel smiled and coloured and patted her husband's arm. 'Mrs Rodd, allow me to present our curate, Mr Henry Barton, who would have used the front door had he known you would be joining us for dinner.'

'But we won't make you go out and come in again,' Arthur said. 'Mrs Rodd will forgive you, because it's all my fault.'

'Yes, of course.' I shook hands with Mr Barton.

Arthur and Rachel were suddenly animated, as if the man had switched them on like the mechanical waxworks that used to tour the country fairgrounds when I was a child. My first impression was of energy blowing into the room with him; a cheerful energy that somehow freshened us and made us sit up straighter. My next impression was that Mr Barton was a good-looking man, well-knit and high-coloured, rude health bursting out of every inch of him.

'Barton is my right arm here,' Arthur said. 'You remember, Mrs Rodd, the muddles I used to get into when it came to practical matters.' (I did indeed.) 'Thanks to Barton, we run like clockwork.'

'If Mrs Rodd will forgive me, I'll get the business matters over with,' said Mr Barton. 'I called on poor old Mrs Goodly, and gave her the money from the burial fund.'

'Of course.' Arthur sighed and rubbed his hair. 'His "confession" rambled on for hours, and frankly didn't make much sense, but he went peacefully at the end, God rest his soul.'

'Amen,' said Mr Barton. He planted his hands in his pockets and smiled around at all of us. 'I don't suppose he happened to confess about stealing my shirts?'

'Barton!' Arthur was smiling yet reproachful. 'You know I can't talk about it.'

'He swiped them off the washing line, Mrs Rodd, and had the cheek to wear one of them to church. His light fingers were absolutely notorious.'

'Do you live in the parish, Mr Barton?' I asked.

'No, I'm three miles away, at Millings Cross.'

'He's in charge of Arthur's other church,' Rachel said. 'It was built twenty years ago, to provide a place of worship for the farm labourers.'

'You can't really describe the place as a village,' Mr Barton said cheerfully. 'It's a cluster of cottages on the edge of the common. Holy Trinity struggles to shake off its reputation as the "poor" church, and it's bursting at the seams, just like the church here – has Somers told you about our great project?'

'I hadn't got around to that,' Arthur said. 'We want to build a new church, Mrs Rodd; a place large enough for everyone.'

Rachel gave him an affectionate smile that made her face strikingly young and pretty. 'Tell her about it tomorrow. It's such a lovely night that I refuse to let you spoil it by unrolling the plans – he spreads them all over the carpet, Mrs Rodd, and they're just a lot of dull blue drawings.'

Arthur and his curate both protested loudly over this accusation, and we made a lively, laughing party when we were called into dinner. It was a very good dinner, just as Mrs Richards had promised, of clear soup, soles, roasted mutton, and a beautiful sharp-sweet rhubarb fool (my dear mother always said this was the only thing you could do with the early rhubarb). Mr Barton, thoroughly at home here, made himself responsible for pouring the wine. He and I ate and drank heartily, while I pretended not to have noticed that Rachel and Arthur took next to nothing at all.

I told them about my case. There was no need to be secretive. Quite the reverse. I actively wanted the whole countryside to help me in my search for the wandering scholar, and their response to the story interested me very much. They had all heard of the man, but only as a kind of local legend.

'I've never seen him,' Arthur said. 'All I can say for sure is that I've seen signs in the woods sometimes, and I know that some of the cottagers give him shelter in cold weather.'

'Some of the people round about are a little suspicious of him,' added Mr Barton, 'because he consorts with the gipsies and appears to move freely amongst them. My opinion is that the gipsies tolerate him as a holy fool. They have a strict code of honour about such things.'

'He was at Magdalen,' Arthur said.

'I'm sure it was John's.'

'He was at Gabriel,' I said. 'Mr Welland has supplied me with a letter of introduction to someone at that college who knew Joshua and – more importantly – claims to have spoken to him since he went into hiding.'

'Jane,' Rachel said to the young maid who was clearing the table, 'have you heard of this man, or ever caught sight of him?'

'Yes, ma'am, everybody's heard of him.' (Jane had been listening to our conversation, of course – I am constantly amazed by the things some people blurt out in front of their servants, as if they were not human creatures with functioning ears.) 'People leave little bits of food out for him for good luck. But I never saw him.'

'I hope you'll tell me if you ever do,' I said. 'I haven't come to do him harm.'

'Yes, ma'am,' said Jane, giving me a cautious smile.

'I have a letter of introduction to a landowner named Daniel Arden.'

'I was just about to suggest you meet Arden,' Mr Barton said. 'He lives at the manor, and is as near as anything our local squire.'

'He's a decent, well-intentioned man,' Arthur said, with a pained expression. 'Unfortunately, you won't see him in church.'

'Is he an ungodly man?'

'Far from it!' Mr Barton was, unmistakably, annoyed. 'He's a Unitarian, very high-principled, and he does a great deal of good around here.'

'I don't dispute the good he does,' Arthur said mildly. 'But I'm still praying to win him back; I tell him so to his face.'

'I'm driving over there tomorrow afternoon,' said Mr Barton. 'You should come with me, Mrs Rodd.'

'I don't like to without an invitation—'

'Arden won't mind, truly; he's told me more than once how much he likes to meet new people.'

'In that case, thank you.' I was interested in this man, and could tell that Mr Barton liked him. 'I accept most gladly.'

A clock chimed sweetly out in the hall. It was late, and I was light-headed with fatigue. This day had been endless. We returned to the drawing room for tea. I swallowed yawns, listening with half an ear as Mr Barton talked to

Arthur about cutting back the bindweed in the church-yard.

I nodded off for a moment, and when I opened my eyes, time had taken a leap forward.

Mr Barton was in the doorway; I had an impression that something had just been said, and was still ringing in the air. Rachel stood close to him, with her back to me. I could see his face clearly, gazing down into hers with a look that told me everything, quite as plainly as if he had said it aloud – the man was in love with her.

But had I really seen that? A moment later I woke up properly, and the two of them were on opposite sides of the room. Rachel held her husband's arm, and Mr Barton was in the middle of a speech about a new storm drain. I decided that I must have been mistaken, and was ashamed that I had jumped to conclusions. I had grown too accustomed to seeing the skull beneath the skin, I told myself. My investigations had introduced me to the worst elements of human nature, until I saw the gravest sins everywhere I looked; now that I was properly awake, I could almost have laughed at myself.

My every instinct told me that these three were the most respectable people on earth, and only sinners in the ordinary sense.

But something troubled me; weary as I was, when I came to the point of lying down in my soft white bed and blowing out the candle, I could not fall asleep.

With hindsight, I am tempted to elevate my sleepless fretting into a full-blown foreboding of the tragedy to come. In fact it was little more than a mild yet persistent sense of disquiet.

But let us be clear, in case I appear to be veering away from my true subject: none of this is a digression.

Five

The Rectory

Hardinsett

31st May

My dear Mary,

You will be glad to know that I have arrived safely. The house is most comfortable and surrounded by very pretty countryside. As usual there are all sorts of instructions that I forgot to give you in the flurry of my departure.

Firstly, the letter of reference for your granddaughter, dear little Anny, is on the round table in the drawing room. Please assure her mother that the Kings of Mill Hill are a highly respectable family; I have placed several girls in service with them, very successfully. You may not care for this, but I have sent for Anny's younger sister, to help you at Well Walk during my absence. I know you will protest that you can manage alone, and that I'm throwing money away – well, too late, the deed is done. I can afford it, and it will be a weight off my mind.

Now for the most important matter. I need a reliable daily source of news regarding Mr Welland – if there are any changes to his condition I would need to know as soon as possible, without having to go through any unnecessary delay. You must call at Rosemount every day to enquire on my behalf. That is the official side of the business. Unofficially, it would be useful if you could strike up acquaintances belowstairs. Servants see and hear everything, and the smallest snippet could turn out to be useful. If poor Mr Welland dies, send to me by express — I have left extra money in the Windsor Castle box to pay for this. And here is a task I know you will enjoy. Please pay the bill at Murphy's, and move our custom to the new butcher's shop in the high street. If Murphy wants a reason you may feel free to mention that awful piece of mutton.

Your devoted friend,

Laetitia Rodd

PS — One more thing! The drugget on the topmost set of stairs is torn, and you must take special care not to trip over it.

Over breakfast the next morning, Arthur and Rachel were the very model of a happy couple. I had once been one half of a happy couple and recognized the language of true intimacy; those little codes and jokes and affectionate squabbles.

Arthur left the house immediately after breakfast.

'He has an engagement over at Swinford,' said Rachel.

'So early?'

'He spends a great deal of time there. He says it makes him feel at one with the sacraments.'

'Oh.' I did my best to hide my dismay. The mere word 'Swinford' was inflammatory in those days, so many years ago. It was a parish near Oxford, which the vicar had turned into a kind of 'monastic' retreat. He had converted the stables into whitewashed 'cells', where numerous earnest young men led a medieval life of prayer, fasting and chastity, and several had ended up becoming Roman Catholics. 'I didn't know that they allowed the attendance of married men.'

'They don't usually, but Father Fogle was Arthur's tutor at one time and they are very old friends. Arthur relies upon him for spiritual guidance.' She would not allow me to ask why Arthur thought he required guidance.

She took me on a tour of the home farm, which I greatly enjoyed. Everything was so sparkling clean, and the sights and smells lifted my spirits. Memories of my country childhood came thick and fast, yet at the same time I could see that the cleanliness was just a little too good to be true; the place looked as if they took it indoors at night.

I asked everyone we met about my wandering scholar. They all knew of him, but by the end of the morning I had a list of about twenty places, spread across miles of countryside, where he was 'definitely' to be found.

The only piece of mildly interesting information came from one of the young dairymaids, who spoke up when another girl mentioned the gipsies on the common.

'He's not with the gipsies, ma'am – the story is that he fell out with them, on account of a gipsy-girl.'

'Indeed,' I said, filing this away in my memory, though I didn't believe it for a moment. All in all, these interviews only left me more confused.

In the early afternoon, Mr Barton arrived in a small open carriage, to drive me to the home of Mr Arden. In the light of what I had seen last night (or thought I had seen), I was interested to observe the curate at close quarters. There was an air of cheerful vigour about him that was very likeable and he was evidently a well-known and popular figure in the neighbourhood; everyone we passed along the way gave him a civil greeting, until his hat was more off his head than on it.

'What a friendly place,' I said.

'Oh, yes – I've met some splendid people since I came here. Even amongst the very poorest, there is a genuine desire to do good, and to help one another, as I'm always telling Somers.' Mr Barton shot me a quick sideways smile.

'It's perfectly possible to be a good Christian without spending all day on your knees. Somers frets that a man's soul is in danger because he hasn't been to church, and I have to remind him that the same man feeds the hungry and gives generously to the poor – which makes his soul positively armour-plated, as far as I'm concerned. And bound for glory just as fast as any of those black-clad ghouls at Swinford.'

'Mr Barton!' I couldn't help laughing at his indignation. 'I take it you don't approve of Arthur spending so much time there. Between ourselves, I quite agree. He always was rather impractical.'

'Impractical!' He was laughing as well now. 'That's putting it mildly – I've never met such a man for muddling dates and times and forgetting to answer letters! I hasten to add that he's also one of the best and holiest men I ever knew – too good to see through certain people, perhaps. But look here, Mrs Somers made me promise not to bore you with church matters.' (He could mention her without blush or tremor, which I took as a sign of a clear conscience; it flashed upon me that he might not know he loved her.) 'I should be showing off the beauty of the scenery.'

'Tell me more about Mr Arden.'

'Most happily. He's an excellent man, and with a remarkable history, though he never speaks of it himself. And Binstock is a remarkable old house.'

'In what way?'

'When he bought the place, about ten years ago, it was falling into ruins. The family that built it had died out, and some distant cousins fought over it in the Court of Chancery. Arden repaired the house and bought back the land that the family had sold. More importantly, he repaired the cottages and mended the roads.'

'A good landowner makes a great difference to a place,' I said. 'Mr Arden must be well liked in the villages.'

'Indeed he is; people thought Binstock would never be sold because there was a curse on it.'

'Oh dear, I wish I knew what makes country people so devoted to curses! My late husband was constantly being asked to lift some curse or other, as if parsons were wizards in their spare time. Ghosts are popular, too.'

'Binstock had a ghost, according to some,' Mr Barton said, smiling. 'The ghost of the last member of the old family, who mysteriously disappeared some thirty years ago.'

'How do you mean?'

'The legend says he walked out of the house one day and was never seen again. Some people are convinced that he was murdered, while others say he was running away from his debts. Whatever happened to the poor chap, his ghost withered away in the light of Arden's pure reasoning; very rational chaps, these Unitarians.'

'Do you know how he came by his wealth?'

'I believe him to be self-made, but I couldn't say what line he was in. The story goes that he was born a few miles from here, into a very poor family, and ran off as a boy to seek his fortune.'

'Like Dick Whittington,' I said. 'How touching that Mr Arden chose to return to the place where he spent his childhood. Does he have a family of his own?'

'He has never married,' Mr Barton said. 'Though local gossips are constantly matching him with eligible ladies. He's bringing up two little orphan boys – cousins, or great-nephews – and they're the reason he summoned me today. They need a tutor, and I mentioned that I was looking for some teaching work.'

He halted the horse outside a pair of tall iron gates. The lodge was a quaint, castellated cottage that spoke volumes for the prosperity of the estate – sparkling clean, with scarlet geraniums on the sills. A neat, smiling young woman emerged from this gingerbread house to open the gates, with two little girls hanging on her skirts.

'Good day, Mrs Woods – hello, Molly; hello, Jessy – yes, I can see you, even when you're hiding your face!' It was pleasant to see how easy he was with the little girls. Once we were through the gates, he added, 'That woman at the lodge is a very good example of Arden's generosity. She was left destitute when her husband died. The man worked on one of his farms and he regarded it as no more than his duty to take care of them.'

'Most admirable!'

'Yes, and practical, too; Arden has a strong belief that people must be helped to help themselves.'

I was, by now, intensely curious about this man. He had reportedly made a great fortune, yet he had not spent his money on empty display. Binstock had no grand avenue of trees, and was surrounded by fields and meadows instead of parkland. The house itself was no mansion, but a welcoming, old-fashioned manor attached to a working farm.

Mr Barton halted the carriage before a stone porch with '1621' carved on the lintel. The heavy wooden door already stood open, giving me a glimpse into the deserted hall. Two large black-and-white collie dogs were stretched luxuriously across the steps; one raised his head when he saw us, the other merely yawned.

The horse stamped, and was still. For a long moment I let the hush of the afternoon wash over me and sink into my bones.

A woman in an apron, briskly drying her hands, trotted out to meet us. Mr Barton explained that we had come to call upon Mr Arden. She shouted, 'Mike!' – and a boy appeared, seemingly from nowhere, to take care of the horse.

And there was our host at the top of the steps. 'Ah, Barton, punctual to the minute!'

Six

I ADMIT THAT I WAS surprised, though I don't know what I had expected. Mr Arden's figure was youthful and upright – all elegance and grace, in fact. His thick hair was iron-grey, but altogether he looked younger than a man of seven-and-forty has any right to look. His face was not handsome, yet somehow vivid and attractive.

'It is a great pleasure to meet you, Mrs Rodd. I know why you're here, and I think I may be able to help you.'

'I always forget how fast news travels in the countryside,' I said, amused by his breezy directness. 'I'll be most grateful for anything you can tell me.'

'And Barton, I've got the boys chained up in my study; please come and inspect them before they escape.'

He led us through the panelled hall into a comfortable room that was partly a drawing room, partly a library. It was the room of a gentleman, and a scholarly gentleman at that; there were piles of books in many languages, and a desk heaped with papers.

'Come out, boys! Jack – Ferdy!'

For a moment, he appeared to be talking to nobody – and then two little boys crawled out from under the desk. They were very alike, with hair so blond as to be almost white, and bright blue eyes, and were shy as two leverets.

'Here are your pupils, Barton.' Mr Arden put his arms around the boys and drew them to his side, smiling in a way that made his lean features positively handsome. 'My twin rascals, John and Ferdinand, eight years old last week. Boys, shake hands with your new tutor.'

The little boys did not move; they stared at Mr Barton with their shining blue eyes.

'Well, here's a fine start,' Mr Arden said, laughing. 'He won't bite!'

'Certainly not,' said Mr Barton. 'I haven't bitten anybody for years. Let me introduce myself properly. I'll be giving you lessons in Latin and arithmetic, and all that sort of thing. I'm also extremely good at cricket and pulling hideous faces. Like this.' He made a silly face, and the boys giggled. 'Did you get any presents for your birthday?'

They nodded eagerly and one of them whispered, 'Ponies!'

'Splendid! I like ponies.' Mr Barton straightened up. 'I think I should meet them as soon as possible.'

A few minutes later he was striding across the lawn, with the boys and the two dogs cavorting around him as if they had known him for years.

'I can't imagine what spell he's cast over them,' Mr Arden said, watching the happy group through the window. 'But I seem to have made a good choice.'

'Yes, indeed,' I said. 'Mr Barton strikes me as an excellent young man. And your nephews are charming.'

'Thank you, Mrs Rodd; they're the best little chaps in the world, but I'm afraid I have let them run wild for too long.' He turned away from the window and I felt his attention fastening upon me. 'They're not my nephews, by the way.'

'I beg your pardon.'

'I adopted them as babies, when their mother died.' Mr Arden's manner was easy and friendly, but his dark eyes were bright and sharp, and I was aware that I was being assessed. 'I have no other children; the twins will inherit everything I have.'

'I see.' (This was interesting; he was easily young enough, and hearty enough, to marry and have children of his own, yet he spoke as if he had ruled this out.)

'I have recently been formalizing my affairs, so that if I drop dead, the estate will be handed on in proper fashion. I've seen what happens to a place, when there is nobody in the immediate family to inherit.'

'Quite so.'

Arden regarded me gravely for a moment, then suddenly smiled. 'The local gossips are convinced that they're my "natural" sons – perhaps that's what you're thinking, Mrs Rodd.'

'No, indeed!' (I tried to make this sound sincere, though it was precisely what I had been thinking.)

'In fact, we're not related at all. My blood relatives are long gone. I should be a lonely man without my boys.'

'The Lord sets the solitary in families,' I said.

'Thank you.' He was touched. 'I see that you understand. Heaven has granted me this joy – and this great responsibility. They must grow up as gentlemen and have a gentleman's education at one of the great schools; this is why I have need of a man like Barton.' He rang the bell and sat down in the armchair opposite to mine. 'I know nothing of such places.'

'Oh dear, it does seem brutal to think of it now, when they're such mites!' (I remembered my anguish at Fred's departure for Harrow when he was only ten years old; I was brave for his sake, but broke down in sobs as soon as the stagecoach turned the corner; our separation was the end of our childhood and my first great sorrow.)

'I've heard tales of the brutality of some public schools,' Mr Arden said. 'Barton assures me, however, that he liked his school. He was at Rugby, in the time of the great Dr Arnold. Thanks to Arnold's influence, many more of those schools are now turning out Christians instead of bullies. Or so Barton maintains.'

The servant we had seen in the hall, a wiry and capable-looking woman of around my own age, came into the room with a heavy tea tray. She was followed by a red-faced maid, puffing beneath the weight of another tray. Mr Arden leapt up, as quick and spry as a much younger man, to assist the servants.

'You look startled, Mrs Rodd,' he said, once we were alone again. 'The fact is that they have instructions to serve up a lavish tea party as soon as they hear the bell – whether I have one guest, or an army of them. This is the time of day I set aside for society; my friends and neighbours know they'll find me at home.'

He made the tea himself and tried to fill my plate with sandwiches, wedges of cake and slices of cold roast ham until I convinced him to let me off with one piece of short-bread.

'Now, as to this business of yours, Mrs Rodd. You are seeking Joshua Welland.'

'Yes,' I said. 'I have a letter of introduction from his brother, who believes you may be able to help us.'

Mr Arden broke the seal of the letter and quickly read the few lines it contained. 'Poor Welland! We met in Argentina, Mrs Rodd. The fact that we were both exiles made us friends. He told me something about the tragedy of his marriage, and his longing to be reconciled with Joshua.'

'Do you know Joshua?'

'I know him,' Mr Arden said, 'but that's not to say I know where to find him.'

His attention was absolute and his attitude so sympathetic that I told him the whole story, including the fact that Joshua's brother was on the point leaving him a fortune.

'I'm not telling most people about the money,' I said. 'I don't want the stories to get even more extravagant.'

'You can trust me to keep it quiet,' Mr Arden said sincerely. 'As far as it's in my power to do so, though I'm sure you know how next-to-impossible it is to keep any kind of secret in the countryside.' He was frowning slightly, deep in thought. 'It's quite right that Joshua should be told of his brother's illness.'

'When you say you know him, Mr Arden, does that mean you've spoken to him – or even seen him?'

'I've spoken to him; not often, and always in some remote place. I believe he trusts me, as much as he trusts anyone. When the nights are bitterly cold, he sometimes creeps into my kitchen here, to sleep beside the embers of the fire. My servants are quite used to him and know not to bother him.'

'What does he look like? What is his manner of speaking? I've heard a dozen fairy tales, without getting hold of one concrete fact.'

Mr Arden smiled. 'The prosaic reality is that he's a quietly spoken man – a gentleman, in fact. My library is a great attraction and I have sometimes lent him books. He has long hair and a long beard, and wears a long black cloak, like a medieval hermit.'

'I don't understand how he manages to live like that in this day and age.'

'Modern life is not as all-encompassing as it seems,' Mr Arden said. 'There are still places it has never penetrated. The last I heard of Joshua Welland, he was living in the woods near Freshley Crossing. My guess is that he'll stay there until after the hay has been got in. He has a great dislike of crowds, and as I'm sure you know, the hay-harvest brings the entire local population out into the fields.' He added, 'I always give a hand myself – I'm incapable of idleness when I'm surrounded by people working. My hands positively itch for the scythe.'

'That must be strange for your labourers,' I said. 'Do they mind you working alongside them?'

He chuckled. 'Opinion is divided. On the one hand, my presence stops the coarse exchanges between the men and the women, and generally spoils all the fun. On the other hand, I provide the strongest beer.'

My liking for this singular man was increasing by the minute. My instincts told me that he was entirely at ease with his humble background, though his speech and bearing were wholly gentlemanly. He drew me a hasty map of the neighbourhood around the woods in which my scholar might be hiding.

'The woods are my property, Mrs Rodd; you must feel free to roam as you wish.'

While he was still drawing his map, we heard shrieks from outside; through the window I saw Mr Barton striding across the lawn, one small boy tucked under each arm. The younger maid ran out to claim them and bear them off to regions unseen. A few minutes later Mr Barton came back into the drawing room.

'Jolly little chaps,' he pronounced. 'And they're far better grounded than you led me to believe, Mr Arden.'

'I have been their only teacher,' Mr Arden said. 'Up to now.'

'In which case, you've been a very good one. They know a lot of irregular Latin verbs for such little fellows, and Master Jack is a veritable tiger with his Greek alphabet. How do you think I ought to proceed?'

The conversation turned to the business of the boys' education. I listened with half an ear, thinking what a fine father Mr Barton would make one of these days, and planning the next stage of my search for Joshua.

Now details begin to be important. Something very unpleasant happened that afternoon, while Mr Barton and I were driving back to Hardinsett. I set it down here because it was later to prove significant.

My guard was down and Mr Barton saw first. To be precise, when we were half a mile from the village in a lonely lane he swore, pulled up the horse and leapt out of the carriage.

I saw three people around a farm gate: a ragged, filthy man and woman – and Rachel.

She was pale as death, on the point of fainting away; I have a vivid picture in my head of her terrified face, the two vagrants menacing her, and the pieces of white calico that had spilled out of her basket strewn across the rough grass at her feet.

In a moment, Mr Barton had dealt the man a mighty punch on the jaw; he drove the pair away with a torrent of the most extraordinary language, while I supported poor Rachel with my arm about her waist.

I see them now – the man was young, with a horrible sort of handsomeness under the dirt, and the toothless, leering crone might have been his mother.

'We'll be back!' the crone shrieked. 'This ain't finished – we'll be back!'

Mr Barton chased them to the bottom of the lane. He then jumped down into the verdant ditch to retrieve his hat which had somehow fallen into the hedge, and returned to us, sucking the knuckles of his right hand.

'Thank you – oh, thank you, I'm perfectly all right.' Rachel did her best to smile. 'I'm sorry to be so silly – they were only begging and I'm sure they didn't mean to hurt me—'

'By God, if that blackguard so much as laid a finger on you—'

Their gazes locked and there was a long moment of silence, during which they both turned scarlet.

This would never do. I ordered Rachel to take my place in the carriage, deaf to her protests that she was utterly recovered. Mr Barton and I gathered up the scattered contents of her basket.

'I beg your pardon if my language offended you, Mrs Rodd.' He could hardly look at me. 'I'm afraid I let my temper get the better of me.'

'Please don't think of it, Mr Barton. I'm profoundly thankful we came along when we did. But what were you doing here, my dear?' I turned to Rachel. 'You must know how dangerous these lonely roads can be at this time of year, when there are so many people in search of work.'

'I was taking a short cut,' Rachel said. 'On my way home from the sewing circle in the village. They must've followed me. They refused to believe I hadn't any money with me.'

I was sure there was more to it than this, but now was not the time to interrogate her, when the colour had only just begun to steal back into her lips. I walked the short distance to the rectory beside the carriage, keeping up a cheerful stream of chatter while the shaken couple pulled themselves together.

'I must ask you both,' Rachel said, just before we entered the house, 'I must beg you – don't tell Arthur.'

'But of course Arthur must know!' I was taken aback. 'I can't keep this from your husband!'

'Please, Mrs Rodd! Nobody must know.'

'The constable should know,' Mr Barton said hotly.

'No harm was done, and I don't want one incident blown up out of all proportion. And Arthur will only be upset, without having the least idea what to do about it.' She had fully recovered now and spoke with ringing firmness. 'I have learnt my lesson and I promise not to take any more short cuts.'

She picked up her skirts and swept into the house.

'Oh dear, I seem to have made a promise,' I said. 'But I'm not sure that I want to keep it; doesn't Arthur have a right to know that his wife was attacked?'

Mr Barton stared after her, with a very unpriestly glint in his eye. 'I'll keep my promise not to tell Somers – but if I see that brute again, I'll thrash him to a pulp.'

'I'll pretend I didn't hear that, Mr Barton,' I said. 'Good afternoon, and please don't get hurt.'

His face cleared and he smiled. 'I beg your pardon, Mrs Rodd – you may trust me not to roll up to Matins with a black eye. Good afternoon.'

Seven

O N THE FOLLOWING DAY I had an appointment with a Mr Silas Jennings of Gabriel College. He had been a student alongside Joshua, and was one of the very few people who had spoken to him since his disappearance.

'I know Jennings,' said Arthur, 'and I know why he wants to meet you at the water meadows.'

'They must be at their loveliest now,' I agreed.

'It has nothing to do with the meadows. He's dodging the Gorgon.'

'I beg your pardon?'

'The Warden's wife, Mrs Watts-Weston – known far and wide as the Gorgon of Gabriel.' He smiled at me, with a flash of the old intimacy we had enjoyed in Herefordshire. 'She pounces on anyone who puts a toe into the porters' lodge, demanding to know all their business. I daresay Jennings is hoping to speak to you without any Gorgons looking over his shoulder.'

It was another fair summer morning. Arthur had kindly undertaken to escort me to Oxford, in the little one-horse open carriage. I was driving – I had forcibly taken the reins away from him the second time he nearly ran us into a ditch. Being a passenger suited him much better. He sat beside me, chattering happily in quite the old way, and it occurred to me that this was the first time we had been alone together since my arrival.

'Do you know Mr Jennings well? I asked.

'Not well. We've met once or twice at Swinford, though I haven't seen him there for a while.'

I had been waiting for a chance to talk to him about that place. 'Rachel told me you are often at Swinford.'

'Yes, I try to walk over at least three times a week. It's only a matter of a few miles as the crow flies. I consider myself very fortunate to be so close.'

'What is the attraction, exactly?'

I spoke lightly, but he knew what was coming; his blue eyes took on the soulful expression that meant I had hit granite; like many gentle people, he was capable of extreme obstinacy.

'It is the most beautiful place on earth – not outwardly, but spiritually,' he said. 'I go to Swinford for the refreshment of my soul.'

'How nice.'

'Nowhere else do I have the sense of standing before the Great Mystery, with my own sinful will annihilated.'

'All well and good,' I said carefully. 'Provided it does not interfere with your duties in the parish.'

Arthur reddened a little and became more soulful. 'I never forget that my chief duty is prayer.'

'Well, of course, that goes without saying.'

'When we came to Hardinsett we found a great deal of ungodliness. People only attended to the outward observances of their religion, believing it was enough to pay their tithes and turn up in church of a Sunday. There was a kind of spiritual famine.'

The word 'fiddlesticks' was in my head, and must have got out into the surrounding ether, for Arthur flushed a deeper red, and said, 'I know that your late husband would not have approved, Mrs Rodd. But times have changed. The hungry souls are clamouring to be fed.'

'I wouldn't know about that,' I said. 'I was a little surprised, however, to observe that you leave a great many matters to your excellent Mr Barton.'

'I'm afraid you're right on that count.' He chuckled suddenly. 'He's so tremendously capable, that's the trouble. I'd be all at sea without him.'

'He should not be making decisions on your behalf.'

'At least he makes the right decisions, which is more than I can say for myself.'

'Arthur dear, I think you ought to take your head out of the clouds occasionally.' I spoke as kindly as I knew how, not wanting to wound him. 'You're the vicar and Mr Barton's the curate, yet you appear sometimes to defer to him as if the positions were reversed.'

'You're quite right, Mrs Rodd – Barton himself has said as much to me more than once.'

'He'll get his own parish one day, and then what will you do? Your next curate might not be such a paragon.'

'I might have known I was in for one of your lectures.' Arthur was smiling now. 'I felt it brewing the first time you heard the word "Swinford". Let me assure you that I'm not about to turn Roman. I mainly go there for the sake of Gerard Fogle. We are very old friends and he has helped me through more than one crisis. I went to him when I had that bout of illness a few years ago – you remember, of course.'

Yes, I did remember, and with a sharp sense of unease. Shortly after the fainting incident that so angered Matt, our young curate fell into a state of weeping exhaustion, and went away to recover. The official reason given was that he had tired himself out with too many devotions, but I had a powerful instinct that there was something else going on, and I had nagged at my husband to tell me, until he said very seriously, 'Please stop asking me, Letty – yes, of course there was more to it, but all I can tell you is that Somers stood in the shadow of a very grievous sin, and I had to tie myself in knots to save the man from absolute disgrace.'

Frankly, I did not understand. What grievous sin had poor Arthur ever committed? Why was he so frightened? And why was Matt so wrathful?

The golden city of Oxford was unspeakably lovely now, at the tail-end of Trinity term. The narrow streets around the colleges were still busy with undergraduates – those that were not on the river, at any rate – but there was a sense of the approaching Long Vacation, when the place would fall into its summer slumber.

We left the carriage in the stables at the Mitre Inn, and Arthur escorted me to the Fellows' Door of Gabriel College; a low door, set into a long blank wall, at which a young clergyman was waiting, rather anxiously, to meet us.

'Mrs Rodd?' Mr Jennings had a fresh pink face, and a dome of a forehead where his light-brown hair was already receding. His eyes, large and of a pale reddish-brown, swam behind thick spectacles. 'I beg your pardon for the informality; I thought you would like to see the gardens, and we can talk there without fear of interruption.'

'Thank you, Mr Jennings; I believe you know Mr Somers.'

'Oh, yes – of course—' For a fraction of a moment, Mr Jennings looked uneasy and the pink in his cheeks deepened. 'From Swinford.'

He and Arthur shook hands.

'It's been many months since we last saw you there,' said Arthur.

'I've been very busy,' Mr Jennings replied. 'And the college authorities don't entirely approve of the place. One has to be so careful.'

He unlocked the low wooden door upon a beautiful garden, one of the secret jewels that hide behind those blank college walls. The velvet lawns led down to a gravelled walk through the meadows beside the river, where swans preened in the reeds, and the dappled fallow deer browsed in the long, sweet grass. It was delightful, and my compliments broke any remaining ice between the three of us.

'We're proud of our gardens,' Mr Jennings said, smiling. 'Naturally, I consider them the very best in the whole city – though men from other colleges might disagree.'

Lovely as the surroundings were, I had not forgotten that I was here on business, and I quickly broached the subject of Joshua Welland.

'Poor old Welland,' Mr Jennings sighed. 'I should very much like to help him. He deserves to be helped. We were close friends at one time.'

'How long have you known him?'

'We entered the college together, as undergraduates. There was nothing singular about him in those days. He was a shabby young scholar, like a hundred others – like myself, in fact. We lived on the same stair and I would've been very lonely without him. I knew nobody and was painfully shy, and Joshua was the first real friend I made here.'

'I'm trying to make up a picture, Mr Jennings; what manner of man was he? What was his character?'

'He was extremely clever – brilliantly clever.' The two of us were strolling side by side, with Arthur keeping a tactful distance behind us. Mr Jennings relaxed a little and stopped looking over his shoulder. 'His talk dazzled me sometimes. I thought he was destined for greatness. But then he left us.'

'Were you surprised when he left?'

'I was astonished,' admitted Mr Jennings. 'I didn't believe the reports at first, they seemed so far-fetched. I was certain he'd be back. This wasn't the first time he'd been absent without leave; the college authorities turned a blind eye for as long as possible.'

'Did he tell you what he'd been doing during these absences?'

'Never. When I asked him, he smiled and said he'd been "seeing sermons in stones".'

'Mr Jennings, you are one of the very few people to have seen Joshua since his so-called disappearance. It would help me very much to hear the details of your encounter.'

'Well – it was an odd sort of business.' The baby-faced clergyman took one more cautious look up and down the path, though there was no one nearby. 'I came across him, quite by accident, more than a year after he left the college. It was on a winter's afternoon, at a lonely river-crossing near the old woods at Freshley. I had been out walking and I was making my way home. The dusk had come on very suddenly, and in the shadows I saw that someone else was waiting there on the riverbank for the ferry. I'm not superstitious by nature, but for a moment I thought he was a ghost – this strange figure, wrapped in a long black cloak. Imagine my astonishment when I heard his voice, quiet and friendly, speaking to me out of the darkness – "Hello, Jennings".'

'He did not try to run away from you?'

'Not at all – he knows I am perfectly harmless, and in that lonely place I could not have betrayed him if I'd wanted to. I think I managed to stammer out a couple of questions, which he brushed off impatiently. He said I was just the man he needed and he had a bundle of papers that he'd like me to keep for him – vital notes for the book he was writing, which he said would be a sensation and cover him with glory.'

'So he had not stopped working,' I said, 'despite living in hedges and ditches.'

'I begged him to come back to college,' said Mr Jennings, 'but he claimed no library in Oxford – or anywhere else – could be of the slightest use to him. I had no idea what he was talking about. Night was falling, and it seemed to be pulling Joshua back into the darkness, until he was nothing more than a black shape. I heard him laughing at me – not at all unkindly, but almost with the old affection. "My dear old Jennings," he says, "don't be so slow! You and I have talked of it more than once – I'm taking inspiration straight from the pages of Joseph Glanvill.' Whereupon I blurted out, "Who?" like a great idiot, and Joshua laughed again.' He halted on the path and turned to face me, engrossed in his story. 'I know I should have asked more questions, but the ferry was approaching and he simply disappeared.'

'Did he give you those papers?' (I was excited; papers were concrete things, and the writing of Joshua would surely contain some clue to his whereabouts.)

'Oh, yes – a thick pile of them, which he abruptly shoved into my hand at the last minute. "Keep them safe," he says. "Don't give them up to any person but me, and tell no one that you have them." Naturally I was wildly curious, and I began to read them the very second I got back to my rooms. But I'm afraid Joshua's masterpiece turned out to be rather a let-down.'

'How do you mean?'

'Oh, dear.' Mr Jennings resumed his strolling, looking uncomfortable. 'The pages were of all shapes and sizes, sometimes torn from parcels, sometimes scraps of rubbish. The handwriting was nearly impossible to make out, beyond a few phrases of Latin and Greek. And quite a few sheets were covered with a language I had never seen; I showed it round the common room and someone said it looked like an attempt to write in Romany, the old language of the gipsies. And that was when I understood why Joshua had mentioned Joseph Glanvill.'

'You have lost me, Mr Jennings.'

'Oh – well – he was a seventeenth-century chap, Mrs Rodd, mainly a fine apologist for religious toleration, but he also believed in witches. Joshua had somehow obtained a mouldy copy of Glanvill's *The Vanity of Dogmatizing*, and we spent many evenings reading what Joshua called "the wondrous nonsense" to one another over the fire. And there was a story in it that he particularly liked, about a certain ragged scholar who left his college and vanished into the surrounding countryside.'

'So when Joshua did his own vanishing,' I said thoughtfully, 'it amounted to a deliberate reference to this story.'

'Yes indeed, and there's more. Glanvill's poor scholar runs into two men from his college, while in some lonely country place – and tells them he is learning the great secrets of the gipsy people, which will one day astound the world. When Joshua met me at the crossing, the similarity to Glanvill clearly struck him at once, which is probably why he was laughing at me.'

'And have you kept the papers that he gave to you?'

'I couldn't have thrown them away, even if they were nonsense. Joshua trusted me to keep them safe.'

'I should like to see them, if that is possible.' The scraps of paper he had described could at least give me clues to Joshua's whereabouts; I had already decided to take the many hints and search the woods at Freshley. 'Thank you, Mr Jennings; you have been most helpful.'

'Watch it!' Arthur suddenly ran to catch up with us. 'The Gorgon approacheth!'

'Mr Jennings! Mr Jennings!'

Mrs Watts-Weston was at our heels in a tumble of grey silk skirts, with a white straw bonnet hastily stuck on top of her blue-ribboned morning cap, positively chasing us along the path.

It was only relatively recently that the Oxford colleges had allowed their dons to marry, and the place was still reeling from the subsequent invasion of petticoats; those slumberous quads and cloisters now rang with the voices of children, and the wives of the great men saw no reason not to interfere with centuries of tradition.

'Mr Jennings—' The Gorgon caught up with us, and we waited while she recovered her breath and settled her skirts. 'If I hadn't been looking out of my parlour window at the exact moment you passed, I should never have known about this – and I'm sure you were present at dinner the other night, when I mentioned that I would like to meet Mrs Rodd!'

'How do you do, Mrs Watts-Weston,' I said quickly, extending my hand. 'I am Laetitia Rodd.'

The introductions were made and I resumed my walk with Mrs Watts-Weston beside me. She was a tall, commanding lady in the early forties, her soldierly figure only slightly softened by childbearing.

'I cannot claim to have met the man you are seeking, Mrs Rodd; he had already left the college when my husband and I arrived here. There was, however, an encounter that you may find interesting.'

'An – encounter?'

'That's all I can call it.' Her lips twitched into a complacent smile; she was enjoying her moment of mystery. 'I'm afraid I'm acting against the wishes of my husband in telling you about it; he is quite rightly concerned with the reputation of this college, and wishes to avoid gossip. In this case, however, I can't see how it can do the college any harm.'

'You may be assured, ma'am, that nothing you say will go any further; discretion is the cornerstone of my work.'

'I don't doubt it, Mrs Rodd – but this is Oxford, where secrets have a way of leaking into the surrounding air and getting into a person's bloodstream!' Her voice was loud and she made no effort to lower it. 'Anyway, my husband and I heard the tale of Joshua Welland shortly after our arrival. A certain book had gone missing from the Founder's Library; a valuable edition of Vico's *Scienza Nuova*. I don't know if you take an interest in philosophy?'

This question startled me. 'I know nothing about it.'

'Never mind, it's not to the point.' She looked, for a moment, a little disappointed. 'The last person to have had possession of the missing book was Joshua Welland. My husband refused to have Welland publicly named as a thief, and undertook to pay the cost of the book from his own pocket, if it was not returned to the college within a year.' She added, 'Frankly, I was very cross when I heard about this; it was a significant sum of money, and while we are comfortably situated, every penny is accounted for.'

'You have a large establishment to run here, of course.' I was assailed by a memory of my own 'establishment' in Bloomsbury when dearest Matt was still beside me; I am thrifty by nature, and was constantly dismayed by the expense of running such a place to the proper standard. 'Husbands often fail to appreciate how much things cost – small, everyday things that they don't even notice until they go missing.'

Mrs Watts-Weston was amused. 'Yours too? I thought only shut-away, scholarly types were thus afflicted! My husband is one of the cleverest men in the world and this country's foremost Latin poet, but he couldn't tell you the price of the bacon he eats every morning, and he seems to think that a family of five children can live on fresh air. That is why I was annoyed by his grand promise. You'll never see that book again, I told him. The man has sold it, or burned it, or wrapped the pages around a hot pie, and we'll be forced to pay for it – so don't you dare complain when we have to spend the Long Vacation in Margate instead of Boulogne!'

She shot me a smile from the corner of her eye, and I was sufficiently off my guard to laugh; I liked the forth-right manner that had made the Gorgon such an object of terror.

'You may be sure,' she went on cheerfully, 'that the whole of Oxford knew every detail of our disagreement. The undergraduates were laying bets on whether or not the missing book would be returned before the year was out. The weeks passed, the months passed, and I had resigned myself to the loss of the money. It was early autumn and very fine weather, and I had taken the children out to Boars Hill to pick blackberries. My son, Alfred – two years old at that time – wandered out of sight for a few minutes. When I found him shortly afterwards, he was holding a square parcel, neatly wrapped in brown sacking.'

'The book?'

'Yes – the Vico, in perfect condition! All my son could tell me was that a man had popped out of a hedge and put it into his hand.'

'You must have been very relieved to see it.'

'I could have turned a cartwheel,' Mrs Watts-Weston said, laughing quietly.

'Did you see anything at all of the man?'

'Not a thing – but it must have been Joshua Welland.'

'So he keeps his ear to the ground,' I said, considering this. 'Someone relays the latest news to him.'

'Evidently – though heaven knows who it is. I have told you everything I know. I hope it will be useful to you.'

'Thank you, Mrs Watts-Weston; the smallest thing can be useful in a case of this kind.' Her story showed, at least, that my wandering scholar was blessed (or afflicted, depending on your point of view) with a sense of humour.

'I know you have already spoken to Daniel Arden, over at Binstock.'

'Yes, and he was most helpful.' (I was by now resigned to the fact that every man, woman and child for miles around knew all my movements, apparently almost before I did myself.)

'What did you make of him?'

'He is most interesting,' I said, rather taken aback by the bluntness of her demand.

'Fascinating – such a shame that he's a dissenter, and we can't be properly acquainted. I took the trouble to meet him because I have a distant family connection to Binstock Manor.' Mrs Watts-Weston absently righted her lopsided bonnet. 'My maternal grandmother was born a Warrender; they built Binstock and lived there for many centuries, until the last one ran off and left the place to fall into ruin.'

'You don't believe the story that the last of the Warrenders was murdered?'

'Certainly not – stuff and nonsense!' the Gorgon said briskly. 'My mother always maintained that the man was a wastrel and ne'er-do-well. He simply ran away from his debts. Generally, where there is any kind of mystery, the dullest explanation turns out to be the truest, don't you find?' She glanced down at the gold watch she wore at her waist. 'I must leave you, Mrs Rodd. It has been a pleasure to meet you – and no thanks to you, Mr Jennings! In future, you will inform me of any visitors you have who might be of interest to me. Good morning!'

Eight

RACHEL AND I HAD a quiet luncheon together, of cold lamb, tender new peas and blancmange. The afternoon was warm and drowsy and we sat out in the garden, in the shade of a great oak tree. Rachel had brought her work for the sewing club; the same pieces of off-white calico that she had been carrying when she was attacked.

'I'll help you,' I said, taking one of the needles from her tortoiseshell case. 'I've made such quantities of babies' caps in my time, I believe I could do it in my sleep!'

Those little caps were very easy to sew, being just a rectangle to cover the top of the head and a gathered piece behind. I liked to stitch in a private prayer sometimes, for the downy pate of the babe who would wear it.

Rachel gazed at the scrap of material in her hands, her expression sorrowful and dreamy, and asked, 'Did it ever make you sad?'

'I beg your pardon?'

'I mean – was it sad for you to sew baby clothes when you had no baby of your own?'

I had been waiting for a chance to broach this subject myself. For a moment I listened to the bees humming and the ducks splashing and quacking in the nearby pond, considering how I could persuade her to confide in me.

'I can see that you are sad, my dear, and you have all my sympathy. I hoped you and Arthur would have a family by now.'

'So did we, but it was not the Lord's will.'

Now I had to choose my words very carefully; I knew that the Lord was sometimes blamed for shortcomings that were purely human.

'You are still young,' I said. 'You should not give up hope too soon. What do the doctors say?'

'I – I don't need to consult a doctor.' Rachel's cheeks were red, and her expression of dumb pain went to my heart. 'I know it won't ever happen, and I am quite resigned to it.' Her gaze dropped away from mine. 'You must have noticed, Mrs Rodd, that we – we do not sleep in the same room.'

'Oh, my dear.' I did not need to say more.

'Arthur is the very best of husbands, and any fault is likely to be mine – because I've failed to be the wife he needed.'

'Rachel!' (I had to prevent myself groaning at this; never had I longed so fiercely to talk to Matt.) 'Are you telling me that the separate rooms were your idea? No, I didn't think so. In which case, the failure is not on your side.' I could go no further without being indelicate, but the plain truth of the matter was that Arthur Somers had bungled yet another of his given duties.

'He is so good, I think sometimes that he is a saint,' Rachel murmured. 'He prays to be freed from the impurities of the flesh.'

Perhaps fortunately, before I could retort that married people were one flesh and there was no impurity about it whatsoever, we heard Mr Barton's whistle, and the man himself walked through the wooden door in the garden wall.

'Ladies, good afternoon.' I had a sense that he was on his guard when he saw me. 'Please forgive my dustiness – I'm looking for Somers.'

'I'm afraid you have missed him,' I said. 'He went out again, almost the minute after we came home from Oxford. I believe he was walking over to Swinford.'

'Hmm,' said Mr Barton. 'No surprise there.'

'He wouldn't stay to eat anything, and it's such a hot walk across the fields.' Rachel was anxious. 'I was hoping he would stay at home this afternoon, to write his sermon.'

(Another memory, rather unwelcome, assailed me; Arthur's awful, rambling sermons, full of scholarly references that nobody understood; Matt used to cough very loudly to shut him up when he could endure no more.)

'I've written this week's sermon,' said Mr Barton. 'It's on the desk.'

'Excellent,' I said. 'I look forward to hearing it.'

'Thank you, Mrs Rodd, but don't expect too much. The most that can be said for my sermons is that they're short and to the point.'

'I'm sure your parishioners are most grateful. Won't you sit down? You look very hot.'

'Yes, do!' Rachel eagerly put aside her sewing and rang the little bell on the table. 'And you must have some of my lemonade. I made it this morning.'

'I'm glad you're still making your lemonade,' I said. 'Mine was never half so delicious, even when I followed your recipe to the letter.'

She smiled, looking very young. 'Mrs Richards thinks I'm a terrible nuisance, but I love being in the kitchen. I think nature intended me for a cook.'

Mr Barton sat down in one of the wicker chairs, fanning himself with his hat. The lemonade was brought out, cool from the larder. Mrs Richards called Rachel indoors

69

to consult about some domestic matter, and the curate and I were alone.

His face darkened – he had been making an effort at cheerfulness, I saw now, for Rachel's sake, and clearly had something heavy on his mind.

'Your meeting at Gabriel was satisfactory, I hope?'

'Most interesting, thank you, Mr Barton.'

'Good.' Mr Barton leant towards me. 'I heard a snippet about Joshua Welland this morning. It might be nothing. I paid a visit to the gipsies on the common.'

This alarmed me, and my work dropped into my lap. 'You were looking for the couple who attacked Mrs Somers.'

'Yes – please don't tell her.'

'Did you find them?'

'Those ruffians did not belong to the camp, and they're not gipsies,' said Mr Barton. 'The old woman who occasionally deigns to give me sixpence-worth of conversation told me they were simply itinerant tramps.' He broke off to gulp down his lemonade.

'The gipsy people do not deserve their bad reputation,' I could not refrain from saying. 'My late husband was constantly defending the poor creatures from every sort of accusation. Did your old woman know where those travellers might be found?'

'She said they might have headed into Freshley Woods. But she added that they'd better watch out for the charcoal burners there, who are very suspicious of strangers.'

'That was certainly true of the charcoal burners we had in Herefordshire. They were insular people, and fiercely territorial.'

'That's when she dropped her hint about your lost scholar, Mrs Rodd,' said Mr Barton. 'She maintains that he was taken in by the charcoal burners after the gipsies expelled him from their camp.'

'He was expelled?' I was startled. 'Did she say why?'

'No; my sixpence had run out, and I had no more change.'

'I must speak with her; I'd be grateful if you could help me, Mr Barton.'

'I'll see what I can do.' He gave me a rueful look. 'Not much to go on, I'm afraid.'

'I have so little that I'm profoundly grateful for anything – thank you.' I remembered the snippet given to me by the dairymaid, which I had dismissed as mere rumour; that Joshua had fallen out with his gipsy friends on account of a woman. At least part of it might be true.

'Arden and I were speaking of your case this morning; he is very anxious to assist you.'

'That's kind of him.'

'He was too polite to ask me outright, but I know he'd like me to pass on anything you tell me about your investigation – if agreeable to you, naturally.'

'It's perfectly agreeable to me, Mr Barton,' I said, wondering why Mr Arden wanted to know. 'I only tell you things I don't mind making public.'

He was amused. 'That makes me sound like a notorious gossip.'

'Not at all,' I said. 'A clergyman must always know the local news. My dear husband maintained that it was part of the job.'

Rachel came back into the garden, followed by Mrs Richards with a tray of tea, and Mr Barton swiftly turned the conversation to mundane parish matters.

The voices began as part of a dream and tugged me gently into wakefulness; low voices, rapid and urgent, so close that for a few sleep-addled seconds I thought they were in the room with me.

Once I was properly awake, I realized that they were outside, under my window. I had left my casement open and uncovered, to make the most of the sweet night air, and Arthur's voice floated up to me on a cloud of fragrance from the stocks in the flower bed.

'It had nothing to do with him; I can't for the life of me understand why you have to drag him into it.'

Another voice – that of Mr Barton – murmured something I could not hear.

I tilted the face of my watch towards a patch of moonlight. It was ten past one in the morning; the household had been asleep for hours.

'But this is precisely why I need him,' Arthur said, his voice weary and tearful. 'He's the only man in the world – but you've never understood—'

I got out of bed, pulled my shawl around my shoulders and crept through the stripes and bars of moonlight to the open window.

(I know eavesdropping is wrong, but must admit that my work had somewhat blunted my conscience in that area.)

Arthur and Mr Barton were directly beneath me and I could see nothing of them except an occasional puff of the curate's cigar-smoke.

'—your duty to the people of this parish, for a start.' Mr Barton's voice was low and tight with anger. 'You don't even know the names of your churchwardens. You hold yourself apart, as if you didn't live here—'

'Not this again! What if I promise to come to the Haymaking Supper? What if I promise to drag poor Rachel out into local society? Won't that be enough?'

'You have no business at Swinford,' said Mr Barton. 'People are starting to talk.'

'People are always talking. And they'll talk more if I suddenly stop going there. You can't mean it!' Arthur's voice shook. 'Please, Henry! Try to understand how important—'

'For God's sake, man!' snapped Mr Barton. 'The japes up at Swinford are only the half of it! Do you honestly think that brute will keep his mouth shut?'

'But you said you'd paid him.'

'Don't be an idiot – he'll be back for more as soon as he's spent it. The sneering impertinence of the fellow made me sick. He could see how much I hated the whole business, and he was revelling in it.'

There was a spell of silence, after which Arthur meekly said, 'I'm really most awfully grateful.'

'You know why I did it, and I wish you'd told me sooner – you should've thought of her, Somers, and your sacred duty to protect her, instead of scuttling off to Swinford like a coward.'

I could hear that something in Mr Barton's manner of speaking to Arthur had changed; he was angry and wounded – but why was Arthur, saintly Arthur, paying off a blackmailer?

'Forgive me, Henry,' pleaded Arthur. 'I'm weak – I confess that I knowingly sought temptation. And that I'm a coward where Rachel is concerned. But how can I look into those great, trustful eyes of hers and tell her the truth about her husband?' He was weeping now. 'That's what I'm praying for – to become the man she thinks I am. And that's one reason I must pay at least a few more visits to Swinford; I'm in the middle of a novena.'

Mr Barton let out a noise that reminded me forcibly of Matt – a combination of groan and snort, like an angry horse.

With a string of oaths and profanities, he asked what a novena might be when it was at home – and when Arthur foolishly started to explain, he launched into another unprintable volley that made my ears tingle.

'Listen to me very carefully.' Mr Barton spoke quietly, but with such intensity that I heard each syllable. 'Your sins are your own business. But if she gets hurt, I swear to God, I'll kill you.'

This struck them into a silence that stretched on for several minutes.

'Henry,' whispered Arthur eventually, 'my dear Henry, please don't be angry with me, don't cast me aside! I know you are right and I'll do everything you say. I acknowledge my transgressions and my sin is ever before me.'

This time the silence lasted so long that I wondered if the two of them had gone.

And then a fox barked, and Arthur said, in more temperate voice, as if nothing had been said, 'It's ridiculously late; you had better sleep here.'

'I can easily walk home,' said Mr Barton. 'It's as bright as day.'

'I'll come to the gate with you.'

They moved away, and I returned to my bed wishing more than ever that I could talk to Matt – though I knew that the first thing he would say was that he had been proved right about Arthur Somers, and I should not have interfered in the making of that marriage.

Nine

ONCE I KNEW THAT Arthur was being black-mailed, how could I help wondering why? Someone knew something that could ruin him, and I went through a mental list of all the usual things that ruined clergymen. I invite the reader to do the same; decency forbids me going into detail. I will simply say that during that long night I made certain connections, and (with no true understanding of the matter) concluded that poor Arthur must have succumbed to a particular and tragic temptation.

I was not ready to face him over the breakfast table, and freely admit that I used my work as an excuse to run away. Next morning, clad in my stoutest boots and plainest black straw bonnet, and carrying a bottle of water, some bread and cheese and Jacob Welland's sealed letter to his brother, I set out as the sun rose and the birds sang their dawn chorus. It was so early that the wild roses in the hedgerows still wore their gleaming diadems of dew; the sheer beauty and freshness of such a morning can lift the heaviest heart, and mine rose up in spite of itself. I made a determined effort to stop worrying about Rachel and Arthur; the ugly things I had overheard last night were none of my business, and had nothing to do with my case. My business was simply to deliver that letter.

I was on a mission to scatter my message to Joshua Welland as near to the ground as possible, in every village, hamlet and settlement around the ancient woodlands at Freshley. The story told to me by Mrs Watts-Weston showed that Joshua had ways of getting information. He knew I was looking for him. If I had to nail notices to every mossy tree and out-of-the-way gatepost, he would hear me – whether he liked it or not.

Knowing that my quarry was shy and solitary, I avoided the busiest roads and quickly lost myself in a maze of narrow lanes and winding paths, so obscure that the grass grew between the cart-tracks and the deep hedges were tunnels of greenery. There is nothing more fair than a midsummer morning in those last days before haymaking, and at first it was glorious.

Everyone I met knew of me, and I spoke to them all – farmers in their fields, cottagers at their open doors, a laughing row of dairymaids sunning themselves upon a fence. I learned nothing new but that was not my purpose; I was calling out to Joshua Welland as forcefully as a town crier with a handbell.

Your brother is dying. I mean you no harm.

The sun climbed in the sky and I stopped to rest on a wooden bench outside a solitary cottage, hidden away within a patch of woodland. For the modest sum of three-pence, the old woman at the cottage brought me a cup of tea (typical cottagers' tea, as I remembered wistfully: they left the teapot stewing all day over the fire until the brew was dark as molasses and strong enough to strip varnish; I hasten to add that it was delicious) and a bowl of straw-berries still warm from the sun.

A wood pigeon called out from a nearby tree, unseen hens fussed and scratched nearby, midges danced; it was very pleasant to sit in the dappled shade, and I stayed far longer than I had intended. My laziness had a good result, however; the carrier's cart came rumbling up the track to the cottage, to deliver a kitchen chair and a large tin bath.

Here was a splendid opportunity to scatter my message and rest my feet at the same time. I asked the carrier if he could take me to Shotton Barrow, where poor Hannah Laurie was buried, and he told me he could let me down at the nearest crossroads for sixpence.

He was a glum, toothless, taciturn old man, who answered my questions about Joshua Welland in grudging monosyllables. I gave up my attempts to talk to him and tried instead to observe where he was taking me. The ancient woods at Freshley had stretched across half the county at one time, and though they had shrunk over the centuries, there were still hamlets and farmsteads that looked as if they had been swallowed up by a tidal wave of trees and forgotten.

The horse halted in a deep green lane, and the carrier said, 'Here you are.'

'Here?'

'Yes'm. Next turning.'

We were only a few miles outside Oxford, yet this was the middle of nowhere. I handed the man his sixpence and climbed off the cart. The 'turning' was narrow, almost hidden by the hedgerows; I walked along it through the afternoon stillness, and presently came upon a little settlement of cottages and barns, clustered around a very small and ancient church.

There is nowhere on earth more peaceful than a country churchyard on a sunny day. I halted for a moment at the lychgate, to let the profound restfulness of this place wrap itself around me. The gravestones were lopsided, splattered with lichen, names and dates worn away by time. Two sheep nuzzled at the grass, in the cool shade of a great yew tree. My beloved parents lie in just such a place, together until the end of days.

I slipped into a reverie ('Truly, can these dry bones live?') and nearly jumped out of my skin when a child appeared at my elbow.

'If you please, ma'am.'

She was a skinny little thing of around twelve years old, in a washed-out calico sun bonnet.

'Good gracious, you startled me! Do you live here?'

'If you please, ma'am,' the child said, frowning and solemn, 'do you want to see the church?'

'Yes, of course – but I'm searching for a certain grave here, a newer grave than any of these. Perhaps you can help me.'

'I know how to show you round the church. The vicar learnt me how.'

'The vicar?' This was promising; the man might remember Hannah, and at the very least he would know where she was buried. 'Where may I find him, my dear?'

'He don't come out no more,' said the little girl flatly. 'He learnt me all the things to say. Now I show people the church.' She added, 'For sixpence.'

It was daylight robbery but I knew I would get nothing out of her until I had crossed her palm with silver; I gave her sixpence and resigned myself to the guided tour. The church was charming, and I was mightily amused by the way my guide rattled out all the information at breakneck speed, to get it over with as quickly as possible.

The most remarkable thing inside the church was a large fifteenth-century tomb, upon which two stone effigies lay stiffly side by side with their hands folded. Their name was Warrender; these figures were all that remained of the great family that had built Binstock.

Once the child had finished her recital, I established that her name was 'Bess' and asked if she could show me Hannah's grave. She duly led me over to a stone under the yew, markedly newer than the others and set a little apart. It was very plain, but of the best York stone, and the inscription finely carved: 'Hannah Elizabeth Welland – Till the day breaks and the shadows flee away'.

'Do you remember this lady?' I asked hopefully.

'No, ma'am.'

'But of course you're too young.'

The plot was well-tended; the grass had been trimmed recently, and someone had planted a clump of forget-me-nots.

'Do you know who takes care of this grave?'

'A man comes,' said Bess.

'A man – what is his name?'

'Dunno his name.'

'Are you able to describe him?'

'He's got a beard, and long hair,' she said promptly. 'And a long black cloak.'

I kept my voice steady, but here was something concrete at last. 'How often does he come?'

'I dunno.'

'I mean, is it once a week, or once a month?'

'I dunno,' repeated Bess. 'He's here sometimes, that's all.'

Joshua, of course; it was no surprise to me that he tended Hannah's grave, though I did wonder who had paid for the stone.

There was a distant shout and Bess ran off through the churchyard before I could ask her anything else. Never mind; I had found my first really solid point of contact. Although I could not risk leaving Jacob's letter in such a place, I wrote a brief note (in faint pencil, on the paper wrapped around my cheese):

To Joshua Welland – I have a letter for you from your brother, who is very ill and begs to see you at Rosemount, Hampstead, London. Yr servant Laetitia Rodd.

I hid my message deep in the heart of the forget-me-nots. The afternoon was advancing, and my most immediate concern now was finding my way back to Hardinsett. I set out along the road, with no real notion of where I was headed, in search of any person or sign that might point me in the right direction. At last, when I felt I had been tramping for ages, and my long black skirts were covered with white dust, I came to a crossroads with a signpost, and recognized one of the place names that Mr Arden had written on the map he made for me – Freshley St Johns, close to both the river and the principal road to Oxford. I followed the road into the very depths of the forest.

Now that I had recovered my sense of direction, I could no longer ignore the fact that I was extremely tired and giddy with hunger. There were no cottages in this part of the wood, and not another living soul in sight; I would have to be satisfied with the unappetizing remains of my bread and cheese.

It was not easy to keep to my path; it had dwindled into a grassy woodland track and vanished altogether in some places. Another hour passed and I was forced to admit to myself that I was thoroughly lost. There were no paths now; I had managed to stray into the very heart of the forest and I suspected I was walking in circles.

There was a pervasive smell of woodsmoke, which I tried to follow; at length I heard voices, and through a space in a grove of trees I saw the sugar-loaf shapes of two large charcoal fires, glowing hot and smouldering lazily. By sheer good luck I had found the famous charcoal burners, who had reportedly given shelter to Joshua after he left the gipsies. Did this mean I had found Joshua himself?

Before I could decide how to make my approach, a large dog with a coarse brown pelt came snuffling angrily towards me; when he found me he barked loudly.

'Who're you? What d'you want with us?' A man in a leathern apron, grimed and striped with soot, came crashing at me through the leaves. 'Get out!'

'I beg your pardon,' I stammered, doing my best to stand my ground with that horrid dog snarling at the hem of my skirts.

'Stop – leave her be!' A young woman ran out after him, swift as a deer. 'It's a lady and she means no harm.'

'Indeed not,' I said quickly. 'I have lost my way.'

'Call him off!' she snapped at the man.

He looked surly, but did as he was told; man and dog vanished into the leaves.

'Thank you,' I said.

My rescuer was a self-possessed young woman, with an intelligent manner. She wore an apron of the roughest sacking and her face and hands were blackened with the grime of making charcoal, yet she bore herself with all the ease of a lady in her drawing room. Beneath the grime her face was decidedly handsome; she had the fine blue eyes, rosy complexion and black hair that recalled the beautiful country girls I had seen in Ireland.

'I will set you on the right path, ma'am; where are you going?'

'I'm looking for any road that will lead me back to Hardinsett.'

The word was barely out of my mouth before the young woman nodded, and set off down the path, so briskly that I could not question her; after that it took all my powers of concentration to keep her in sight and not lose her in the trees; she led me with the blind assurance of someone who knew every stick and stone.

At length she halted and waited for me to catch up, and I saw that she had brought me to a most enchanting little glade, a sunny clearing with a ruin of some kind at its centre; I could only make out a heap of mossy stones beneath a glorious blanket of ivy.

When I reached her, the young woman pointed to an opening at the other side of the glade. 'Follow that path and you'll come out by the signpost; then it's not more than ten minutes to the Oxford road.' She turned around and began to walk away from me, without a backward glance.

'Wait!' I called after her. 'You have been very kind; please let me give you something for your trouble!'

Reluctantly she stopped, and turned to me with a look of amusement. 'I don't want money just for showing you home, Mrs Rodd.'

'You – you know who I am?'

She was openly smiling at me now. 'You're the lady who's looking for Joshua Welland.'

'Yes – and I heard that he lives with the charcoal burners – perhaps you know him?'

'Perhaps I do.'

'If you see him, please assure him that I mean no harm,' I said.

'He don't trust you.'

'I beg your pardon – why not?'

'He dares not, that's why.'

'If you will give him this letter from his brother, I will stop bothering him. My business with him is simply to inform him that his brother is near death and wishes to see him; won't you at least do this?'

Those vivid blue eyes of hers regarded me charily for a moment and then she nodded once, took the letter from my hand and ran off into the trees.

I was alone once more; she had gone before I could protest that I was no more 'dangerous' than a newborn lamb.

The strangeness of this encounter already felt dreamlike; had I been reckless to trust her with Jacob's letter? The light was paler now, for the afternoon was wearing on; with sinking spirits I contemplated the long walk ahead of me and sat down upon one of the mossy stones to gather my strength; the inch or two of water left in the bottle was disagreeably warm and did not refresh me. I was dreadfully tired; I had not walked so far in twenty years.

'Mrs Rodd!'

This new voice startled me; I scrambled to my feet to see Daniel Arden. He had a book tucked under one arm, and was plainly surprised to find me in that secluded place. 'I beg your pardon, I didn't mean to disturb you – but you're alone, and I thought I heard talking.'

'Good afternoon, Mr Arden.' I settled my dusty skirts. 'I was talking to a young woman from the charcoalers' camp; I got lost and she kindly set me back on my path.'

'You were looking for Welland, I suppose.'

'I stumbled across the camp quite by mistake,' I said. 'My purpose today was simply to make sure I had delivered my message.'

'I'm sure that you have,' said Mr Arden, smiling at me. 'You have spread your word far and wide, and no one can hide for ever.'

'Can't they?'

'People don't just disappear.'

'My dear Mr Arden, people disappear *all the time!*' I said. 'In some cases because they wish to disappear; in some cases because they have been unlawfully killed and their bodies concealed or destroyed.'

'Oh—' He was startled by my bluntness.

'I beg your pardon, I didn't mean to be so grisly; I'm afraid my aching feet have soured my temper.'

He smiled again. 'In which case, you must share my provisions; I have a flask of sherry and some biscuits.'

The sherry, poured from his silver flask, was old and fine; it scented the air and filled me with well-being. Mr Arden sat down upon a nearby stone and we drank in a companionable silence.

'You are a long way from home, ma'am; my horse and gig are at your service, if you will allow me to drive you there.'

'I'm sure it's many miles out of your way, Mr Arden, but I accept most gratefully.' This was heaven-sent; I could almost have wept with relief. 'I do hope I haven't upset your plans.'

'Nothing important,' Mr Arden said cheerfully. 'I came here to read for an hour or two, that's all. It's one of my favourite spots.'

'I can see why – it's lovely, and the ruins look so romantic.'

'This was an unromantic limekiln when I was a boy, and when I bought the land decay had made it so beautiful that I couldn't bear to spoil it; I decided to allow myself this one piece of sentimentality. In every other matter I am highly practical.'

Mr Arden's modest horse and gig were waiting about a hundred yards away from the old kiln; he led me to it as if he knew every untrodden path, every blade of grass. It was a long drive, and very pleasant; Mr Arden wanted to know where I had been that day, and he raised his eyebrows when I told him I had got myself as far as Shotton Barrow.

'You have covered a lot of ground, Mrs Rodd. What were you hoping to find there?'

'It was mainly curiosity,' I said. 'I wanted to visit the grave of Mr Welland's wife, and perhaps talk to someone who knew her. The only person I came across, however, was a little girl – and all she could give me was a few facts, which she claimed had been imparted to her by the vicar. But she ran off before I could discover where he lived.'

'That's Collins,' said Mr Arden. 'He's very old and on his last legs, poor chap; I doubt he could tell you much about anything.'

'I admired the tomb of the Warrenders,' I said. 'I believe I have met their last representative on earth.'

'I beg your pardon?'

'Mrs Watts-Weston, at Gabriel College.'

Mr Arden laughed softly. 'To be sure – how could I forget? The lady presented herself to me at a charity bazaar, quite unabashed by the fact that we had not been introduced. But how on earth did you come across her?'

'I was visiting a Gabriel man who knew Joshua Welland, and Mrs Watts-Weston chose to interrupt us.'

We were both laughing now, and I decided to entertain Mr Arden with a brief account of my meeting with the redoubtable Gorgon. After this we fell into easy conversation about local matters – the impending haymaking, Mr Barton's lessons with the little boys, and Arthur's long vigil with the dying man who wished to 'confess'.

'Now, there's a thoroughly good young fellow,' declared Mr Arden. 'Some people say he's too fond of flummery and outward show, but I cannot criticize his manner of worship when I know his faith to be deep and true. I have seen for myself his tenderness towards the sick. I have seen how fervently he prays with them, until you think he won't leave off until he has delivered them to the very gates of Heaven.'

'Yes, indeed.' My respect for Mr Arden increased; he was without prejudice, and shrewd enough to see beyond dear Arthur's 'flummery' to the essential sweetness of his soul. 'This confession business worries me a little – but that is simply personal prejudice, and I have to honour his sincerity. He's not a man to do things by halves; I truly believe he'd sooner die than break the sanctity of the confessional. When Mr Barton teases him about it, as I'm afraid he is inclined to do, Arthur only smiles with saintly patience – like one of those early Christians who sang hymns while they were being eaten by lions.'

'Great of faith,' said Mr Arden, 'and pure of heart.'

He had to stop the carriage while a farm wagon came out of a gate, and all mysticism was at an end.

Ten

TWO DAYS AFTER MY long tramp around the countryside, which had worn me out more than I cared to admit (I had spent the intervening day writing letters and resting my feet), I came down to breakfast to find a letter from Mrs Watts-Weston.

Gabriel College

Wednesday

Dear Mrs Rodd,

We have had a drama, in which you may have an interest. I can tell you the particulars if you will be good enough to call between ten o'clock and noon today.

Yours,

Caroline Watts-Weston

PS – The matter is STRICTLY CONFIDENTIAL

I did not need to state my business; the porter at the lodge took one look at me and marched me straight to the Gorgon's lair, otherwise known as the Warden's House.

'Good morning, Mrs Rodd; I knew you would be prompt.' Mrs Watts-Weston came out into the hall to meet me. 'The long and short of it is that we've been robbed.' She uttered the last word with a certain grim relish.

'I beg your pardon?'

'We believe it happened during dinner last night. And before you ask, nobody saw a single thing – not a thing! – which I find quite extraordinary.'

'What happened – was anyone hurt?'

'Nobody was hurt, but considerable damage was done to college property,' said Mrs Watts-Weston. 'Mr Jennings returned to his rooms and found a scene of dreadful destruction – his possessions strewn about, his books torn, his papers all over the place—'

'And what exactly was stolen?' My mind flew instantly to the papers given to Mr Jennings by my wandering scholar.

'Well, that's the most curious thing – but you must ask him yourself.' She ushered me into a small sitting room, in which I found a very uncomfortable-looking Mr Jennings. 'I've been keeping him here until you came.'

The young clergyman stood up when he saw me. 'Mrs Rodd – good morning.'

'Mr Jennings.' I shook his hand. 'I'm glad to see you're not hurt.'

'No, not in the least,' said Mr Jennings. 'I didn't see anything except the damage.' His brown eyes, behind his spectacles, were those of a trapped animal. 'Mrs Watts-Weston has been most kind.'

'His rooms were not fit to sleep in,' said Mrs Watts-Weston. 'I insisted that he slept here; I would not hear of a refusal.'

We sat down in three chintz-covered armchairs beside the empty fireplace. I saw that this room was Mrs Watts-Weston's own domain; an elegant oasis of femininity, with a quaint mullioned window that had a splendid view of the gardens (the homely basket of mending on the window-seat told me this was her accustomed watchtower).

She handed me a cup of excellent coffee and looked expectantly at Mr Jennings.

'There's not an awful lot to tell,' he said. 'When I returned to my rooms just after midnight, I found a scene of absolute chaos – smoke everywhere, because the robber had thrown a bundle of my papers on the fire – and spilled a bottle of ink over the desk.'

'But nothing was missing,' said Mrs Watts-Weston impatiently. 'Which leads me to believe the robber was looking for something. And of course I recalled the bundle of papers given to Mr Jennings by Joshua Welland – well, isn't it obvious? Joshua Welland was our robber!'

It was not obvious to me; I believed I knew my scholar well enough to know that this was not his manner. Joshua could appear and disappear like a mist. He was not destructive. And if he had wanted something from his old friend, he would simply have asked. Mrs Watts-Weston, however, had made up her mind and was not to be budged.

'Naturally, my husband wants to hush the matter up as far as possible, for the sake of the college. He thinks this robbery is a sign that Welland is a lunatic, who is seeking some kind of revenge against the college because he could not get preferment. My husband does not approve of the difficulties put in the way of the poorest scholars.'

Every door is barred with gold, and opens but to golden keys.

My employer Jacob Welland had quoted this line (from Tennyson's 'Locksley Hall') in his letter and I heard its echo now – had poverty and obscurity driven poor Joshua out of his mind? I did not believe it, nor did Mr Jennings, but we could not talk openly in front of Mrs Watts-Weston. Very fortunately, however, while I was wondering how on earth to shake her off, she was called away to some emergency belowstairs.

'How very annoying! I beg your pardon for leaving you, Mrs Rodd – and for a footling matter in the kitchen! Mr Jennings will show you to his rooms, so that you may see the damage for yourself. I gave strict orders that nothing was to be touched.'

Mr Jennings could not hide his relief at leaving the house; it flooded his rosy face the moment we were out in the garden.

'You've had a hard night of it, Mr Jennings,' I suggested.

'Rather – she forced me to stay with them, and the mattress was like a bed of nails. I'd have been far more comfortable in my rooms.'

'She has decided Joshua is the culprit.'

'He had nothing to do with it,' said Mr Jennings emphatically. 'But she wouldn't listen to me and it's impossible to argue with her.'

'Do you have any idea who the real culprit might be?' I could not imagine this mildest of young men having any enemies. 'Could it have been some undergraduate prank that got out of hand?'

'I'd say absolutely not; most of our undergraduates are reading for the Church, and are far too serious to play any sort of "prank".'

He led me into one of Gabriel's quadrangles, and for a moment I was distracted by its beauty; the soft stone cloisters were mellow gold where the sunlight fell upon them, and the square of grass in the middle was as smooth as velvet.

'Is this the way you came last night?' I asked.

'Yes.'

'I know that you were not in college; where were you coming from?'

'I spent the evening with an old friend.' His gaze did not waver, but his blush deepened. 'A couple of miles outside the city.'

'When you got back, did you see anything out of the ordinary?'

'No – that is, I wasn't really looking,' said Mr Jennings. 'Not a soul was about, as far as I could see. It was just after midnight – I know because I heard the clamour of the bells while I was on my way. This is my stair.'

He gestured towards a dim entry at the foot of a stone staircase. A wooden board on the wall listed the occupants, including 'No. 3, The Revd Mr S. Jennings'.

'Mind the steps, Mrs Rodd; they are very uneven here.' He stopped on the first landing. 'This is where I was when I noticed a smell of smoke. The door of my room stood wide open and the smoke came from a heap of papers that had fallen out of the fireplace on to the hearthrug. I'd say the fire had been lit in a hurry; it was only smouldering, and easily put out.'

He unlocked his door and pushed it open; I had been prepared for disorder, but the mess was extraordinary, as if the room had been caught in a blizzard of paper. Sheets and sheets of paper – some half-burnt – covered the floor, the desk and the chair, and the bed in the adjoining room. The burglar had stuffed the tiny fireplace to overflowing.

'Oh dear—' Poor Mr Jennings was very downcast. 'It looks worse in daylight. This is going to take untold ages to sort out.'

'Mr Jennings, are you absolutely certain that nothing was taken? I don't see how you could tell in so short a time – and in the dark.'

'Oh, yes—' He was flustered now, and would not meet my gaze. 'My few valuables – my father's gold watch, for instance – were left untouched. It was the first thing I checked.'

'But you could not have checked all your books and papers.'

'Well – no. I'm afraid I only said it to get Mrs Watts-Weston out of my rooms.'

'What makes her so sure that Joshua did all this?'

'I mentioned that some of the papers belonged to him,' said Mr Jennings. 'And that was all she needed.' He bent down to pick up a grubby, scorched piece of paper from the floor, which he held out to me. 'This is one of his.'

I had wondered a great deal about the famous bundle of Joshua's papers, and was intrigued to see his handwriting – small, close and neat, but the lines were barely legible due to the quality of the ink he had used, already in some places fading into nothing. The other side of the paper was part of a printed notice for an auction.

'He wrote on anything he could find,' said Mr Jennings. 'And with a goose-quill, like Shakespeare.'

'Can you make sense of any of this?'

'Well, it's mostly in Greek, with intervals of Latin,' said Mr Jennings. 'I don't believe these papers contain the ravings of a lunatic – though it's jolly hard work to decipher because he obviously makes his own ink.'

'I find it strange that he would try to destroy his work, after taking such pains to preserve it.'

'I know he had nothing whatever to do with this.' His voice was firm, yet his gaze swerved away from mine, and the colour deepened in his round cheeks. 'I'm sure of it.'

'But how can you be sure? Mr Jennings, let's not waste more time; there is something you have not told me.'

'Oh – no—'

'You know it wasn't Joshua, because you saw him somewhere else!'

This was a bold guess, but Mr Jennings's scarlet face showed that I had (as my nephews would say) hit the bullseye.

I made my manner as gentle as I could. 'Where did you see him – was he here?'

'No. We were both miles away, in Freshley Woods.' He became easier; telling the story was a relief to him. 'Joshua sent me a note yesterday afternoon – a scrap of paper shoved under my door – in which he begged me, in the name of heaven, to meet him in a certain cowshed, beside a certain village tavern.'

'Can you say exactly where?'

'I gave my solemn oath never to reveal the exact place,' said Mr Jennings. 'Though I don't think I could if I tried. For a start, the so-called "tavern" was simply the front parlour of someone's cottage, and the green outside it was crowded with the poorest people – men and women – drinking themselves into a state of oblivion.'

'And it was there that you met Joshua Welland?'

'Yes.' He paused; I could see that he was weighing up how much he could tell me without breaking his promise. 'He dragged me through the woods for what seemed like miles, until we came upon a sort of camp where the charcoal burners had built their fires.'

'Joshua was taking you to his home!' I was excited. 'But why did he want you?'

Mr Jennings blushed brick-red. 'Because he needed a clergyman. A very discreet clergyman. I can't say any more, I'm afraid. I gave my word.'

'Thank you, Mr Jennings.' I longed to know why the charcoal burners had wanted a clergyman in a hurry, and under conditions of such secrecy, but it had little or no bearing on my case. 'I'm quite satisfied that Joshua Welland could not possibly have carried out this ransacking of your rooms. But if it wasn't him, who on earth was it?'

'Honestly,' said Mr Jennings, 'I haven't the faintest idea.'

Meek and mild as he appeared to be, I knew he would disclose nothing more. I thanked him again and left the college (taking a more round-about path to avoid Mrs Watts-Weston's parlour window), dispirited because the most I could claim to my employer was that I had delivered his message, when I had set my heart on seeing the brothers reunited. Whether or not I was personally satisfied by the outcome, however, I saw now that my work for Jacob Welland was done.

Eleven

Dear Mary,

My investigation appears to be at an end. I have written to Mr Welland, regretfully informing him that though I believe I have delivered the message to his brother, I have not managed to speak to him directly or discover precisely where he lives. Perhaps, if I had more time – but time is running out, and I don't like to take any more money from a dying man when I don't feel I can offer him any return.

I will tell you more when I receive Mr Welland's reply, but expect to be coming home inside a week. And while I'm looking forward to seeing you, dear Mary, I shall be very sorry to leave my kind hosts and their supremely comfortable house. Never mind – we have funds enough now for one or two small luxuries! You must overcome your horror of spending money and lay in the following items against my return: butter, new milk, half a pound of Orange Pekoe tea, a lemon, a half-pound of loaf sugar and a half-quartern of the better brandy from the tavern.

I will send the exact day as soon as possible, to give you plenty of warning.

Your affectionate friend,

Laetitia Rodd

'I'VE HAD A DELIGHTFUL time here,' I told Rachel. 'But Mr Welland is not paying me to have a holiday. Much as I hate to admit it, I have failed him.'

'You're being too hard on yourself, Mrs Rodd; I don't see what more you could have done.'

'I wanted to deliver Joshua in person. I wish I knew why he did not dare to trust me. And I have such a dislike of loose ends.'

'But you won't be leaving us immediately?'

'I'm awaiting my employer's further instructions,' I said. 'I can only stay until I hear from him.'

'Surely, since you've delivered the message, you could stay a little longer? Do stay!'

'My dear Rachel, you and Arthur have made me far too comfortable here; I can't thank you enough and I only wish I could stay until Christmas.'

'You will be here for the Haymaking Supper tomorrow, anyway,' said Rachel, smiling. 'I positively forbid you to miss that!'

She looked very pretty this evening, I thought, strikingly so; her pale blue silk dress brought out the splendid colour of her hair, that rare shade of dark auburn like my mother's garnet necklace.

It was after dinner and we were in the drawing room – myself, Mr Barton, Rachel and Arthur. All the windows stood open, so that we could hear the harvesters shouting to each other across the fields.

Arthur was in high spirits. 'You mustn't even think of missing our rustic bunfight, Mrs Rodd! It's positively the jewel of our social calendar, when the rude forefathers of the hamlet celebrate the hay-harvest with violent country dancing – and also with drinking and licentiousness. It's a frightful occasion, which I've done my best to avoid in the past. This year – for my sins –' he shot a teasing glance at

Mr Barton '– I shall be attending. Your presence will help me through the ordeal.'

'Nonsense,' I said, laughing. 'You used to love country dances! Have you suddenly decided that dancing is sinful?'

'Certainly not – I'm thinking only of my poor feet, trodden black and blue by the local maidens in their hobnailed boots. I expect you to save me by dancing with me as much as possible.'

'Don't be silly, I haven't danced for years. I've forgotten all the steps.'

'I don't believe a word of it,' Arthur declared. 'You'll hear the first notes of "Packington's Pound" and your feet will start dancing before you know what you're doing – like an elderly circus horse when it hears a trumpet.'

This piece of impertinence made me laugh, for I knew he was right; I have loved country dances all my life. (My dear father would not have understood these modern churchmen who hold dancing to be improper for a man in holy orders; he was a country parson of the old school, and could dance a lively Gathering Peascods until well into his seventies.)

The Haymaking Supper was held in an empty threshing barn, the property of the ever-generous Mr Arden, who had also provided beer and the best fiddler in the county. In the mellow summer dusk, crowds of people were trooping in from several miles around, and the whole countryside was alive with noisy merriment.

The dancing took place on the green outside the barn, so that the sweet music was for once not drowned out by the din of stomping feet. I gave myself up to the pleasure of dancing the dear, familiar measures, and found myself with all kinds of partners, including the taciturn carrier who had taken me to Shotton Barrow (he was surprisingly nimble), and Mr Arden, who danced as gracefully as he did everything else.

There were paper lanterns hung in the trees around the green, and when the sky darkened the effect was most picturesque.

'This was another of your ideas, I suspect,' I said to Mr Arden, while we were catching our breath on a wooden bench between dances. 'You have made us all look wonderfully romantic.'

'How does your investigation go, Mrs Rodd? Have you discovered Joshua's whereabouts?'

'Not really.' I could not tell him about Mr Jennings and the business with the charcoal burners; it was not my secret to share. 'It seems he does not wish to be found.'

'I have a certain amount of sympathy,' Mr Arden said, his face thoughtful. 'He's had so many years of hiding in hedges and ditches that he has turned into a kind of wild creature, and fears returning to the world.'

'You may very well be right, Mr Arden, but I don't have enough time to try coaxing him from his burrow with a piece of cheese. He must know by now about his brother.'

'If you are able, I hope you will carry my regards to poor Welland.'

'Most happily.'

'Thank you. He will know that I am praying for him.'

The dance ended, and there was a loud outbreak of applause. I was glad to observe that dear Arthur (possibly mindful of Mr Barton's rebukes) had embraced this occasion with his whole heart; I had not seen him sparkle like this since he was our curate in Herefordshire. He had danced with grandmothers and little girls with a radiant good nature that delighted his parishioners.

Catching my eye, Arthur came to sit beside me. He collapsed on the bench with such a comical groan of exhaustion that Mr Arden and I could not help laughing.

'My feet, my poor feet! I have danced like a dervish, and now I couldn't strip another willow if you paid me!'

'Mr Somers! Mr Somers!' A small girl came scampering across the grass. "Tis the Barley Mow, Mr Somers – you promised!'

'It's Molly, from the lodge.' Mr Arden stood up, and for a moment his face was suffused with a tenderness that made him almost handsome. 'Leave Mr Somers to rest, Molly; come and dance the Barley Mow with me.'

Arthur and I smiled at the grave courtesy with which he took the child's grubby paw and led her out to the lines of dancers.

'Look at her,' said Arthur. 'Proud as a little duchess! That man is a constant puzzle to me.'

'How do you mean?'

'I don't know – he holds himself in reserve, somehow, and shows nothing but his public face. He is never off guard.'

'His manner is cautious, certainly,' I said. 'I have always assumed it was because he was mindful of his origins and fearful of making a mistake.'

'Oh, I don't mean to criticize the man,' Arthur said quickly. 'This entire evening is evidence of his boundless generosity. He has never forgotten what it means to be poor; I must respect him for that.'

'You deserve a rest now,' I said. 'You have done your duty splendidly.'

'Haven't I, though? I only hope Barton saw how bravely I tackled all the most hideous undanceables – he's the one I'm trying to impress.'

The Barley Mow began, and my eyes were drawn to two handsome figures in the midst of the crowd – Mr Barton and Rachel.

If I had not been off my guard that night, what might I have seen?

*

My summons came the following morning; the briefest note from Mr Welland, requesting a meeting at the first opportunity. I took leave of my hosts and set off at once for London.

'I'm very annoyed with myself for not getting any further,' I told my brother the next day, as we walked together up Christchurch Hill towards Rosemount. 'The plain fact is that I was in Joshua's hands the entire time and he led me wherever he pleased, as if he had me at the end of a string.'

'You hate to admit defeat, that's your trouble,' Fred said, with an aggravating grin. 'And you can't bear a secret that you can't prise open.'

'I'm afraid that's perfectly true.' I was too glad to see my brother to let him annoy me. 'I must tell Mr Welland that I have hit a brick wall, when I'd set my heart on a full reconciliation.'

'Well, you delivered the message, anyway,' said Fred. 'You can lead a horse to water, but you can't make him forgive his brother – not even you. And I'm jolly glad to have you home in time for the pipkin's christening. We've changed her name, by the way.'

'Again? What on earth was wrong with Agnes Matilda?'

'Fanny can't get over the novelty of choosing names for a girl; I think she's been storing them up over the years.' (Fred's enormous family mainly ran to boys; this latest child was only their third daughter, after dearest Tishy and sweet, six-year-old May.) 'Now she's decided that the little pipsicle must be known as Geraldine Helen.'

'Beautiful!' I said, laughing at him. 'But I'll try not to get used to it – there's many a slip between here and the font.'

'I should warn you, old thing,' said Fred. 'If Fanny thinks you're at leisure, she'll do her best to dragoon you into helping with the move to the seaside.'

They had rented a large villa for the summer at Bon-church, in the Isle of Wight; it cost a shocking amount of money, but in those days there were still outbreaks of cholera during the hottest months, and everyone who could took their children out of the city.

'Please tell her I'd be happy to help.' It was so pleasant to be at home and hearing the family news that my bosom was filled with charity for even my sister-in-law. 'Packing up a family of thirteen plus servants is no small undertaking.'

'Now that you have no case on your hands, you can come with us,' said Fred coaxingly. 'It would be a lovely rest for you.'

'A rest? My dear Fred, I'd have more rest with a tribe of savages!' Though my bosom was still filled with the afore-said charity, I knew perfectly well that Fanny mainly wanted me as an extra pair of hands. 'I'll think about it – but not if you nag me.'

We had reached the gate of Rosemount. The door was opened by the same fresh young maidservant we had seen on our last visit, and the handsome brigand met us in the hall. I had assumed that we would find Mr Welland closer to death, and was glad to see that his health appeared to be no worse than the last time I had seen him. Though dreadfully weak, he was calm and doing his best to smile.

'I am here to close our account, Mr Welland,' I told him, once the young manservant had bowed himself out of the conservatory (oh, the heat! The shades had been pulled down over the glass roof to cut out the worst of the glare, but it was a positive inferno). 'I believe I have come to the end of my usefulness to you, unless there is anything more you wish me to do.'

As concisely as possible, I outlined everything relating to my search for Joshua, up to his taking Mr Jennings to the charcoal burners.

'By God, it gets more romantic by the minute!' This was the first Fred had heard of the story and he was enchanted, as I had known he would be. 'But can it possibly be true? Isn't it rather operatic for the outskirts of Oxford in the nineteenth century?'

'Perhaps, but I'm sure Mr Jennings was telling the truth.'

'Mrs Rodd,' whispered Mr Welland, 'you have delivered my message with admirable speed and efficiency. Thank you.'

'I'm only sorry that I could not do more.'

Mr Welland smiled (it was painful to see the concertina-folds of his wasted cheeks). After a short spell of silence, he said, 'You must have done more than you know. Joshua came to me.'

'Here? Your brother came here?' This was the last thing I had expected; Fred and I exchanged doubtful glances. 'Are you certain it was him?'

'I promise you, this is not delirium.' Welland was clearly amused by our startled reaction. 'Three nights ago Joshua appeared at my bedside.'

'But how did he get into the house without rousing the servants?'

'According to the housekeeper, he forced the window in the scullery and slipped through it like an eel. He did not even disturb my poor Carlos, who sleeps in the chamber next to mine.'

'Good grief,' said Fred. 'Are you saying he simply appeared, like a demon in the pantomime?'

If he had been able, Mr Welland would have laughed at this; I sensed that he was proud of Joshua. 'We spoke together and prayed together, and he told me that he forgave me with his whole heart.'

'I'm very glad to hear it,' I said sincerely. 'Does this mean he has come out of hiding?'

'No – he said he must disappear again – and that I must not ask why. He said, we are brothers again – and will meet again in Heaven.'

He was coming to the end of his strength, fighting for every wisp of breath, yet I sensed that he was peaceful. The fire had gone out and he had one foot in the next world. Fred and I took respectful leave of him and rang the bell for the servant.

Carlos appeared, and my thoughts began to collect themselves as soon as we stepped out of the stifling conservatory into the cool hall. Someone was waiting for us; a stout, grey man with a bald crown and tremendous sidewhiskers, very elegantly dressed.

'Mrs Rodd – Mr Tyson.' He bowed to us. 'I am William Chauncey. My patient instructed me to make myself scarce, but I wanted to be sure that you know – this is likely to be your last meeting.'

'Thank you, Doctor,' I said. 'I'm not surprised to hear it; how long would you—?'

'A matter of days, ma'am,' said Dr Chauncey abruptly. 'Perhaps hours. His wits are wandering.'

'We suspected as much,' said Fred. 'Is there any truth in the story of his brother's clandestine visit?'

'I'd say not; such visions are commonplace when a person is dying.' The doctor shot a sharp glance at young Carlos. 'The man couldn't possibly have broken into my house without disturbing someone. The bare notion is nonsense!'

For a fraction of a moment, my eyes met the lustrous dark eyes of Carlos, and I was certain there was something he wanted to say to me – but it was impossible to question him when we were being hurried out of the house. And my case was officially closed, so it was none of my business anyway.

'I don't believe Mr Welland was dreaming,' I told Fred, when we were back on Christchurch Hill. 'He struck me as perfectly lucid. I'd love to know why Joshua is hiding; it's most annoying not to get the rest of the story.'

'Ah, that's the trouble with reality,' Fred said, with a comical sigh. 'It doesn't come with a third volume, in which all the ends are neatly tied up.'

'But why were Mr Jennings's rooms ransacked? And how on earth did Joshua manage to get himself to the outskirts of London without being seen – a man without money, dressed in that outlandish medieval costume?'

'My dear old thing, the man's obviously as mad as a hatter!' As far as Fred was concerned, the business was closed. 'Your job is done; nobody's paying you any extra to fret about it.'

'He believes he is in danger. I think we should take him seriously.'

'Pooh!' said Fred. 'I can't take anything seriously when I've just been broiled like a pork chop. For two pins I'd rip off my clothes and jump into the pond. Take a leaf out of my book and stop thinking about crime for a week or two; we all deserve a bit of peace.'

Oh, how that last word came to haunt me later!

Twelve

I MUST NOW LEAP FORWARD to the third week in August, when I was in the Isle of Wight with Fred and his family. It cannot be described as a holiday, for I have never laboured harder in my life. Fanny fell ill with a fever, and then nearly died of terror when some of the children came out in a rash; she was convinced they had scarlet fever, but it turned out to be chickenpox, to which the smaller children had not yet been exposed. They were woefully short-handed for such a crisis, there was no local help to be had at the height of the season, and so Fred summoned me.

The worst had passed by the time the fateful letter arrived, and I was enjoying a (relatively) quiet afternoon in the garden. The grey stone villa, on the south coast of the island, sat in a gaudy nest of summer flowers. The long lawn stretched down to the beach, where Fred was playing cricket with the bigger boys while the little ones made sand-pies under the eye of the nursemaid. My oldest niece, dear Tishy (short for Laetitia; she is my godchild), sat a little way off, reading a story to the bundle of shawls in a basket chair that was poor May, who had taken longest to recover.

It was a few years before the wondrous convenience of telegrams; the single sheet of paper that shattered my peace was brought by special messenger (who had to be paid a vast sum of money) and it was from Mrs Watts-Weston.

The Warden's House

Gabriel College

Oxford

22nd August 1851

Dear Mrs Rodd,

If you have not already heard the dreadful news, you must pardon my bluntness. The whole world will know of it soon enough.

Arthur Somers is dead, and Mrs Somers and Mr Barton have been arrested for murder.

Whatever the facts of the matter, I am concerned about Mrs Somers; she has no family, and you appear to be her only close friend. I think you must come here to stand by the poor creature, and you are most welcome to stay with me at the Warden's House for as long as is necessary. Shall not the merciful obtain mercy?

Yours sincerely,

Caroline Watts-Weston

My heart breaking and my mind whirling, I left for Oxford the following morning. The journey was complicated and uncomfortable – carriage, paddle steamer, two trains – and the cost was colossal. Fred provided the money, partly from kindness, partly from professional interest (seeing my distress, my brother did his best to hide his glee, but he did love a good murder).

Arthur, dear Arthur, was dead.

I spent the long hours of that sorrowful journey praying for the repose of his soul.

Dear Fred,

Since you always seem to know about crimes practically before they are committed, I'm sure you will already have heard the bare facts. It is all over the newspapers by now. People are saying that Rachel and Mr Barton were lovers, and that they killed Arthur to get him out of the way.

I do not believe it for a moment – but I am aware of certain things I know, which will only make everything look worse if I reveal them! What am I to do?

I told you of the conversation I overheard, between Arthur and Mr Barton, which I am now bound to report to the person conducting the investigation. And it makes me quite wretched to think of what a jury might make of my evidence – let alone the counsel for the prosecution. A worse punishment for eavesdropping can scarcely be imagined.

As for Rachel, I would swear before the Court of Heaven itself that she is innocent.

They will both need the very finest defence that can be got, regardless of cost. I beg you to recommend a suitable man or men to defend them – if they are hanged because of my evidence, I think the remorse will kill me.

Here is what I know so far. On the 18th of this month, Arthur Somers left his house at around noon, with the intention of walking over to Swinford. Rachel was seen to give him a bottle of lemonade. He did not come home.

On the morning of the 19th, very early, the household was roused by the local constable, a Mr Pye, and a clergyman, Gerard Fogle.

107

They were the bearers of the terrible news that Arthur had been found dead in the room he sometimes used at Swinford.

A Dr Jaques examined the corpse and announced that he had been poisoned 'by the ingestion of atropine'. At first the talk was of suicide, though Arthur left no letter behind.

An inquest took place in Oxford on August the 21st. Three people testified under oath that they had seen Arthur and Mr Barton engaged in heated disagreement on the evening of the dance — one of these witnesses being Mr Daniel Arden. The verdict was Murder.

On August the 22nd, Mr Barton and Rachel were arrested.

Please forgive the rambling nature of this letter — it is nearly three in the morning and the lamp is at its last gasp, but I am too upset to think of sleeping. The Warden's House is perfectly well-appointed and my chamber very comfortable, and Mrs W-W has been endlessly kind. I must stay here for as long as Rachel needs me; she has no one else. And in any case, I am involved now — this plea is personal rather than professional.

Your affectionate sister,

Letty

PS — Please tell Fanny I am sorry she was put out by my hasty departure.

'Mrs Rodd — I'm so very glad to see you!'

'Rachel, my dear!'

I will never forget — it is branded on my memory for all time — my first sight of poor Rachel in her widowhood. Her face was deathly pale; she wore a plain black gown from which all trimmings had been removed and her beautiful hair was quenched beneath a widow's cap.

She made a faint attempt at a smile. 'What do you think of my prison?'

The town lock-up, with its pitiful population of vagrants and unfortunates, had not been thought suitable for a gentlewoman or for a clergyman. Mr Barton was lodged in the house of the local magistrate. Rachel's 'prison' was a red-brick vicarage on the Banbury road, and her 'warders' were the vicar and his sister. It so happened that the vicar, Mr Philip Martindale, had once sat on a committee with my dearest Matt, and this emboldened me to turn up unannounced on his doorstep. He had very kindly allowed me this private audience with Rachel in his drawing room. We sat down on the sofa and I clasped her cold hands.

'Are you comfortable here? Do you have everything you need?'

'Thank you, I'm perfectly comfortable. The Martindales are very good to me. They do not judge me.' Rachel's red eyes brimmed with tears. 'They know my heart is breaking and they pity my sorrow. Oh, Mrs Rodd – how has this happened to us? As if I'd ever hurt my darling Arthur!'

'I know you did not murder him,' I said. 'The very idea is ridiculous.'

'And – and I did not betray him.' She held her head up proudly. 'It is very important to me that you believe me.'

'I do, my dear.' I spoke soothingly, for this was no time to air my own suspicions about her feelings for Mr Barton. 'Now you must try to recall for me every detail of poor Arthur's last day on earth. I understand that he left for Swinford just before noon.'

'Yes, and I sent him off with a bottle of poisoned lemonade, which I placed in his pocket in front of several witnesses.'

'I'm afraid you will be asked a great many questions about that bottle of lemonade,' I said. 'For example, who filled it – and when?'

'I did, naturally. I'll give you the entire history, if you like, right back to the lemon tree.'

'Rachel, please; I am not against you.'

'I beg your pardon, I shouldn't snap at you, of all people.' She was meek now. 'I had made the lemonade the previous day. I drank some, with no ill effects, so it wasn't poisonous yet. I left the pitcher in the dairy overnight to keep it cool, and I filled the bottle for Arthur a few minutes before he left.' She sighed softly, and was quiet for a few moments. 'Everyone in the house must have heard me calling out to him to wait while I fetched it – which I surely would not have done if I meant to commit a crime.'

'No, indeed,' I said. 'I hope you examined the contents of that pitcher.'

'It was tested, but nothing was found; the atropine was only in the bottle I gave to Arthur.'

'So it is established that the poison must have been added somewhere outside the house.'

'I know Mr Barton had nothing to do with it; he loved Arthur.'

(And threatened to kill him, I couldn't help remembering.) 'Let's go back to that day. Did you know that Arthur would be spending the night at Swinford?'

'No, but he often stayed there,' said Rachel. 'That's why I wasn't unduly worried when he didn't come home. He was perfectly well that day, and perfectly happy. I was completely unprepared for the news of his death; I don't think I truly believe it yet.' She added, 'I know how ridiculous that sounds, but I keep catching myself thinking of him as if he were still here.'

(This was a sensation I remembered only too well from the commencement of my own widowhood; in the midst of all the shock and pain of my husband's sudden death, I found myself storing up things to tell him.)

'It's because they wouldn't let me see him,' said Rachel, with a catch in her voice that went to my heart. 'And Miss Martindale says he is to be buried tomorrow.'

'He has not yet been buried?'

'The coroner has only just released the body. He is at Swinford now.'

I shuddered to think of the state of the corpse so many days after death; it was just as well Rachel could not see it. 'Remember that it's not Arthur any more,' I said gently. 'The true Arthur is now rejoicing in the light of the next world.'

'Mrs Rodd, will you go to him at Swinford?'

'Yes, if you wish it.' I had already decided to do exactly that, while I still had the use of Mrs Watts-Weston's neat little one-horse carriage (and while the lady herself was otherwise engaged and could not interfere). 'I will go this very day.'

'Please pray for me.' Rachel clutched at my hand. 'I mean – please pray on my behalf. My own prayers aren't any good.'

'You know that's not true.'

'In my mind I know it,' said Rachel. 'But my heart feels nothing; when I try to pray it's like banging on a locked door.'

I glanced up at the wooden clock on the chimney-piece; Mr Martindale had only allowed us a very few minutes and might come in at any moment. 'When you are tried,' I said, 'the prosecuting counsel will do everything in his power to convince the jury that you and Henry Barton were lovers. And whether it's true or not, the jury is likely to take it as evidence that you conspired to kill your husband. If you have held anything back, I entreat you to tell me at once.'

'I have told you everything.' It was an effort for her to meet my eyes. 'Before Heaven, we are innocent.'

Thirteen

THE NOTORIOUS 'MONASTIC' COMMUNITY at Swinford held a fascination in those days that younger readers might find hard to comprehend. In the popular imagination it was a sinister place, a hotbed of Jesuitical intrigue, where innocent young men were lured away from their respectable families into the Roman Catholic priesthood.

Since there is nothing duller than dead Church politics, I will sketch the background as briefly as possible. Mr Gerard Fogle (I saw no reason to address the man as 'Father' in the Roman manner) was a great figure in the so-called Oxford Movement. He was expelled from his college amidst claims that he presented a moral danger to his students (there were comparisons to Socrates, though not from my dear husband, whose comments on the matter are not fit to print). Mr Fogle was given the living of St Alphage and All Saints at Swinford, a small village a few miles to the south of Oxford. He famously kept to the 'monastic rule' of a medieval monk, and such numbers of young admirers flocked around him that he had the nearby stables made into bare white cells.

Arthur had walked to Swinford across the fields. The journey was longer by road; I drove myself there directly after taking leave of Rachel, in Mrs W-W's little one-horse trap, and it was not an agreeable experience. Vulgar people always feel free to shout insults at a lone female driver, and there were knots of loafers at every corner, apparently with nothing better to do; I was almost glad when the rain drove them all indoors (though I worried about the dye coming out of my second-best bonnet). I was by this stage absolutely famished for concrete facts.

I was also intensely curious to see the real Swinford. Well, as far as I was concerned it was a thorough let-down. I stopped the natty little carriage outside a perfectly ordinary country church, in a perfectly commonplace village. The famous 'community' was nothing more than a huddle of farm buildings – all dripping thatch and puddles, most unlike the romantic picture conjured in my mind by the word 'monastery'.

Nothing stirred, nobody came out – no brown-kirtled friars, nor anyone else. I left the horse under a chestnut tree, nuzzling at the grass; he was a good-natured, patient, biddable creature (as all creatures around Mrs W-W, including husband, children and the kitchen cat, tended to be).

The rectory was a large house of red brick that took up one side of the village green. I knocked loudly on the front door, and listened to the sound dying away into emptiness. Just as I was debating with myself whether to knock again, I heard footsteps hurrying towards me. The door opened about six inches and a young man peered out.

'Good afternoon,' I said. 'I wish to speak to Mr Fogle, on a very urgent matter; please tell him that I am here.' I held out one of my visiting cards. 'My name is Laetitia Rodd.'

The young man stared at it anxiously. 'Oh – er – I'm afraid I can't disturb him.'

'I am calling on behalf of Mrs Somers. I'll wait if necessary.'

114

'You see, the thing is, they don't generally have ladies here.'

'If I am not allowed inside this house, Mr Fogle must meet me somewhere else,' I said, more forcefully. 'I am determined to speak to him.'

'It's all right, Rivers; I will see to this.' The voice was arrestingly soft and sweet. 'You may admit this lady.'

'Yes, Father.' He opened the door and stepped aside for me to enter.

The large hall was bare and clean, with no furnishings save one gloomy brown painting of someone being martyred. There was a smell of old cooking and carbolic soap, cut through with a tang of incense. The young man bowed to me quickly and scuttled away through a door under the stairs, leaving me alone with one of the most celebrated and argued-about churchmen in England.

Gerard Fogle was tall and very thin, clad in a priestly black suit and Roman collar, and handsomer than the soulful portraits I had seen in the newspapers. He was in his middle forties, with smooth dark hair. His grey eyes were large and expressive, and if they had belonged to a young girl they would have been beautiful; in Mr Fogle's thin, beaky face the effect was disconcerting.

'You are welcome here, Mrs Rodd; please come into my study.' His voice had a feminine lilt to it, and his manner was unexpectedly charming; it was easy to see why he exerted such power over his devotees. 'There is a fire; I find this damp weather very trying.'

It was a very small fire. Mr Fogle's study was not a comfortable room (I could not help comparing it to Matt's study in Herefordshire which was absolutely consecrated to the dear man's comfort, with its roaring fires, easy chairs and decanters).

This room was as sparsely furnished as possible. The floor was of bare wood and the walls not covered with

115

books were of whitewashed plaster. A large mahogany crucifix, of the kind seen in foreign churches, loomed over Mr Fogle's desk. We sat down beside the fire in two hard wooden chairs.

'I am very glad to see that poor Mrs Somers has someone to speak on her behalf. I have not been in a position to help her; this house of holiness is now the scene of a crime.' His great, girlish eyes filled with tears. 'When you knocked I thought you were another policeman. They have sent some men from London.'

I was on the alert at once; I had known someone would be sent from Scotland Yard, but I had hoped to steal a march on them (they made such an awful mess of a crime scene in those early days). Never mind. I forced myself to concentrate upon Rachel, the true reason for my visit; I had given her my solemn promise that I would pray, on her behalf, over Arthur's remains. It was the only comfort that I could bring her.

'Mr Fogle, I understand that Arthur is still here.'

'Yes, he lies in our chapel; he was brought back to us as soon as the coroner released him. He will be buried here tomorrow.' The tears rolled down his cheeks; he made no attempt to hide them from me. 'In the place he was happiest.'

'I know that he was very happy here,' I said. 'He spoke of it more than once. He spoke of his friendship with you.'

'It was more than friendship. I loved him beyond expression.'

'Oh.' I was a little taken aback by the extravagance of this declaration.

'I know that you loved him too, Mrs Rodd; you must not be afraid to use the word. Arthur often spoke of you and your late husband, and the kindness you showed to him.'

'I'm afraid he and my husband didn't always see eye to eye.'

'Not in some matters, perhaps,' said Mr Fogle. 'But your husband – at considerable risk to himself – did Arthur a great service, which he never forgot.'

I did not know what he meant; I could not remember anything in the shape of a 'great service' done to Arthur by Matt (unless you counted teaching him whist).

I hurried on, a little flustered by those radiant eyes. 'During my last visit to Oxfordshire, I was struck by the amount of time he spent here. He seemed to walk to Swinford nearly every day.'

'Yes, he came often.' Mr Fogle was as mild as ever, yet I sensed a wariness. 'There was no formal attachment to our community; it was simply that he and I were very old friends. He was troubled; it was natural for him to turn to me.'

I must confess that, for once, my courage failed me; I simply could not bring myself to utter a word about the wretched matter of the blackmail, never mind the sin attached to it; in my time I have faced up to murderers and here I was, smitten into silence by a wraith of a man I could easily have knocked down. But how were such things to be spoken of before a creature of such refinement?

Quickly changing direction (and with the strangest sense that this ethereal being could read my mind), I said, 'The shock of his death must have been quite dreadful.'

'I felt it as a bolt of lightning,' said Mr Fogle. 'As an arrow in my heart.'

'Who was the first to discover the body?'

'One of my young men; Edward Rivers, whom you saw in the hall just now. It was very early in the morning. Rivers had arranged to pray with Arthur, as preparation for the six o'clock service in our chapel. When he failed to appear, Rivers assumed he had overslept and went to his room. There was no response to his knocking. He went into the room—' Mr Fogle's face creased up in anguish and he could not continue.

I pitied the man, but there were things I needed to know and, now that Scotland Yard had taken over, I was aware that I might not get a chance to question Mr Edward Rivers myself. 'When did you hear of it?'

'I was in my bedchamber, engaged in my morning devotions,' said Mr Fogle. 'I was summoned at once – the sight is burned into my memory for all time. Rivers had not touched Arthur's body, for he was quite obviously dead. He lay halfway between the bed and the floor, with his eyes wide open and staring at nothing, and his face frozen into the most ghastly, snarling expression – forgive me.' He was struggling to compose himself. 'He looked like a stranger.'

'The distorted face can be a sign of atropine poisoning.'

'He was not given poison in this house,' said Mr Fogle. 'The Coroner's Court decided that it was administered at some time in the afternoon of that day, before his arrival at Swinford.'

'At what time was that?'

'Six o'clock. He stayed in his room for an hour and came to me here at seven.'

He stopped suddenly, and I had a strong sense that there was something he did not want me to know (my instinct is very reliable; I can always smell a secret). 'Can you tell me what the two of you talked about that evening?'

'It was a private matter.' Mr Fogle's mild voice now had the faintest crackle of frost. 'A religious matter, between two consecrated priests of God.'

'Can you tell me about his mood? Was he cheerful – had the poison started to affect him?'

There was another spell of silence, during which Mr Fogle looked cagey and was clearly weighing up how much he should reveal to me. Eventually he shook his head and said, 'I cannot betray the secrets of his inmost soul, but you may as well know, since everyone here must have heard – towards the end of our meeting, Arthur became very agitated. I could make nothing of it at the time. I have since learnt that atropine can work upon people in this way.'

'At what time did he leave you?'

'Just after eight o'clock,' said Mr Fogle. 'He – he wished me goodnight and went to his own room. It was the last time I saw him. I cannot bear to think that he suffered so much and died alone – in such a dreadful way!'

'Yes, I'm afraid he must have suffered.' My knowledge of poisons was limited, but atropine is derived from the common plant known as 'deadly nightshade' – and all country-bred people know those purple berries can bring a death that is truly agonizing. 'But did no one hear him? I cannot believe he died without making a single sound!'

'By a most unhappy chance, all the other rooms in the old stables were empty that night.'

Once again I had a strong sense that he was hiding something. Of course he was; the greater part of Arthur's last day on earth was still unaccounted for. And before that, where had Arthur been between leaving Hardinsett and arriving at Swinford? But I decided not to press him and changed course.

'You have been most kind to receive me, Mr Fogle. Before I leave you, I would very much like to see Arthur's body.'

'I would advise against it.'

'You need not worry that I'll faint or go into hysterics. I have no fear of the dead. His wife is in great distress because she could not pray beside him; I promised to do so on her behalf.'

'You are on an errand of mercy,' said Mr Fogle. 'I cannot deny you. The poor woman must save her soul before she dies.'

He thought Rachel was guilty. I swallowed my anger, for I could not afford to argue with him now.

Meek and mild as ever, yet somehow still conveying unwillingness, Mr Fogle led me out of the house through a back door. I had seen a picture of the famous 'retreat' he had built here, and was prepared for the oddity of the place; the stableyard had been dug up and laid to lawn, and the stable building itself whitewashed, with a cross placed above the door, but there was still a lingering atmosphere of horse.

A young policeman stood at the door, which was wide open.

'They are everywhere,' Mr Fogle murmured to me, his face creased with pain. 'My holy house has been violated.'

'The police must be allowed to do their work,' I could not help pointing out. 'And you can't blame them for violating your holy house – the murderer did that.'

'Lord bless me!' cried someone behind the door. 'Is that Mrs Rodd?'

And out stepped the stiff, drab, soldierly figure of the best policeman in London (to give him his due), who had caused me a not little annoyance in several of my past cases.

'Inspector Blackbeard!'

Fourteen

FOR A MOMENT I had an unholy desire to laugh. Inspector Thomas Blackbeard's hooded eyes had a kindly glint to them, which I recognized as humour.

'Well, Mrs Rodd – I might have known you'd come into it somewhere!'

'This is not one of my cases, Inspector,' I said quickly, aware that Mr Fogle was frowning. 'My involvement is personal.'

'I'm very sorry to hear that, ma'am.'

'Mr Somers was a dear friend of mine. I'm afraid you will want to speak to me, but first I wish to see him.'

'Not a pretty sight,' said Blackbeard, shaking his head solemnly. 'But I know you've seen worse, Mrs Rodd. And you're just in time, too – I was about to tell the undertaker's man to put the lid on and nail him down.'

Mr Fogle winced at his bluntness. 'I beg you, Inspector, to remember that this is a place of prayer.'

'It's a place of murder,' said Blackbeard shortly. 'I need to speak with you, Mr Fogle; I'd be obliged if you'd suggest a time.' (He was of my mind, I noted, and would not address Fogle as 'Father'.)

'I shall be at your service, after I have shown Mrs Rodd into our chapel.'

'Thank you, sir.' The inspector gave us a stiff little bow. 'And I shall be interested to hear anything you have to tell me, ma'am.'

Mr Fogle led me into the old stables. The stalls had been turned into tiny white 'cells', their open doors revealing each with a crucifix on the bare wall above the narrow bed, and a little high window.

'This was the room he stayed in, when he was here.' Mr Fogle opened the door at the end of the short passage.

I looked at the room. It was white and bare and exactly like all the others; the last place that poor Arthur had seen on earth.

'It has been cleaned,' I said.

'Yes,' said Mr Fogle. 'As I have explained to the police, at first we had no idea that this was the scene of a murder.'

'But – what else could it have been?' I tried not to snap at him. 'Surely you did not assume he had taken his own life?'

'Naturally it crossed my mind, Mrs Rodd, until I saw how unlikely it was that he – or indeed anyone – would have chosen a method so painful. I concluded in the end that it must have been a simple accident.'

Mr Fogle opened the door of the chapel, and startled me by suddenly dropping a curtsey and crossing himself.

After that I had no eyes for anything but Arthur.

His open coffin stood in the aisle of that small, bare chapel; I wept freely when I saw him.

The ingestion of poison does not improve the appearance of a corpse, and this one had been further disfigured by the passing of time. Mercifully, the 'snarling' expression of his features caused by the poison had faded, but I had to search for the man I knew in the fragments of his wrecked beauty.

I prayed beside Arthur for a long time, trying not to be distracted by the shouts and footsteps outside. I imagined my beloved Matt greeting him in the next world, as he had too often greeted him in this one: 'Good grief, Somers, what daft thing have you done now?'

I had my chance to speak properly to the inspector when he accepted a ride in my carriage.

'Thank you, ma'am; some of us ain't as young as we were, and a ride back to Oxford would be most welcome.' He climbed into the seat beside me. 'Particularly now the rain's stopped. It's wetter than the rain we get in London, if you ask me.'

'Very true,' I said. 'Did you speak to Mr Fogle?'

'He put me off till after the funeral tomorrow,' said Blackbeard. 'And he wasn't too pleased when I told him I was in no hurry. Rum sort of place, eh?'

'To put it mildly, Inspector, I must admit that I'm rather glad to get away; there's something oppressive in the atmosphere.'

'As well there might be, ma'am, at the scene of a murder.'

'The Coroner's Court found that Arthur Somers merely died at Swinford,' I reminded him. 'And the actual murder took place elsewhere – somewhere between here and Hardinsett.'

'With respect, Mrs Rodd, all we've got on that is the word of them vicars.'

'Are you saying that you don't believe them?' I tried not to smile at 'them vicars', for this was important. 'My dear Inspector, they're clergymen!'

'All I'm saying is that they could be wrong about the time of the victim's arrival at Swinford, and that could make a difference. When did he run into Barton, and where? That's what I need to know.'

It was all coming back to me now; the peculiar and contradictory nature of my feelings about this man, so spare and grey and self-contained. Before he joined the Metropolitan Police, Blackbeard had been a sergeant in the army, and he still held himself like a soldier. In several of my cases he had infuriated me with his obstinacy, his dogged sticking to one line of thinking, his dismissal of anything in the shape of an instinct. But I had the greatest respect for his intelligence, and my heart sank a little, for if Blackbeard had made up his mind to send Rachel and Mr Barton to the gallows, I had a hard fight on my hands.

'You seem to be assuming,' I said carefully, 'that they are guilty.'

'I don't assume anything,' said Blackbeard. 'But it does rather look that way.'

'Appearances can be deceiving. I visited Mrs Somers this morning, and I'm as sure of her innocence as I am of my own!'

'Hmm,' said Blackbeard. 'Who let you go a-visiting, ma'am? It's the first I've heard of it.'

I began to explain my old acquaintance with Mr Martindale, but Blackbeard made a sound like two sheets of sandpaper being rubbed together, which I knew to be his version of laughter.

'I should've guessed! Is there any vicar on earth you don't know, Mrs Rodd? I just wish I had a shilling for every time you've gone behind my back because you know the vicar! Well, it won't wash this time. In future nobody visits Mrs Somers unless they apply to me. And that goes for Mr Barton, too.'

'I know Mr Barton. He's a fine young man – and the last person on earth to commit a murder. I'm sure of it.'

'Hmm,' said Blackbeard (oh, that 'hmm' of his, how it annoyed me!). 'Here we go.'

'I beg your pardon?'

'You're going to tell me about your instincts and your feelings. And then you'll get up on your high horse when I ask for some proper evidence.'

'You and I are on the same side, Mr Blackbeard,' I said firmly. 'We both want to find the person or persons who murdered Arthur Somers. My friends are victims of a terrible injustice.'

'Well, I hope you're right, ma'am; I don't like to think of hanging ladies and clergymen. But even ladies and clergyman need decent alibis, and they ain't got one.'

'I haven't been able to examine all the reports; where do they both claim to have been, on the afternoon of the murder?'

Blackbeard did not reply for a moment, but looked at me with the faintest hint of a smile. 'Here you go, firing out questions! But the boot's on the other foot this time. You could be a witness.'

'A witness? Nonsense.'

'It may be that I have to ask you about certain events that occurred during your visit.'

'Mr Blackbeard, you have my solemn promise that I will tell you absolutely everything – but I know in my very bones that they are innocent.'

'You and your bones won't hold up in court, ma'am. Find me someone who saw them. Mrs Somers says she was sleeping; Barton says he went a-walking in the woods, and never met a living soul.'

'That's possible, surely.'

'Lots of things are possible,' said Mr Blackbeard. 'As things stand, however, I have two good reasons for thinking Barton's guilty. The first being the testimony of Mr Daniel Arden.'

'I know Mr Arden. He is a very good man; how can he be involved?'

'He made the poison.'

'Oh.' I had not heard this detail.

'He's something of a chemist and he distilled some deadly nightshade as part of an old recipe for eyedrops,' said Mr Blackbeard. 'He saw Barton put the bottle into his pocket, allegedly to keep it away from the little boys.'

'Oh.' This was bad. 'And what is your second reason?'

'Well, it's a rule I follow in all cases of murder.' Blackbeard's dry voice was matter-of-fact, but he was very serious. 'When you boil it down, there's only three reasons why people do it – love, money and the fear of being found out. If I have a suspect who's driven by one of those three, it's ten to one he – or she – is my killer.'

I wanted to argue, but could not; the truth was that most murders could be made to fit into this crude model, and it was only too obvious what drove Rachel and Mr Barton. I was suddenly horribly aware that anything I told Mr Blackbeard could send them to the gallows.

Fifteen

A T THE EXACT HOUR of Arthur's burial at Swinford the following morning, I knelt in the empty chapel at Gabriel and read through the service in the prayer book. The great and all-too-familiar words brought me, for the first time in many days, a sense of peace. I had no doubt that dear Arthur was now in the Celestial City – no matter who had sent him there.

Afterwards, not quite ready to face Mrs Watts-Weston, I went wandering through the college gardens. The sun was warm, yet the air had a smoky tang of approaching autumn. Though the official start of the new term was several weeks away, Oxford had begun to shake itself awake. Young voices echoed in the stairwells and cloisters, and the narrow streets were absolutely black with clergymen.

'Mrs Rodd! This is a bit of luck; I was on my way to call on you.'

It was Mr Jennings, who trotted along the path to catch me up.

'Mr Jennings, how nice to see you.' We shook hands.

'I wanted to say how sorry I was about Arthur Somers; I know he was a friend of yours.'

'Yes, I was very fond of him – which made the brutal manner of his death yet more distressing.'

'I didn't know him well,' said Mr Jennings. 'But he was a good man, with a pure heart.'

He looked very well, as I belatedly noticed; his plump, fresh face had lost its harried expression and he wore a fine new suit of clothes.

'You have been away,' I said.

'Yes, Mrs Rodd,' said Mr Jennings. 'I spent the past month down in Sussex, with my mother. I knew nothing of the murder until I saw the newspapers at the railway station. But I wanted to talk to you about something else.'

'Oh?'

'Let's just walk a little further along the path – out of range of the parlour window.' He led me into the shelter of a great weeping willow tree beside the river, where only the swans could see us. 'I wondered if you had heard the news about Joshua Welland.'

'I have heard nothing.' The truth was that, thanks to chickenpox and then murder, I had not even thought of my wandering scholar for weeks.

'I'm very sorry to tell you that he has died.'

'Good heavens!' I was so shocked that for a long moment I could not speak. 'When did this happen? How?'

'In July, some weeks after you had left Hardinsett.'

'He feared for his life. I wish we had listened!'

'There was no crime involved,' said Mr Jennings sadly. 'The poor chap died of pneumonia. He sent for me at the end; I thank God that I had not yet left town and was there to tend to him.'

It made a melancholy postscript to the story, though I was glad the man had not been murdered after all. 'Was he able to speak to you?'

Mr Jennings nodded. 'He was very weak, yet he had all his wits about him. He wanted to give me certain instructions about his burial. He had purchased a plot for himself at—'

'Shotton Barrow,' I could not help interrupting. 'Next to the grave of Hannah Laurie.'

'Yes.' He was startled that I knew this.

'And I assume you performed the burial.'

'I did, and it was an odd sort of affair,' said Mr Jennings. 'I was rather taken aback by the crowd of people in the churchyard. They came from miles around. Even the charcoal burners came.'

For a few minutes we were quiet.

'I am most grateful to you for telling me,' I said. 'I take it his brother was informed.'

'I wrote to him and his doctor sent a reply, saying he had relayed the news, but didn't know if Jacob had understood.'

'Jacob must have gone himself by now, God rest his soul.'

'Amen,' said Mr Jennings.

'I'm afraid I have no idea when he died; he was very close to it when I last saw him.'

'They're together now, at any rate.' His eyes glazed with tears; he muttered, 'Please excuse me,' pulled his handkerchief from his pocket and loudly blew his nose.

'You were a true friend to Joshua, Mr Jennings,' I said. 'I'm glad to know that you were with him at the end.'

'Thank you,' he said shakily. 'I did my duty as a clergyman, but it was a sorrowful duty. I couldn't help regretting all that wasted promise. And I don't even have those papers of his to remember him by, because the servant threw them away. Now every trace of his existence has vanished.'

'He stood on the very brink of inheriting his brother's fortune,' I said, wondering who would get it now. 'I do wish I had managed to help that story to a happier outcome!'

Mr Jennings gave me a watery smile. 'Joshua left me one more surprise. When I arrived at my mother's house, a few days after the funeral, there was a letter waiting for me. It contained a bundle of banknotes, and an unsigned message: "For God's sake man, buy some new clothes!"'

'I see that you obeyed him,' I said, smiling at Joshua's final piece of impudence, and touched by his final act of generosity. 'You are most elegant.'

'Thank you,' he said earnestly. 'I know a better man would have given the money to the poor – but my mother and I are poor, and it came as an absolute boon. I was getting awfully shabby, and certain Gorgons had started to make public complaints about my frayed shirt-cuffs. Joshua's bequest has turned me respectable again.'

We left our tent of green willow branches to resume our walk beside the river.

Mr Jennings broke the silence. 'I wish I could be more useful to you in the matter of Arthur Somers.'

'You were not in Oxford at the time,' I said. 'Or I would have asked you if you'd happened to see him on the day of his death.'

'We were never close friends,' said Mr Jennings, 'yet I have the clearest memory of our last encounter. It has quite haunted me.'

'When was this?'

'A week or so after the end of last term. We met in a lane near Freshley St Johns. There was a sudden shower of rain; we took shelter together in the porch of the church.'

'How did he seem to you?'

'He was very well, as far as I could see – perhaps a little careworn and distracted. He said he was getting sick of all the gossip about the old man who had "confessed" on his deathbed. We fell to talking about the sacrament of confession; Somers spoke of the difference between carrying one's own sins and carrying the sins of other people.'

'Good heavens, what a subject to while away a downpour!'

'As you will remember, Mrs Rodd, he took the whole business very seriously.'

'Mrs Rodd! Mrs Rodd – are you there?'

Mrs Watts-Weston came dashing along the path behind us (she ran surprisingly fast, like a well-dressed antelope). 'Mrs Rodd!'

'Good morning, Mr Jennings,' I said, laughing. 'You have my permission to flee!'

He gave me a hasty bow – and fled.

'Good God, how time gallops! It's no time at all since I could carry that boy on my shoulders – and now he towers over me and corrects my Latin! When did he turn into a copy of Papa?'

My brother, having eaten a gargantuan luncheon, was indulging in a little sentimentality – quite forgivably, as far as I was concerned. It was the day after my encounter with Mr Jennings and Fred was in Oxford to deliver his oldest boy, dear Augustus, to his new college, well before the beginning of term; to my joy he had chosen to read for the Church.

'If only Papa could see him,' I said. 'He'd be so happy, and so proud!'

'Gus is the son he wanted me to be,' said Fred. 'Sometimes he fixes me with an absolute replica of the old man's famous disapproving look.'

'I wouldn't know,' I said, laughing. 'I didn't see that look as often as you did. You were a rascal from the day you were born.'

We were in a cosy private parlour at the Mitre Inn. A waiter came in to draw the cloth and Fred's whole attention turned back to the important business of his stomach. I needed to talk to him about the murder, but knew there was no point until he was settled, and waited patiently while he ordered another bottle of claret, Stilton cheese and biscuits, and more coal on the fire.

Once his mouth was full and his ears were free, I gave a quick account of my progress so far – very quick, since I had made no progress at all. 'Fred, I'm so dreadfully anxious about Rachel – about both of them.'

'As well you might be, my dear old thing,' said Fred. 'When every fresh turn of events makes the pair of them seem worse!' He grinned at me. 'Looks hopeless, doesn't it? But you know I can never resist a challenge. Though I might come to regret it, yesterday I agreed to defend Mrs Somers.'

'Oh, my dear!' This was such a great relief, for so many reasons, that tears came to my eyes.

'I have one question,' said Fred. 'You must promise not to be cross.'

'Of course I won't.'

'I want to be sure that you still believe they are innocent – that is, innocent of murder. They're not on trial for the other business.'

'Yes, I believe it with all my heart,' I said at once. 'They did not kill Arthur. And as for what you call the "other business" – they didn't do that either.'

'Don't get in a bate! Obviously, I'll tell the jury they're whiter than the snow and therefore had no reason to et cetera et cetera. But I bet they were doing it.'

'Fred!' I was outraged. 'That's a shameful accusation!'

'I beg your pardon for my jaded view of the world,' said Fred. 'In my experience, everybody's doing it – and then lying about it afterwards.'

'Not Rachel Somers!'

'Stop flapping! This is only my private opinion. As far as the rest of the world is concerned, I hold them to be as pure as a pair of angels.' He refilled his wine glass. 'How much do you know about the witnesses?'

'Next to nothing; just what I have read in the newspapers of the inquest.'

'Did you hear of the fight?'

'What fight?'

Fred chuckled. 'It happened at the haymaking dance, after you'd gone to bed. The vicar and his curate had a blazing row—'

'But this is nonsense – wicked nonsense!' I was horrified.

'There are four witnesses, who claim they heard Somers shout out "Bloody Judas", and saw him knock Barton flat on his back.'

'It can't be true,' I said fiercely. 'I would have noticed something amiss the next morning. Rachel would have told me.' (Would she? Could I be sure of anything?)

'Three of the witnesses can be dismissed quite easily, having admitted to being in liquor at the time. The fourth, however, presents us with a problem.'

'Mr Arden,' I said wretchedly.

'It's well-nigh impossible to turn a jury against such a man.' Fred's eyes gleamed. 'As things stand, his evidence is enough to hang Barton several times over.'

'Stop smirking!'

'I'm not smirking,' said Fred. 'Merely pointing out the obstacles in front of us. It would help if you could find someone else with a motive to murder Arthur Somers.'

'I daresay it would,' I returned, rather shortly. 'Until I do, however, we must work with what we have. Who is to defend Mr Barton?'

'A young tyro from my chambers, Mr Patrick Flint,' said Fred. 'He's the chap who made such a stir a few months back, in the matter of the Enfield Cesspit Murders.'

'Oh, yes.' I was a little more hopeful, remembering that this Mr Flint had saved a man everyone believed to be guilty. 'And you think he's capable?'

'Very much so; Flint has a way of sinking his teeth into an argument.' Fred paused to cut himself a slice of Stilton. 'You'll meet him when you're back in London. He has no social graces whatsoever, but you mustn't mind that.' He leant over to tug briskly at the bell. 'Let's have another bottle '

'Another?'

'You got most of the last one.'

'Frederick Tyson, that is a bare-faced lie!'

It was impossible to carry on being serious with Fred when he was tired of seriousness, and I burst out laughing, quite against my will.

Sixteen

THE ACCOUNT OF THE fight filled me with dismay. I had taken it for granted that clergymen could not possibly behave in this manner. Especially Arthur. Yes, I had seen for myself Mr Barton's quick temper and readiness with his fists, but – *Arthur!* Gentle Arthur, whom my husband once described as 'the epitome of the word "milksop"'. I longed to talk to Rachel again, but before I could get Blackbeard's permission, both defendants were carried off to London, to await their trial at the Old Bailey. There were one or two things I had to do before I followed.

Mrs Bentley sent me a letter that had come to Hampstead; it was waiting for me on my plate at breakfast. Mrs Watts-Weston eyed it so beadily that I felt obliged to open it immediately. It was from Mr Harold Mitchell, the attorney who dealt with the affairs of Jacob Welland.

'Bad news, Mrs Rodd?'

'Nothing unexpected,' I said. 'Poor Mr Jacob Welland has died at last.' (And Mitchell requested a meeting with me, regarding a 'confidential matter', but I kept that to myself.)

'Dear, dear!' sighed Mrs W-W. 'Such a sad end to a sad story! Cedric, my dear.'

'Hmm?' Her husband raised his scholarly nose from his book (he brought a book to every meal if he could get away with it; the Warden was a dapper little egg of a man, round and bald and amiable, and I could not imagine how he had ever got up the gumption to propose to his whirl-wind of a wife).

'My dear, Jacob Welland is dead,' said Mrs Watts-Weston. 'Joshua's older brother.'

'I'm sorry to hear it,' said the Warden. 'I always felt that Joshua's history was a stain upon this college. When you told us of his death, Mrs Rodd, I was mostly dismayed by the wanton waste of a good brain. The fact that he died in such abject poverty—'

'I can't get hold of Mr Jennings for all the details,' interrupted Mrs W-W. 'I positively think the man is avoiding me! Cedric, if you see him skulking about in the common room you must send him to me at once.'

'Yes, my dear.'

'There would be a lot more talk about it, if not for the murder, which is all anybody can talk about these days. And that reminds me, Cedric—' She glared at her hus-band. 'Some very impertinent young men were singing that horrid song about the cup of cold poison, right under-neath my window! I know who it was – the Parrish boy, and that grubby youth who is always with him—'

She launched into a tirade of complaints about certain undergraduates who were particularly offensive to her, and I allowed my attention to wander. The letter from Mitchell pricked my curiosity; had Jacob Welland sent me one final message?

'—and I'm sure you've heard the latest rumour, Mrs Rodd.'

'I beg your pardon?'

Mrs Watts-Weston tutted impatiently. 'About the inci-dent at Banbury Fair!' She smiled to see my blank face, for she lived to be first with news. 'Apparently, Mr Barton was seen fighting a man there.'

'Oh,' I said faintly, trying to hide my horror. I had heard nothing of this.

'People are now saying this man had some connection to Arthur Somers; a most unsavoury connection. Well, it's quite clearly blackmail – for the usual reasons that cannot be uttered before servants and children.'

'Caroline!' the Warden protested.

'Oh, fiddlesticks! We're all people of the world. I know of such a case in the history of my own family! One of the tales that circulated about Sir Christopher Warrender was that he was being blackmailed by a local ploughboy.'

'My dear!'

'Mark my words, this blackmailer will turn out to be the murderer,' said Mrs Watts-Weston happily. 'More tea, Mrs Rodd?'

'No, that's all wrong.' The Warden snapped his book shut and spoke with a sudden forcefulness that took me by surprise. 'What would be his motive? It would not be in his interest to murder a reliable source of money. The scandalous side of all this is simply a most unfortunate distraction, and the love of scandal is making people look in the wrong places.'

I was intrigued, for the Warden had shown no sign of particular interest in the case, and he had touched upon one of my own deep-seated fears. 'Where would you look?'

'On his doorstep,' said the Warden. 'I don't mean his wife and curate; as a clergyman, Somers was witness to all the essential dramas in the lives of the local people. Consider the fuss he stirred up when he heard that man's so-called confession. Somebody was clearly afraid that he knew some secret or other – whether or not it was so – and that is the most convincing motive we have seen so far.'

137

'Nonsense!' declared Mrs W-W. 'Anyone can see that this amounts to far more than some crude village scandal!'

'I really doubt it,' said the Warden mildly. 'You are too fond of melodrama, my dear.'

He opened his book and his attention left us, like a light being extinguished.

His wife tutted and shrugged and refilled my teacup. 'Don't listen to him, Mrs Rodd – melodrama, indeed!'

I don't know what I said in reply, for the Warden's intervention was deeply unsettling, and made me think of Inspector Blackbeard and his three motives for murder – love, money or the fear of being found out. We had all been so caught up with motive number one that we had scarcely bothered with number three.

Fear of being found out.

Could we all, in our love of melodrama, have overlooked what my brother called 'the stark and the staring'?

Someone had daubed the word 'Whore' on the wall of the barn at Hardinsett, in whitewash letters a foot high. The word hit me like a slap and I stopped Mrs W-W's dashing little chariot rather sharply. The fine September morning was utterly spoiled.

It was in the process of being scrubbed off by two labourers with long brushes and pails of water.

'Mrs Rodd, good morning.' One of the labourers turned around and I saw that it was Mr Arden, unfamiliar in his shirtsleeves.

He dropped his brush and came to my side, before I could decide how I felt about him. I could hardly treat him as an enemy, when he was scrubbing the foul word off Rachel's barn with his own hands.

'This is very good of you, Mr Arden.'

'I took it on myself to remove it as soon as possible. It's a disgraceful piece of cowardice.'

'I quite agree,' I said warmly. 'Nobody around here would dare to insult Mrs Somers openly.'

'It's one thing I can do for the poor woman,' said Mr Arden, very earnest. 'And with all my heart I wish I wasn't involved. Please understand, Mrs Rodd, that I'm a very unwilling participant in this matter. But I can only tell the truth.'

'Naturally I understand.'

'I have a great liking for Barton, and I don't for a second believe that he is a murderer. I cannot deny, however, that I made the poison and saw Barton put the bottle into his pocket. And I'm very sorry for it.'

'Yes, that fact is particularly awkward.' I could not keep the exasperation from my voice. 'Why on earth did you make it, anyway?'

'As a remedy for an eye-complaint,' said Mr Arden. 'Two drops of atropine in a half-pint of distilled water. And I distilled the atropine myself. I am an enthusiastic amateur chemist. To my eternal regret I left the bottle on my desk, one of the boys got hold of it and Barton very properly took it away from them. That's all.'

He was absolutely sincere and I softened in spite of myself. 'I'm not blaming you for telling the truth, Mr Arden. The sad fact is that, in this case, I don't like the truth when I hear it.'

'You should have more faith,' he said, smiling. 'Once the truth is properly revealed, it is always beautiful.'

'Oh – yes—' (I had no idea how I should respond to this sudden piece of mysticism, and was a little depressed to think how a jury would enjoy it; oh, why did this man have to be on the other side?) 'But I'm sure you did not reveal the truth to your boys.'

'Certainly not!' Mr Arden was startled, and then amused. 'You've unmasked me as a hypocrite, Mrs Rodd. I told the boys that Barton had gone away on a long visit. They're devoted to him.'

'They must miss him.'

'Very much,' said Mr Arden, his face glowing and youthful as it always was when he spoke of the twins. 'You saw how quickly he won the trust of those wild creatures, and their progress has been marvellous. He managed to stop them running off in the middle of lessons, which I never could. And they had a habit of stuffing food into their pockets for "the man in the woods" – whom I assumed to be a figment of their riotous imaginations, until they suddenly announced that the man had "gone away"—'

'Joshua Welland!' I exclaimed.

He nodded. 'It must've been Joshua; they described his big cloak and long beard and so forth, and it could hardly have been anyone else.'

'But where on earth did the twins meet him? Did he come into your garden?'

'He would not have needed to do that.' Mr Arden was a little sheepish now. 'My estate is a large one, and I'm afraid I gave Jack and Ferdy too much freedom to roam about – as I did myself when I was a child. Barton very tactfully explained to me that a genteel upbringing must be far more restricted.' He gave me a wry smile. 'Shades of the prison-house must close about my growing boys.'

'This is very curious, Mr Arden,' I said. 'What else did they tell you about this mysterious man? I don't believe Joshua ran into the boys by chance – but what could he want with them?'

'Whatever it was, he has taken the secret to his grave,' said Mr Arden. 'The twins said he told them stories. When

140

we heard of Joshua's death, it was Barton's opinion that they should be encouraged to forget him as quickly as possible. He's determined to lick my cubs into shape – or he was before he was arrested for murder.'

'Do you think he did it?'

'No,' said Mr Arden. 'I do not. And Mrs Somers is utterly blameless. Believe me, I'd be overjoyed if you find out something to clear their names. Let's pray that justice will be done; we are all in God's hands.'

'Indeed we are,' I said, suppressing an impious wish that the Almighty would move in his mysterious ways a little faster. 'I'm on my way to the rectory now, to talk to the servants.'

'I'm afraid Mrs Richards is the only servant still to be found there. The others all ran off.'

'Never mind,' I said stoutly. 'Mrs Richards will do very well.'

'I wish you luck, ma'am, if that is allowed.'

'Thank you, Mr Arden.'

We exchanged bows and I drove off along the lane towards the vicarage, feigning a confidence I did not feel, wondering where I should start digging for the choicest village scandals.

It was sad to see that charming house with all the blinds drawn and an air of neglect. I stopped the carriage in the gravelled drive, and while I was tying up the horse, Mrs Richards emerged from the front door.

With many apologies, she led me through the hall into the kitchen. 'All the other rooms are shut up; it's not so tidy as I'd like, but there's a nice fire.'

'You are very good to stay here by yourself,' I said.

'Someone had to,' said Mrs Richards. 'I can't leave the place empty.'

'It must be lonely for you, especially at night.'

'I don't mind it, ma'am.' She gave me a cautious half-smile. 'There's a story going about that the place is haunted, and I encourage it because it keeps the children away.' She placed a Windsor chair in front of the range. 'Will you have a cup of tea?'

It was the powerful 'country' tea that I liked so much. We sat a little too near the fire; I was almost too comfortable. There was no danger of drowsiness, however, for Mrs Richards was more talkative than I had ever known her.

'This is a sad sort of return for you, ma'am.'

'The saddest possible!'

'And it all happened so quick, I don't know if I'm on my head or my heels.' She eyed me cautiously. 'Have you come to help Miss Rachel?'

'Yes, if I can.'

'I'm thankful she has somebody to stand by her. She didn't do it, ma'am. The policeman from London came here right after it happened, and tried to trip me up and confuse me. But he couldn't make me change my story. I know she is innocent.' Mrs Richards set her cup down on the table and folded her arms with an air of defiance. 'And I will swear before any court in this land that she didn't go putting poison into her own lemonade. Stuff and nonsense, I told him.'

(What a splendid witness she would make; Blackbeard had met his match at last.)

'There's not a bad bone in her body, Mrs Rodd, and it bothers me that people are so quick to condemn her, with pretty much no evidence against her. What's more, she loved her husband with all her heart. She was not carrying on with Mr Barton. You mention that again, I said to the policeman, and you'll get the back of my hand.'

'I don't understand,' I said, 'how such a shocking rumour has come to be so widely believed.'

'You've Maggy Woods to thank for that,' said Mrs Richards. 'The young widow from the lodge at Binstock. She says she saw them kissing, ma'am. At that blessed Haymaking Supper.'

'But that can't be true – she must be mistaken—'

Mrs Richards simply pursed her lips and looked at me, and I had no more strength left to argue. Why was I wasting time in arguing with witnesses, anyway? If I carried on telling people they were 'mistaken', we would get nowhere.

'I will try to talk to Mrs Woods before I leave,' I said. 'I'll admit to you, Mrs Richards, that I saw several signs of an attachment, but only on the part of Mr Barton.'

She gave me a curt nod, as if satisfied. 'You saw it, and I saw it, plain as day. That young man is in love with Miss Rachel.'

'I'm afraid so.'

'But that's not her fault, is it?'

'Certainly not!' I said warmly.

Mrs Richards nodded again, and seemed to relax a little. 'Would you care for something to eat, ma'am? I've got an apple pie ready to come out.'

'Yes, please!' I was very hungry and hours away from my next meal. 'I remember your famous pies from the good old days. My late husband always maintained that you had a touch of genius.'

'I couldn't think what else to do with the apples,' said Mrs Richards. 'The orchard was knee-deep this morning. Nobody's come to pick them and they're just falling off the trees.'

It was a splendid pie, beautifully garnished with pastry leaves. We ate it hot at the kitchen table, and fell to reminiscing about the happy times in Herefordshire. Mrs Richards produced glasses of sherry, and softened enough to tell a droll story about Rachel's aunt and her stinginess.

We agreed that Rachel's wedding day, ten years ago, seemed like yesterday.

'I helped her to dress,' I said, 'and I'll never forget how lovely she looked. They were both so happy!'

'That's right,' said Mrs Richards, gazing thoughtfully into the kitchen fire, glowing through the open door of the range. 'Miss Rachel was never anything less than a good and loving wife to him. If you'll pardon me, Mrs Rodd, Mr Somers was too fond of religion. He took it too far and I told him so, when he was going off to Swinford, on the very day he was murdered.'

'Was he annoyed?'

'Not a bit of it,' she said sadly. 'He burst out laughing. That was the last I saw of him.'

'And Mrs Somers was at home for the whole afternoon – she did not go out at all?'

'No she did not,' said Mrs Richards. 'She had a headache and went upstairs to lie down.'

'Did anyone call at the house?'

'No.' She was on her guard again, I thought. 'Mr Arden called to ask for Mr Somers, and the ribbon-man came to the back door. That's all.'

It was time to change tack. 'When I was last here, Mr Somers unwittingly made trouble for himself with the business of Tom Goodly's deathbed confession.'

'Oh, yes, ma'am.' Mrs Richards sighed and rolled her eyes. 'Poor man, he should've known better! He stirred up a right lot of silly talk.'

'Did the fuss die down after I had gone back to London?'

'It got worse.'

'In what way?'

'The stories got taller,' said Mrs Richards. 'Until everyone thought Mr Somers knew all their dark secrets.'

'I remember that the night at Goodly's deathbed made Mr Somers very anxious.' My heart was beating harder now, though my voice was light and level. 'But he did say that most of the famous confession seemed to be nonsense.'

'So did his wife,' said Mrs Richards. 'She was listening with all her ears because she thought Goodly had been in a big robbery and hid the gold in the house.'

'A robbery!' This was the last thing I had expected. 'Surely the man was far too old?'

Mrs Richards chuckled. 'It was thirty years ago, ma'am, and nobody can recall any robbery at that time. She must've imagined it all, but still she insists that Goodly brought home a sack of gold sovereigns and hid it away from her.'

'It does sound rather unlikely; Mr Somers told me they lived in terrible poverty.'

'She searched every corner of that cottage, ma'am, and whenever she was in liquor – which was often – she used to nag him about it. But there was never any gold, and not a word of it came out in what she heard of Goodly's confession.'

'Perhaps I'll speak to her anyway,' I said. 'Where does she live?'

'In Pig Lane, but you won't find her there now; her daughter took her off to Abingdon.'

'Is she very infirm?'

'She's as fit as a fiddle, ma'am,' said Mrs Richards. 'She had to leave because she went funny and her neighbours threw her out.'

'That was rather harsh, surely!'

'They had no choice, Mrs Rodd; first she went ripping up her own thatch, and that was bad enough. But then she was caught ripping up the thatch of the house next door, and accusing them of stealing that fairy gold of hers.'

145

'Oh, dear.' I could not see why this unfortunate old woman would want to kill Arthur. 'Were you aware of any other rumours going round?'

'There were quite a few,' said Mrs Richards, with grim amusement. 'Some folks wanted to know if Goodly had confessed to being the true father of George Baines up at the mill. And other folks said Baines's nose did the confessing for him.'

We both smiled at this, and I said, 'You make me remember the distinctive flavour of village gossip, which I rather missed when we moved to Bloomsbury.'

'Crimes and scandals stand out more in the country,' said Mrs Richards decidedly. 'That's why I don't care for the city. You can't hide anything in a country place.'

'And yet,' I said, 'I have a feeling someone is doing exactly that – trying to hide something that Mr Somers threatened to expose. Do you have any idea what this might be?'

She had nothing more to tell me and I was a little disappointed; I had allowed myself to hope for another suspect, another line of enquiry. I took my leave, with many thanks.

Seventeen

THE QUAINT LODGE AT Binstock looked very pretty when I drove myself there next morning, sparkling in the early autumn sunshine like an iced cake. Mrs Woods ran out at once to open the great gates. She was a little taken aback that I stopped the carriage and stepped down to speak with her.

'You are the reason I'm here, Mrs Woods,' I told her. 'I wanted to ask you a few questions about the Haymaking Supper.'

She was nervous and I suddenly saw how young she was, scarcely older than my Tishy, though she was already a widow and a mother. I immediately softened my tone, and asked, 'But where are Molly and Jessy?'

'They're at school, ma'am.' The mention of their names made her smile. 'Down yonder in the village. All the estate children go to school.'

(Mr Arden's doing, I was certain, and typical of his liberality.)

'This is a very pretty situation, Mrs Woods.'

'Yes, ma'am.'

'How long is it now, since your husband died?'

'Going on for three years, ma'am. Jessy wasn't weaned yet. If Mr Arden hadn't took care of us, I don't know what would've become of us. Mr Arden said he felt obliged because Woods was doing a job for him when it happened.

He was clearing the ivy off an old wall, and it fell down and crushed him.'

'What a dreadful tragedy,' I said warmly. 'I honour Mr Arden for his decency. I hear the man's praises sung wherever I go.'

'Yes, ma'am.'

'I'll never forget the sight of him dancing with your Molly.'

She giggled. 'Oh, she was that proud!'

I had brought us to the subject of the dance and knew that I must choose my words with extreme care, so as not to frighten her.

'Mrs Woods, I think you know why I'm here.'

Her round, childish cheeks reddened. 'It's about what I said to the policeman.'

'Yes,' I said. 'And I'd be most grateful if you could repeat it to me.'

'I swear it's the truth!'

'I don't doubt it, for I can see that you are a truthful person.'

'I saw Mrs Somers and Mr Barton, on the night of the dance. They had their arms about each other and they was kissing.'

The words, uttered with such guileless conviction, rained down upon me like blows. 'My dear, could you possibly have been mistaken?'

'No,' Mrs Woods said promptly. 'I saw what I saw.'

'Of course you did,' I said hastily. 'Thank you, Mrs Woods.' I gave her two sixpences, one for each of her girls, and left her smiling.

My own spirits, however, were very low. If Mrs Woods was called to give evidence in court, poor Rachel's good name would be damaged beyond repair. Fred was right, I thought; every new twist and turn makes the two of them look even more culpable.

The weather was pleasant and I could not face Mrs Watts-Weston's soul-stripping gaze while my mind was in turmoil. On an impulse, coming across a signpost, I drove the little carriage towards Shotton Barrow, so that I could pay my last respects to Joshua Welland.

The journey took longer than I had expected; the tracks and lanes I had traversed on foot were too narrow for the carriage. I secured the horse on a verdant patch of ground outside the wall of the churchyard. Someone was there already – a grizzled, threadbare figure, perched on a tombstone, who jumped to his feet when he saw me.

'Mrs Rodd!' It was Blackbeard, as startled by the meeting as I was. 'Bless my soul, what brings you here, ma'am?'

'Good day, Inspector. I am visiting a grave.'

'So am I,' said Blackbeard. 'But it's nothing to do with police business – I'm paying respects to my wife's parents.' He rested his hand upon a nearby headstone, as if introducing them. 'My wife rests in Clerkenwell, where I can keep an eye on her, so to speak. But she was born here, and loved this place; she always said she was a country maid at heart.'

I remembered now that Blackbeard had lost his wife around the same time that I lost my husband, and softened in spite of myself. 'I'm sorry to disturb you.'

'Not at all, ma'am.'

'I came here to satisfy my curiosity about my last case.'

'Hmm,' said Blackbeard. 'Would that be the Welland chap?'

'Yes – I should have guessed you'd know about it. I have only recently heard of his death.'

'You'll find him over by the wall, where the ground is broken.'

'Thank you.'

Just as Mr Jennings had said, my scholar lay beside his true love Hannah Laurie, to wander no more. I gazed at the mound of earth and said a prayer for the peace of his soul.

Blackbeard's shadow fell across the grave; he was beside me, his hat in his hands. 'Rum sort of story, don't you think?'

'Very.'

'It only goes to show what a hard world it can be, for a man without friends or money.'

This was most unexpected, and I dared to ask, 'Do you speak from experience?' (I knew almost nothing of his background, beyond this new snippet about his wife.)

'You could say that, ma'am.' He eyed me cautiously. 'But I wasn't your scholarly sort, not like this fellow. In a better world, he'd be alive and well and working in his college. It's a shame to see a good brain wasted.'

'Indeed it is,' I said.

'I suppose Mr Collins did the service.'

'No, it was Joshua's friend Mr Jennings.'

'Well, of course,' said Blackbeard, 'Collins must be as old as the hills by now. He lives in that queer old place over the road.' He added, 'It was a great house once upon a time. But most of it fell down, or was pulled down, and that's what remains.'

'Another relic of the Warrenders, I suppose.'

'Oh, yes, my wife was full of old tales about them Warrenders.' Blackbeard's granite face was almost smiling. 'She knew their history, right back to Noah's flood. And she swore that the last of them was murdered.'

My interest sharpened – I had been wondering a great deal about the facts behind this legend. 'Did Mrs Blackbeard have a theory about who murdered him?'

'None that held water, bless her heart. And they never found a body. There was another story going the rounds, that Sir Christopher Warrender was living in a lodging-house in

Plymouth, in somewhat sinful circumstances, ma'am.' He sighed to himself. 'But she wouldn't have it. She made me promise I'd look into it one day. Well, it's an old case now, if it's even a case – it must be more than thirty years ago.'

'Thirty years ago seems quite recent to me these days, Inspector.'

'Very true, ma'am.'

'Was there an official search for the man when he vanished?'

'He had an old aunt, and she searched high and low. But then she died and people lost interest. It didn't help that everyone knew she'd fallen out with him and was after him for money.'

'Oh.' The noble line of Warrenders had died out rather ignobly, it seemed. 'My hostess, who is distantly related to the family, hinted at rumours of blackmail.'

'By the by, Mrs Rodd—' Blackbeard's hat was back on his head, and he was businesslike again. 'I believe you have something to tell me in that department.'

'Oh – yes.' My spirits sank again, for in the cold light of those hooded slits of eyes, what I had overheard seemed yet more awful. 'But how did you—'

'Come along now, ma'am. I can see why you'd want to cover it up, but you're too late.'

'I don't like to discuss such matters in a churchyard,' I said. 'Would you be kind enough to join me in the carriage?'

'Well, if you could give me a ride as far as the Oxford road,' said Blackbeard, 'I wouldn't say no.'

We walked back to the carriage in prickly silence. Once we were moving I told my sordid tale of eavesdropping and blackmail as briefly as possible, but leaving out nothing.

He was not shocked. Blackbeard had a low opinion of human nature and nothing shocked him.

'Hmm,' he said, once I had finished my recital. 'Thank you, Mrs Rodd.'

'Will this evidence of mine make matters worse for Mr Barton?'

'I couldn't say.'

'He was angry, Inspector; he simply lost his temper.'

'Hmm,' said Blackbeard. 'You heard him threaten to kill Mr Somers.'

'For goodness' sake, Mr Blackbeard – my late husband used to threaten to kill him at least once a week! It really didn't mean anything.'

'I don't like to speak ill of the dead,' said Blackbeard, 'let alone a vicar. But I'm sure you heard about the set-to at Banbury Fair.'

'I heard that Mr Barton was seen in yet another fight.'

'Well, that was more of the same.'

'I beg your pardon?'

'The talk is that he was dealing with the blackmailer.'

'Again?' I could not hide my dismay.

'So it seems, ma'am,' said Blackbeard, looking (I thought) pleased with himself. 'You're out of your depth with this case. Ladies like yourself don't know the half of what goes on. Where a certain crime is concerned, the law being what it is, respectable men lay themselves open to disgrace. I beg your pardon if I've shocked you.'

'Not at all.' (I was deeply shocked, but strove to hide it.)

'It's like I always say, Mrs Rodd,' said Blackbeard, with a gleam of inner satisfaction on his face. 'Love, money, or fear of discovery. And this murder is all about love.'

'I'm beginning to think it has more to do with some-one's fear of discovery.'

'No, no, it's love all right – whether you like it or not. Sometimes it happens that a thing is exactly as it appears to be. And that's what we have here. You're just refusing to look facts in the face because the main players are friends of yours.'

He was cutting deep now, and he knew it. While I was still casting about for a reply, we came to a crossroads and Mr Blackbeard asked to be put down.

'Thank you, Mrs Rodd.' He jumped into the road and gave me a stiff bow. 'We'll meet in London, I daresay. Good day to you, ma'am.'

'One moment, Inspector; what must I do to convince you of their innocence?'

'Give me a convincing suspect, ma'am, with an obvious motive; give me good evidence and reliable witnesses.'

'Thank you.' I tried to speak lightly though my heart was heavy. 'I promise not to bother you with any new theory until I can provide every single item on that list.'

Eighteen

Mrs Watts-Weston had planned a dinner party, and would not allow me to miss it.

'You are the great attraction, Mrs Rodd; you can't possibly go back to London until I have shown you off. You're the talk of Oxford, and everybody wants a glimpse of you. I've had to put two extra leaves on the dining-room table.'

'You're most kind, and of course I'll be happy to attend.' I did not want to in the least, but how could I refuse when Mrs W-W had been so hospitable? 'I hope I won't be too much of a disappointment.'

'You'll meet some of the finest brains in the country,' said Mrs W-W, with great satisfaction. 'If we apply those brains to the question of the murder, we'll have it solved before pudding, I daresay.'

This made me laugh; the fact was that during my sojourn under her roof I had grown rather fond of the Gorgon. Her household management was nothing short of brilliant, but she was also a fine scholar who taught her children Latin and Greek. What was more, she could inhabit both realms at the same time; I once saw her reading Homer with two of her sons at the kitchen table, whilst making beeswax polish for the furniture – now show me the man who could do this.

I was careful to be early downstairs, after an hour spent cleaning the hem of my hard-working black silk. My hostess had made lavish preparations; I caught a glimpse of the extended dining-room table laden with silver and flowers, glasses gleaming in the candlelight. The guests were shown into the drawing room, to shake hands with the Warden and his wife and to be introduced to me, after which they were given glasses of sherry.

'I knew they'd all descend at once,' said Mrs W-W. 'Nobody is late in Oxford, because there's never anything else to do.'

At least three-quarters of the guests were clergymen. They talked loudly, and with somewhat improper jollity, about poor Arthur's death. Each man had his theory, and very little sense was spoken. I sipped sherry and nodded politely.

'Mrs Rodd!' Mrs Watts-Weston appeared at my side, firmly gripping the arm of a shy, rather colourless young woman. 'Allow me to introduce my niece, Miss Isobel Drewitt, and her fiancé, Mr Rivers.'

She extracted from the nearest group of clergymen a short, broadly built young man with cropped dark hair and eyeglasses on a long gold chain; he looked vaguely familiar, and I was still trying to place him when Mrs W-W hauled her niece away to be introduced to a group of ladies.

'We met at Swinford, Mrs Rodd.' Mr Rivers spoke very softly, so that I strained to hear him. 'I was the chap who opened the door to you.'

'Oh, Mr Rivers, of course I remember you now.'

'You wrote me a letter, to which I did not reply,' murmured Mr Rivers (I had sent him a brief note requesting a meeting on the day after my visit). 'I'm sorry for it now and would be grateful if you could spare me a few minutes.'

'Yes, of course; I shall look for you after dinner.' This was interesting. Had I not guessed that Mr Fogle was holding something back?

There was now a general surge towards the dining room, and I was claimed by the Warden, who was taking me into dinner. The food was excellent, the conversation pleasant and dull. Afterwards, when the gentlemen had finished their port and cigars and returned to the drawing room, and Mrs Watts-Weston was distracted by the task of making tea, Mr Rivers and I sat down on the window-seat. There was by now such a roar of conversation that it was easy to be confidential.

'I left Swinford on the day after we met,' said Mr Rivers. 'And I haven't been back since. The shock of it all made me ill.'

'I'm not surprised to hear it,' I said. 'The discovery of a dead body is always a dreadful thing, and the sight of poor Arthur would have upset anyone.'

'I had to give evidence at the inquest. And the police-man from London made me relive the experience at least fifty times.'

'Mr Blackbeard is very thorough,' I agreed.

'I told no lies,' said Mr Rivers, 'but not the whole truth – which I now know to be as bad as lying.'

'Mr Fogle told me of an argument between himself and Arthur, on the night before Arthur's death.'

'Oh yes, there was an argument.' Mr Rivers was com-posed, and spoke rapidly, as if he had been preparing what to say to me. 'I was sworn to silence and said nothing about it when I gave my account to the police. But I've been very uneasy, and now think I must confide in some-one.'

'If you know anything significant,' I said, 'you must confide in Scotland Yard.'

'No, no, I can't do that.' His voice had shrunk to a cau-tious murmur.

'Why not?'

157

'Because it would cause such a scandal.'

'Oh dear – what sort of scandal might that be, Mr Rivers?'

'I told the police and so forth that I heard "raised voices", but could not make out what they were saying.'

'But you could.'

'Yes, Mrs Rodd. And I was rather less than candid regarding my encounter with Somers on the day of his death.'

'As I understand from the report of the inquest, you admitted to exchanging greetings with him,' I said. 'And to settling that you would meet next morning.'

'Perfectly true,' said Mr Rivers. 'But there was more. I had been reading out in the garden. I came upon Somers whilst I was on my way back to the house – I'm not sure of the precise time; it was between five and six. He was sitting on a low wall, and he didn't have a hat – which later struck me as odd.'

'How did he seem to you? Had the poison started to affect him?'

'His face was red, as if he had been running,' said Mr Rivers. 'When he saw me, he called out, "Oh, it's Rivers – hello, Rivers! You have the air of a man whose mind is made up – is it to be Romance or Rome?"'

'What did he mean?'

The young man looked pained. 'He was referring to the conflict I was wrestling with at the time, between turning Catholic and proposing to Isobel. He saw that I was annoyed to hear it spoken of so lightly, and quickly gabbled, "Don't mind me, I've spent this afternoon wrangling with someone who thinks Rome is a harlot and her sacraments so much moonshine!'

My interest intensified, for here at last was a clue to where Arthur had spent his last afternoon. 'Did he tell you who it was?'

'Not precisely,' said Mr Rivers. 'It was at this point that I asked if he felt unwell, for he appeared to be in pain. He said he had a headache. And then he asked, "Do you know Henry Barton?"'

This was a heavy blow, though I kept my face a mask of polite interest. 'Was he saying he had just met with Mr Barton? Please think carefully, Mr Rivers; the police are searching for any evidence that places the two of them together on that day.'

'I assumed that's what he meant, Mrs Rodd. I said I did not know Barton. Whereupon he gave me a dazed sort of look, and said, "Henry upset me and we parted in anger."'

'But he didn't say where or when they met?'

'No. He was confused and he staggered as he stood up, and I'm afraid I thought he had been drinking.' His prim, bespectacled face became warmer, and younger. 'I feel awful about it now.'

'Don't reproach yourself too much,' I said. 'Even if you had known about the poison, there was nothing you could have done for him.' I breathed more easily, for this new piece of evidence was starting to look decidedly flimsy. 'Was it your idea to meet next morning?'

'No, it was his,' said Mr Rivers. 'He wanted me to pray with him, before early communion.' He stiffened irritably. 'His exact words were – "Rivers, you're a dim-witted prig with no sense of humour, but you have the pure soul of an angel."'

I nearly laughed out loud, and with a stab of pain, for this was the authentic Arthur. 'Dear me, how rude of him!' I hastened to say. 'That must have been the effect of the poison, for he would never have said such a thing in his right mind.' (Not to your face, anyway, I mentally added: behind your back was another matter; I'm sure Arthur did a marvellous imitation of you and I wish I had seen it.) 'You did not sleep in the stables that night, I understand.'

'I did not,' said Mr Rivers. 'I had a cold; the cells are places of penitence and prayer. And to be frank – kindly don't repeat this, Mrs Rodd – I was getting a little impatient with all the praying and so forth at Swinford. I slept in a room on the first floor of the house. That's where I went that night, directly after a miserable supper of cabbage and boiled potatoes.' He glanced across the room and suddenly smiled. 'I had by this time fallen in love with Isobel, and the food was yet another reason not to embrace a monastic life. Anyway, I began to read a life of Thomas à Kempis, and for some reason fell asleep.'

'Your cold made you drowsy,' I suggested (swallowing another laugh at the 'for some reason' and wishing I could catch Arthur's eye).

'I woke to the sound of shouts and noises downstairs.' Mr Rivers's gaze dropped away from mine. 'It was Father Fogle and Arthur Somers.'

'Mr Fogle told me about it,' I said. 'Perhaps not willingly, but readily enough. He said they had a disagreement.'

He was uncomfortable. 'In my statement I said I heard "raised voices". Which is perfectly true, only it's not quite strong enough.'

'Can you tell me what you heard, Mr Rivers?'

'I can't repeat the exact words – certainly not here.'

'That won't be necessary,' I assured him. 'Just give me a general idea, if you can.'

'Well – both voices were loud, and Arthur was absolutely screeching. He was beside himself, Mrs Rodd, raving like a lunatic. I rushed downstairs; the door to the study stood open and when I went inside … he shouted certain unrepeatable epithets.'

'Did he threaten you – how was his behaviour?'

'He was angry,' said Mr Rivers. 'His face was flushed; he kept picking things up and dropping them. I know now

160

that the poison was working its wickedness. At the time, however, I still thought – I should have been more … '

'How was Mr Fogle?'

'I found him weeping. He begged Somers to "have mercy". And then Somers said, "How dare you condemn me, you of all people? You're ready enough to make excuses for yourself!"'

'Were those his exact words?'

'Yes, pretty much. And then the poor man lurched off towards the cells, and that was the last time I saw him alive.' Mr Rivers sighed and lowered his voice. 'I know that there was nothing I could have done to help him – but I could have stayed beside him, and given him the benefit of my prim, dim-witted prayers.'

There was a movement amongst the crowd in the room, in the direction of the piano.

'Thank you, Mr Rivers,' I said. 'You have been very helpful.'

'Could you keep my name out of it, as far as you can? I swore I would not speak of it.'

'Mrs Rodd, you won't hear a thing stuck in that corner!' Mrs Watts-Weston was upon us, ablaze with the success of the evening. 'Mr Rivers, dear Isobel has agreed to sing for us, and nobody accompanies her better than you do; the two of you are positively harmonious!'

Our interview was at an end; Mr Rivers was marched to the piano and I was kindly-but-firmly chivvied into a chair in the front row. Miss Drewitt had a very pleasing soprano, and sang for us Handel's 'How Beautiful Are the Feet' most affectingly.

I had promised Mr Rivers I would keep his name out of it, but that was not going to stop me going back to Swinford.

Nineteen

I DROVE MYSELF OVER TO Swinford in Mrs W-W's little chariot, directly after breakfast the following morning. The weather was warm, stuffy and grey, the September sun muffled behind a thick quilt of cloud. As I secured the horse on the scrap of green in front of the main house, I heard a dismal chanting from the direction of the old stables; a not-very-tuneful attempt at medieval plainsong. If they were in the middle of one of their peculiar services, I would have to wait to see Mr Fogle.

Never mind. This meant that I could wander about the place without anyone looking over my shoulder. The church itself was commonplace enough; like so many village churches at that time, it was a new construction, built on the site of the old one that had become too small. I stepped inside for a moment to say a brief prayer; I love the peace of an empty church.

When I emerged into the churchyard, I was surprised to see a thin, stooping, black-clad figure, in the shadow of a great yew that was older than the church by several centuries.

'Mr Fogle!' This was so providential that I approached him quite boldly. 'I thought you would be in the chapel.'

'Mrs Rodd.' He turned those radiant, unsettling, tearful eyes towards me, not the least discomposed. 'It's not a service; the men in the chapel are at prayer.'

'Oh.'

'They are singing praises to the Queen of Heaven, this being the month of her nativity.'

'Really.'

'Your lip is curling, Mrs Rodd; I take it you don't approve of such things.'

'You are quite wrong, Mr Fogle,' I said. 'I have the highest respect for the Queen of Heaven; she has always struck me as a woman of excellent good sense.' (I refer the reader to her intervention at the wedding in Cana.)

He surprised me by suddenly smiling, like sunshine through rain. 'Indeed she was; I may use that as the motif for a sermon.'

'This is Arthur's grave, isn't it?' We were standing over a bare brown mound of earth.

'Yes. There will be a tombstone in place eventually. I often come out here to pray; even in death he draws me to him.'

'Mr Fogle, I would very much like to talk to you again about that night.'

'Why?' The man appeared to be genuinely puzzled. 'I'm sure I've said everything I could possibly say on the subject.'

'We can't talk here. Is there somewhere—?'

'Let us move to the garden.'

He led me through a door in the old wall of the churchyard, into a very pretty and sheltered little patch of garden, still bright with cottage flowers left over from the hot summer. He gestured to me to sit down upon a wooden bench while he chose to stand, his long white hands folded behind him.

'I'm at your service, Mrs Rodd.'

'Well—' (Where to start? But I could not allow him to intimidate me.) 'I was curious about the argument you had, you and Arthur.'

'Oh, the argument,' said Mr Fogle. 'Oh, yes, yes, of course. You've been speaking to Edward Rivers.'

'How did you—?' I had not expected this, and was dismayed because I had made a promise to Mr Rivers that I could not keep.

'I thought as much,' he said mildly. 'He was the only person who could possibly have overheard us. And I suspected that his conscience would lead him into telling someone. I hope he is well. It is some weeks now since I saw him.'

'He is very well,' I said. 'And is engaged to be married.'

'I wish him happiness,' said Mr Fogle. 'Not everyone is destined for the higher calling.'

I repeated, word for word, everything Mr Rivers had told me. Mr Fogle listened, with an air of what I can only describe as distant contempt, as at the footling concerns of lesser beings.

When I had finished, we fell into silence for a long moment.

'It is all perfectly true,' said Mr Fogle eventually. 'Our meeting began as all our private meetings did, with prayer and confession. It was apparent to me at once that Arthur was not in his right mind. He lost his temper at my suggestion that Henry Barton had been a thoroughly bad influence on him.'

'A bad influence? From what I observed, Mr Barton was if anything rather a good influence. I'm sure Arthur told you of the unfortunate matter of the blackmail, and how Mr Barton helped him.'

'Indeed,' Mr Fogle said coldly. 'But Barton also betrayed him, by lusting after his wife. It was poor Arthur's misfortune that he trusted the two of them.'

'They did not betray him, Mr Fogle!' I protested. 'And kindly remember that Mrs Somers is a friend of mine.'

'I don't wish to offend you, Mrs Rodd, but I must speak plainly. Her licentious nature has been the ruin of two good men.'

'That is shameful nonsense!' I gasped indignantly.

'I do not condemn her. I pray every day for the redemption of her soul.'

My dear mother would have said, seeing that one of my outbursts was imminent, take a deep breath and count to ten; I did this now and managed not to shout at him, though I was very angry.

'She wanted to pay for his monument here,' said Mr Fogle. 'Naturally I did not permit it. I warned Arthur against that marriage.'

It was painful to be reminded that I had done the exact opposite. 'Mr Fogle, what did Arthur mean, when he accused you of "making excuses for yourself"?'

His grasshopper's figure stretched into proud nobility. 'It was my great love for Arthur that got me expelled from my college. The love that grew between us was very much misunderstood by the authorities. But it was a love of minds, of souls, without the slightest impurity – and not to be compared with Arthur's highly unsuitable feelings for Henry Barton. I had said as much to him before; this time he flew off the handle. Dreadful things were said, threats were made.'

'Did you have the impression that Arthur had seen Mr Barton that afternoon?' I asked.

'I did,' said Mr Fogle.

'I mean, did he tell you in so many words?'

'Well—' His eyes narrowed disdainfully. 'I suppose I assumed it; Arthur spoke as if he had come fresh from an encounter with Barton. But he was not in his right mind; I shouldn't set too much store by it. He spoke of his encounters with a number of people, including St John the Divine.'

'Oh.'

'You will understand why I did not tell the police, Mrs Rodd; these ravings would hardly be permissible in a court of law.'

'No, they would not.' This was a great relief to me; any solid evidence of a meeting between Arthur and Mr Barton, from a reliable witness, would have finished us.

'I'll admit that I was afraid,' said Mr Fogle. 'Not of physical harm, but of the consequences if he carried out the wild threats he was making. And God knows, the tragedy has already left its stain upon this place.' He was silent for a moment, and when he spoke again, his voice was soft and feminine. 'I built Swinford as a sweet, holy refuge from the sinful world. I don't understand how or why we came to be mired in scandal. My only desire was the greater glorification of God. Would you mind if I sat down?'

'Please do.' I moved my skirts to make room for him on the bench.

He folded his long body to sit beside me. 'I believe I have just presented you with a motive for murder.'

'Fear of scandal is certainly a plausible motive,' I said. 'But you did not kill Arthur.'

'Can you be sure of that?'

'I'm not sure of anything. I do know, however, that he was not poisoned here. If I want to make you into a suspect, Mr Fogle, I will need a witness who saw you and Arthur together much earlier in the day. And I have nothing of the kind.'

'I'm glad to hear it. I could not have hurt a hair of him – though he hurt me most grievously. That is why Edward Rivers saw me weeping. Arthur cut me to the heart. The love that existed between us was never defiled by earthly lust, and never grossly acted upon. I beg your pardon for my candour.'

'Thank you, Mr Fogle; I quite understand.'

'Naturally, it did not take me long to see that he was out of his mind – even without the accusations apparently levelled at me by St John.'

'Was there anything significant revealed in his confession?'

'I'll tell you what I told Mr Blackbeard; though I venerate the secrecy of the confessional, I would never hold back anything that might help to identify the murderer.'

Over in the old stables, a bell pealed flatly.

'They've finished,' said Mr Fogle. 'I must leave you, Mrs Rodd.' He rose and gave me a deep, old-fashioned bow. 'Good morning.'

Twenty

'THIS IS THE WAY I see it,' said Mr Flint. 'The other side will lean heavily upon the matter of the adultery. They will seek to put the defendants on trial for committing adultery, in order to establish common purpose – surely their only hope, when the evidence is so meagre. My task will be to convince the jury that Barton is innocent on both counts. I will tell them precisely what I told you, Tyson – I would not have taken this case if I suspected for a moment that I was being asked to defend an adulterer. It's all or nothing. I will remind them at every turn of the monstrous black stain a wrongful verdict will leave upon their consciences – upon their immortal souls—'

'Flint – my dear Flint!' Fred cut in, shaking with laughter. 'Stop! How many times must I tell you? A juror is a tender creature, my boy – especially where personal morality is concerned – and you won't win them over by threatening them with hellfire!'

'You'd have me buttering them up, I daresay.'

'A little butter wouldn't go amiss, now that you mention it,' said Fred. 'I thought you Irish chaps were supposed to have a gift for that sort of thing.'

'I'm not that sort of Irishman,' Mr Flint said sternly. 'You're thinking of someone more like yourself, Mr Tyson. And that approach won't answer here.'

'Stop, I beg of you!' Fred gave another yelp of laughter, not in the least offended by the man's rudeness. 'You're alarming my sister.'

'Not at all,' I said faintly.

This was my first encounter with Mr Patrick Flint, the 'young tyro' from Fred's chambers who would be defending Mr Barton, and I was overwhelmed rather than alarmed – and quite unable to see why my brother considered him to be the ideal man for the job. Mr Flint was a black-browed, black-haired creature, whose clean-shaven features might have been handsome without the permanent scowl. His clothes and linen were of fine quality, yet worn so carelessly that his shirt-cuffs were spotted with ink, and there were several buttons missing from his coat.

We were at Fred's house in Highgate, in his study that overlooked the old village green, on a damp and chilly afternoon. I had returned to London the previous day. My brother lounged royally at his desk and Mr Flint stood before the fire – literally, with one large foot on the tiles in the grate, which he did not appear to have noticed.

'There can be no half-measures,' said Mr Flint. 'They must be made aware of the peril to their souls.'

'You can do that without thundering at the poor chaps.' My brother poured himself another glass of sherry from the decanter on his desk. 'If you frighten them too much, you'll be handing a golden opportunity to the other side.'

'What is "common purpose"?' I asked.

Mr Flint gaped at me, as if he had only just seen me (he did this every time I opened my mouth).

'Well now, common purpose,' said Fred, with a sherry-scented sigh. 'If two people express a wish to do away with a third person, and one of them goes ahead and does the deed, the law says they're both guilty. Flint is quite right that the prosecution will have no choice; without clearly establishing common purpose, they barely have a case at all.'

'Mr Flint,' I said, 'you have seen Mr Barton today.'

'Yes.' He frowned down at me. 'I was at Newgate this morning.'

'What do you make of him?'

'He's a decent man,' Mr Flint said sternly. 'A Christian gentleman, a priest of God, and not afraid to use his fists in order to protect a lady.'

'I meant – did you like him?'

'That's neither here nor there, Mrs Rodd. My personal feelings don't come into it.'

'It's a blessing that the victim's crazed pronouncements won't stand up,' said Fred. 'But we're still pining away for want of a decent alibi. I hoped you'd return from Oxford carrying somebody who saw the pair of them at the time in question, and miles away from those wretched woods. What about the housekeeper – could she have been throwing you a line regarding the movements of Mrs Somers?'

'Possibly,' I said. 'But I doubt it; I've known Mrs Richards for many years.'

'She's on our side, anyway, and won't rock the boat.'

'I know Arthur was out of his mind – but I think you should tell Mr Barton what he said, and ask outright if there's any truth in it.'

'With respect, ma'am,' growled Mr Flint (with no respect whatsoever as far as I could see), 'what passes between myself and my client does not concern you.'

'Ignore him,' Fred put in quickly. 'The victim's ramblings won't stand up in court, but that's not to say you can't follow them up in your own investigations, my dear. Two innocent people are on trial for murder. I'm more certain with each passing day that they did not kill Arthur Somers, whether or not they were lovers.'

'Fred! For the last time—'

'Oh, all right! All that matters is the fact that they are innocent of murder.'

'All that matters?' Mr Flint was stern. 'My client swears there was never so much as an impure glance between them. Are you calling him a liar?'

'Oh, Flinty, do pipe down,' said Fred jovially. 'As far as the jury's concerned, I'll make them out to be paragons of spotless virtue. We'll get mostly city shopkeepers, with an occasional publican thrown in for good measure, and they can be surprisingly broad-minded if handled in the right way. There's always a chance, however, that one of them will be a rabid evangelical, and just one Bible-basher is all it takes to turn a jury; I always try to spot them in advance.'

'Fred, stop teasing; I know you're far less cynical than you make out.' I was still annoyed, but also had to stop myself laughing. 'Don't mind him, Mr Flint. He doesn't mean to insult evangelicals.'

'Yes I do! They're never any fun.'

'Fred, really!'

Mr Flint began to mutter angrily about 'parlour games', and ten minutes later took his leave.

The moment the door closed behind him, I got up to fetch the hearth-brush, for Mr Flint had left an ashy foot-print in the middle of the rug. After I had dealt with the rug I set the fire irons straight where he had pushed them over and swept up the stray cinders in the grate.

'Well, Letty, what's the verdict?' Fred was proud, like a showman with a wild beast. 'What do you think of my man?'

'I don't know what to think,' I said. 'I was too distracted by those missing sleeve-buttons, and those terrible cuffs – and he seems to have thrown a broken wine glass into the fire—'

'Oh, I know, and you're a trump to tidy up after him. He's been working here for the past week, and driving Fanny and Mrs Gibson to distraction. Only Tishy is kind to him – she went round the house and rescued seven of his handkerchiefs, which he tends to discard when dirty and stuff down the sides of chairs.'

'Bless her,' I said. 'She seems to have inherited your fondness for a lost cause.'

'Patrick Flint is a very clever young fellow.' Fred refilled his glass. 'He never jokes, never cajoles, flatters nor entertains. The beauty of the man is that he never takes a case he does not believe in with every fibre of his soul. It goes down an absolute treat with a jury.'

'I'll take your word for it,' I said, somewhat reassured, 'if you promise to do something about his appearance – perhaps find a wife for him, with an endless supply of fresh sleeve-buttons.'

'He was married once,' said Fred, 'though he never speaks of it, to a girl from his home in County Antrim. After a year or so, she had a stillborn child and died, and Flint reverted to being a bachelor.'

'How very sad!' This sorrowful fact, imparted as an afterthought, seemed to me to be the keystone of Mr Flint's character.

'I always remember it when the man infuriates me,' said Fred. 'Poor young fellow, he makes me count my blessings – all eleven of them.'

At that very moment, several of my brother's smaller blessings erupted in shrieks outside the door; it made us both laugh, and Fred rose up from his desk with a great roar, to end our meeting with a noisy game of 'Bears' in the hall.

It was dark when I got home to Well Walk, and to my very great surprise, I found Mrs Bentley entertaining a most magnificent young stranger in our basement kitchen; a fine gentleman in a fine black suit, with a gold watch-chain and immaculate linen.

'There now, she don't know you!' said Mrs Bentley, most amused. 'Didn't I say? It's Carlos, ma'am!'

'Oh – I beg your pardon—'

Mr Welland's absurdly handsome footman rose from my rickety old kitchen chair and bowed to me with the grace of a Spanish nobleman. 'Mrs Rodd, I hope I do not intrude.'

'Not in the least,' I said. 'Please accept my condolences for the death of your master.'

'Thank you.'

'He don't live in Rosemount these days,' said Mrs B proudly. 'He has rooms at a private hotel – isn't that right, dearie?'

'Yes,' said Carlos. 'It is very comfortable, but I do not see so many people.'

'This'll be the talk of Hampstead by the morning,' said Mrs Bentley. 'Mr Welland left him a fortune! He's a gentleman now.'

I was very glad to hear it, for I had seen the love between Jacob Welland and his young servant, and it was good to know that he had not left Carlos friendless and alone. Fine feathers do not make fine birds, but I thought his new clothes suited him very well.

'Will you have a little brandy, ma'am? I've just this minute made up a fresh jug.'

'I bring, Mrs Rodd,' said Carlos, showing me a whole bottle of what looked like good cognac (and which explained Mrs B's unwonted liveliness).

'That is most kind of you.' I removed my mantle and bonnet, sat down in the chair that Carlos set for me beside the fire and accepted some hot, sweet (and powerful) brandy-and-water. 'May I ask why you are here – is there anything we can do for you?'

'He's lonely, that's what,' said Mrs Bentley, refilling her own glass. 'His only friends are the servants at Rosemount, and he's not allowed back now his master's gone.'

'What a shame,' I said kindly (though I really did not believe this handsome, wealthy young man would be 'lonely' for long).

'I go there today—'

'Went,' said Mrs B.

'I *went* there today.' Carlos smiled at her with real affection, and I remembered that I had asked Mrs Bentley to make friends with the servants at Rosemount. 'Dr Chauncey has a new patient and says I must stay away. Mr Mitchell says I am no longer a servant and must not mix with servants. But I say these are my friends, the only people I know in the world now that my master is gone.'

'I have an appointment with Mr Mitchell tomorrow,' I said. 'I'm glad to hear that you have someone to advise you, but you mustn't be shy about standing up to the man.'

'He is my guardian for next six months,' said Carlos gloomily. 'Until I am aged twenty-one.'

'You'll be your own master soon enough,' said Mrs Bentley, patting his arm. 'And then you can do as you please.'

'London is strange.' The fortunate-but-lonely young man turned his melting, mournful eyes towards me. 'I have been here for one year. My English is not good because my master speaks to me in Spanish.'

'How long were you with Mr Welland?' I asked.

'How long—?'

'How many years?'

'This number.' He held up one hand.

'Five, dearie,' said Mrs Bentley. She reached across and counted off his fingers. 'One, two, three, four—'

'Five,' said Carlos, laughing softly. 'Five years.'

I was touched by his evident fondness for Mrs B, and the gentle chivalry with which he treated her; it was impossible not to warm to him, with or without brandy. 'Were you with Mr Welland when he died?'

'Yes, Mrs Rodd.'

'I'm very thankful that the poor man was not alone, and can only hope he did not suffer too much.'

'He is quiet,' said Carlos. 'He cannot speak. He moves his lips and I understand. He says – "Hannah".'

'Oh, poor man!' I have kept vigil at many deathbeds, and often observed the burning-away, at the very end, of everything but the greatest love. 'Was that his last word?'

'No, madam,' said Carlos softly. 'The last words were for me – "*mi amado hijo*". My beloved son.'

The three of us were silent for a moment.

'Well, bless my soul!' Mrs B chuckled, in a great effluvium of hot brandy. 'So that's why he left you all that money!'

Twenty-one

THE FOLLOWING MORNING, MY brother kindly sent his carriage to take me to Barnard's Inn in Holborn, where I was to meet Mr Mitchell. I was very grateful, for the day was damp, the crowded roads were plastered with wet, sooty mud and I was anxious about my best black silk gown.

Mr Mitchell received me in his office, on the first floor of the ramshackle old building. He was tall and loosely made, with a small pot belly, and wary little eyes behind gold-rimmed spectacles.

'This is good of you, Mrs Rodd; the estate is nearly wound up, but my client particularly wished me to meet you in person, and to put this into no other hand but yours.'

He took an envelope from his desk, sealed in the old-fashioned manner with red wax, and placed it in my hand with a formal bow. This was very unexpected and I was too curious to wait, so I broke the seal at once. The envelope contained a number of new white banknotes, amounting to a sum of money that fairly took my breath away.

'I don't understand – Mr Welland owed me nothing! Why has he done this?'

'The money is yours absolutely,' said Mr Mitchell. 'Whether or not you act upon his request.'

'Request?'

'He was near the end when I saw him,' said Mr Mitchell. 'But I judged him to be perfectly lucid, and I am satisfied that I understood him correctly. He wished you to find the person or persons who murdered Arthur Somers.'

'I beg your pardon?' This was the last thing I had expected to hear, and I was for a moment deeply confused; surely these two cases were entirely unconnected? 'Mr Welland did not know Arthur Somers, as far as I'm aware; why was he so anxious for me to discover his murderer?'

'To be frank, Mrs Rodd, I have no idea. The man could barely speak; it was painful to watch him struggling to form the words. It appeared to be something about Joshua. I reminded him that his brother had passed away, but he would have none of it.'

'That is understandable; the poor man was dying.'

'I am merely delivering the message,' said Mr Mitchell. 'He kept repeating three words – "Hannah", "Arden" and "Desolation".'

Hannah – Arden – Desolation.

Now I was bewildered; what did Mr Arden have to do with Hannah Laurie, and what did either of them have to do with desolation?

'Hannah was the name of Jacob Welland's late wife,' I said. 'I am acquainted with Mr Arden, who was a friend of his many years ago. Did he leave me any further instructions?'

'No, ma'am,' said Mr Mitchell. 'That was all.'

'And what is the connection with the murder – if there is a connection?'

'Once again, I have no idea; I am simply carrying out my client's instructions. He also left you a small cedar-wood box of sundry papers, but to my very great annoyance, it has gone missing.'

This latest revelation only increased my confusion. 'Do you mean it has been stolen?'

'That's possible,' Mr Mitchell said. 'Since it contained nothing of value, however, I think it far more likely that it has simply gone astray. It was placed in the carrier's van yesterday afternoon, to be delivered to the carrier's office in Smithfield and thence to me. Somewhere between Hampstead and here, however, it vanished. One of my clerks spoke to the driver of the van. The man swore that he had delivered the box as far as Smithfield, but it could not be found.'

'I'm sure it will turn up,' I said (privately certain it would do nothing of the kind; this latest incident was all of a piece with the ransacking of Mr Jennings's rooms at Gabriel, and told me that Joshua's famous scraps of paper had not been thrown away, as he had assumed). 'You have discharged your duties admirably, Mr Mitchell; you should not be troubled further. You may leave the finding of the box to me.'

'Thank you, ma'am.' Mr Mitchell thawed a degree or two. 'It was destined for Smithfield, as I said; an inn near the London Wall, the Cross Keys.'

'I know it.' Here was some good news – Mrs B's son, Mr Joe Bentley, was under-manager of the stables at the Cross Keys. He had his mother's excellent powers of observation, and he would have noticed the smallest thing amiss in his domain.

Mr Mitchell coughed and looked pointedly at the clock on the chimney-piece, and appeared to think our interview was at an end. I had another matter to discuss, however, that had nothing to do with stolen boxes.

'I saw Mr Carlos yesterday,' I said, 'in all his newfound splendour. He's a nice boy; I don't believe the sudden turn in his fortunes will spoil him.'

'That remains to be seen,' said Mr Mitchell coldly. 'Welland appointed me as his guardian and instructed me to educate him in the ways of polite society. He is to be a gentleman. There will be talk, of course, about Welland's reasons for leaving a fortune to a handsome young servant.'

'Carlos is his son.'

'So you have heard this claim, Mrs Rodd.' Mr Mitchell's long nose twitched disdainfully. 'Whatever the truth of the matter, my personal opinion is that the six months of my guardianship will not be sufficient to eradicate the servant in him.'

'He only needs a little time and patience!' I spoke as persuasively as I could, though I wanted to snap at this sneering, superior man; no wonder poor Carlos was so miserable, when he ought to have been rejoicing. Snapping, however, would get us nowhere. 'If you will pardon me, Mr Mitchell,' I said sweetly, 'you should not be burdened with such a responsibility. You are a very busy man.'

'I cannot deny it,' said Mr Mitchell, eyeing me cagily.

'In my opinion, the best way to prepare Mr Carlos for his new circumstances would be to place him in the heart of a respectable household. I can recommend an excellent tutor, Mr John Bourne, the vicar of St Luke's in Knightsbridge.'

'Oh?' He was definitely interested now.

'Mr Bourne is a thorough gentleman, and while I would not accuse him of being "worldly", he is very well versed in the ways of polite society. His wife is charming, and they do not have any daughters, so there can be no vulgar gossip about fortune-hunting. More to the point, they lived in Spain for several years when Mr Bourne was chaplain at the Embassy, and speak the language.'

He could not hide his relief. 'It would be a weight off my mind, ma'am, I can't deny it. I have no idea what to do with the boy. I am a bachelor. I couldn't very well take him into my own household; it consists of three rooms and one servant. He is lodged at a private hotel in Half Moon Street. I would be most grateful if you could write me a letter of introduction to your Mr Bourne. I won't expect him to make a silk purse out of a sow's ear.' Mitchell had stopped glaring at the clock and trying to get rid of me. 'The boy's money will cover a multitude of sins.'

'Mr Carlos is hardly a sow's ear,' I pointed out. 'I think he will surprise you.'

'I'm sure I hope so, Mrs Rodd. Jacob Welland was a valued client of mine, who became a valued friend – though never close enough to tell me he had a son. It is my duty to carry out his instructions to the very best of my ability.'

The rain had stopped by the time I emerged from Barnard's Inn, and a watery sun gleamed out intermittently between banks of cloud. There was no question of my walking to Smithfield, for the streets teemed with carts, vans, carriages, horses and people, all jostling against each other. A lone female being invisible in such a tumult, I asked Mr Mitchell's chief clerk to summon me a cab from the nearby stand. The cab driver appeared to be sober and was wholly civil to me, but he had a terrible habit of roaring profanities at other drivers from the box, and it was not a pleasant journey.

The Cross Keys was a large and prosperous establishment in the heart of the city, near to the old London Wall. It was past midday when I arrived and I breathed the rich atmosphere of meat and gravy rather wistfully. A waiter showed me to a dismal 'coffee room' tucked out of sight, supposedly designed for ladies but empty and lacking a fire.

I did not have to wait long, for Mr Joe Bentley appeared after a very few minutes; a burly man in a rough jacket and leather gaiters, with the remains of the bright-red hair that was the family hallmark.

'Mr Joe.' We shook hands. 'It's very good of you to see me, and you must not worry that I'm bringing bad news about your mother; she is in marvellous health.'

'Thank you, ma'am,' said Mr Joe. 'I'm glad to hear it – if I ask her how she is, she bites my head off.'

'You know how stubborn she is, Mr Joe; she won't admit to being in the least bit elderly, and I have to hide any attempts I make to help her.' I remembered, with a momentary lifting of my spirits, the money left to me by Jacob Welland, and all the small comforts it would buy us. 'Before I leave I must talk to you about sending one of your daughters to help us out – but I am here to enquire after a certain box, addressed to me, care of Mitchell, that has apparently gone missing.'

He knew of it, and interrupted my explanation. 'Well, that box has now been found, ma'am.'

'Indeed?'

'It turned up this morning, in the alley behind the stables. The driver confessed that he had left the van unattended for some time, outside a public house in Kentish Town. He reckons that's where the box was filched.'

'Has it been opened? Are the contents intact?'

'I wouldn't know about the contents, Mrs Rodd,' said Mr Joe, 'but I'd be grateful if you could sign it off in the ledger.'

The so-called 'coffee room', as I had already guessed by the smell, was at the rear of the inn and conveniently placed for the stables. Mr Joe took me to a tiny office, crammed with ledgers and papers, in which the business of leaving and picking up luggage was transacted. The cedarwood box, about the size of a large shoebox, stood upon the counter.

The lock had been broken, but it was quite impossible to know if anything had been removed; I looked inside just long enough to see a jumbled heap of Joshua's shabby scraps of paper, and arranged to have it carried up to Well Walk (Mr Joe would take no fee for this, on account of the 'mix-up').

How did Jacob have those famous papers? The only possible explanation was that Joshua had given them to him; which meant that he really had come to Hampstead to take leave of his brother. I made a mental note to talk again to Mr Carlos.

Once I had left the Cross Keys, I made my way through the scrum of men towards the cab-stand.

'Mrs Rodd!'

I was very surprised to see Mr Daniel Arden at my elbow, strikingly elegant in a black suit and grey silk waistcoat, and positively laughing at me. 'We are destined to run into each other, ma'am; may I be of any assistance?'

'Mr Arden, it's always a pleasure to run into you,' I said, 'and it would be most helpful if you could find me a cab – a clean one, if possible, with a sober driver.'

'I have a carriage at my disposal, ma'am; the driver is as sober as a bishop, if not a judge, and this maelstrom is no place for a lady.'

He held out his hand with such winning cordiality that I momentarily forgot he was a witness for the prosecution, and allowed him to help me into a small and luxuriously appointed hired carriage that waited nearby.

'Where may I take you, ma'am?'

'I'm on my way home to Hampstead,' I began. 'If you could take me as far as the old turnpike at St Giles—'

Mr Arden would not allow me to finish. 'Then let me carry you back to Hampstead; I am at leisure this afternoon, and very much in want of good company.'

It was pleasant to lean back against the red plush cushions, with Mr Arden sitting opposite, so close that my black silk skirts lapped around his knees.

'I don't care for life in London,' he told me cheerfully. 'In the country there are always a dozen things to do. In the city I devote hours to doing absolutely nothing, and it's hard work.'

'I know that you are in London because of the trial,' I said. 'I suppose we should agree not to speak of it.'

'I suppose so – but I would be very happy to hear that you are homing in on the true criminal.'

'To be frank with you, Mr Arden, we are still floundering.'

'That's a shame; I wake every morning with the hope that the whole thing will be stopped before it gets to court.'

'Amen to that!'

Mr Arden opened a little cupboard in the carriage door, to reveal a silver flask and two small glasses. 'Once again, I am able to offer you refreshment, just as I did on the day we met in the woods.'

The sherry was delicious, and very soothing to my aching feet.

'It was at the old limekiln in the woods at Freshley,' I said. 'I'd just had my strange encounter with the charcoal burners. And you appeared out of nowhere, Mr Arden, exactly as you did today, like a genie in *The Arabian Nights*.'

He smiled. 'A genie would have whisked you home on a flying carpet. Are you any closer to discovering where the victim spent his final hours? But perhaps I should not ask.'

'Your tact is admirable; I only wish I could boast to you about our progress.'

'You must have faith,' said Mr Arden. 'The Lord will reveal the truth – in his own time, and on his own terms.'

'We are waiting for him to reveal someone – anyone! – who saw either Arthur Somers or the defendants on the day of the murder,' I said. 'Thus far, we have no one. Between the hours of noon and six o'clock, the three of them might as well have been invisible!'

'I saw Arthur Somers two days before, if that helps.'

'I'm afraid not – though it's a kind offer from a witness for the other side.'

'We met by chance at that same old kiln,' said Mr Arden. 'It's a sorrowful memory to me now. Somers loved the peace and beauty of that place as much as I do; I had come across him there before.' He smiled suddenly. 'On this occasion, I found him fast asleep on a soft bank of moss, like one of Shakespeare's enchanted lovers. I did not intend to disturb him; my dog woke him.'

'Dear Arthur!'

'He was very much amused,' said Mr Arden. 'We had our usual good-natured dispute about Church politics. And then he spent some time trying to teach my dog tricks – with no success whatsoever.'

'Your last sight of him was a happy one,' I said. 'I shall try to think of it; he wasn't designed for tragedy.'

'Would you care for a sandwich?' Mr Arden opened the little cupboard to produce a tin box. 'I never travel without provisions.'

The sandwiches were tiny, perfectly symmetrical, and delicious.

To move us away from the subject of the murder, I told Mr Arden of my meeting with Mr Mitchell. 'Here is more proof that you are a genie; your name was mentioned.'

'My name?'

'When Jacob Welland lay dying,' I said, 'he had no breath to speak, but shaped three words, over and over. "Hannah", "Arden" and "Desolation".'

Mr Arden was visibly shaken; the colour drained from his face, and for a moment he looked years older.

'Do you know what he was trying to say, Mr Arden?'

'Did he say anything more?'

'He did not.'

'Well—' He had recovered his composure now. 'Good God! And this is no profanity, but sober truth; his goodness is infinite. Jacob's last words are proof to me that his soul was saved at the end.'

'How do you mean?'

'Forgive me, Mrs Rodd; I'm not about to preach at you. The experience that I shared with Jacob Welland – I would be happy to tell you of it, but not while I'm shut away in here. I am pining for a breath of air and a glimpse of the sky. Would you do me the honour of walking with me on Hampstead Heath?'

'Most happily,' I said. 'You must take me home first, however, so that I may change into more suitable clothes. And I am concerned about your shoes, Mr Arden; they may be too fine to withstand the mud.'

'I don't care about my shoes.' He smiled at me, thoroughly in command of himself once more. 'I would positively welcome the sight of some honest mud!'

We had now left behind the snarl of narrow city streets, and were driving smoothly past the sheds, small taverns and market gardens that lined Kentish Town Road, in those last days before it was torn up by the railway.

Our conversation was easy and amiable; we kept to the safe subject of news from Mr Arden's home. His local knowledge was impressive; he had heard all about Tom Goodly's famous deathbed 'confession'.

'His wife was treated shamefully by her neighbours,' said Mr Arden. 'If her daughter had not come to claim her, the poor soul would have ended her days in the town asylum.'

He declined my invitation to come into my house, although he did permit me to send Mrs Bentley out to his carriage with a cup of tea while I hurriedly changed my dress, shoes and bonnet.

Hampstead Heath is never empty, and the better paths were fairly busy, even on such a damp afternoon. There are always out-of-the-way places, however, if one is prepared to put up with the puddles, and I led Mr Arden along a favourite path of mine that ran alongside the wall of Caen Wood.

Mr Arden walked quickly and spoke little, until we sat down together upon the trunk of a fallen tree. He took off his hat and raked his fingers through his plentiful dark-grey hair. 'When you spoke of "desolation", Mrs Rodd, you touched upon the greatest, the most solemn experience of my life. It happened on an island off the coast of Chile; the Spaniards named it "Desolacion" and it was certainly desolate. Jacob Welland and I were partners in misfortune. We had fallen into one another's company several months before, and endured terrible hardship together, but this time we knew that we had come to the end. The two of us lay, half-starved and shivering with fever, and confessed to one another the sins we had committed that would haunt us to our graves. We prayed with all our hearts for a chance to redeem ourselves.' He looked at me in silence for a moment. 'Please note that we were not praying for our physical bodies, but our immortal souls; I believe this is the reason we were heard.

'Jacob told me, for the first time, of his ill-fated marriage to Hannah Laurie. He also told me of a dalliance

187

he'd had with a certain woman. He deserted this woman
and their child, and now he yearned to atone for his sin.
We were ready to surrender our souls to God, and were
granted another chance to do God's work in the world.'

'What sins did you confess to, Mr Arden?'

'Many and various,' he said. 'Large and small. The
fact that I am alive and well is proof that my sins were
forgiven. Jacob and I were born again.' He spoke quietly
and earnestly, his eyes pinned to me. 'Everything I do at
Binstock springs from my sense of atonement. He spared
me so that I could give the poor all the things I never
had – food, shelter, education, a chance to get on in life.'

'I have seen many examples of your success.'

'Thank you; I can't help being proud of the improve-
ments I've been able to make. I like to believe that I was
granted my wealth on the condition that I used it properly.'

'Do you mind my asking where you acquired it?'

He smiled. 'It certainly didn't appear out of nowhere,
but my experience on the island was the turning-point; I
had sunk all my money into a mining enterprise, and the
mine suddenly came good.'

'Did you and Jacob Welland stay together?'

'We went our different ways soon after Desolacion, but
that was not a reflection of our friendship. We met God
together on a bare hillside, and it bound us for all time.'

'Did you know about his son?'

'I know that the boy's mother sang and danced in the
streets, and that Welland had left her destitute. And I know
that he vowed to find her, though I couldn't say when he
did.' said Mr Arden, 'I've seen Mr Carlos, however; we
happen to be staying at the same hotel in Half Moon
Street. He is a fine young man.'

'I must confess,' I said, 'that I cannot see any resemblance to his father.'

'Oh, it's there,' said Mr Arden. 'Especially around the eyes and forehead. Jacob's eyes were blue and his son's are dark, yet their shape is exactly the same. I can never forget. Once upon a time, I thought they would be the last thing I saw on earth. He was a good man, Mrs Rodd.'

'I don't doubt it.'

He was silent for a few moments, then said abruptly, 'I did not ask for much in return for my work. I have lived quietly – trying not to be selfish, trying not to think of my own gratification. But I've lately begun to wonder if following my heart's desire might not be selfish after all.'

'Your heart's desire?' I was all ears now. 'Do you mean you are thinking of getting married?'

'Let's say that it has crossed my mind – but only in the most general sense. There is no particular lady. It's simply that I am feeling my solitary state. And I could do so much more of God's work with a wife at my side.' He was quiet for a moment. 'But perhaps I'm too old.'

'Nonsense!' I declared. 'You are not too old in the least!'

'Thank you, Mrs Rodd.'

The light was fading now, and the wind began to be cold. Mr Arden gave me his arm to escort me back to Well Walk.

Twenty-two

MY BROTHER WAS VERY well-known inside Newgate Prison; he often said he spent more time in
that dreadful, sorrowful place than he did in his
chambers. It was a blackened, eyeless hulk of a building,
crouching at the feet of the Old Bailey, just across the
street. The cells inside the prison were grouped around a
central courtyard, with the common prisoners upon one
side, and upon the other the prisoners who could afford to
pay for slightly better quarters.

'But you won't find Barton hanging out with even the
better sort of felon,' said Fred drily. 'He's being kept in the
rooms of the prison governor, by virtue of his collar. And
he's receiving us in the splendour of the governor's private
office.'

The young clergyman was waiting for us there, perfectly at ease; it came as a slight shock to see him quite
unchanged, as if he had not been living in the very shadow
of the scaffold.

'Mrs Rodd, this is a pleasure.' He shook hands with all
of us and we sat down beside a fine fire, in the well-
appointed office that the governor had kindly vacated for
us.

'She wants to talk to you,' said Mr Flint, looking sour. 'I
can't stop her if you don't mind it.'

'Flint!' my brother snapped. 'Manners!'

'I'm delighted to see you, Mrs Rodd,' said Mr Barton, almost laughing. 'And I hope you will talk to me; you have been in Hardinsett, and can give me news of home.'

'I can,' I said, 'though none of it is very happy.'

His face darkened now; we were both thinking of Rachel.

After a short silence, he asked, 'How is the church – has anyone stepped in to take the services?'

'Yes, a Mr Whitely, from Iffley. He can only do one service a week, unfortunately.'

'Better than nothing,' said Mr Barton. 'I'm glad to hear the place is ticking over.'

'And I know you will want to hear about your boys; they are well, and know nothing of your true situation.'

'Thank God! They're far too little to understand.'

'Mr Arden told them you had gone away.'

'Good, let them think that while they can,' said Mr Barton. 'I miss them like fury.'

'So you spoke to Arden,' Mr Flint cut in. 'What did he have to say for himself?'

'He's a most unwilling witness,' I began.

'He's a liar, with no respect for the established Church,' said Mr Flint hotly. 'And that lodge-keeper of his is another one. If they are not exposed as liars, the jury has no choice but to believe their disgraceful piece of slander is the truth!'

'You must not torment poor Mrs Woods,' I said, quailing at the thought of that timid young woman being mauled in the witness box. 'I judged her to be a very truthful person – don't you agree, Mr Barton?'

His gaze fell away from mine, and he was silent.

'But this is irrelevant!' protested Mr Flint.

'Shut up,' said Fred, staring intently at Mr Barton's bowed head.

'Mr Barton,' I said, as gently as I knew how. 'Consider what you are doing. You know Mrs Woods; are you really prepared to watch her being torn apart in court? We are all your friends; we know you did not murder Arthur Somers. We cannot help you, however, unless you tell the whole truth – my dear, it's too late to be delicate – this is the only way that you can save Mrs Somers!'

I was very sorry for him; at my words his bravado melted away, exposing all his bewilderment and terror.

'And I mean everything,' I went on, 'including the business of the blackmail. Arthur would not have wanted you to give your life for the sake of his reputation.'

'Don't imagine you can shock her,' said Fred happily. He produced a large silver flask from his pocket. 'Have a nip of brandy to keep your strength up.'

He would not allow Mr Barton to refuse and firmly handed him one of the little silver cups, filled to the brim.

Mr Flint was very still, and suddenly sickly pale. 'If Mrs Woods is not lying – but I know that Mrs Somers—'

'She's blameless,' Mr Barton said emphatically. 'That must be understood from the start.'

'Maggy Woods says she saw you and Mrs Somers kissing,' said Fred. 'Did she?'

'Yes,' said Mr Barton. 'But it wasn't Mrs Somers's fault, and if we hadn't been in a public place, she would have resisted more forcefully – I acted impulsively and without her permission. The blame is entirely mine.'

Mr Flint breathed heavily and I wondered what was the matter with the man.

'Whoops-a-daisy,' said Fred. 'That could give me trouble. Still, forewarned is forearmed. While we're talking about that infamous dance, what about the punch-up you had with the victim?'

'As I told Flint,' said Mr Barton testily, 'that is unfortunately true. Somers and I had a difference of opinion.'

'What about?'

'I'm not prepared to say.'

'And here we hit the wall!' said Fred. 'You're not prepared to say what matter you were discussing, though it
obviously wasn't the nature of the Trinity. Give it up, my
boy. The jury will hear that Somers shouted "Bloody
Judas" and knocked you down flat.'

'Yes.'

'Where does Judas come into it?'

(I was also very curious about this, and increasingly
annoyed with myself for going to bed early on that fateful
night and missing the whole drama.)

Mr Barton reddened and frowned and the silence
stretched into minutes, yet I sensed a yielding in him, and
even a certain relief, and hoped most devoutly that Mr
Flint would not jump in and spoil it all.

'I have not been keeping quiet to protect myself or my
own reputation.' His voice was low, he was deeply in earnest. 'It was all for her sake. I know that I have wronged
Mrs Somers. I was trying not to make things worse for her
– if they could be any worse.'

Poor young man, he had sunk to the lowest level of
misery, where there is no longer any point in trying to
obscure the truth.

'I saw for myself how fond you were of Arthur Somers,'
I said. 'I know you couldn't possibly have murdered him. I
am absolutely sure of your innocence. But I observed
many things while I was at Hardinsett. My dear Mr
Barton, it was as plain as the nose on my face that you
were in love with Rachel.' He could redden and wince all
he liked; there was no more time for niceties. 'Your behaviour towards her was perfectly proper – but if your

194

attachment was obvious to me, it must have been so to Arthur. Was that the cause of the fight?'

'Yes,' said Mr Barton. 'You remember that ghastly evening, Mrs Rodd; after you retired, Somers and I had to see off the last stragglers. We were both tired and overwrought. He accused me and I confessed my – my feelings for his wife.'

'And then he knocked you down,' said Fred. 'Which is more than understandable, heaven knows, though Somers didn't strike me as the knocking-down type.'

'He wasn't,' I said. 'He was the mildest of men.'

'Rather ungrateful of him to whack you, after everything you'd done for him,' said Fred. 'Let's talk about the blackmail, shall we?'

'I'd rather not,' snapped Mr Barton.

'Mr Barton, I have a confession to make to you.' The time had come to tell him what I had overheard while eavesdropping.

He was mortified; as for Mr Flint, he was pale with anger, and scowled at me as if to blame me for the sordid events I had described.

'I was forced to take a fresh look at certain incidents in the past,' I said. 'And a great deal became clear to me. For instance, that time in Herefordshire – my husband couldn't tell me, but Arthur was being blackmailed then, wasn't he?'

'Yes,' said Mr Barton. 'He told me it had happened before, and that your late husband somehow managed to save him.'

'You were angry with him.'

'I was angry for *her* sake, for his wife's sake. I could not bear her to be defiled by the evil rumours going about. And I was angry with Somers for involving me in the filthy business.'

'Tell us about Banbury Fair,' said Fred.

195

'The man wanted more money, as I had warned Somers he would. I met him at the fair and knocked him down for his impudence regarding a certain lady. And I'd do it again.'

'But you're in holy orders!' I was shocked by such shameless belligerence.

'If I had not been in holy orders,' said Mr Barton, 'I would've killed him.'

'Mr Barton—!'

'Any half-decent man would have done the same.'

'Yes, by God!' cried out Mr Flint, clenching his fists.

'Bravo,' said Fred, beaming round at us all. 'That'll go down very nicely – you can remind the jury of their red-blooded manhood, Flint – the Sir Galahad card is always a strong player.'

'Fred, how can you?' I protested. 'Am I the only Christian in this room, as well as the only female? Violence can never be condoned!'

'Sometimes it can,' Mr Barton said quietly. 'God gave me these fists, Mrs Rodd, to use on his behalf. I thrashed that man in order to defend two persons I loved and honoured. Arthur Somers was no saint, but his weaknesses must not be allowed to cancel out his virtues. He was one of the best men I've ever met, and a better man than I am.'

'That's good,' my brother cut in briskly, 'but not good enough. We're still struggling with that lost afternoon of yours, upon the day of the murder.'

'I went walking in the old forest around Freshley St Johns.' His expression turned shuttered and stubborn. 'I didn't see anyone, and no one saw me.'

He was lying; we all knew it.

'Wherever you were,' said Fred, 'someone saw you; I beg you to spill the beans before the other side springs it on us in court.'

'Mr Barton—' I was mindful of the time ticking past; we could not afford to waste a moment of this precious interview. 'I have heard that Arthur said he saw you, hours before his death, and claimed that you "upset" him.'

His eyes flashed anger at me, and I hit the 'brick wall' with almost physical force. 'I did not meet Somers on that day. I did not argue with him, and I did not put poison in his lemonade.'

'This is irrelevant,' Mr Flint put in crossly. 'The victim's ramblings simply won't stand up, as I have already explained to you.'

I ignored him. 'I've also been making enquiries about Tom Goodly and his deathbed confession.'

'Oh?' Mr Barton was startled.

'Could Arthur have been killed because of something Goodly confessed to him?'

'It's possible, I suppose,' he said thoughtfully. 'Somers didn't reveal a word of what passed between them, but that wasn't enough to stop all kinds of extravagant rumours.'

'Do you recall any rumours in particular?'

'Well—' He made a visible effort to draw this into focus.

'The hidden gold, for instance?'

'Gold?' He looked blank for a moment, then reluctantly smiled. 'Oh, to be sure – Arthur did tell me that he had trouble keeping Mrs Goodly out of the way. And that the poor deluded woman kept begging him to ask her dying husband about the gold.'

'Might there have been a grain of truth in the story? Was that what Goodly wanted to confess?'

'I very much doubt it,' said Mr Barton.

'Did Arthur ever tell you about anything else he heard that night?'

'Never; the secrets of the confessional were sacred to him.'

'I remember that he was anxious about something,' I said. 'When I asked him, he told me that he felt other people's secrets as a burden upon his own soul.'

'Oho, he must've heard something good and meaty!' For the very first time, my brother showed a spark of interest in this line of enquiry. 'A lovely confession of murder, perhaps; are there any unsolved killings in the neighbourhood?'

'None that I know of,' said Mr Barton.

'What about Sir Christopher Warrender?' I demanded. 'He disappeared, but I'm beginning to believe—'

'No!' Fred interrupted me with a rude groan. 'For pity's sake, don't distract us with some old piece of folklore!'

'Aren't you interested in finding the true killer?'

'That's a matter for the police, Mrs Rodd,' said Mr Flint. 'My business is purely to build a case for Barton's defence. I'd like to talk to him alone now, if you please.'

My brother and I took our leave of the prisoner; I shook his hand, trying to stifle the thought that it might be the last time I saw him before he stood in the dock. He seemed to guess what I was thinking; he held my hand a little longer than was necessary, and smiled at me with special warmth.

'Thank you for everything, Mrs Rodd.'

Fred and I left the room, and out in the corridor I immediately fumbled for my handkerchief, to wipe my eyes.

'Oh, my dear!' sighed Fred. 'I have learnt over the years not to have feelings about my customers, but that young man would move a stone!'

'Don't take any notice of me; I didn't mean to give way.'

'We have made progress, of a sort. You got him to own up about the canoodling with Mrs Somers.'

The 'canoodling' made me wince. 'I wouldn't call that progress; it shows Mr Barton in a very bad light.'

'Again, forewarned is forearmed,' said Fred, smiling. 'You must trust Flint to trim it and dress it, and serve it up to the jury as a delicacy.'

'Fred, I can't bear to think of Rachel in court; it will kill her! Is there nothing we can do?'

'I'll protect her as far as I can, you know I will.'

'She shouldn't be there at all!' I whispered fiercely. 'She's innocent, they're both innocent! We should be doing everything we can to find the true criminal!'

Twenty-three

THE CEDARWOOD BOX THAT had been through so many adventures stood on the kitchen floor, on the faded rag-rug in front of the fire. It was the evening of the day after my visit to Newgate, and I had spent most of it toiling through Joshua's papers. This was the first time I had been able to examine these at my leisure and, though I had not found anything remotely useful to my investigation, I was intrigued.

Once I had got used to the odd appearance of the writing, and had scrutinized the faded lines through a strong magnifying glass, I found that many of the passages in Latin and Greek were long extracts from various famous works, as if Joshua had tried to preserve everything that he remembered in a kind of private library. My Latin was rusty, but Papa had taught me well and I remembered enough to translate several passages that were not taken from classical literature. There were also a few pages in English.

To discover a stolen horse, bury the harness and build a fire above it, saying, 'Who stole thee/ Sick may he be.'

Take a sucking babe to a stream; hold it over the water while saying, 'Tell me, Oh Nivaseha,/ By this child's hand,' and the water will flow in the direction of the stolen beast.

These strange snippets (including a rather horrid recipe for love-sickness, which involved cutting open a dead crow and observing the behaviour of the maggots) I took to be part of Joshua's great work about the ancient wisdom of the gipsy people – cut short when the gipsies expelled him from their encampment. I also found many sketches, ranging in quality from detailed drawings of animals and flowers to rough maps and diagrams whose meaning was anybody's guess.

Mrs Bentley did not like the scraps of dirty paper strewn about her kitchen. 'I can't see what you want with it all, ma'am, I'm sure.'

'I want to know why the box went missing; what could the thief have been looking for?'

'Hmm.' She was sceptical.

'I'm curious, Mary,' I said teasingly.

'I used to say to my boys, curiosity killed the cat.'

'And it's a welcome distraction from my anxiety about the trial.'

I cleared the papers away when our visitor appeared. Mr Carlos had sent me a note that morning, asking if he could call later. The note had been delivered by an impossibly superior ticket-porter from the hotel in Piccadilly. Mr Carlos himself arrived with a homely basket of dear Mrs B's favourite delicacies, including a parcel of pigs' trotters – ungenteel but delicious.

She would not hear of anybody else preparing them. Mr Carlos and I were banished to the drawing room upstairs, where I had lit a fire. The young man seemed easier; he was becoming accustomed to drawing rooms. Mr Bourne, the vicar of St Luke's, Knightsbridge, had called on him, and Mr Carlos had been much impressed by his kindness.

'He does not think I am stupid because I cannot read English books. He brings me Spanish books and speaks to me in Spanish. I shall be very happy to move myself to his house. Could you please tell me, madam, the money I should pay to him?'

I mentioned a suitable sum of money.

'Thank you, madam,' said Mr Carlos. 'I do not like the hotel. The servants are rude to me, and they look at my things.'

'You are a great object of curiosity to them. Mr Bourne's servants will be far better behaved.'

I took the opportunity, while I had Mr Carlos before me, of asking him about Joshua's bundle of papers.

'I'm sure these are the same papers that I saw in Oxford, in the rooms of Joshua's friend, Silas Jennings. They can only have been brought to Rosemount by Joshua himself. I did not believe poor Jacob when he told me of his brother's nocturnal visit, nor did Dr Chauncey. But it seems he was being entirely truthful.'

'Yes, madam.'

'Did you see or hear anything?'

'I was sad that I did not wake,' said Mr Carlos. 'In the morning, my master's bed is covered with papers. He says I must tell nobody that he has them.'

'Why the secrecy?'

'My master says there is a map amongst the papers, that shows where gold is buried.'

'Oh.' I could not hide my disappointment, yet even as I dismissed this as nonsense, I was struck by how that rumour of lost gold persisted. 'Surely he did not believe such a wild story?'

'I do not know, madam.'

Mrs Bentley called that supper was ready and Mr Carlos and I descended to the kitchen.

There are few things more alarming than being roused at the dead of night.

I was rudely woken by violent pounding on the front door. Imagining every kind of dreadful news, I hurriedly lit my chamber-candle, pulled on my flannel wrapper and hurtled downstairs.

It was my brother – he assured me at once that all was well at home, and he was radiant with excitement. 'I had to tell you at once, my dear; events have taken such a splendid turn!'

He was on the point of revealing all to me when Mrs Bentley appeared at the top of the stairs, a white, wispy-haired wraith, wrapped in a black shawl, and brandishing a poker to defend herself. Fred was very much at home in our house, and while I assured Mrs B that we were not in danger, and persuaded her to return to her bed, he revived the kitchen fire, commandeered the best brandy and raided my tiny larder for cake.

'A thousand pardons, my dear, but I was too wrought-up to go home,' he said, when I joined him. 'I came here directly from a meeting with the Home Secretary – no, not waving a full pardon, but he has agreed to postpone the trial; there's been another murder!'

'What – who?'

'You'd better sit down and have some brandy.'

'Is it someone I know?' I dropped into the Windsor chair he had drawn up close to the fire. 'Who, for pity's sake?'

'Gerard Fogle,' said Fred.

'*What?*'

'Found dead in his bed this morning. Smothered with a pillow.'

'Dear God!'

'I'm sorry, Letty – but isn't it delicious?'

'No! There's nothing remotely "delicious" about any murder.'

'But don't you see?' my brother demanded. 'A second corpse at Swinford puts the first in a whole new light! Our defendants cannot possibly have been responsible for this one. Naturally, I tried to convince the Home Secretary to release Barton and Mrs Somers at once, but it is far too soon for anything of that sort. And his hands are rather tied until the coroner has given his verdict.'

'Gerard Fogle! Tell me slowly. When is the inquest?'

'Tomorrow.' Fred glanced up at the clock on the shelf. 'I mean, today.'

'How did you hear about it so quickly?' I rubbed my forehead distractedly, as if this would calm the turmoil in my mind; the murder of such a controversial and cele-brated churchman would be an enormous sensation. No wonder Fred was gleeful.

'My chap at Scotland Yard told me, as soon as the news came by express. Never was half-a-crown a week better spent!'

'How can they be sure Mr Fogle was murdered – smoth-ered, you say – and did not die of natural causes?'

'Apparently it was only too obvious,' said Fred. 'The man's eyes and mouth were gaping open, there were livid bruises across his chest and on his hands. And there are some uncanny similarities to last time – I mean, the morn-ing they found Arthur Somers.'

'At what time was Mr Fogle's body discovered?'

'A quarter past six. He failed to turn up for some ghastly early-morning service in that chapel of theirs. This time, there were a number of weedy young clergymen staying in "cells" at the old stables. One of them ran back to the house and found the body. The doctor who examined it later had no doubt about the cause of death.'

'Do you know who was in the house that night?'

'The house was only sparsely populated – two elderly manservants, one coachman in an outbuilding.'

'Someone could easily have broken in, and killed Fogle without being heard.'

'I daresay, but I don't know anything more. You must go back to Oxford. Find out who bumped off Fogle. I'd bet any money it's the same man who did for Arthur Somers.'

'But where is the connection?'

'Oh, come on!' cried Fred joyfully. 'Two clergymen found horribly murdered in the same place? That's enough of a connection for me!'

Twenty-four

TWO YOUTHFUL POLICEMEN STOOD in the lane at Swinford, the modern equivalent of angels with flaming swords. They had orders to admit no one, and it was easy to see the sense of this, for the small, dull village was swarming like a hill of ants. My carriage could take me no further than the Red Dragon, the nearest inn of any consequence, more than a mile from the rectory. The inn yard and the surrounding roads were jammed with carriages of every size, the smoky saloon bar was packed with reporters from the newspapers, and all was noise and confusion. This murder had caused a sensation across the country, and I was in the eye of the storm.

'Is Inspector Blackbeard here?' I asked the policemen. 'Please inform him that I wish to speak to him. I don't mind waiting, but I won't leave until I have seen him.'

One of the policemen hurried up the lane and re-appeared in a few minutes with Blackbeard beside him. 'So here we are again, Mrs Rodd!'

'Good morning, Mr Blackbeard. You are not surprised to see me.'

'I don't have any surprise left in me, ma'am.' He was closely buttoned into a long brown coat, and wore a battered brown hat that was just the right side of respectable. 'I daresay you want a little peek at the scene of the murder.'

'If you please, Inspector; I promise not to disturb anything.'

'Well, seeing as you've come all this way ... ' said Blackbeard.

He nodded at the two policemen, who immediately stood aside to let me pass. Blackbeard and I walked together towards the rectory – woefully turned inside-out, as I saw from across the small village green, with windows agape and two more policemen at the front door.

'I'll be candid with you,' said Blackbeard. 'I haven't a single suspect; not one.'

'Did you receive the letter I sent you about Mr Rivers?'

'I received it, and I have read it.'

'Well – what do you make of it?'

'Not much, ma'am,' said Blackbeard. 'But Mr Rivers did indicate a possible motive; there's been some funny doings here that any number of folks might want covered up. I'd like to know what Fogle knew.' A glint of humour briefly appeared in the depths of those hard, suspicious grey eyes of his. 'I must say, I'm thankful you didn't come right at me with "I told you so"!'

This made me smile in spite of myself. 'I shall take that as an admission that you've changed your view of Mr Barton and Mrs Somers.'

'They ain't off the hook yet, Mrs Rodd. They're still in the picture where Somers is concerned. But this is a different kettle of fish. If you're looking for a motive, half the country was against that man.'

'That is perfectly true,' I said. 'I have been studying the newspapers. One Low Church bishop is even claiming that Mr Fogle was struck down by Heaven, as punishment for his High Church opinions. And one publication this morning has called it the "First Oxford Movement Murder". But ecclesiastical squabbles don't get people

208

murdered, Inspector – or the nation's clergy would all have killed each other years ago.'

Before we entered the rectory, Mr Blackbeard asked one of the policemen, 'Where are the vicars – still praying in the stables?'

'Yessir.'

'Best place for them,' said Blackbeard. 'Keep them out of my way for as long as you can.'

'Yessir.'

'Five vicars, Mrs Rodd! All shrieking and shivering like wet hens! And that's only the vicars who were present on the fateful night. At least twenty more vicars turned up this morning, to pray over Fogle's coffin.'

'So the coroner released the body,' I said. 'I would very much like to see it, if you would permit me.'

'Not possible, ma'am; I told 'em to put the lid on.'

'Oh.'

'I had to,' said Blackbeard. 'You wouldn't credit what they wanted to do with that corpse!'

'What do you mean, Mr Blackbeard?'

'The vicars wanted him left open, clutching his beads in his fingers, and I don't know what.'

'Mr Fogle had a great fondness for the rituals of the Roman Catholic Church, and took great comfort from them,' I said. 'Let us not be prejudiced.'

'Hmm,' the inspector said shortly. 'I have nothing against Catholics, I assure you. They're often Irish and can't help it. I'll tell you what's rubbing me up the wrong way – some of them vicars are making out that the corpse was a saint.'

'Surely not!'

'One of them says to me that Fogle's body was so holy, it didn't give off a bad smell! I said they couldn't smell anything in that place on account of all the smoke.'

'Smoke? Oh, you mean incense.'

'Whatever they call the stuff, Mrs Rodd, it's another obstruction put in my way.'

'This talk of saints is very silly,' I said. 'But only to be expected, when Gerard Fogle had such a devoted following. My impression of the man was that he was only too human.'

'I was present at the inquest,' said Blackbeard. 'And I can assure you, ma'am, that he smelt just like any other corpse, when it's in a crowded room on a warm day.'

'I can quite believe it, Inspector.'

We walked into the red-brick rectory through the open door. Here I was once more, in the bare and gloomy hall where I had first met the murdered man. The tiled floor was now criss-crossed with muddy footprints. The solemnity of the atmosphere took hold of us both; we walked upstairs in silence and Blackbeard removed his hat.

Mr Fogle's bedchamber, on the first floor, was white and empty, and of a penitential plainness. There was a narrow bed, with a crucifix nailed to the wall above it, and a prie-dieu before a sort of shrine in one corner, where there were spent candles and a small brass Calvary. An open door showed a dressing room with a large tin bath in the middle of the floor.

'I haven't let them touch the bed,' said Mr Blackbeard. 'It's near enough like when he was found.'

I turned my attention to Mr Fogle's bed, a disordered tangle of sheets and blankets; a place of violent struggle and death. I said a short prayer to myself for the repose of his soul.

'I have read a rather imperfect account of the inquest,' I said. 'Who discovered the body?'

'One of the vicars, a young chap named Yates,' said Blackbeard. 'It was before dawn and pitch dark. Mr Yates knocks and gets no response. So he goes in with his candle and sees Mr Fogle lying there with a pillow over his face.'

'And the servants heard nothing?'

'Not a squeak, ma'am. But they're both elderly and hard of hearing.'

'Were there any signs of a break-in?'

'None that I could see – which is not to say that it didn't happen. They don't lock doors or windows here like they should.'

'I see. Thank you, Mr Blackbeard.'

We left the room in silence. When we were halfway down the stairs, the sound of singing suddenly broke out from the direction of the old stables; a mournful chant in medieval plainsong. Mr Blackbeard said nothing, but seemed to harden all over with disapproval.

I could quite see how the torrent of piety was hampering his investigation. The patch of green outside the old stables was dark with clergymen, all kneeling, hands clasped in prayer, and all droning out some dismal Latin incantation. Even in the open air, the reek of incense (Mowbray's 'Rosa Mystica') from the chapel was over-powering.

'No wonder they can't smell him,' said Blackbeard. 'You couldn't smell a crate of bad fish in there.'

I was a little shocked by my desire to smile at this dour observation, and we retreated into the house. The door to Mr Fogle's study stood open and I asked the inspector's leave to take a rapid look around it before I left.

The room was exactly as I remembered, yet the atmosphere had changed somehow and there was a great serenity. I had a vivid sense of the sweetness that is true holiness, when all wickedness, all sorrow has been shed away; I believe that such a thing as a 'state of grace' exists, and this was what I felt here.

The desk was bare, save for a tidy pile of paper in the middle of the blotter.

'Sermon,' said Blackbeard. 'You can read it if you like, ma'am. I couldn't get through it.'

I picked up the unpreached sermon and read the heading: 'For I Acknowledge My Transgressions and My Sin is Ever Before Me; The Holy Sacrament of Confession.'

I folded the papers carefully and stowed the bundle in my pocket; Mr Blackbeard did not appear to know the value of what he had given me. This was nothing less than the saint's last sermon; the chanting clergymen outside would be outraged to see the precious document in my unhallowed hands.

There were six sheets, closely written on both sides, and I was not at all surprised that Mr Blackbeard had been unable to finish it. Fogle's style was flowery, dense with scholarship, and of a medieval severity that must sometimes have puzzled his parishioners.

Love must be without flesh, for all flesh is of the earth, and in flesh resides our downfall.

I read it over the little fire in my private parlour at the Mitre, after an excellent supper of beefsteak pie, and nearly nodded off at several points. There were no great revelations; he had not known that this sermon would be his last.

Redemption will only come with true and wholehearted contrition. And contrition will be incomplete, unless the sinner surrenders every atom of self-will. He can never justify his sinful actions, even if the outcome of those actions appears to be a good one. Human creatures

may 'make allowances' when judging their imperfect fellow-humans.
God, in all his stern perfection, will not.

It was a very solemn thing, to remember that the author of these implacable words now stood himself in the light of that 'stern perfection'. I said a prayer for his soul and stowed his last sermon carefully in my glove-box.

Twenty-five

THE FOLLOWING AFTERNOON, AS I was finishing a long letter to Fred, a waiter came to the door of my little upstairs parlour at the Mitre, to inform me that Mrs Watts-Weston requested an interview.

Before I could instruct him to show her up, the lady herself pushed him aside and swooped into the room.

'My dear Mrs Rodd, how splendid to see you!' She righted her eternally lopsided bonnet. 'I ran here the very moment I heard you had come back to Oxford. I know you have come because of the murder at Swinford; I have always maintained that there was something sinister about that place.'

Well, I had not expected to keep the Gorgon out of my affairs for long, and at that moment I was very glad to have her company. I told the waiter to bring us some tea and invited her to sit down beside the fire.

It was some time before I could seize hold of the conversation. First I had to hear her denunciations of the Catholic revival in general and Swinford in particular.

'My husband says Gerard Fogle had a baleful influence upon his young followers, but you'll find many people who venerate his supposed "holiness". The news of the murder divided the whole of Oxford; we are all back in our factions, Mrs Rodd, and the atmosphere is simply savage; High Church set against Low Church, liberals against conservatives, and countless dinner parties ruined! My husband and I consider ourselves to be "Broad Church" and above petty sectarianism, but that doesn't do us any good; it simply means that we annoy everyone.'

I made the tea, thinking how I had missed Mrs Watts-Weston's rattling powers of conversation, quite content to listen to her.

'My husband is to preach the sermon in the University Church this coming Sunday, Mrs Rodd; it will be widely reported and he is anxious to strike a note of reconciliation.'

'Very proper,' I said.

'He feels that the Church must show a united front. He utterly refuses to speculate about the murder, and is peevish with me when I speak of it. My belief is that it was a robbery, although I'm sure there is nothing in that dreary house worth stealing. The one bright spark in the whole business is that it calls into question the guilt of Barton and Mrs Somers; you must be very happy about that.'

'As happy as I dare to be. They have not yet been exonerated. I have actually reached the point of praying for witnesses.'

'Something will turn up,' said Mrs Watts-Weston. 'In the meantime, a fresh murder has stirred up all the stories about Sir Christopher Warrender, and set me wondering if I could possibly have been wrong.'

I had to hide a smile; she presented the notion that she might have been wrong about something as such a tremendous novelty. 'You now think he could have been murdered?'

'I wouldn't go quite so far as murder; but I am curious to know how the last of the Warrenders met his end. If you're free tomorrow morning, Mrs Rodd, you must come with me to Shotton Barrow; I'm visiting old Humphrey

Collins and he has spent a lifetime tracing the lines of all the great families in the neighbourhood.'

'I am calling at Shotton Barrow with a particular purpose,' Mrs Watts-Weston told me next morning. 'It has nothing to do with old murders. The living is in the gift of our college and poor old Collins can't last much longer. I want to take a quick look at the place, in order to assess its suitability; I'm determined to bag the living for Edward Rivers, so that he is able to marry my niece before they both go grey. You may feel free to condemn me for plotting and scheming, but it's what everyone else will do.'

I was amused by her cheerful lack of contrition. 'I won't condemn you; I've done plenty of plotting and scheming myself in my time.'

It was one of those still, cold, autumnal mornings, with bright sunlight that dazzles without warming. The Warden's elegant closed carriage drove us through brown fields and hedgerows heavy with blackberries, while Mrs W-W speculated about the number of bedrooms in the rectory, and the state of the drains.

When we reached the little village, she stood in front of the queer, quaint old house, stared in silence for a few moments, then said, 'Too near the road!' She tugged vigorously at the bell. 'Such a shame that it was so cut up; now there is scarcely room for a family. And those old casements must make it very dark inside.'

The heavy door was opened by a housekeeper, most civil and respectful, with a rosy, weather-worn face and a bunch of keys at her waist. She introduced herself as Mrs Potter, and said that we had chosen a good time to call.

'Mr Collins is sharpest in the mornings; there's nothing ails him but old age. Last month he turned ninety-four!'

'Ninety-four!' echoed Mrs Watts-Weston. 'This situation must be more wholesome than it looks.'

The interior of the old house, all smoke-blackened beams and woodwormed panelling, was decidedly charming.

'You'll find him sitting up in his book-room,' said Mrs Potter.

She showed us into a room at the back of the house, and my first impression of Mr Collins reminded me strongly of a dead beetle lashed into the web of a spider. There was no telling the true size and shape of the room; the walls were covered, floor to ceiling, with piles of papers and rolls of parchment, and the floor was covered with boxes of more papers, until there was only just enough space for a desk and a few chairs, and the frail old man appeared to be on the very point of being swallowed up.

He shook our hands and permitted the housekeeper to move a heap or two, so that we could sit down; though his eyes were dim and his voice a whispered pipe, his understanding was perfectly good.

Conversation was difficult at first, for like many very elderly people, his deafness was selective, and he looked blank when Mrs Watts-Weston fired out questions about the house and its situation. At last, giving up, she told him of her connection to the Warrenders. The name brought a gleam to his eye, and a firmer note to his quavering voice.

'To be sure! Your grandmother married into the Fortescues of Northumberland – the better branch of that family.'

She was gratified. 'You have a most excellent memory, Mr Collins!'

Frankly curious to try what could be got out of the old man, I asked, 'Were you acquainted with the Warrenders?'

'I was well acquainted with the old baronet, Sir Henry Warrender; when I came here – dear me, more than fifty years ago! – he was a fine man. Young Sir Christopher was his grandson, and he was a fine scoundrel. Lady Tremlett was Henry's sister and therefore Christopher's great-aunt.'

'I shouldn't have started him off,' Mrs Watts-Weston murmured to me. 'How are we to stop him?'

Mr Collins went on, 'Lady Tremlett made a great to-do when Sir Christopher ran away.'

'Not because she was fond of him,' said Mrs Watts-Weston. 'The story was that she was pursuing him for money. I have sometimes wondered if there was one last piece of family treasure, and he made off with it.'

'No treasure left there, ma'am,' said Mr Collins. 'Long gone!'

'How disappointing!' Mrs Watts-Weston was losing patience. 'It's just as well Sir Christopher was the last of that line.'

'But he was not the last!' cried Mr Collins, now positively animated. 'No, ma'am, not strictly speaking. Sir Christopher inherited Binstock from his uncle, when the man died shortly after the old baronet, and left only an illegitimate son. But I found good evidence of the uncle's marriage, which means that the son ought to have inherited after all. He would have had a good case for the courts, if he had not died young. He had a daughter – his true heir, had there been anything left to inherit.'

'Most interesting!' said Mrs Watts-Weston loudly. 'You have a great many papers, Mr Collins; if they were removed, this room would make a very pleasant breakfast parlour. Is the drawing room of a similar size?'

The old gentleman was not to be diverted until he had finished his recital. 'The daughter married a man of no particular lineage, by the name of Laurie.'

'Laurie!' I was all attention now. 'Was this the father of Hannah?'

'Why yes!' said Mr Collins, with a happy smile. 'You have guessed it, ma'am – is it not singular? The last of the Warrenders lies in my own churchyard! I did not know of this when I buried her, for she went by the name of Mrs Welland.'

'Did you ever meet her?'

'I did not; she never attended my church.'

'Do you happen to recall who paid for her tombstone?'

'It was Mr Daniel Arden. And it was quite proper, for he adopted her twin boys.'

This was such a surprise to me that it took a moment to digest; the mother of those beautiful children was none other than Hannah Laurie.

And this surely meant that their true father was Joshua Welland – but why had he never claimed his own sons?

'It's quite appropriate, when you think about it,' said Mrs Watts-Weston. 'There is poetic justice in the fact that those boys will inherit Binstock after all! Was Mr Arden aware of the connection?'

'Oh, yes,' said Mr Collins. 'When he acquired the estate, he asked me many questions about the history of the Warrenders. He spent hours here, studying my documents. He told me that he was guided by the hand of God.'

Why hadn't Mr Arden told me the truth about his beloved twins? I remembered Arthur observing that the man was always on his guard.

'I've seen enough to be going on with,' said Mrs W-W, no longer bothering to whisper. 'Let's go, before we have to hear the lineage of every family in the county!'

We took our leave of Mr Collins, and once we were outside again, Mrs Watts-Weston rather embarrassed me by walking along the length of the house, brazenly looking into every window, with not the slightest care for the two labourers staring at her from across the road. Finally, she climbed into the carriage, smiling with great satisfaction.

'I am pleased with the house; it can easily be made fit for a new incumbent, once all that rubbish has been thrown away. I do wish I'd been able to see the attics, and to ask about the lease of the home farm. Never mind, I have enough to commence my campaign.' She frowned and exclaimed, 'Price!'

'I beg your pardon?'

'I was trying to recall the name of Lady Tremlett's paid companion. It was Miss Price, and later Mrs Wainright, and according to my mother, the old lady led her a terrible life.'

She produced a silver pencil and a piece of paper and began to make notes about the house.

I fell to thinking of the latest piece of information, and vainly trying to fit it into the picture.

I was still as blind as Bartimeus, but the reader's eye may already have seen the truth – namely, that the key to absolutely everything was Hannah Laurie.

Twenty-six

'I THOUGHT I'D LOOK IN while I was passing,' said Inspector Blackbeard. 'Something rum turned up this morning, that might be of interest to you, ma'am.'

It was past ten in the evening and Blackbeard had materialized, like a dingy apparition, in the doorway of the small private dining room at the Mitre, where I was 'treating' my nephew, dear Gus, to supper (I cannot resist adding that he was a great deal cheaper to entertain than his greedy father; this handsome, earnest, young protoclergyman took after Fanny's side of the family; her brothers are as slender and as finely built as gazelles).

'I'm glad you looked in, Inspector; please join us.' My heart rose up with hope, for I knew Blackbeard well enough by now to catch the excitement in his laconic tone.

'I don't like to intrude, ma'am.'

Gus quickly said he had to return to his desk in college; I introduced him to the inspector.

'How do, Mr Tyson,' said Blackbeard, shaking his hand. 'I know your father, sir. I daresay we'll be seeing you in court one of these days.'

'Not unless I commit a crime,' said Gus (with a droll glance aside at me that suddenly made him astoundingly like Fred). 'I'm hoping to enter the Church.'

After my nephew had taken his leave, Blackbeard said, 'Fine young man. You must be proud of him.'

'I'm as proud as a peacock! But you shouldn't encourage me, or I'll brag about him all night, and I would much rather hear what you have come to tell me; please sit down.'

Blackbeard was not a man to be hurried; no matter how momentous the news, he had to filter it through the unknowable layers of his brain before he could utter a word. He sat himself beside the fire and shook his head when I offered refreshment.

'But I'd be obliged if you would permit my pipe, Mrs Rodd. It helps me think. And this latest turn is a thinker, if ever I saw one.'

'Of course.'

'Thankee.' Out came the short, blackened clay pipe I had so often seen (the tobacco he smoked was of the roughest sort, yet I always found the smell of it less offensive than the indelible reek of Fred's cigars). After a few minutes of frowning at the fire, he said, 'I was called out to Hardinsett this morning.'

'Oh?'

'The message came from the man I left there, to keep an eye on the place. That old cottage of Tom Goodly's caught afire and burned to the ground. The farmer who owns it decided to tear it down to make more space for his pigs. They had to dig deep to take out the foundations. They dug up the cesspit, ma'am. And hid right down at the very bottom – what do you think was found?'

'I can't imagine.'

The inspector laid his pipe down on the hearth and took from his pocket an old piece of sacking. Slowly and carefully, he opened it to reveal –

'Gold!' I gasped out.

The coins were clean, and the lamplight gave them a rich gleam.

'Twenty gold sovereigns,' said Blackbeard. 'Enough money to send a poor woman out of her wits! The farmer, by the name of Grimley, is an honest chap and turned it over to the constable, who gave it to me.'

'I don't understand it; such a sum would have set the man up for life! Why did he never touch it?'

'My guess is that there was someone else in the picture,' said Blackbeard. 'Goodly didn't touch the money on account of being too scared.'

'Something made Goodly afraid for his soul. That is why he wanted to make his confession to Arthur Somers when he lay dying. And that is the reason Arthur was murdered!'

'We have our motive – but who does it belong to? There's more digging to be done, and I would be glad of your help, Mrs Rodd, for time is short and two heads are better than one.'

'With all my heart, Inspector! Where should we go first?'

'Abingdon,' he said promptly. 'To meet an old woman who ain't as mad as she's been painted.'

Inspector Blackbeard arrived at the Mitre next morning, just as every bell in that city of bells rang out eight o'clock. He was to escort me to Abingdon, and as we set out in the plain closed carriage, my spirits rose in spite of everything; the weather was fine and sunny, the sound of bells is always cheerful to me, and it was good to have Blackbeard on my side, for the moment, at least.

Abingdon is six miles from Oxford, in the beautiful countryside known as the Vale of the White Horse. Before we came to the town itself, we turned off the principal road and into a maze of narrow lanes and tall hedgerows.

The old woman's daughter was a Mrs Squires; she lived in a lopsided row of labourers' cottages, cheek-by-jowl with a large cattle-byre. The cottages were dilapidated, the thatched roof sagged and one of the cob walls bulged dangerously. It was a typical scene of rural poverty, only too familiar to me from my years as the wife of a country vicar. I knew enough to look beyond the dilapidation, which was the fault of the landlord, to the well-tended vegetable patches and lines of washing that were signs of hard-working tenants. As we picked our way along the muddy path before the row of little houses, we heard hens and smelt pigs. It was a relief to know that the daughter was in far less wretched circumstances than her mother had been.

Mrs Squires was in the patch of garden before her front door, hanging a piece of coarse linen on the washing line, to make the most of what might be the last good drying-day of the year.

The woman could not have been older than me, and was probably much younger, but she was wizened and stooping, and half her teeth were gone. When spoken to, however, she revealed a perfectly sound intelligence; her eyes were bright and watchful. Saying nothing of the gold, Mr Blackbeard asked if we could see her mother.

'Yessir, if you want,' said Mrs Squires. 'She's not bad today.'

'How has she been, since you brought her here?' I asked.

'Sits quiet, mostly. She's no trouble, ma'am.'

'You are good to take care of her, Mrs Squires.'

'I don't mind it, now the old man's gone.' She was sour. 'I wouldn't have him near me. We don't drink nothing but small ale in this house, and my mother's all the better for it. She's not mad. The drink sent her off her head.'

The door of the cottage was so low that we had to bend our heads to get inside. There we found ourselves in one room, humbly furnished yet well-kept, where a truly ancient woman sat before the kitchen fire, slowly and deliberately paring a heap of potatoes into a bowl on her lap.

'She makes herself useful,' said Mrs Squires, 'if you don't mind waiting all morning.'

Mr Blackbeard, I was interested to see, was absolutely at home and at ease in this setting; not for the first time, I wondered where he had spent his youth.

He drew two more rough wooden chairs up to the fire-side, and – ignoring the old woman's expression of bewilderment – sat down close to her, as if he had been her nephew.

'I was at Hardinsett yesterday, Mrs Goodly. The old place is just the same – but I'm sorry to tell you that your cottage got pulled down.'

She blinked at him in silence for a moment, as if sieving the facts through her fractured brain. 'They said I was mad.'

'You're not mad,' said Blackbeard. 'That's right, isn't it, Mother? It was the drink that did for you.'

'Yessir,' said Mrs Goodly. 'The measure was the same as usual, but I got to drink it all, for once.'

'She means on account of my father being gone,' put in Mrs Squires. 'When he was alive she had to sneak her sups of gin without him seeing. If he caught her at it, he beat her black and blue.'

Mrs Goodly nodded, and murmured, 'She's a good girl, is my Em.'

It was pleasant to see how the daughter's face softened, though all she said was, 'How's the potatoes coming, then?'

'Nearly done!' Mrs Goodly resumed her slow work and I had a sense of someone coming back to their senses after long imprisonment. She was not insane, only a little dazed by the light of freedom (I was forming a lower and lower opinion of her unlamented husband) and the novel experience of sobriety.

'I'd like you to tell me a story,' said Blackbeard, in what was for him a coaxing voice. 'It's an old story; you've been telling it for more than thirty years.'

'Not that dratted gold!' groaned Mrs Squires.

He shot her a stern look and carried on, 'That man of yours was given to thieving, wasn't he?'

'I dunno, sir.'

'Come along, Mrs Goodly! Nothing you say can touch him now.'

'He was a thief, all right,' said Mrs Squires. 'I left home for good and all when he tried to filch my first summer's wages.'

'Yes, yes, he was terrible light-fingered!' her mother sighed. 'Everybody knew it, till I was ready to die from shame. He kept bad company, too – every rogue for miles about!'

'I want you to think very hard, Mother.' Blackbeard's voice was low and (for him) tender. 'Let's see how much you can recall about the supposed "robbery" all those years ago. Do you know who got robbed?' He shot a warning glance at Mrs Squires, before she could interrupt again.

'The first I knew was when he came home,' said Mrs Goodly. 'It was past midnight, which I know because I was lying awake, and heard the church clock. When Goodly got in, I pretended to be deep asleep upstairs. He wasn't always fooled, but this time he was and let me alone. I heard him walking about and mumbling, so I crept to the top of the stairs to see what he was up to.' With a hint of drama, she added, 'And that's when I saw the gold!'

(Mrs Squires pursed her lips, obviously longing to speak.)

'Carry on, Mrs Goodly!'

'It was all spread across the table and it had such a shine in the candlelight that I knew it was gold!'

'You must've been happy to see it.'

'No, sir,' said Mrs Goodly. 'I was scared. But I saw what I saw, and Goodly never managed to beat it out of me. I knew he had it – but not a penny could I ever get out of him, even when the children cried with hunger.'

'Well, well,' said Blackbeard. 'And did you ever find out where it came from?'

'No, sir. Never.'

'He wasn't working alone, was he?'

'No, sir.'

'Let's have some names!' He leant a little closer to her. 'I'm sure you remember some of them "rogues" he hung out with!'

'Oh yes, sir,' said Mrs Goodly. 'Will Tapp, John Gore, Dan Smith, Kit Warrender, Jack Barker, Dan Cummings—'

One name in that list leapt out at me. 'Warrender – could that be Sir Christopher?'

'Yes'm.'

'Oh, yes indeed!' Mrs Squires burst out. 'That young fellow was a bad 'un, ma'am; the whole countryside knew it. He drank and gambled until Binstock fell into ruins.'

'There was a story that he was murdered,' said Mr Blackbeard (speaking mildly, but with eyes like gimlets). 'What do you say to that?'

'It's nonsense, sir,' said Mrs Squires. 'Warrender ran off because of his debts. And because the old lady was after him.'

'What old lady?'

'I heard that he had an aunt, a Lady Tremlett,' I put in.

'That's right, ma'am,' said Mrs Squires. 'After Warrender ran off, she searched high and low for him, the story being that he'd stole something from her, I don't know what it was. But there was another story going about.'

'Plymouth,' I suggested.

She needed no more prompting. 'Yes, ma'am – that he was living there in scandal and shame, with a local boy who disappeared at the same time.'

'Do you recall his name?'

'Dan Smith,' piped up Mrs Goodly. 'Young devil that he was.'

There were other questions I would have liked to ask, but Blackbeard appeared to be satisfied. He gave Mrs Squires half-a-crown (telling her to 'buy some comforts for Mother') and we took our leave.

He would not speak until we were in the carriage and well on the road back to Oxford.

And then he said, 'Nice morning's work.'

'I'm glad you think so, Inspector,' I said. 'My head is still whirling! Did Goodly conspire with Warrender to rob Lady Tremlett? He must've known something about the man's disappearance; should I go down to Plymouth?'

'I wouldn't,' said Blackbeard. 'The truth is nearer home, Mrs Rodd. As it usually is. If you don't see me for a day or two, it'll be because I'm out and about looking up some of them names.'

'But it was so long ago,' I said. 'Those men must all be dead by now!'

'I'm banking on at least one of them being alive and in his right mind. Twenty golden coins don't spring out of nowhere.'

Twenty-seven

'I LOOKED IN CROCKFORD'S FOR the name of Wainright,' said Mrs Watts-Weston. 'And I looked in vain, until I suddenly remembered that the man was actually called Belling. He is dead, but his widow still lives nearby. I cannot imagine how old she must be now.'

I was in the Warden's carriage once more, driving along the principal road towards the town of Wallingford. Inspector Blackbeard had expressed a cautious interest in Lady Tremlett's paid companion, and that was the only hint I needed to seek the Gorgon's help that morning. She was delighted, and ordered such handsome provisions for the journey (game pie, claret from the college cellar, ham sandwiches) that we might have been headed for Timbuctoo.

'This is quite a holiday for me, Mrs Rodd! Domestic matters will have to take care of themselves for once.'

'It is most kind of you,' I said. 'And it may lead nowhere. We are clutching at straws.' I had not told her about the gold.

'Never mind, I am simply intrigued. May I help you to more pie?'

'No thank you.'

'I've warned my husband for years – one bright morning, I shall simply run away, just like Joshua Welland.'

'I can't see you living in the forest,' I said, smiling (and thinking that it would need to be a very orderly forest). 'Is life at the college so terrible?'

'Life at the college is perfectly beautiful, Mrs Rodd, for those allowed to spend their days in the library. My days are spent in wash houses, kitchens, nurseries, and the drawing rooms of other women that I don't much like.'

I laughed outright at this. 'Have you found no congenial society here?'

'Not really. I know only too well how it feels to be denied an education. Joshua Welland merely wanted more money. My situation was far worse.'

'How do you mean?'

'Because I'm a woman, of course!'

'Oh – yes.'

'Every door is barred with gold, Mrs Rodd, and opens but to golden keys – unless you're a woman, in which case there are no keys at all. I have sometimes wondered why the Almighty bothers to create clever women in the first place. It seems such a waste.'

'He creates nothing without a purpose,' I said decidedly. 'If he gave us females brains, it follows that he meant us to use them; he is not to be blamed for wrongheadedness that is entirely human in origin.'

'Good heavens, I didn't expect you to be such a radical!' cried Mrs Watts-Weston, smiling in a way that suddenly gave me a glimpse of how handsome she had been as a girl. 'There are some advocates of female education in Oxford, but nobody asks them to dinner or takes them at all seriously. And they are so badly dressed!'

She broke off to pull down the window of the carriage, and to stick her head out of it, as she had done every ten minutes or so since we started.

'Robbins! ROBBINS! Why are we so slow? What IS the obstruction?'

Robbins, up on the box, shouted down something about the traffic.

Mrs Watts-Weston whisked her head back inside and shut the window. 'It'll be easier once we take the turning to Barncott. Mrs Belling lives in Lower Barncott.'

'I'm a little uneasy about descending on her like this,' I ventured. 'Without any warning.'

'Pish!' said Mrs Watts-Weston. 'I don't imagine she's doing anything else.'

The carriage turned off the main road, and she once more stuck her head out of the window to shout instructions at Robbins, and at a farmer who was blocking the way with his wagon. We passed through the main village, a busy and bustling place. Lower Barncott was a mile or so beyond it, a scattering of pretty thatched houses surrounded by fields.

Larkspur Cottage, the home of Mrs Belling, was the largest and most genteel of the houses; a long, low cob cottage set in a walled garden. The door was opened by a neat young servant-girl, and Mrs W-W's loud preamble was cut short by a voice from somewhere nearby.

'Show them in, my dear; they will not mind a little informality.'

Mrs Belling was in her drawing room, in the middle of washing some delicate pieces of china in a small bowl of warm water, on the table at her elbow.

'Please sit down, ladies, and forgive me for not getting up; I suppose you are here on behalf of the Winter Relief Club. Good heavens, it comes round earlier every year!'

She had grey hair, covered with a muslin cap of antiquated design, a rounded, unlined face and cordial manner. I judged her to be around seventy-five years old,

233

and as hale as a much younger woman. Mrs Watts-Weston began her explanation, and the face of the former Miss Price lit up when she heard the name of Warrender.

'You must be little Caroline!'

'Why – yes—' For once, Mrs Watts-Weston was thoroughly rattled. 'But how can you possibly—?'

'I had you all by heart,' said Mrs Belling. 'The family tree and its ramifications were all my employer liked to talk about. You were the only girl in your family, and the apple of your father's eye.'

'No, you're quite wrong,' said Mrs Watts-Weston, her cheeks reddening. 'My father didn't approve of me at all!'

'He was very proud of you,' said Mrs Belling. 'But clever little girls must not be cleverer than their brothers.'

'Oh—'

'Mrs Belling,' I said quickly (we could not afford too much ancient history), 'we are trying to find out about the time of Sir Christopher's disappearance.'

'Are you, indeed! Well, there can't be any harm in speaking of it now.' For the first time, her smile took on a hint of sourness. 'When everybody has been dead for years.'

I chose my words carefully. 'Lady Tremlett made a great noise about her nephew's disappearance, I believe.'

'That she did,' said Mrs Belling. 'She had notices printed, she placed advertisements in newspapers, she offered a reward and I don't know what. She was very angry, ma'am. And she died angry.'

'It was all about money, apparently,' said Mrs Watts-Weston, now recovered from the glimpse into her childhood. 'We wondered if he'd run off with something of value.'

'Ha! Did you, now?' Mrs Belling's reaction was intriguing; though she chuckled, as if at a private joke, her expression was grim. 'It was bound to come out eventually.'

She would say no more until she had called to the maid for glasses of Madeira and a plate of sugary biscuits that crumbled like dust.

'I didn't care for Sir Christopher Warrender,' she said. 'And I cannot pretend I was sorry to see the back of him.'

'Did you live at Binstock?' I asked.

'Yes,' said Mrs Belling. 'My employer considered herself the head of the family, and took up residence at Binstock when the old baronet died. The story was that she was keeping house for Sir Christopher. The plain truth of the matter, however, was that she was too poor to keep her own establishment. By the time I came to her, the house was in a shocking state – and she made me do the work of at least three servants. The term "paid companion", as I'm sure you know, covers a multitude of sins. I was a very distant cousin – which meant that I was expected to live upon crumbs and be grateful.'

As she talked, she dried her little pieces of china with a soft linen cloth, before placing them carefully in a cabinet with glass doors (beautiful china, very like the blue-and-white pieces that I inherited from my dear mother, who also washed her china with her own hands; servants simply can't be trusted with such fragility).

'From what I've heard,' said Mrs Watts-Weston, 'Lady Tremlett was rather a horrid old thing.'

Mrs Belling laughed softly, not at all put out by Mrs W-W's bluntness. 'She was an angry woman, and a disappointed woman, who never stopped complaining. And I'm sorry to say that I thought her extremely horrid. It was an unpleasant house. Sir Christopher was a drunkard, and the one thing that can be said for Lady Tremlett is that her presence protected me from his dreadful friends. I knew that she was at the end of her life, and I was frankly rather impatient for the end to come. The shameful fact is that I was secretly engaged to the local curate, my dear late husband; at the time of the disappearance, I was longing to be married – but I could not leave Lady Tremlett, for she had no one else in the world.'

'That was decent of you,' said Mrs Watts-Weston. 'And I know for a fact that she never paid you a bean.'

Mrs Belling opened her mouth to say something, then closed it again and looked at us both, a little warily. 'I might as well let it out now, though I have never told a soul except my husband. Lady Tremlett was stingy but that's not even the half of it – she was a thief!'

'I knew it!' gasped Mrs Watts-Weston, alight with excitement. 'The Romney!'

'Yes, Miss Caroline; that picture truly existed. And Lady Tremlett truly took it off to London wrapped in sacking. Sir Christopher had nothing to do with it. There were other things, too; an enamel clock, a set of fine glasses – the house was in such chaos that it was possible for her to filch little bits and pieces without being found out. She felt that she had a right to the things because she had been born a Warrender. But there was something else – something that I was not supposed to know. The wicked old lady was invited to a large house party, from which she returned with a valuable necklace; it looked valuable to me, at any rate. She tried to hide it at the bottom of her work-box. But Sir Christopher managed to find it, and take it with him when he disappeared.'

'That explains why Lady Tremlett was in such a state,' I said. 'She could hardly advertise for the return of a stolen necklace!'

'Quite,' said Mrs Belling tartly. 'Her fury was a sight to behold; I'm sure it was the cause of the seizure that killed her. I hope you will believe that I did my best for her, but she died raging.'

'Was there no response to her campaign?' I asked. 'Did she find out what happened to the necklace?'

'There was a story going round, a few months after she died, that the necklace had been sold at a horse fair for one hundred pounds – a fraction of what it was worth.'

'One hundred pounds!' cried Mrs Watts-Weston. 'So much for all the rumours of stolen fortunes!'

My mind had gone back to the gold sovereigns, gleaming in Blackbeard's hand.

Had Sir Christopher been murdered for the sake of a few gold coins?

Men have been murdered for a lot less.

Twenty-eight

'INTERESTING,' SAID MR BLACKBEARD. 'In a round-about sort of way.'

'I know it's not much, and might be nothing,' I said. 'But Mrs Belling's story does explain why there is no record of a robbery at the time of Sir Christopher's disappearance. According to her, it happened somewhere else, at this house party, when the old lady stole a certain necklace and her nephew exchanged it for gold.'

'Hmm.'

'I was afraid you would make that irritating noise, Inspector! Don't you think it warrants further investigation?'

'Indeed I do, Mrs Rodd, but it's slow work that can't be hurried.'

There was a gleam of satisfaction about him this morning, almost invisible to the naked eye but enough to make me intensely curious; he had turned up quite unannounced, to request my company, but so far he had revealed nothing. I did not even know where we were going, for the windows of that plain black carriage of his were small and thick with dirt.

'I thought I'd take a look at Binstock,' said Mr Blackbeard. 'I know that Mr Arden is in London, but it ain't him I'm after. I'm still chasing after some of those names, and I'm betting that they were local rascals – if a

239

man wishes to go to the bad, ma'am, he never has to look very far for company.'

'Very true,' I said.

'Will Tapp, John Gore, Dan Smith, Jack Barker and Dan Cummings.' He rattled out the names. 'I've had my constables searching through all the parish records for miles about, and I've already scratched John Gore off the list; he was hanged for sheep-stealing twenty years ago. And then ten years ago, Jack Barker got drunk and drowned in the river. But it won't be easy finding the others, after so many years. Times passes, ma'am, and memories fade.'

'They may not all be dead,' I said stoutly. 'And country memories never fade, Inspector! If we ask the right questions of the right people, we will find the truth.'

'Hmm,' said Blackbeard. 'You're light-hearted today, Mrs Rodd!'

'I wouldn't go so far as light-hearted,' I said, smiling at his accusatory tone. 'But this new line of yours makes me hopeful for my poor friends.'

'The papers have lost interest in them, anyhow,' said Mr Blackbeard. 'All eyes are on Swinford now.' (This was perfectly true, as those of my years will remember; at the time the scandal was enormous, splashed across every publication and preached about from every pulpit.)

'Have you discovered anything new there?' I dared to ask him a direct question.

'No,' he said flatly.

'Oh, dear!'

'The trouble is, I've been distracted for too long by a load of tittle-tattle.' His stony eyes glinted humorously; this was the nearest he would get to admitting he had been wrong about Rachel and Mr Barton. 'But gold is gold, and that's a good solid thing to chase after.'

'Again, very true,' I said. 'How should we proceed? And did you bring me along for a particular purpose – or simply to assist in the general stirring-up of old village gossip?'

'If there's one thing I've learnt from you, ma'am, it's that nobody knows a place better than the vicar. And you have the knack of shaking them down.'

I could not help smiling again at this rather doubtful compliment. 'Whom would you like me to "shake down", Inspector? Is it anyone I know?'

'A curate,' said Blackbeard, 'by the name of Charles Yates.'

'Yates?' I was puzzled for a moment, and then remembered where I had heard the name before. 'Oh, of course; the young man who discovered Mr Fogle's body at Swinford!'

'That's the fellow.' A ghost of a smile flitted across his face. 'When he ain't praying in a stable, Mr Yates is curate-in-charge at Binstock church. And I'm sorry to say that he don't like the police.'

'I suppose it's understandable,' I said thoughtfully. 'The whole experience must have been quite shocking to him. I wrote to request an interview, but he refused, saying that he was ill.'

'Well, he ain't,' said Blackbeard shortly. 'The inquest put him into a fright, that's all.'

'Really? From what I have read, I thought the coroner's questions were perfectly civil.'

'It's what happened outside the court that got him. Someone who don't like Catholics chucked a bad egg at him.'

'Poor man – how horrid!'

'Now he runs a mile whenever he sees me, Mrs Rodd. So you see why I need you; I want all the local information and Mr Yates won't give me the time of day.'

'In which case, I shall be tact itself,' I said. 'Would you be kind enough to open the window?'

Blackbeard jerked down the dirty window, so that I was able to see where we were going; we passed the lodge at Binstock and followed the road for a mile or so, until we came to the village.

This was Mr Arden's 'pet' village, held up as a model for miles around. Blackbeard stopped the carriage when we came to a trim little green, overlooked by a row of trim little cottages; every thatch was new here, every wall was freshly whitewashed, and even the cows that grazed in the field behind the single street looked as if they had been polished. I was strongly reminded of the bucolic picture upon the lid of Mrs B's sewing-box.

The church was an old one with a square tower, set well back from the road behind a large and wondrously tidy churchyard.

'You'll see some familiar names in here, ma'am.' Mr Blackbeard nodded towards the tipsy-looking gravestones in the cropped grass. 'There's a Gore, and a Tapp, and a Cummings. Some folks spend their lives on one small patch of earth, until they end up being buried in it.'

'When I was a girl,' I said (wondering yet again where the man had spent his childhood), 'people stayed where they were born, and regarded twenty miles as a great distance. There were always one or two, however, that managed to leave.'

'Like Arden.'

'Yes – but Mr Arden came back to his patch.'

'Do you happen to know, ma'am, exactly where Arden was born?'

'Not exactly; I understood that he grew up within a few miles of here, but was not attached to any village in particular.'

The entrance to the church, through a quaint lychgate, was situated in a turning off the road, faced by the small, neat, grey stone vicarage. I had been prepared to send in my card, but Mr Yates was out in the garden to one side of the house; a slender young man with fair hair and a permanent dint of anxiety over the bridge of his nose. He wore an apron of brown holland over his black suit, and brown holland sleeve-guards, and the young woman beside him was similarly attired. They were pulling the pelargoniums from a row of pots and cutting them right back to the roots to store over the winter (my mother and I used to do this; it seems brutal, but the reward is a profusion of flowers when you plant them again the following year).

The sight of Mr Blackbeard made the young man stiff and defensive. Blackbeard, however, took his leave as soon as he had made the introductions, leaving Mr Yates openly relieved, although still a trace suspicious of me.

'What a charming garden you have here, Mr Yates,' I said. Of course I was 'buttering him up', as Fred would say, yet the garden truly was very pretty, even at the beginning of autumn, and most beautifully maintained.

'Thank you,' he said curtly. 'This is my sister, Minna, who keeps house for me here.'

'How do you do, Mrs Rodd.' Miss Yates was small and pale and delicate-looking, with a plain, peaky little face and a gentle, hesitant manner. 'Won't you come inside, out of the wind?'

She showed me into a small sitting room at the back of the house. 'I hope you won't mind the parlour, Mrs Rodd; we never have a fire in the drawing room at this time.'

I assured her that I did not mind in the least, for it was a comfortable room and the fire was generous.

'It may appear to be rather extravagant,' said Mr Yates, once his sister had left us alone together. 'Minna is not strong, however, and I always insist that she must have a decent fire.'

'Very sensible,' I said.

He did not sit down in the other armchair, but stood at attention on the hearthrug. 'I beg your pardon if this seems rude, Mrs Rodd, but I have nothing more to say about the terrible events at Swinford. I told that policeman everything he could possibly want to know.'

'That is not the reason I'm here, Mr Yates. And you must not mind Mr Blackbeard; he is all bark and very little bite.'

'His behaviour at Swinford was disrespectful and occasionally downright ungodly.'

'I'm sorry to hear it.' I was longing to ask him about the murder, but there was no point when he was on his guard and prickling like a hedgehog. 'He is looking into something quite different today, concerning a robbery that occurred many years ago.'

'A robbery?' The surprise opened out his face, and he looked years younger.

'This must be in the strictest confidence, Mr Yates – but naturally I know that I can rely upon your discretion.'

As briefly as possible, I recounted the whole story of the stolen gold. It was the last thing he had expected to hear, and he was clearly fascinated; he climbed down off his high horse and sat down to listen, sometimes interrupting with questions. I finished with a recital of the names given by Mrs Goodly, and then allowed the silence to stretch while he thought it all over.

'I had heard of the business with the old woman; if she had been one of my parishioners, I would've tried to prevent her being sent away.'

'It was a blessing in disguise, Mr Yates; she has a comfortable home with her daughter now.'

'And the gold was real after all!'

'Do you know if any of those men are still living?'

'No – but you'll find the same names in every church-yard this side of Oxford. We have a Tapp family here, and a Cummings – look here, you'd better ask my sister, who knows far more about the people of that class than I do.'

Miss Yates was at that moment coming into the room with a tray of tea-things, which her brother hastened to wrest from her hands; I was touched by his concern for her, and the good-natured scolding he gave her because the tray was too heavy. When she was with us the atmosphere was markedly easier; the last shred of the curate's pompous disapproval melted away and he rattled out the story like an eager schoolboy.

'You'll know, Minna; was it the Tapps had a death in the family just before we came here, or was that the Carters?'

'The Tapps,' said Miss Yates, in her soft voice.

'Yes, to be sure – one of the names you mentioned, Mrs Rodd! He died of an attack of pleurisy—'

'No, that was old Enoch Carter,' said Miss Yates, laughing at him in a way that lit up her timid little face. 'Will Tapp was run over by a brewer's dray.'

'You see, Mrs Rodd, my sister puts me to shame; I have lived in this village for five years and know nothing of my neighbours. Minna knew everybody in five minutes.'

'The Tapps are good, respectable people,' she said quickly. 'Will was their only scapegrace; he was wild in his youth, and given to drink in his old age. As to Dan Cummings, he died last winter of pneumonia.'

'Despite the comforts rained down upon him by our esteemed Mr Arden.' The curate's voice took on a bitter tang. 'The great philanthropist who turns his back on the church at his very gates!'

Miss Yates winced and her thin cheeks reddened.

'Smith is the only name left,' I said, pretending I had not noticed this. 'Are there any in this parish?'

'Not here,' said Miss Yates. 'I know of several Smith families, however, in several directions; it is a very common name in this part of the country.'

The clock upon the chimney-piece whirred and chimed the hour.

'I must leave you, Mrs Rodd,' said Mr Yates. 'Please finish your tea; my sister will look after you.'

'You have been most helpful, Mr Yates,' I said. 'I really should apologize for calling unannounced.'

'Not at all; I'm sorry I was suspicious of you at first.' He spoke to me, yet his eyes were fixed to his sister. 'These dreadful events cannot be allowed to damage the reputation of the Church, and we must all be on our guard.'

He looked at her mildly enough, but Miss Yates's pale face was suddenly scarlet.

Twenty-nine

I PRETENDED NOT TO NOTICE her confusion, and after Mr Yates had left the house, I began to talk about pelargoniums; it was a solo performance at first, but after a few minutes the fierce blush faded and Miss Yates regained her self-possession. We drank second cups of tea and I dared to move the conversation in a more personal direction.

'Were you and your brother brought up in this part of the country, Miss Yates?'

'No, we grew up in Hale, near Manchester. Our father was a clergyman.'

'That is something we have in common,' I said. 'I am another daughter of the parsonage; mine was in the deepest depths of Gloucestershire – I don't like to think how many years ago! Are your parents still living?'

'Our mother died when Charles and I were very young,' said Miss Yates. 'And we lost our father six years ago; I can only be thankful that he lived to see his son ordained.'

'I'm sure he was most happy and proud! My own dear father would have loved to see my naughty little brother made a clergyman, but Providence had other plans and he was called to the bar instead. Did your brother consider other professions, or was he always set on the Church?'

'Always! That is – when we were children, I was the religious one, while Charles took his faith more lightly. It was only when he went to Oxford that he experienced it as something profound. He was greatly influenced by Gerard Fogle.'

'Dear me, that must have made the experience of his death a hundred times more painful!'

'You must forgive him for snapping at you, Mrs Rodd. It's only because some people have been so unkind. My brother's name was made public and linked to Swinford. That was enough to bring him a fine batch of anonymous letters. And we would have had trouble in the parish itself if Mr Arden had not intervened; he made a special point of shaking Charley's hand in the street and speaking out against the gossips.'

'Your brother didn't seem to approve of Mr Arden,' I observed softly.

The blood surged back to her cheeks at once, as if I had shot her in the heart; I allowed the silence to stretch, worried that I had gone too far.

At length she ventured, 'They have had some differences of opinion.'

'About wretched Church politics, I suppose, and the awkward fact that Mr Arden is an unrepentant Unitarian!'

I was as cheerful as can be and she responded with a smile; I noticed that, in some lights, her nondescript features became absolutely beautiful, and when a plain girl suddenly turns pretty, I am always interested.

'Mr Arden doesn't try to convert anybody else,' she said earnestly, 'and he has nothing but respect for the established Church. My brother feels, however, that he is a bad influence in the neighbourhood, and ought to set a better example.'

'In my opinion, Miss Yates, his generosity to the poor is example enough.'

'Oh, yes! My brother's position here meant that we couldn't call upon Mr Arden, but I couldn't avoid making his acquaintance informally. I often met him in the houses of people I visited and he was compassion itself. I dared to ask him outright for money to improve the school; he took a personal interest in the project, which led to us becoming … friends.'

The last word fell into another chasm of silence. Hold your nerve, I told myself; she has no one she can confide in, and there are some secrets a young woman cannot bear to keep to herself.

'There was nothing improper between us, Mrs Rodd, please believe me,' she said eventually.

'Of course I do, my dear! You could hardly have ignored him.'

'I tried to explain as much to Charles,' said Miss Yates, rather pitifully grateful that I did not chide her. 'But I couldn't overcome his prejudice; he believes Unitarians to be next door to heretics.'

'I'm afraid that particular intolerance can be traced back to Swinford; my poor late friend Arthur Somers was constantly flinging out all sorts of accusations against nonconformists.'

'Mr Arden and I never spoke of religion when we met; there were too many other things to discuss – practical things. But I know his mission to be noble: to root out the causes of poverty, and to help people to the means of helping themselves!'

'The signs of his success are everywhere,' I said. 'Surely there can be no possible objection to him, when he does so much good?'

(On I chattered, watching her like a hawk; she was too innocent to be aware of how much she was giving away, yet it was quite plain to me – she was in love with Mr

Arden; naturally my mind flashed back to what he had said to me when we walked on the Heath together; was Minna Yates the reason he had allowed himself to think of marriage?)

'My brother says he encourages disrespect for the Church, and he has forbidden me to meet with him in private.'

'That must be rather awkward,' I said, 'in a small place like this.'

'It was on account of those anonymous letters,' said Miss Yates, raising her head proudly. 'One of them made disgusting insinuations about my friendship with Mr Arden.'

'How dreadful!'

'And now the gossips are saying there's no smoke without fire. I tried to explain to Charles that the two of us had only ever discussed things like the salary for the schoolteacher, but he was too angry to listen. And he blamed me for being a cause of scandal.'

'You? My dear Miss Yates!' I could not hide my indignation at the sheer unfairness of this. 'You are not to blame in the least! It would be a great pity if your brother's prejudice stopped you and Mr Arden helping your neighbours!'

'Thank you.' She was as red as a turkey-cock, but relieved that I took her part. 'I should hate you to think ill of me! That's what I cannot endure, Mrs Rodd; my brother and I have always been of one mind and spirit, and the coldness of his expression cut me to the heart. He seemed to believe I had somehow set out to "entrap" Mr Arden. I hope you will believe I did nothing of the kind.'

'Of course I do!' I said stoutly. 'If he were a few years younger, I'd box his ears for being such a lout! A gentleman – particularly a clerical gentleman – does not insult his sister.'

Miss Yates smiled. 'It is the only disagreement we've ever had; I put it down to his anxiety about the murder at Swinford. Do you know if the police have found out anything new?'

'Not yet.'

'Mr Arden thinks it was a robbery that went wrong.'

'When did you see Mr Arden?'

'Yesterday morning,' said Miss Yates, meeting my gaze boldly. 'We met by chance, at the market in Culverton – quite by chance.'

'Oh, I'm sure of that!' I said (not sure at all). 'And in such a public situation, of course you were forced to acknowledge him. But I thought he was in London.'

'The delay in the trial brought him back to Binstock,' explained Miss Yates. 'He never can endure being away for long. And I wanted to speak to him about the wild behaviour of a certain local boy and the necessity of helping him. It was not a personal conversation in the least.'

'No, of course not.'

'Mr Arden will always stand up for the wild lads, to stop them falling into criminality.'

'Perhaps he's thinking of his own boyhood,' I said. 'He has spoken to me of his wish to give others all the things he never had himself.'

'He is reticent to a fault about his history,' said Miss Yates. 'Once, however, he admitted to me that he had been a criminal in his youth.'

'Oh?'

'He was locked up many times when he was a boy, for petty stealing, and for poaching. And he narrowly missed being transported for rick-burning – he was only saved because someone had heart enough to speak up for him. But this is confidential; I should not have said so much.'

'I'm always discreet, Miss Yates,' I reassured her.

251

'He told me how he had suffered, and how sin and suffering are two sides of the same coin – if you eliminate the suffering, the sin will go too. And there is so much to be done! Mr Arden makes no distinction between the "deserving" and the "undeserving" poor. He says only the Almighty has the right to make such judgements and that the rich have a sacred duty to share their good fortune, because the less fortunate are our brothers and sisters and not another race of beings!' The words poured out of her in a rush of exaltation. 'The woman in the lodge at Binstock is an example of his practical goodness.'

'Ah, yes,' I said, 'I know Mrs Woods.'

'Her husband was killed when part of the old limekiln collapsed on top of him; Mr Arden consulted me at the time about how best to help the poor widow. I cannot begin to describe the marvellous things he has wrought here since he came! My brother says he's a radical and does not approve, but Mr Arden says the Gospels themselves are radical.' She added, 'I beg your pardon if I have shocked you.'

I assured her that she had not – all the time observing that unmistakable light in her eyes.

It was possible that this innocent creature was unaware of the fact that she was in love I took my leave of her, thinking what a fine wife she would make for Mr Arden, if only her brother could be brought round.

Blackbeard was sitting on the wall of the churchyard, in a contemplative cloud of pipe-smoke. He tapped out the pipe when he saw me, and escorted me to the carriage that waited along the road; once we were heading back to Oxford I gave an account of my visit, omitting the romance.

'Mr Yates and his sister have lived here only five years,' I said. 'They couldn't tell me much about local history

– except for Mr Arden's boyhood brushes with the law. I hope you did better, Inspector.'

'Hmm,' said Blackbeard. 'Not much. All I've learned is that this is a terrible place for violent deaths. Apart from the chap that died of pnuemonia, every name on Mother Goodly's list has been hanged or drowned, or knocked down by a brewer's dray, until there's just one man I can't account for.'

'Dan Smith,' I said. 'She called him a "young devil". But we know he's not here, Mr Blackbeard; the story was that he ran off to Plymouth with Sir Christopher and was never seen again.'

'I told you not to bother with Plymouth before, ma'am; now I'm a bit more interested.' He cleared his throat. 'Do you happen to know any vicars down there?'

Thirty

THAT AFTERNOON, AFTER A heartening luncheon of lamb chops and fried potatoes, I sat down beside the fire in the empty coffee room at the Mitre, to write to my connection in Plymouth – for of course I had one.

To the Revd Wilfred Bone, The Seamen's Mission, Union Street, Plymouth

The Mitre

Oxford

14th October

Dear Cousin Wilfred,

A shocking amount of time has passed since our last exchange of letters. I make no apology; I know that you do not care to receive 'frivolous' letters not concerned with the business of the Mission, but I am writing with a request for information. I shall never forget how very useful you were in the Heaton case – especially with your knowledge of the inns and taverns around the docks.

This case may be less straightforward and I shall quite understand if you tell me it is impossible. You will need to cast your mind back all the way to 1819. I am searching for two men last seen in Plymouth during that year and never seen since: a young man who went by the name of Dan Smith, and a gentleman, Sir Christopher Warrender.

Sir Christopher's aunt, Lady Tremlett, made a great stir in the town when he disappeared, which I daresay you remember. But there the scent grows cold. I would like to hear any snippet you can tell me about those two men – and I mean ANY little scrap of information, even if it seems inconsequential.

You and the Mission (I don't think the two can be separated) are always in my prayers.

Yours affectionately,

Laetitia Rodd

PS – Please send any reply to my address in London

The following day was to be my last in Oxford, and I therefore had a long list of very dull things to do (settling my bill at the Mitre, sewing a new black ribbon to my second-best bonnet, mending a tear in my umbrella, et cetera). In the afternoon I was due at Mrs Watts-Weston's At-Home; the weather was dreadfully wet and I did not see how I was to get to the college in my good shoes; I wished I had a pair of homely wooden pattens to protect them.

This was my train of thought when I was summoned downstairs, directly after breakfast, to find Inspector Blackbeard dripping all over the flagstone floor.

'Good morning, Mrs Rodd!' I could read the signs by now and by Blackbeard standards he was positively jaunty. 'It's shocking wet today, ma'am.'

'You are soaked through, Mr Blackbeard! Take off your coat and come to the fire.'

'I can't stop,' said Blackbeard. 'You and I are going on another journey, Mrs Rodd; the carriage should be here in ten minutes or so.'

I knew better than to nag him for more information, though my instinct told me this was something significant; I hurried into my thick cloak and walking shoes, and when I got downstairs again, the carriage was already waiting in the yard.

'We're off to Millings Cross, ma'am,' said Blackbeard.

'I know it; Mr Barton lives at Millings Cross.'

'So he does.'

'Why are we going there?'

'It's on account of a man in the town lock-up,' said Blackbeard. 'Gives his name as "Pauly O'Hare" and he's one of the gipsies from the common. I don't say they're all thieves, ma'am, but this man is most definitely a thief, with a record to show for it as long as your arm. This time he runs the risk of being hanged.'

'Oh.' I had not expected this and was intensely curious.

'He tried to make a bargain with me, along the lines that if I let him out, his dear old mother had something to tell me about the murder. Now, I'm not in the habit of striking bargains with blackguards, but I thought I'd pay the old woman a visit, to see what I can get out of her.'

'There was an old woman that spoke to Mr Barton sometimes,' I said thoughtfully. 'If he paid her.'

'We won't need cash today, ma'am; I have it in my power to make life a bit easier for her son. She'll have every incentive to be truthful.'

'Do you know what information she has?'

'Maybe nothing,' said Mr Blackbeard. 'Then again, she might be a witness.'

'To Arthur's murder?'

'No.'

'To what, then?'

'Let's wait and see, ma'am.'

I had to be content with this, for Blackbeard pursed his thin lips and turned his attention to a copy of *Jackson's Oxford Journal*, wet from the rain and folded very small. At least the rain had cleaned the windows of the carriage; I was able to see when we turned off the Hardinsett road, down the narrow and grievously muddy lane that led to Millings Cross.

As Mr Barton had said, the place was barely a village. I was a little ashamed that I had never taken the trouble to visit his church; it was a small and modest building of raw red brick, with a churchyard at the very edge of the rough common. There was only one house that looked remotely genteel enough for a clergyman: a low-built thatched cottage.

'You're to wait in the house, Mrs Rodd,' said Blackbeard. 'The camp's no place for you.'

I could have argued that I had been in far worse places, but knew him well enough to know that his mind was made up and argument was futile.

The rain had by now abated to a thin drizzle. I climbed out of the carriage, on to a very imperfect road, and looked at the gipsy encampment on the other side of the common; a dismal collection of carts and caravans, wreathed in grey smoke from several sluggish fires.

The door of Mr Barton's cottage was opened by a young policeman.

'No servants here,' said Blackbeard. 'Barton lived alone, ma'am; the woman next door came a few days a week to do his cleaning and washing and suchlike.'

I was shown into a small sitting room, plainly but decently furnished with a desk and easy chair. There was a bitter smell of smoke, for the policeman had tried – and failed – to build a fire in the cold grate. When Mr Blackbeard left to fetch the old gipsy-woman, I knelt down on the hearthrug to make a proper blaze (people will never use sufficient kindling, but damp coal needs every encouragement) and by the time he returned the fire was burning merrily.

Mrs O'Hare, the gipsy-woman, was as battered, grimed and ragged as anyone who has spent a lifetime out of doors. She was suspicious and cagey and shot glances of pure loathing at Blackbeard, but then she saw the fire and flung herself at it as if embracing an old friend. I believe she would have climbed into it if she could.

'Let's hear it, then,' said Blackbeard, eyeing her keenly. 'Your son reckons you know something.'

'My Pauly never done it.'

'It don't look good for him, not as things stand. If his old mother decides to turn witness, however, all kinds of things are possible.'

'What things?'

'Depends what you've got for me,' said Blackbeard. 'Who knows, eh? You might even save his life!'

She drew back from the fire then, and her eyes, so bright and black in her wrinkled face, were full of calculation.

'Mrs O'Hare,' I put in, as gently as possible, 'you have nothing to fear from telling us the truth; I promise that you will not lose by it.'

'Give me my son first.'

I murmured to Blackbeard, 'Are you able to do that?'

'I can't spring him just like that,' he said. 'But some of those charges might disappear before the next assizes. She knows the game, ma'am.'

Mrs O'Hare considered for a moment, then said, 'I saw Barton on the day of the murder. And I saw her, too.'

'You saw Mrs Somers?' I blurted this out and was all set to protest that she must have been mistaken – but Blackbeard shot me one of his looks and smote me into silence.

'Where did you see them?' he asked.

'Right here,' said Mrs O'Hare. 'Right in this house. And he was a-waiting for her. There wasn't another soul about save for the ribbon-man, and I shooed him away. And then I crept up to look in the window. And the two of them was a-hugging and a-kissing of each other and went at it – right there, on that couch.'

The reader may imagine the horror, the dismay I felt upon hearing this crudely worded statement. Rachel – angelic Rachel – had lied to me.

If this was the answer to my prayers for an alibi, it was hardly a matter for rejoicing – proof that the lovers could not have broken the Sixth Commandment on the fateful day, because they had been too busy breaking the Seventh. Sickened by the sense of their shame, I opted to allow Blackbeard to question the old woman for the details.

She claimed to have seen Mr Barton and Rachel in the early afternoon of the 18th of August.

'I came here to see Mr Barton.'

'To beg off him, I suppose,' said Blackbeard.

'What if I did? Barton's a good man, and I had no food for the children. But afore I could get to the door, I saw the lady running down the lane so I hid myself in the hedge.'

'Are you sure the lady you saw here was Mrs Somers?'

'Yessir.'

'Sure enough to say it in court?'

'Yessir – if you free my Pauly. She was in a blue gown and all in a tremble, and when Barton comes to the door, she says, "I should not have come." And he says, "We are quite alone." And then they went inside.'

I found my voice at last. 'Do you know how long she stayed in the house?'

'I saw Mrs Somers coming out,' said Mrs O'Hare, 'round about evening milking.'

'Do you know where she was going?'

'No, missis. I came to the door here, and Barton gave me a sixpence. Now what about Pauly?'

'If that's your story and you stick to it,' said Blackbeard, 'your Pauly will get off with a five-bob fine.'

She was not satisfied, and not sure she trusted him, but knew it was the best she could expect. Despite Blackbeard saying no money would be necessary, when we left I gave her a shilling; the largest coin in my purse.

'Bless you, missis!'

'I wonder,' I said, on an impulse, 'was it you that spoke to Mr Barton of Joshua Welland?'

She gazed fondly at the coin in her grubby palm. 'Yes, missis.'

'Well now, you may as well get your full bob's-worth,' said Blackbeard.

'You said Joshua was expelled from your encampment on account of a woman,' I said. 'Is this true?'

'He was living with one of our girls,' said Mrs O'Hare. 'And then he ran off with the whore that was his brother's wife.'

I flinched at the word she uttered so carelessly. 'Thank you.'

Inside the carriage, on the jolting, muddy journey back to Oxford, I was too sore at heart to speak for the first mile or so – during which Blackbeard maintained a tactful and even sympathetic silence.

Eventually he said, 'She's not the witness I'd have chosen, ma'am.'

'No, indeed.'

'And it ain't the prettiest story she's telling.'

'No,' I said wretchedly. 'But I have to believe it's the truth.'

'Come along now, Mrs Rodd!' There was a slight mellowing of his face, and a hint of cheerfulness about him.

'I'll get that ribbon-man to back her up, and then we've got your friends a fine alibi.'

'You're quite right, Inspector.' I was suddenly ashamed of my lack of thankfulness when my prayers had been answered so decisively. 'I know that this ghastly revelation could save their lives; I'm simply trying to digest it.'

'Mrs Richards lied to you,' Blackbeard went on. 'She said Mrs Somers was at home all afternoon.'

'I thought she was hiding something,' I said. 'She might think she's helping Rachel. Or she might have been out of the house herself. I must speak with her again; I'm sure she will tell the truth this time. I will put off my return to London for another day. Do we have enough for them to be released without a trial?'

'That's not my area, Mrs Rodd. That's business for the lawyers. If Barton and Mrs Somers are off the hook, it means I must start looking for my murderer somewhere else. And we already know they didn't do away with Gerard Fogle.'

'You will pursue the matter of Goodly's confession, I suppose,' I said. 'Although I fail to see how Mr Fogle could be connected with an old piece of village scandal about a robbery.'

'People confessed things to him,' said Blackbeard. 'There's your connection. Let's say Somers knew something from Goodly, and he went and confessed the same to Fogle. Let's say somebody has a secret, and didn't trust those vicars to keep it.'

Thirty-one

THE RAIN HAD STOPPED by the afternoon, and a faint sun gave the puddles a sheen of silver. I simply could not risk my best black silk on the wet streets, and presented myself to Mrs Watts-Weston in my second-best alpaca. The At-Home was in full swing when I arrived; the drawing room of the Warden's House was packed (mostly with ladies on this occasion, though clergymen made up a sizeable minority).

Mrs Watts-Weston, magnificent in dark-red silk, greeted me with great complacency. 'You are not the main attraction today, Mrs Rodd; only look at my triumph! Nobody else has managed it, he never goes into society – yet there he stands, large as life, eating macaroons!'

I was pleased and surprised to see Mr Daniel Arden; as usual utterly at ease and very elegant in his black coat and grey silk waistcoat.

'If you're looking for Mr Jennings,' said Mrs Watts-Weston, 'I'm afraid you will be disappointed. He is unwell and has gone home to his mother.'

I said I was sorry to hear it and hoped it was nothing serious.

'Oh, he's not at death's door. He ate some bad fish a couple of nights ago – or so he claims, though I must emphasize that no one else in the college was affected. And then yesterday he fainted in the street.'

'Dear me, poor Mr Jennings!'

'Simply dropped down without warning, right in the middle of Queen Street – and a horse trampled his hat. He was carried into the stationer's and upon coming to himself was mortified. I'm sure that's why he scuttled off home.'

From the other side of the room, through a forest of heads, Mr Arden caught my eye and gave me a rather rueful smile.

'Oh dear,' said Mrs Watts-Weston, annoyed. 'He's seen you and now he's coming over, and it's not your turn to talk to him! There are at least three people in front of you.'

'I can drive him away, if you like,' I offered, unable to help smiling at her fondness for organization. 'And I promise not to monopolize him.'

Someone important arrived at that moment, and Mrs Watts-Weston charged off across the room.

'I hoped I would see you here, Mrs Rodd,' said Mr Arden, coming to my side. 'I know hardly anyone, and everyone I meet wishes to interrogate me! I was told this would be a "small" gathering.'

'You are the lion of the moment, Mr Arden,' I said. 'And I'm afraid you will simply have to put up with it.'

'I shouldn't complain. It's high time I contributed a little more to what is called polite society, for the sake of the boys if nothing else.'

(And a possible future wife, I mentally added; was he deliberately preparing himself to propose to Minna Yates? My instincts are very sharp where this sort of thing is concerned.)

'The official reason for my presence is my business with the Warden; we are in the process of setting up a fund to assist the poorest scholars.'

'How splendid!'

'Joshua Welland was our inspiration,' said Mr Arden, looking at me keenly. 'It's not official yet, and I'd be obliged if you would keep it to yourself – but I imagine you have quite a gift for that.'

'I like to think so; you may rely on me to be discreet about this.'

'The Warden feels, as I do, the shameful injustice of the system as it stands. Joshua was a sizar and did not pay for his tuition because he also worked as a college servant. People seem to think that the system is perfectly fair and that prevents them from seeing the reality.' Mr Arden's enthusiasm made his face youthful and handsome. 'Which is that these young men are grievously overworked and underfed, and must sacrifice food and fuel in order to study. My money would award full scholarships, and enable poor men to live decently while they are studying.'

'It is most generous of you,' I said. 'Let there be no more ragged scholars.'

'Speaking of which,' he said, smiling, 'I heard of Joshua Welland's final bequest to Mr Jennings; your scholar was a generous soul and I wish now that I had managed to know him better. My boys still talk about him, though I have told them of his death more than once; the poor little fellows are too innocent of grief to accept it.'

This was neither time nor place to ask him about Hannah Laurie, nor his reasons for adopting her twins. I suspected, however, that he was motivated by nothing more mysterious than love – and loneliness. I changed the subject to Mr Jennings's sudden indisposition.

'I believe I was present at the dinner where Jennings ate the fateful fish,' said Mr Arden. 'He was involved with the discussion about the scholars' fund, and made several very sensible suggestions. I wish him a speedy recovery.'

'I don't think he is gravely ill.'

'By the by, Mrs Rodd, I hear you were at Binstock.'

'Yes, the day before yesterday, and I thought it a very pretty place.'

'I'm guilty of the sin of pride where that village is concerned; when I bought the place it had fallen into a sorry state.'

'I met Mr Yates and his sister.' (I said the name as casually as possible, all the time watching Mr Arden's response; he did not blush, yet a kind of light came into his face, and his attention intensified.) 'I found Miss Yates most charming.'

'More than that,' said Mr Arden quietly. 'I never thought I would meet anyone whose thoughts were in such perfect harmony with my own.' He did not want to speak of her, but could not help it. 'You mustn't think we only meet to talk about politics. Minna – Miss Yates – is practical, and quite fearless in her demands if the cause is good enough. I have worried sometimes that she takes too much upon herself.' (He could not have denied it if he tried: the love shone out of him; I could not help judging these pure, principled lovers alongside Rachel and Mr Barton.)

'Her brother was rather prickly.'

His smile soured. 'Mr Yates does not approve of me. And I don't have time to win the man round.'

'You should be patient,' I said, longing to speak frankly about a possible match. 'The business at Swinford upset him more than he will admit.'

'Now you sound just like her, Mrs Rodd. She's utterly devoted to that brother of hers.' He reached across to take a cup and saucer from a passing servant and hand it to me. 'I beg your pardon, I'm forgetting my manners; would you care for some sugar?'

'No thank you.'

'I'm glad you have met Minna Yates, and wish you might come to know her better – but we're both bound for London very soon. Are you any closer to finding an alibi for your friends?'

'I can tell you – if you swear not to repeat it – that Inspector Blackbeard has made a certain promising discovery.'

He laughed softly. 'You have given me just enough to intrigue, and no more; I'll take the hint and forbear from pestering you with questions.'

'Mr Arden, I did not invite you here to wait upon everybody!' Mrs Watts-Weston appeared at his side, and very firmly took possession of his arm. 'It has been the Dean's turn to meet you for nearly ten minutes!'

Thirty-two

'You'll be happy to hear that I've spoke to that ribbon-peddler, Mrs Rodd. And he backs up the old woman's story.'

'That is good news, Inspector,' I said warmly.

'Assuming we can get Mrs Richards to sing another tune, your friends will be off the hook.'

'I sincerely hope so!'

It was the morning after the At-Home, fine and fresh, with warm sun and a crisp, chill breeze. Mr Blackbeard was escorting me to Hardinsett so that we could give Mrs Richards a chance to change her statement. Despite the breeze, I had opened the window of that plain black police carriage, and was gazing out at hedgerows heavy with blackberries and rosehips.

Mr Blackbeard folded his arms and gave me what I privately called his 'tortoise' look, because it reminded me of a dreadful stuffed tortoise I once saw in the house of a retired colonial bishop; cold and blank of expression, with hard slits for eyes and a long, somehow disapproving mouth.

'You don't look happy,' he said. 'Not like you should.'

'I won't be truly happy until they are freed, and the charges dropped.'

'You're still shocked, ma'am,' said Blackbeard, 'that's the trouble. They're not murderers, for sure – but they're not saints, and that's what you can't abide.'

I was nettled, for there was more than a grain of truth in this. 'It's not merely that they lied to me so boldly, Inspector – although I was very hurt – it's hard for me to understand how two such people could so far forget themselves.'

'Hmm.'

'I beg your pardon?'

'In my opinion, you should go a bit easier on them.'

'Are you saying my judgement is too harsh?'

'It's the sin everybody lies about,' said Blackbeard. 'People go to extraordinary lengths to hide it, like Adam and Eve trying to hide their shame from God. Your friends were so ashamed of what they'd done, they were ready to die for it!'

'No – they were waiting for the true murderer to be found, so that they could return to something like normal life without anyone finding out.'

'Come along now, Mrs Rodd! They are not criminals. All they did was commit a sin that thousands commit every day. They fell in love – you may frown, ma'am, but you'll never stop folks doing that.'

'I don't want to do anything of the kind – even if such a thing were possible. I suppose I assumed Rachel and Mr Barton would have more self-control.' I sighed resignedly, already giving in. 'But how many of us are models of self-control when we fall in love? You are right to rebuke me.'

Now, at last, I let go of my prejudices and all my old fondness for Rachel, and my liking for Henry Barton, came surging back. My mind flashed to practicalities (where should they go if they were released? could they marry? could Mr Barton keep his holy orders?), which I set aside until I could talk to my brother.

'No rebuke intended, ma'am,' said Blackbeard. 'Just trying to cheer you up.'

It was kind of him, but there was little to 'cheer me up' in the appearance of the rectory at Hardinsett. The air of neglect was more pronounced this time – there were weeds growing in the gravelled drive, and all the curtains and shutters were drawn across the windows. It made me sad to remember what a pretty house it had once been.

Mrs Richards was suspicious and very much on her guard when I appeared with Blackbeard at my side. She led us to the kitchen, which was perfectly clean and orderly, but held signs of someone living there; she whipped away a rack of clothes drying before the fire. My instincts come into their own at a time like this, and I was sure she was covering something up; we needed to play on her loyalty to Rachel.

I kept up a soothing stream of chatter, until the three of us were sat down and drinking cups of tea. Mrs Richards stared at Blackbeard, and at myself, and gave me nothing but monosyllables.

'We have had some hopeful news about the trial, Mrs Richards,' I said.

'Oh?'

'We have two witnesses, who are prepared to swear they saw Mrs Somers and Mr Barton upon the day of the murder.' Briefly, and in language more refined than that used by Mrs O'Hare, I related the facts to Mrs Richards.

She was startled and discomfited, and could not meet my eye.

'It's all well and good,' said Blackbeard. 'Trouble is, Mrs Richards, you swore Mrs Somers stayed here all that afternoon. And you also swore that you stayed here, too. Without accusing anybody of telling lies, I do seem to have two different versions of the truth.'

'I know that you want to help Mrs Somers,' I said gently. 'You can help her now by setting the record to rights. I would suggest that you went out somewhere.'

She looked at us then, her dark eyes flicking between our faces. 'I'd prefer to speak with you alone, Mrs Rodd, if I may.'

I expected Mr Blackbeard to object, but he stood up at once and puzzled me by letting out a dry snivel, indicative of amusement, as he left the room.

'This is awkward, ma'am,' said Mrs Richards (very red about the face). 'I did leave the house that day – I thought Mrs Somers was asleep in her chamber, so I slipped out to – to see a friend.'

'I see.' (I did not.) 'When was this, exactly?'

'It was directly after I spoke to the ribbon-man at the back door. The other servants were out on account of their half-day. It was in the early part of the afternoon.'

'At what time did you return?'

'Round about sunset.'

'You were away for a long time,' I said. 'Was Mrs Somers here when you returned?'

'She – she left her bedchamber and came downstairs about twenty minutes after.'

'Can you say where you were?'

'No,' said Mrs Richards. 'What I mean is – no disrespect to you, ma'am – I'd much rather not.'

'You know I will be as discreet as possible.'

She looked me in the eye at last. 'Nobody can know about it. My friend can't be seen with me. On account of his wife.'

'Oh.' I understood at last, and had an effort to keep my voice level, but – really! Was everyone in the entire world, even sensible Mrs Richards, enjoying an illicit romance?

'His name's Robert Melks,' said Mrs Richards. 'He has a farm at Uppershot, two miles along the Swinford road, and his wife ran off three years ago. They didn't have any children. We weren't harming anybody.'

'I'm sure you were not,' I said quickly. 'And the rights and wrongs of it are none of my business. I'm very grateful to you for your honesty.'

'But you can't ask Melks to back me up, ma'am, or the whole world will know.'

'Did anyone else see you in that neighbourhood?'

'I was doing my best *not* to be seen!' said Mrs Richards. 'Dinah Hatch from the inn – I ran into her when I passed by Burnt House Lane just outside Uppershot. She'll say she saw me. And Mr Daniel Arden came by on horseback and gave me a greeting.'

'Oh, if Mr Arden is able to place you away from the rectory at that time, we may be able to spare Mr Melks.'

I thanked her sincerely, and left with a lighter heart, to report to Mr Blackbeard in the carriage. 'She was dreadfully ashamed,' I told him. 'And I don't wonder!'

'Didn't I say, ma'am?' was his response. 'It's the sin everybody lies about.'

'I'm beginning to think you are right, Inspector. This case will broaden my mind, if nothing else. Frankly, the more I consider the facts of Mrs Richards's dalliance, the less I am inclined to condemn her for it. As she said, she was harming nobody; the man's wife deserted him.'

'It's a pity Mrs Somers don't have the same excuse,' said Blackbeard. 'She was carrying on right under her husband's nose. I'm afraid no jury's going to love her for it.'

I could not reply, for my mind veered back to the conversation I had with Rachel about her marriage. She had allowed me to believe that their separate bedchambers were a recent arrangement. I had failed to understand what she was really trying to tell me – which was that Arthur had never fulfilled his duties in that area and, in the strictest sense, Rachel had never had a husband to deceive.

Thirty-three

O<small>N THE FOLLOWING DAY</small>, I finally managed to leave Oxford. I might have been sorrier to say goodbye to this most beautiful of cities if the weather had not been so gusty and damp and generally disagreeable.

'Mrs Rodd!'

I had been thinking only of my luggage, and had not noticed Mr Yates and his sister in the crowd on the station platform.

'This is a piece of good fortune,' said Mr Yates. 'I was just looking out for someone to keep an eye on Minna – I'm forced to send her to London all alone, and it would be a weight off my mind to know that she has a companion.'

'Charley, you mustn't worry so!' Miss Yates touched his arm. 'Don't mind him, Mrs Rodd; he doesn't mean to bother you.'

I replied, quickly and sincerely, that I would be glad to have Miss Yates's company on the journey. Her brother, greatly relieved, settled us in a very comfortable First Class compartment, which we had to ourselves.

'I'm going to see a doctor,' Miss Yates told me, once we were under way and rushing through the fields. 'A very important and expensive doctor, because Charles cannot stop himself fretting about my health.'

'Have you been ill, Miss Yates?'

'Not at all! I often catch cold in the winter, otherwise I'm perfectly healthy. I would far rather save the money.'

'London is hardly a healthy place for you.'

'I'll be staying with our great-aunt; she has a villa in Putney, well out of the smoke.'

We produced the books we had brought for the journey. I was reading a volume of Gerard Fogle's *Collected Sermons*, in the hopes of finding either spiritual refreshment or some little thing that gave a clue to his murder (as yet I had found neither). Miss Yates read a small, shabby book with great attention and I covertly studied her; though she did not appear to be ill, I could see why her brother worried about her health. She was very pale and transparently thin; I drifted into wondering if Mr Yates was able to take her to Italy or the South of France, to spare her another English winter.

My book slipped from my hands to the floor. Miss Yates picked it up and handed it back to me with a shy smile. 'Mr Fogle's sermons! What do you make of them?'

'Not much, I'm afraid. Too many roses and lilies for my taste. I know this book has been enormously influential, but have managed to avoid it up to now.'

'It's very well-known to me,' said Miss Yates. 'Charles has often read it aloud to me; there is much that I don't understand, but a great sense of the Beauty of Holiness.'

'How well did you know Mr Fogle?'

'Oh, I don't claim to have known him; I only met him once, when he came to visit my brother. And I was too much in awe of him to do anything more than shake his hand.'

'Your brother knew him much better,' I suggested.

'As well as anyone,' said Miss Yates. 'On the very night before his death, Charley prayed with Father Fogle in his bedchamber – which made his discovery next morning yet more frightful.'

'Poor man, I can quite imagine.'

'He was very agitated that day.' She paused and then said in a rush, 'That was my fault.'

'Yours, Miss Yates?'

'I don't see any harm in telling you, for I know you will keep it to yourself. Charley had come fresh from a dispute with Mr Arden.'

'Were you the cause of this dispute?'

'Indirectly, yes,' said Miss Yates. 'Mr Arden had given me a certain book, of which my brother disapproved.'

'And did you know of his disapproval?'

'Well – yes.' Her thin skin flushed painfully. 'When he found me reading it, he made me promise to send it straight back. But I did not keep my promise, as you see – for this is that very book.' She held the book out to me; I opened it to discover that it was *Rights of Man*, by Thomas Paine.

(I will admit that I was not as shocked as perhaps I ought to have been, for I had my own guilty history with this book; when I was a girl I heard my dear father preach a withering sermon against it, and that made me so curious that I read it at the first opportunity when I discovered a copy hidden in the sewing-basket of a friend's governess.)

'It is Mr Arden's own copy. He meant no harm – but Charley was very angry.'

'Has he ever read it himself?'

'Never.'

'I have read *Rights of Man*, Miss Yates; I found the writing to be crudely sensational, but I thought parts of the argument highly sensible and just – and perfectly compatible with a religious point of view.'

'Just what Mr Arden says!' All of a sudden, her pale face was radiant. 'He simply wished me to understand him more fully, and was surprised that my brother was so angry.'

'And their disagreement took place on the day of Mr Fogle's murder?'

'It was only a disagreement on Charley's side; Mr Arden is a great believer in the soft answer that turneth away wrath.'

'Most sensible,' I said. 'I'm sure I ought to disapprove of your deceit, but I cannot approve of your brother telling you what you may or may not read.'

'He is only trying to protect me, Mrs Rodd – as he promised our father he would.'

I decided to change the subject by opening my basket of provisions and persuading my companion to share them with me. Later, when she had fallen asleep, I fell into dreaming of a match between Minna Yates and Daniel Arden, and the good they could do together.

Upon our arrival in London, Miss Yates was claimed by a manservant of respectable appearance and I took a cab to Hampstead, where dear Mary welcomed me with a home-coming feast of sliced ham, bread-and-butter, pound cake and a fragrant pot of my favourite Orange Pekoe tea.

'And I mustn't forget to tell you, ma'am,' said Mrs Bentley, 'Mr Tyson looked in this afternoon. He's picking you up in his carriage tomorrow morning first thing.'

I fought off yet another yawn. 'Oh, dear – I was hoping to rest tomorrow! Did he say why?'

Mrs Bentley, who had a soft spot for Fred, chuckled fondly. 'He said he needed you to stop him throwing Mr Patrick Flint out of the nearest window.'

Thirty-four

'**I** FAIL TO SEE WHY Mrs Rodd is here,' growled Mr Flint. 'It is thoroughly improper.'

'Pish!' said Fred. 'The only "improper" element in this room is you, Flinty. I'm here to stop you preaching one of your hellfire sermons, or we'll never get to the truth of the thing. I brought my sister because tact is called for and you don't have a tactful bone in your body.'

It was early in the morning; my brother's carriage had pulled up in Well Walk before I had properly digested my porridge, to bring me to Newgate Prison. We were not in the governor's office on this occasion, but a large room of whitewashed brick, lit by a jet of gas and one high window. It was bare and echoing, furnished with a plain deal table and a few chairs. Fred and I sat at the table; Mr Flint roved about the room like a thunderstorm.

'Tact!' He spat the word out contemptuously. 'The whole rigmarole sickens me! He's a liar, he's a libertine – he has disgraced his priesthood!'

'But he hasn't broken the law,' said Fred. 'Do bear that in mind.' He brushed a few stray crumbs from the front of his waistcoat (he had spent the entire journey eating). 'The jury must be made to see that this encounter – sordid as it may be – is proof that Barton could not have committed the murder, the only matter for which he is on trial. Morality doesn't come into it.'

'That's where we differ,' said Mr Flint coldly. 'I believe morality comes into everything.'

'Indeed it does,' I put in quickly. 'I quite understand your feelings, Mr Flint, for I was dreadfully shocked when I first heard Mrs O'Hare's story. If we can't set aside our moral judgements, however, we'll get nowhere.'

'I cannot defend a man I despise.'

This was very bad and I looked at Fred in dismay.

'Fear not, my dear,' my brother said, not in the least put out, 'I'll bring him round.'

Mr Flint had no chance to protest, for the door opened – with a great rattling of locks, as if any of us could forget we were inside a prison – and Mr Barton entered, with a uniformed warder. Once more I was struck by how out of place he looked here; this handsome young clergyman in his black suit and white collar, still apparently unaffected by his imprisonment.

The warder retreated to a chair beside the door. Mr Barton greeted us all very courteously and sat down at the table. Mr Flint remained standing.

'And so the wall is breached at last!' said my brother. 'We have two witnesses who saw you and Mrs Somers on the day of the murder. As I said in the little note I sent you, it's all out now.'

The young man reddened and squared his shoulders. 'I won't admit to anything that might hurt Mrs Somers.'

'The truth can only help her now,' I said, as persuasively as I could manage in Flint's glowering presence. 'We haven't come here to condemn you.'

He held my gaze defiantly for a moment, then looked away with a sigh of resignation. 'You couldn't condemn me as heartily as I condemn myself, Mrs Rodd. I'm ashamed to remember that I accused poor Arthur Somers of weakness in the face of temptation. My own behaviour was a thousand times worse.'

'During my visit to Hardinsett last summer,' I said, 'I noticed that you were in love with Mrs Somers; was the Haymaking Supper the first time you declared yourself? And I wish you would explain what made Arthur so angry with you that he knocked you down.'

'And why he called you "Judas",' said Fred, eyeing him keenly.

'No mystery there!' snapped Mr Flint. 'You betrayed him by falling in love with his wife!'

There was a spell of silence, during which I was interested to watch Mr Barton's face. We had him cornered and he knew it, yet I saw a spark of defiance.

'I don't deny that I fell in love with Mrs Somers – what would be the point?' he said. 'Yes, I love her. Yes, I would happily die for her. She is an angel.'

Mr Flint snorted angrily.

'Did I fall in love with her at first sight? No, I did not.' Mr Barton, clearly uncomfortable, reddened, but carried on. 'When I took up my post as Arthur's curate, two years ago, I thought his wife was very beautiful and very kind – but love never entered my head. Never! May heaven be my witness, Mrs Rodd, my work in the parish was my only concern. As someone I once counted among my friends, I'm particularly anxious that you should know everything – not that I'm making excuses—'

'I am still your friend, Mr Barton,' I said, as gently as possible (and turning my back on Flint). 'Let us have the whole story at last.'

'It's outrageously indelicate,' said Mr Barton. 'I know you are broad-minded; I hope you won't be offended. I have to touch on … certain things.'

'I'm beyond offence, Mr Barton,' I told him sincerely. 'When I first came to Hardinsett, I decided you were in love with Rachel Somers, but had not yet admitted as much to yourself. Was that right?'

He blushed until his eyes watered. 'Pretty much.'

'And was the Haymaking Supper the start of it all?'

'Not quite. You were present. It was when Ra— – Mrs Somers – was attacked by that blackmailing villain. That's when I knew that I was in love with her. I was bitterly ashamed of the fact, and did my best to overcome my sinful emotions. But we – but I – honestly didn't intend—'

(Flint took his watch from his pocket and glared at it; my brother quelled him with the awful frown he sometimes used in court in the process of destroying a witness.)

'She came to me asking about the blackmail – begging me to tell her why Somers was so anxious. She was weeping. It seemed only natural to take her in my arms.'

'And then it was only natural that her husband would call you "Judas" when he caught you at it,' said Fred. 'That much is obvious.'

'Not to me,' I said, thinking of everything I had observed during my visit, and suddenly determined to get at the truth. 'Mr Barton, what was the great spiritual crisis that drove Arthur to Swinford?'

'This is completely beside the point,' interrupted Mr Flint. 'You and Mrs Somers were lovers; now that is established, the jury will have every reason to think you lied about everything else – I ask you again, Tyson: how am I to defend such a man?'

Mr Barton's temper broke at last; he leapt to his feet and his voice had the same quiet intensity I had overheard at Hardinsett. 'Very well, you may have the true reason that Arthur struck me – it was nothing to do with his wife – he claimed that he was in love with me!'

'Good grief!' muttered Fred. 'You can't say things like that, my boy.'

'Not even when I'm about to be hanged for murder? I'm sick of saying nothing. Must we die because something is unmentionable? Arthur struck me because he was jealous – because I had given my heart to Rachel and not to him – now, how will that look in the *Morning Post*? Does this give me yet another motive for murder? I'm as good as dead – she's all I care about now.'

As soon as the words were uttered, I remembered certain things I had witnessed last summer and knew Mr Barton spoke the truth.

'I must be blunt, Mr Barton,' I said. 'I can think of no polite way to phrase this. Was her maidenhood intact?'

He had been red in the face and now he turned white. He nodded.

'After ten years of marriage!' Fred, the father of eleven, could scarcely imagine such a thing. 'Never once?'

'Somers admitted it to me himself,' said Mr Barton, very quiet. 'The situation made him miserable, for he loved his wife deeply, and really longed to be a husband to her in the truest sense. That's why he did all that praying at Swinford.'

'Dear me, you're a victim of the most monstrous bad luck!' Fred shook his head and pulled from his pocket the inevitable flask of spirits. 'If Somers hadn't got himself murdered, none of this would've seen the light of day – the vicar and his wife both in love with the curate!'

'For pity's sake, Tyson, how can you treat this lightly?' Mr Flint burst out. 'You seem to imagine this disgraceful story will somehow clear Barton's name, when it exposes him as an adulterer!'

'I beg your pardon for my flippancy,' said Fred. 'Naturally, we'll dress it up for the jury; the whole matter of the blackmail, and Somers's fondness for getting himself into trouble at horse fairs, will win them over. Adultery's a small thing – even an understandable thing – when you set it alongside such a great unmentionable.'

'Will that really be necessary?' The prospect of such a scandal absolutely sickened me. 'Must you make out that poor Arthur was a villain?'

'This is precisely what I was trying to avoid,' said Mr Barton. 'If this comes out it will make people forget how good he was – like that line in Shakespeare – the evil lives on while the good is oft interred with their bones. Or something like that.' He paused for a moment. 'Look here, Flint, I know I ought to have told you everything when we first met, and I'm sorry for it, but it was only another of my clumsy attempts to protect the woman I love. As far as I'm concerned, we are man and wife – and I would be glad to die for her. But if you want to drop me, I'll understand.'

'Well, I don't,' said Mr Flint, who had listened to this in perfect stillness and silence. 'I have no intention of "dropping" you.'

'Thank you,' said Mr Barton.

'Phew!' said Fred. 'You had me worried; I won't ask what prompted this rare about-face.'

'It's because I respect a man who defends those he loves,' said Mr Flint, with an inward expression that made me wonder if he could be recalling something about his lost wife. 'And so will the jury, by the time I'm done with them.'

'Splendid!' My brother beamed around at us all. 'Now, before we're chucked out of here, is there anything you need?'

'You're very kind,' said Mr Barton, with a half-smile. 'I'm very well-off for comforts, however; my situation and the surrounding publicity has won me many admirers, and complete strangers have showered me with gifts. I've had flowers, bottles of ink – someone even sent a boiled lobster.'

'Well then, is there anything I can do for you?'

'If I'm condemned,' said Mr Barton, 'if we are both condemned ... I wish to marry Mrs Somers before I face my maker.'

There was a silence amongst us, during which I sent up a quick prayer for the two unfortunate lovers.

'We'll cross that bridge when we come to it, my boy, and we're not there yet.' My brother hated to admit the slightest possibility of defeat. 'The police will find the real culprit – any day now!'

Thirty-five

'I NEARLY REFUSED TO SEE you, Mrs Rodd,' said Rachel. 'If you know everything, as your brother says, you will know how wicked I have been.'

I see her now, her face palely composed in the shadow of that hideous widow's cap, her slight figure framed by the long rain-spotted window. She was lodged with a Mrs Dunster, widow of a clergyman (we have all sorts of uses), in a narrow house that overlooked a small, out-of-the-way city square.

'My dear,' I said, 'I have not come to scold you; won't you sit beside me?'

Rachel sat down at the other end of the hard, shabby sofa. 'Have you seen him?'

'If you mean Henry Barton, I visited him this morning.'

'How is he?'

'In good health,' I said. 'And in reasonable spirits; his courage is a thing to behold.'

'When I heard that the old woman had seen us – oh, the mortification! This is Heaven's punishment, and it is all my fault!'

'Mr Barton says it's his fault,' I said. 'We'll say you are both equally at fault and leave it there.'

She gave me a faint smile. 'I was especially worried about what you would think of me, Mrs Rodd, your standards being so high.'

'And my mind being so narrow!' (I was a little hurt to be cast in this forbidding role.) 'Let me assure you, however, that my mind has lately broadened to such an extent that you could now drive a coach through it. We'll get on much better if we forget about moral judgements and concentrate upon facts. I would be interested to know about Arthur's state of mind, in the days leading up to the crime.'

Rachel's gaze moved wistfully to the window. 'It's like recalling another world!'

'Did anything strike you as odd, or unusual?'

'Not really.'

'I heard that the confession-business made him anxious,' I said.

She nodded.

'Rachel, if he told you anything about it, I implore you to tell me!'

'Arthur did not confide that sort of thing; you saw how serious he was about the sanctity of confession.'

'Mr Arden claims that he met Arthur two days before the murder, at the old limekiln; did he mention it to you?'

'No – how odd!' Rachel became more animated. 'Arthur would certainly have told me; Mr Arden fascinated him.'

'Mr Arden has volunteered to me, more than once, how he liked Arthur.'

'Oh? I don't think there was much liking on Arthur's side,' said Rachel. 'He gave the man the respect he was due and no more.'

'Perhaps Mr Arden got his dates muddled,' I said. 'Or perhaps I misunderstood him. Do you recall anything else about those last few days?'

'No – that is, I remember that the weather was very warm and close, which made everyone short-tempered.' Her eyes flooded with tears. 'That might be one reason why Henry and I did what we did, but I'm not trying to make excuses for us.'

'When did the two of you arrange that meeting at Millings Cross?'

'The day before – oh, of course we knew it was wicked of us, and a dreadful sin – and of course I don't expect you to believe me when I say I couldn't help it – and yet I felt helpless, utterly unable to stop myself – and worse – utterly unwilling!' The tears streamed down her white cheeks. 'And now we are to die for it!'

'No, no, my dear—'

'I can't describe the force of it – the power – after I had resigned myself – or thought I had – to never being touched, never kissed! Mrs Rodd, you cannot imagine the sadness of my honeymoon!'

'My dear!' My heart ached for her; no, I could not imagine it; I remembered the intense happiness of my own honeymoon and was dismayed to think that I was at least partly to blame for this most ill-assorted match. 'Keep up your courage; we will find the truth!'

'Two letters for you, ma'am,' said Mrs Bentley, when I got home to Hampstead late that afternoon. 'You go and change your gown and then you can read them by the fire with a nice bit of toasted cheese.'

In these comfortable conditions I settled down to read my letters about twenty minutes later. The first was in the small, tight hand of Cousin Wilfred.

Dear Cousin Laetitia,

I read your letter with great interest and your request pricked my conscience, for I remembered that I never properly acknowledged the very generous donation of ten pounds, fifteen shillings and eight-pence that you sent last year after your charity bazaar. I fear my thanks were swept away by the disagreement I had with your brother.

You are asking me to cast my mind back a very long time, to when I was newly arrived at the Mission. The name of Sir Christopher Warrender meant nothing to me at first, until I recalled, all of a sudden, the hue and cry created by his aunt. She or her agents made enquiries here, knowing how many people take refuge with us.

As for 'Dan Smith', however, I did recall someone of that name, from around that time. He was very young, scarcely out of child-hood, and with a singular air of self-possession that set him apart from the other men. Youthful as he was, he had a good sum of money – about fifty pounds – and he had already secured passage on a ship (I don't know which ship, or where it was bound). He could read and write, and gave me the impression that he had received some kind of education.

The Mission, as you know, besides sheltering the very poor (and the very drunk), provides a decent lodging for sailors and other tran-sients, at a very low cost. Upon arrival here, these men surrender any valuables, so that I can put them in the safe. I write the sum down in the ledger, and the man either signs his name or – far more common – makes his mark.

Dan Smith particularly sticks in my mind because he left us with a most extraordinary donation of a golden guinea; such a sum that I hardly liked to accept, and even wondered if the boy was a little soft in the head. But he assured me, with great sincerity, that he wanted his last act in his native land to be one of charity. He went on his way and I have never heard of him since. I hope this information is helpful.

You and Frederick are always in my prayers. Please be assured that I have forgiven Frederick for his intemperate and unfeeling remarks last time we met, when I had simply suggested that the number of his offspring indicated an inability to subdue certain appetites.

Yours affectionately,

Cousin Wilfred

Setting aside that last paragraph (Fred had told me of the regrettable incident), Cousin Wilfred's letter interested me very much. Here was Dan Smith, but we had been seeking a ploughboy in the company of a gentleman, and this Dan Smith was alone.

Now my mind made one of its leaps, which were often so annoying to Inspector Blackbeard.

The description made me think irresistibly of Daniel Arden; it was the guinea that did it. Mr Arden was known to have left the country at around the time of Sir Christopher's disappearance. Why could it not be him? I was eager to speak to him again; I had never asked him about his youth in any detail.

Were Mr Arden and the fabled 'Dan Smith' one and the same?

If so, he must have known Warrender.

And what about that money?

The questions were positively swarming now. I decided to call at Mr Arden's hotel at the earliest opportunity, and to leave an urgent message if he was not there.

The other letter, in a hand I did not recognize, was from Mr Jennings's mother:

Dear Mrs Rodd,

You were kind enough to write to my son expressing concern for his health. Silas is unable to reply himself; the doctor has forbidden him all reading and writing. Although he is not seriously ill in body, his nerves are suffering greatly, for which I blame far too much study. I am assured that a few weeks of complete rest will restore him.

Yours respectfully,

Agnes Jennings

No mention of the bad fish – that was my first thought. Mr Jennings was suffering from 'nerves', the cover-all word that was used for anything from dangerous insanity to mild laziness. Wondering if something – someone – had frightened him away, I pushed him to the back of my mind.

As things turned out, he did not stay there for long.

Thirty-six

THE FOLLOWING DAY, WHICH was to be so momentous, dawned bright and clear. In the normal way of things, I was perfectly able to travel across the city either on foot or by public omnibus. Today, however, my best black silk was required yet again (I apologize to the reader for 'harping on' about that precious dress, but it was my only good one, and its maintenance took up a great deal of our time).

'It's still wet underfoot, ma'am,' said Mrs Bentley. 'You can't risk those shoes.'

'I suppose not, but my boots won't do in Piccadilly.'

'You'll just have to take a cab, and that's all there is to it.'

She was quite right; I resigned myself to the extravagance and gave the little boy next door a penny to fetch me a cab from the nearest stand. I was going to call on Daniel Arden, for Cousin Wilfred's letter had kept me awake half the night, and I wanted to speak to him before I said anything to Inspector Blackbeard.

Stoppard's Hotel, in Half Moon Street, was as discreet in its appearance as a private house and much favoured by rich foreigners (the noble Portuguese girls I took round the Great Exhibition had been staying there). The door was opened by a haughty young footman, who showed me into a beautifully appointed public drawing room which had that hush I always associate with the houses of the very wealthy, as if money muffled the noises of the vulgar outside world.

'Mrs Rodd, you have a delightful habit of surprising me!' Mr Arden came hurriedly into the room, attired in a black riding coat and high black boots. His face, which had been anxious, cleared and he smiled as he shook my hand. 'I have been out riding with the swells on Rotten Row and very dull I found it; I could swear that my horse yawned.'

'I beg your pardon for descending on you at ten in the morning,' I said. 'I know it is considered very early in this part of town.'

'You and I still keep to our country hours, Mrs Rodd! How may I help you?'

It struck me that he looked youthful, even dashing, and Minna Yates flashed into my mind; was he aware that she was in London?

'I wanted to hear your opinion of a certain letter,' I said. 'From the Reverend Wilfred Bone.'

'Should I know him?'

'That remains to be seen; it might be nothing at all. Mr Bone lives in Plymouth.'

'Ah.' Though his manner remained casual, I knew he was on his guard. 'Yes, to be sure; you are pursuing the ghost of Warrender, according to the tallest stories.'

'Wilfred Bone is in charge of the Seamen's Mission in Union Street. He was replying to my enquiry about a youth by the name of Dan Smith.'

'I see.' Mr Arden sighed, and then puzzled me by laughing softly to himself. 'I take it Bone is one of your famous clerical connections.'

'My cousin,' I said. 'On my mother's side.'

'Give me ten minutes to change my clothes; I'll have them send in some coffee, if that is agreeable to you.'

It was highly agreeable; the coffee arrived quickly and was excellent. Mr Arden returned a very short time later, and I had that sense of being wrapped in his attention, so deep was his concentration when I read him my cousin's letter.

He was silent afterwards and I let the silence stretch into minutes.

'You are Dan Smith,' I said boldly. 'I wonder that nobody recognized you when you came home.'

'Dan Smith was a boy of fourteen when he left,' said Mr Arden. 'A small and scrawny imp, who could easily have passed for a child of ten. I waited for someone to recognize me, and no one did, though I made no secret of the fact that I had grown up in that part of the country. Without actually telling lies, I have been less than truthful.'

'Where were you born, Mr Arden?'

'In Binstock – more accurately, in a ditch nearby. My mother's name was Ellen Smith. She was the daughter of a farm worker, and her family disowned her for being with child. I can't claim to remember her, for she died when I was very young.'

'Do you know who your father was?'

'There are no official records, but none were needed. It was widely known that my father was a Frenchman, driven into exile by the Revolution. He earned his bread as a tutor of French and dancing, and vanished before I was born. Naturally I made enquiries about him when I returned to this part of the country, but he had left barely a trace behind him. Slightly to my disappointment, he was not an aristocrat, but a minor clerk in one of the palaces.'

'My cousin thought you'd had an education,' I said. 'How did you come by such a thing?'

'I made the acquaintance of a gentleman who taught me to read and write, and encouraged me to explore his library – the remnants of it, anyway.'

'Was that Sir Christopher Warrender?'

'Yes.'

'It was kind of him to teach you.'

'I paid a heavy price for it,' said Mr Arden, his face unreadable. 'Not with money, but another currency entirely – all that I had, in fact.'

He watched me steadily, allowing this dark and troubling information to sink in, and knowing full well that I would not pursue it.

'He was a scoundrel,' said Mr Arden, eyeing me with steady calm. 'Doubly so because he was born with every advantage, and laid waste to all that Heaven had granted him. The old squire was by all accounts a very decent and godly man. Sir Christopher drank heavily and by the time he disappeared, as I remember it, he was a sorry, shambling figure.'

'There is a story that the two of you ran off to Plymouth together.'

'We did not,' said Mr Arden. 'I was quite alone.'

'What about the money – so vast a sum for a boy like Dan Smith? Where did you get it?'

'You asked me what sins I confessed to Jacob Welland, when we both thought we were dying. I stole that money.'

'From Sir Christopher?'

'Yes – indirectly.'

'How do you mean?'

Mr Arden stood up to tug at the bell-pull beside the fireplace. 'It's not an easy subject to talk about; I need the assistance of food and wine and hope you have time to share it with me.'

I assured him that I had all the time in the world; though I was impatient to hear his version of events, I was not going to turn down the hospitality of the best hotel in London. The waiter arrived and, though it was not yet noon, Mr Arden ordered wine, cold game pie and a plate of ratafia cakes. It was impossible to talk openly when a seeming regiment of starched waiters descended on us with plates and cutlery.

'Well, here it is, at last!' He was affable, almost cheerful when we were once more alone together. 'The truth behind my great atonement, Mrs Rodd. Everything that I own, everything good that I have built, has its origins in the crime that I committed thirty years ago. I stole something – not from Sir Christopher, but from the old lady.'

'A necklace?'

'Ah – you know of the necklace.'

'I spoke to a Mrs Belling, formerly Miss Price.'

'Price?'

'Lady Tremlett's companion.'

'Of course, of course!' murmured Mr Arden, his quick dark eyes fixed upon me. 'She comes back to me now.'

Briefly, I told him everything I had heard from Mrs Belling; he listened politely and with the faintest spark of humour.

'She was half-right,' was his comment when I had finished. 'It was all Sir Christopher's idea – he had seen his aunt hiding the jewels in the bottom of her work-box. But she kept it under her bed and was the type to sleep with one eye open; he would've woken her in a moment with his blundering and cursing. Whereas I was as supple and quick as a monkey. I took the necklace, waited for him to drink himself insensible and then ran off.'

'Was it you that sold it for a hundred pounds?'

'I sold it – but actually for forty pounds.'

'Now you must satisfy my curiosity; "Dan Smith" was one of the names given to me by old Mrs Goodly; was it you who gave Goodly the twenty pounds in gold?'

'I gave the man nothing,' said Mr Arden.

'But you knew him?'

'I did.'

'The gold was discovered,' I said, watching him closely, 'when the cottage was pulled down.'

He was quiet for a moment, and then he observed, 'I always wondered what he did with it.'

'Where did it come from, if you didn't give it to him?'

'He stole it from me,' said Mr Arden. 'He heard of my transaction at the horse fair and waylaid me on the way home; he was a burly fellow and I was easily overpowered. Fortunately I had tied the money up in two handkerchiefs and he only got one of them.'

'Do you know why he never spent any of it?'

'I have no idea; perhaps such a large sum was simply too much for his mind to take in.'

'You had fifty pounds when you arrived at the Mission; where did the rest come from?'

He was distantly amused. 'I'm afraid you've hit upon another of my sins, Mrs Rodd. Before I got to Plymouth, I replenished my coffers by picking pockets at the races.'

'How did you make so much?'

'I had a natural talent for picking pockets,' said Mr Arden with a half-smile. 'And also quite a talent for coercing other boys into stealing on my behalf. Now you are shocked.'

'I must admit that I am, a little!'

'I was a thoroughly bad lot, and if I am able to speak of my past without blushing it's not due to a lack of shame on my part. My whole life since Desolacion has been one long act of contrition. Before you condemn me for any of my actions, Mrs Rodd, I urge you to consider the end result.'

'No one disputes the good you have done.'

'Does a good action count for less when it springs from a bad one?'

'I – I really couldn't say.' I was not prepared for philosophy, and was flustered. 'It sounds suspiciously like trying to strike bargains with the Almighty – though I'm sure He blesses any act of true repentance.'

'Precisely!' Mr Arden's eagerness made his face boyish. 'I'm not in the business of saving my own soul; it is more that I am constantly aware of my duty to wash away the stains my sins have left upon the world; everything I took must be given back a hundredfold!'

'That is right and good,' I said. 'I am grateful for your candour, Mr Arden – especially when you know that I am bound to pass this on to Inspector Blackbeard.'

'If he wants to arrest me for my ancient crimes, so be it.'

'After all this time, I think he'll be inclined to let sleeping dogs lie.' I could say this with some conviction; Arden had not given me anything 'hard' enough to interest Blackbeard.

'I must not be afraid of the truth,' said Mr Arden, intense and serious. 'I know that Barton and Mrs Somers are not murderers; their innocent faces haunt my dreams.'

'And mine!'

'I am praying for them both, Mrs Rodd.'

'The poor souls are being wondrously brave,' I said. 'Their circumstances have been made a little easier by the fact that all the public attention has now turned to Swinford.'

'Indeed.'

I could not resist. 'I heard that you were in that vicinity, on the day of Mr Fogle's murder.'

'Me?' He was visibly startled, though still smiling. 'Where on earth did you hear that?'

'From Miss Yates, of course; I assume that you know she is in town.'

'Well – yes.'

'She must have mentioned that we travelled together. I'm sure the two of you have met since we arrived, and I beg you not to think I'm condemning you for it.'

'We have been underhand,' said Mr Arden. 'Her brother rather forced her into that position when he declared that she was forbidden any contact with me. She told me that you and she had talked about a certain book, also "forbidden".'

'Mr Yates is devoted to Minna,' I said. 'Possibly a little over-protective; I doubt he can afford the opinion of a West End doctor.'

'She has some slight irregularity of the pulse,' said Mr Arden. 'I rode beside her carriage yesterday, while she was driving through the park. She had just seen a famous specialist who assured her that her condition is not serious, and dismissed her with the usual prescription for port wine and rest.'

'Very sensible advice,' I said, 'though anyone might have given it free of charge.'

'And as they all do, he recommended a move to a warmer climate.'

'I'm afraid that would be beyond their means.'

'I would give anything—' Mr Arden leant forward, eager and intense. 'Anything – if I could carry her off to Nice or Florence.'

'Have you visited her in Putney?'

'I have not, for she made a solemn promise to her brother that she and I would not meet there. I took a short ride alongside her carriage, and that is all. We were in a public place where anyone might have seen us.' He paused and shot me a wary look. 'You once asked me, Mrs Rodd, if I were considering marriage, and I think you and I understood one another very well on that occasion. You know where my heart lies.'

'I believe I do,' I said. 'When you and Miss Yates met on the day of Mr Fogle's murder, was it by accident or design?'

'We had arranged it in advance,' said Mr Arden. 'Miss Yates was attending a tea party at a house named The Beeches, a big place a few miles from Swinford. We met, supposedly by chance, in the middle of the village – and had the misfortune to run into Charles Yates, who made a scene that hurt his sister's feelings very much.'

'Oh, dear!'

'I managed to keep hold of my temper,' said Mr Arden. 'As I generally do. Yates is a young man, and has a tendency to hysteria – I should not like him to suffer for it. The merciful shall obtain mercy, and the Lord's justice shall be done.'

My mouth was full of cake and I could not say 'Amen'.

Thirty-seven

OUR MEETING ENDED CORDIALLY, with Mr Arden insisting that I should be conveyed home to Hampstead in one of the hotel's private carriages. There was no time to mull over the strange story he had told me, for I was due at a charitable tea party near to the Spaniards Inn, and barely had time to draw breath before I set out again. I scribbled a very hasty account to Mr Blackbeard – *Dan Smith and Daniel Arden are one and the same* – very curious to know what he would do with the information.

Darkness had fallen when I finally returned to Well Walk. I was very tired after such a busy day, and thinking only of removing my painful second-best shoes. Fate had other ideas, however; to my great surprise, an anonymous black carriage was waiting outside my house.

'Mr Blackbeard sent it over, about half an hour ago,' said Mrs Bentley. 'He's after you to go off somewhere right away.' She took a scrap of folded paper from the pocket of her apron and held it out to me.

Dear Mrs Rodd, I wd be obliged for you to come into town, respectfully, T. Blackbeard.

My exhaustion melted away at once, for I could smell adventure in the air and possibly danger, and the excitement of driving into the heart of the city at night made my blood fizz and sparkle.

The cab took me back to the fashionable quarter that I had visited this morning. I was set down on the shabbier side of Hyde Park, close to where the old gallows had been at Tyburn. The streets here were well-lit and still bustling with traffic.

'This is good of you, Mrs Rodd.' The inspector came out to the pavement to meet me, and handed me out of the cab with his usual old-fashioned gallantry. 'Something odd has turned up, ma'am.'

'Did you receive the letter I sent you this afternoon?'

'Letter? Oh, yes ma'am, and very interesting it was too. But this is something else. And I must admit, I can't make head or tail of it.'

'I'm always glad to assist, Mr Blackbeard; where have you brought me?'

'This is a temporary police lock-up for the Great Exhibition,' said Mr Blackbeard. 'In case of trouble, you know, though there hasn't been any trouble to speak of.'

The lock-up was at the end of a small terrace, and consisted of one bare room, where a police constable perched at a tall desk. A man in a dark coat lay dozing morosely, on two chairs before the tiny fireplace. He sat up briefly when Mr Blackbeard ushered me inside.

'Well? Am I to be allowed in?'

'All in good time, Doctor,' said Blackbeard.

'It's a great nuisance to hang about in this way – and I'm not to be blamed if he dies.' He lay down again and shut his eyes.

'Police surgeon,' said Blackbeard, by way of explanation. 'Dr Taggart. Called out in the middle of his dinner.'

'I'm dreadfully curious, Mr Blackbeard, and you are making it worse! What on earth is going on?'

'I wish I knew, and that's a fact! Inside that cell yonder, ma'am, I have a man who's been shot.'

'I beg your pardon?'

'He came in here some hours back,' said Blackbeard. 'He said he'd been shot, and demanded to be locked up for his own protection. He was dripping blood all over the floor, but wouldn't let the surgeon near him.'

'Did he tell you his name?'

'Herring, ma'am; Richard Herring. Do you know it?'

'No,' I said, 'I know nobody of that name. Where did he claim the shooting took place?'

'In this very park, that's crowded with people and police, if you can believe it.'

'But someone must have seen it, or at least heard the shot!' I said. 'And how long has his injury gone without treatment?'

'That, Mrs Rodd, is anybody's guess. He rolled in here saying he was in fear of his life. But he won't trust the surgeon and fights us off if we try to bring him out – until I'm afraid to agitate him any further, in case it kills him.'

'He accused me of trying to poison him,' Dr Taggart said, sitting up again on his makeshift couch. 'For God's sake, calm him down before he bleeds to death.'

The story seemed preposterous to me at first, but I saw that Mr Blackbeard was deadly serious. 'What I do not understand,' I said, 'is why you needed to fetch me; what can I do?'

'Well, that's the thing,' said Blackbeard. 'He asked to see you, ma'am.'

'Me? But I've never heard of him!'

'He's heard of you!' Blackbeard was enjoying my confusion. 'While he could speak, he said, "I must see Mrs Rodd" – ain't that so, Kennedy?' He looked at the policeman.

'Yessir,' Kennedy said. 'First he wants Mr Blackbeard. Then it was "I must see Mrs Rodd". He said it twice, and very clear.'

'Let me see him.' My protestations were helping nobody, and there was clearly no time to waste. 'At the very least I can persuade the poor man to allow Dr Taggart to tend to him.'

Kennedy produced a clanking bunch of enormous keys. The surgeon yawned irritably and grabbed his leather bag. The three small cells were located down a flight of stone stairs, in a large cellar with tiled walls and a dismal echo. Only one cell was occupied. A still figure, swathed in a voluminous tweed garment, lay on the hard bench. He was so very still, and the section of his face that was visible so ghastly pale, that I was sure he was dead.

The moment I put a foot into the cell, however, a shudder ran through him; he mumbled, 'No, no, no – I will not be moved!'

I sat down beside him on the single chair, taking care to leave room for Dr Taggart. The doctor immediately tried to move aside the cape of the tweed coat or cloak, upon which there was a dark stain of blood; but Mr Herring let out a feeble wail of alarm, and he was forced to withdraw.

'Mr Herring,' I said. 'It's Mrs Rodd; you wanted to see me and here I am; I beg you to let the doctor help you!'

'No!' This was uttered in the feeblest of whispers; a moment later, the man lost consciousness entirely and Dr Taggart was able to expose the great wound in his left shoulder.

'He's been shot all right. I'll need to get the bullet out of him, and it can't be done here.'

There was something in the man's white, anguished face and close-cropped fair hair that was naggingly familiar. And then Mr Jennings came into my mind and I realized why he had fainted in Queen Street. He had, quite literally, seen a ghost.

'Well, ma'am?' asked Blackbeard. 'You look as if you'd seen a ghost!'

'R. Herring, indeed!' I cried out. 'Oh, what fools he must think us! That is Joshua Welland!'

At long last I was face to face with my wandering scholar.

There was no time to argue about the identity of the man, though I was more certain with every passing minute that I was right; shorn of his hair and beard, 'Mr Herring' bore an unmistakable resemblance to his late brother. Our overriding concern now, however, was keeping him alive.

Knowing who he was, I also knew that money would be no object. I wrote a rapid note to Mr Mitchell, and took it upon myself to have Joshua carried to Stoppard's Hotel, as it was just a short distance away. The manager, a Swiss gentleman named M. Marchier, was doubtful about allowing him into the exquisite establishment, but Blackbeard simply ignored him and settled the unconscious patient in two of the very best rooms on the first floor.

It was Mr Arden who put a stop to the manager's objections. His rooms being nearby, he emerged on to the landing to find out what the noise was, and instantly offered to underwrite any expenses incurred.

'Let's hope they ain't funeral expenses,' said Blackbeard. 'You'll never get a coffin down them stairs.'

M. Marchier let out a little bleat of horror.

'I'm sure it can all be discreetly managed, Marchier,' said Mr Arden. 'People have been ill here before now.' He bowed to me. 'You may trust Mrs Rodd to do what is required.'

His intervention removed the last difficulties, and Dr Taggart was finally allowed to cut the bullet from our unconscious patient. I have long experience of sickrooms, and I rather alarmed the hotel servants with my various commands. The windows overlooked the street, busy with traffic even at this late hour, and could not be left open due to the noise and dirt. Knowing the vital importance of fresh air, I had the heavy plush curtains taken away, and also the thick rugs around the bed – which immediately made the atmosphere less dusty. I had them pull Joshua's bed away from the wall so that what air there was could circulate freely, and personally attended to the fire (the coals were plentiful and of the highest quality, but a fire will smoke if not properly tended, and the smoke from a coal-fire is thoroughly unhygienic). I sent for an excellent and highly respectable nurse I knew, by the name of Mrs Hurley. I sent to the kitchen for beef tea, to keep ready on the hob in case the patient awoke.

'You've turned the whole place upside down, Mrs Rodd,' was Mr Blackbeard's comment, when I stopped to draw breath. 'You're a regular whirlwind!'

'I know how things should be done, Inspector.' Mrs Hurley had arrived by this time and established herself in a hard chair beside the bed. Blackbeard and I had retreated to the adjoining room.

'And this nurse is all right, is she?'

'I have employed her on several occasions, very successfully.'

'I'll take your word for it, ma'am.' He was thoughtful. 'I'll wait till this fellow speaks before I go digging up any graves – though I'm curious to know who got buried, if it wasn't him. I suppose you're certain he's Joshua Welland?'

'Yes.'

'Who shot him, then?'

'I have no idea!'

'Hmm,' said Blackbeard. 'I'll leave a constable here, in case whoever it is takes another crack at him.'

'That's comforting to know, though I cannot believe he's in any danger here, in so public a place.'

'Do you have anyone in the frame, ma'am?'

'I know of only one person who might have a motive.' Painful as it was to me, I had to say it. 'Mr Carlos, who must surely surrender at least half his fortune if Joshua is alive.'

'His nephew,' said Blackbeard. 'What do your instincts say about him, then?'

'He's a good young man, Inspector, and I simply cannot imagine him daring to shoot someone in a crowded London park! Didn't anyone see anything, or hear anything?'

'I sent my men out as quick as possible looking for witnesses, but there was too much noise and bustle,' said Blackbeard, shaking his head. 'Some street tumblers was letting off firecrackers, which has confused matters. Everybody heard any number of shots.' A gilt clock on the chimney-piece softly chimed the midnight hour. 'You should get home, ma'am, and I'm very much obliged to you for your assistance.'

Thirty-eight

I HAD TRIED, MORE THAN once, to persuade Mrs Bentley
not to wait up for me when I was late home. She would
never hear of going to bed, however, and I was fully
expecting to find her sleeping upright beside the embers of
the kitchen fire as usual. I was most surprised, therefore,
when I got to Well Walk at nearly one o'clock, to see the
window of my drawing room all aglow with lamplight.

Mrs B, not remotely drowsy, pounced on me in the hall.
'He turned up a couple of hours ago, ma'am, ever so
polite but wouldn't go away – says his name's Jennings. I
put him in here and made a pot of tea.'

'Mr Jennings?' I was so tired that my brain could hardly
take it in. 'Good heavens, what has got into everyone
today? Thank you for keeping him here, my dear Mary.
Now you must go to bed.'

'Not likely! I'll be listening outside like I always do.'
She opened the drawing-room door. 'Here she is, Mr
Jennings!'

And there he stood, in the middle of my hearthrug. He
looked a little thinner about the face but healthy, and not
in the least like someone suffering with his 'nerves'.

'Mrs Rodd, I know this is the most fearful imposition—'

'Mr Jennings!' I cut short his torrent of apologies. 'I'm
very sorry you were kept waiting, and I'm glad to see you
looking so well.'

'I'm perfectly well now,' said Mr Jennings. 'I'm returning to college next week, but I couldn't face it until I had spoken to you. My – my conscience troubles me.'

Mrs Bentley poured me a cup of tea (the pot was still warm), and left us alone together.

'There are certain things I did not tell you,' said Mr Jennings. 'Certain pieces of information …'

It was ridiculously late and I decided to help him out. 'This is about Joshua Welland, isn't it?'

'Yes.'

'And the fact that he is not dead.'

His rosy face flamed, as if someone had put a match to it. 'You know?'

'I have just left the bedside of a man I believe to be Joshua.'

I told him all that had happened, watching him keenly; he was mainly relieved that I had already heard the tallest part of this tall tale.

'Will he live now?'

'The doctor says we may be hopeful,' I said. 'Do you have any idea who might have fired that bullet?'

'All I know is that he was mortally afraid of someone – hence the assumed name.' The young man was easier with me now, and let out a long sigh. 'He's got me into no end of hot water, that I do know. What on earth am I to say to the Church authorities – let alone the college? I shudder to think who – or what – I buried in that grave!'

'Don't torment yourself too much; I think your friend Joshua took advantage of your honesty. If there was some great secret thing he knew, I wish he had reported it to the police, and don't quite understand why he did not.'

'I told you, when I described him to you, that Joshua was once a normal sort of undergraduate, but when I look back he was always eccentric.' He reached for his cup of tea.

312

'Oh dear, that tea is cold,' I said loudly, so that Mrs B would hear me. 'I wish we had more hot water!'

There was a scuffling outside the door, followed by the deliberate thump-thump-thump of Mrs Bentley's feet going down the basement stairs.

Mr Jennings did not seem to hear this, but looked thoughtfully into the fire. 'I was sometimes worried that Joshua truly believed in witches and sorcery, and so forth. He made a bit of a joke of it – but he used to cast spells.'

'Did any of them work?'

'None that I saw,' said Mr Jennings.

'I take it that Joshua was the reason you fainted in Queen Street?'

'I saw his face in the crowd on the pavement; he stopped and looked me in the eye – in proper clothes and his tangled locks shorn away – exactly like Joshua as I first knew him!'

'It must have been a dreadful shock,' I said. 'When did you know for certain that he was still living, and not a ghost?'

'He wrote to me at my mother's house. I will show you the letter; it's mostly an apology for nearly scaring his old friend to death. And another apology for misleading me.'

'How did Joshua mislead you?' I asked.

'By not dying, for one thing. I saw him desperately sick with pneumonia and I judged him to be on the very brink of death. I didn't think it mattered terribly that I was hustled away before I had witnessed his last breath. I took it on trust and wrote and signed a letter to certify the fact. And now he's made an utter ass of me.'

'Not at all, Mr Jennings. You acted in good faith, and should not blame yourself too much.'

'He called himself "R. Herring" as a joke, but there was no joke about his reason for doing it. Did he say anything, after he was wounded?'

'All he did, as far as I can gather, was to beg for sanctuary.'

'Ah,' said Mr Jennings. 'The thing is, Mrs Rodd – has anyone told his wife?'

'His wife! I guessed that was the reason Joshua wanted a clergyman in a hurry! Yes, Mary, you may come in.'

Mrs Bentley appeared a little too quickly with a jug of hot water.

'How thoughtful – thank you.' I set about replenishing the teapot, and managed to extract two passable cups of tea.

'There was nothing unseemly in Joshua's haste to be married,' said Mr Jennings, pink and solemn, once we were alone again. 'He wanted his wife to be in a position to claim his fortune. More than this, he wanted to solemnize their relationship before Heaven.'

'She has not been informed of her husband's injury,' I said. 'She must be informed at once; do you know where I can find her?'

Mr Jennings reached into a breast pocket inside his frock-coat and pulled out a folded piece of paper, which he handed to me.

It was a letter from Joshua; his handwriting was greatly improved by the use of a good steel pen and a bottle of Stephen's black ink. I skimmed the few lines impatiently until I came upon his final words: *Mr and Mrs Herring are currently domiciled at Moon Lodge, Terence Crescent, St John's Wood.*

Naturally, I set out at once, pausing only to write a few explanatory lines to Inspector Blackbeard. Late as it was, this was not a matter that could be delayed for another moment; if Joshua's wife knew nothing of what had happened to him, she must be beside herself with anxiety.

Mr Jennings readily offered to escort me in the cab he had kept waiting outside. The outer reaches of London had a ghostly emptiness in the small hours of the morning; the clatter of the horse's hooves was unnaturally loud as we hastened through those still streets. It was too dark to see anything we passed, only the occasional house with a light showing (I could not help wondering about the stories behind those lonely windows; at this bleak hour it could only be a death, or a birth).

'The funny thing is that I'm not tired,' said Mr Jennings. 'I should be tired, and I'm actually wide awake.'

'That is the excitement carrying you along, Mr Jennings; you are young and well able to bear the after-effects of a night like this. I am not young, and know full well that I'll spend the next two days feeling that I've been run over by an omnibus. At this moment, however, I can think of nothing but Joshua's wife – whom you have met, of course. What was your opinion of the woman?'

'I had a low opinion of the entire business,' said Mr Jennings. 'To be frank with you, I thought he was cracked. I tried to explain to him that I didn't know whether the marriage he wanted me to do was legal. Joshua said he only cared about the laws of Heaven – he could always talk me round. And I must admit that I was a little fearful for my safety among the charcoal burners.'

I recalled the snarling dog and his scowling master who had tried to drive me away from the camp. 'Did anyone threaten you?'

'No – that is, not in so many words. I felt it in the atmosphere.'

'I met a young woman from the camp, who showed me the way when I was lost.' I saw her in my mind's eye, and felt sure that this woman was Joshua's wife (based on little more than instinct and the fact that I had liked her). 'She was handsome, I thought. Is Mrs Welland handsome?'

'Rather,' said Mr Jennings. 'She has raven hair and very fine blue eyes.'

'I knew it! There can't be two of them.'

'I was hustled away, almost the moment the ceremony was finished, and met the new-made Mrs Welland only briefly on that occasion. Her name is Philomena.'

'Very pretty.'

'We met properly last Friday; Joshua nearly knocked me for six by turning up at my mother's house.' He smiled. 'All shaven and shorn, and with a wife upon his arm! My mother was very taken with both of them – and had not a clue that the origins of Mrs Welland were anything but perfectly genteel.'

'The young woman I met could have passed as a lady quite easily. It's not a difficult thing to achieve, with a good helping of native intelligence.'

As may be imagined, I was famished with curiosity; partly because I was convinced that this woman knew her husband's dangerous secret, and partly because I wanted to know the woman Joshua had chosen for his wife.

Moon Lodge was a square white villa, set amidst gardens and amongst other white villas; St John's Wood was already a desirable suburb in those days, though dear Mrs Bentley, who had been born there, remembered fields and hayricks. Two long windows – one on either side of the front door – were lit, showing that the household was awake.

The front door opened as soon as our cab stopped, and a woman ran down the path to meet us, calling out, 'Joshua, is that you?'

She stepped into the light shed by the lamps upon the cab; as I had guessed, it was the same young woman I had encountered in the woods, amazingly transformed by a gown of rustling violet silk. Those shining eyes of hers filled with anguish as she realized we had not brought her husband.

'Where is he? What's happened to him?'

I reached out to take her hand, and gave her the news about Joshua as concisely as possible. She flinched, but did not lose her self-possession. 'I know you – you are Mrs Rodd. And I know Mr Jennings. I will come with you at once.'

Thirty-nine

'HE LEFT THE HOUSE this morning, saying he would be back before nightfall. I knew something dreadful must've happened to him, or he would've sent word. I've been half sick with worrying.'

Mrs Welland sat opposite me in the cab and I studied her as best I could in the dim light. She had wrapped herself in a beautiful mantle of blue velvet, lined with fur. Her bonnet, put on in careless haste, was of the latest fashion. Her voice was soft and very pleasant, with the faintest hint of a country 'burr'.

'Do you know who tried to kill your husband?' I asked.

'Would to God that I did!'

'If he confided in you, Mrs Welland, I beg you to tell us now.'

'He did not confide in me. He never has confided in me – for the sake of my safety, so he says. We argued over it again only last night. I accused him of making the whole thing up – oh God forgive me, it was nothing but the truth!'

'Please try not to worry too much; the doctor who attended him was most hopeful.' I reached across to take her hand again. It was so cold that I felt its chill through my glove. 'The bullet was removed cleanly, without splinters of bone, and it was nowhere near his heart. And he is quite safe now, for Mr Blackbeard left a police guard.'

'Joshua doesn't trust the police,' said Mrs Welland. 'That was reasonable enough when he was poor and lived in a hedge – but now he has money enough to hire a whole army – and yet he won't!' Her fingers tightened around mine. 'What is money, if we have to live under a false name, like criminals?'

'I'm glad to see that your husband has claimed his fortune,' I said approvingly.

'Jacob left instructions about that,' said Mrs Welland. 'It was all in the letter that you gave to me, Mrs Rodd. Joshua was in such haste to get married because he wanted to be certain that I would get it all if he died.'

'When did he begin to hint that he was in danger?'

'Oh, that man has been fleeing from danger since the day I met him!' She was exasperated, in the wifely manner that springs from deep affection. 'He's been hanging about us charcoal burners since I was a girl. In those days he was afeard of some gipsy-men who were after him. He had jumped over the broomstick with their sister, and then run off with his brother's wife.'

'Did they take up residence with you?'

'Not exactly – the two of them were on the edge of things and nobody asked questions. Joshua was tolerated due to his learning, for there always had to be someone who could read and write. And folks pitied him when his girl died, for he was fairly out of his mind with sorrow – in no state to care for those twins.'

'Who cared for them before Mr Arden adopted them?'

'They were passed between the handful of nursing mothers in our little settlement, but it wasn't enough and they were so tiny! If Mr Arden hadn't stepped in, they would likely have died.'

'How did Joshua feel about giving up his sons?'

'At first, he was just thankful,' said Mrs Welland. 'Arden could pay for the best wet-nurses, and the boys were bonny and thriving for the whole world to see. Until recently, he was content to watch them from a distance. And then, a year or so ago, he started to talk about his wish to claim them for himself.'

'What made him change his mind?' I asked.

'He is their father, Mrs Rodd; it was only natural.'

'Of course.' I should not have been surprised to learn that Joshua loved his children, when his entire history had been driven by his love for Hannah. 'But why all this fear, this secrecy?'

'As I told you, he will not confide in me – though we are married.' A passing light caught the silver tracks of tears on her cheeks. 'And I accused him of storytelling!'

There were lighted streets around us now, though the lights were pin-pricks in the black immensity of London by night. The prosperous crescents and squares we passed through were utterly silent, yet I knew there was another, invisible city living alongside this one; a city of wickedness and danger, peopled by murderers and thieves.

Blackbeard had left a policeman on guard in the foyer of Stoppard's Hotel, and he opened the door to us after one soft knock; he had been playing cards with the night porter beside the fire.

Mrs Welland stepped into the light and I saw her properly for the first time; she was dressed exquisitely in whispering silks and glinting jewels, and despite her dreadful anxiety she was a striking beauty (what a couple they would make, I could not help thinking: high society would love this woman; her charcoal-burning history would only add to her mystique).

Another policeman stood on the landing outside Joshua's door. Mrs Welland thrust the door open at once and ran across the room to her husband's bedside.

'My dearest – my darling!' She sank to her knees and covered his limp hand with kisses.

'He's coming along nicely, ma'am.' The nurse, Mrs Hurley, was in her early forties, with a friendly face and intelligent manner, not at all discomposed by the sudden appearance of a weeping wife at the bedside of her patient. 'Weak, to be sure, but no hint of a fever; I saw to it that the surgeon washed his hands.' (She was a stickler for hygiene, still imperfectly understood in those days.) 'His breath is easy and he opened his eyes once – didn't say anything, but he's had a good deal of laudanum for the pain.'

'Is he – I mean—?' Mr Jennings hung back fearfully, his gaze fixed upon Joshua's face, so white and still upon the pillow. 'Will he recover?'

'I'd say so, sir,' said Mrs Hurley. 'If everyone does as I tell them.'

'Thank God!' He went to Mrs Welland and laid a gentle hand upon her shoulder.

She straightened herself proudly, her face flushed and wet with tears. 'I can endure no more of this,' she said softly, never taking her eyes from Joshua. 'He made me swear I'd never tell it – when he took the papers to his brother, he kept back that stupid map—'

'Map?' I remembered how Mr Carlos had spoken of a map, and I had dismissed it as nonsense.

'No, no, no – there's no buried treasure!' Mrs Welland cried out passionately, before I could mention the gold. 'It's a drawing, like the plan for a house – Joshua said I must never tell, for he was in constant fear of his life, and one man had already died from knowing! I don't know what there was to know – but it is a drawing of the old limekiln!'

I fired off an urgent message to Inspector Blackbeard and wrote a short note to my brother. And then I spent the next twenty-four hours in a stupor of fatigue. My feet were so blistered by those agonizing second-best shoes that I hobbled about in my woollen slippers, my bones creaking like the hinges on an old gate.

'You're not as young as you think you are, ma'am,' said Mrs Bentley (who had weathered the night a great deal better than I had, and was now, I felt, rather smug in her sprightliness). 'You can't expect to go gallivanting about in cabs without paying a price for it later. Not at your age.'

'Don't remind me,' I groaned, 'for I feel every year of it!'

She insisted upon making a fire in the drawing room, and I sat myself down beneath my dear husband's painted gaze. I was on the point of dozing off when the postman came, bearing a letter from Minna Yates.

Minerva Cottage

West Hill

Putney

Dear Mrs Rodd,

I know that you have spoken to Mr Arden, and I am afraid you must think very badly of me. You have listened to me with such sympathy, however, that I find I have a great desire to tell you everything. I beg you not to think that I am making excuses for myself. I know that I was wrong to deceive my dear brother, who is moved only by his love for me. Since the death of our father, we have been all in all to each other and he worries so dreadfully about my health – in fact, my health is Charley's sole extravagance.

I suffer from a small irregularity of the heartbeat, which I regard as little more than a nuisance; I am forced to rest when I would rather be active and that is the worst of it. But poor Charley heard of various wonders performed by a certain fashionable physician in Wimpole Street, and nagged at me until I had agreed to consult him.

As I told you on our journey together, I am staying with our dear Aunt Emma in Putney. Her house is very pleasantly situated near to the river, surrounded by trees and gardens, and so comfortable that I am in a fair way to being spoilt! Aunt Emma (actually our great-aunt) is a cheerful soul who plies me with delicacies and expects me to 'sit on a cushion and sew a fine seam' all day long. When I expressed an interest in doing some work for the poor, she replied, 'Pish! There aren't any poor folks in Putney, so you must get used to doing nothing!'

Aunt Emma escorted me to Wimpole Street, for she was also consulting the great man, though I don't believe there is anything the matter with her beyond the fact that she is seventy-eight years old. I had told her nothing about Mr Arden and tried to pass off our meeting in the park as a coincidence.

She was not fooled, however, and saw the truth of the situation at once. I poured the whole story out to her and though she scolded me for lying to Charley, she declared herself to be sympathetic. Being from an earlier and more worldly generation, my aunt could not help fastening upon Mr Arden's wealth, and congratulated me for my 'catch' until I really could not blush harder without bursting into flames!

Sir Digby Pyle is a shining, smooth, immaculate creature, who listened to my pulse as if chatting to it in a drawing room. His advice was perfectly sound, but did not amount to much more than plain common sense. And he annoyed Aunt Emma, by suggesting that her gout would trouble her less if she gave up all her favourite eatables and drinkables.

Aunt Emma is confident that Charley can be 'talked round', and thinks his religious objections absurd. He is afraid of losing me, whether or not I decide to turn dissenter – which I certainly will not. Mr Arden has assured me that his only concern is to marry me, and for the sake of marrying me 'I would gladly change my religion to anything you like from Hindoo to Albigensian!'

He uttered these words in a state of exasperation, during the terrible argument he had with my brother when they met by chance in Swinford, upon the day of Fr Fogle's murder.

We had arranged to meet in advance, when we happened to attend the same tea party. Oh, it was so sordid that I felt sick with shame – though I must emphasize that the two of us only met in public places, and did nothing more reprehensible than declaring our feelings for one another.

Mr Arden kept hold of his temper, even though Charley actually called him a 'heretic', a 'denier of Christ' and 'an enemy of the established Church'. (You may imagine how painful this was for me.) But here is the part I did not tell – that none of us told – namely that the altercation was interrupted by Gerard Fogle himself. He was returning from a walk, heard Charley's voice raised in anger and intervened at once.

He spoke sternly to Charley, saying, 'I expected better of you.'

To Mr Arden he was civil and I left the two of them conversing – perfectly amiably – while my brother insisted upon whisking me home. Much later, Mr Arden told me that they had engaged in a 'fascinating' discussion – something that Fr Fogle was currently writing about for a sermon.

My dear brother apologized to me for losing his temper and begged my pardon very sweetly. As you observed, Mrs Rodd, there was no shadow left between us by the time we parted at the railway station.

I have written reams, and only intended this to be a short letter, so I will cease now – but I wish very much that you could come to visit me in Putney. My aunt claims she is 'too old and too indolent' to keep to a special day for receiving. You are not merely formal 'company', however, and if you make the long journey at an early hour, I can promise you a most delightful day.

Yours in sure and certain hope of the Resurrection,

Minna Yates

The letter moved me greatly, and I wrote a quick reply, to the effect that I would come to Putney on the next day but one.

I wanted to know why Daniel Arden had not told me of his 'fascinating' discussion with Mr Fogle upon the day of the murder. I had a good idea of their subject, for I had seen the sermon.

I acknowledge my transgressions and my sin is ever before me.

Forty

I HEARD HIS VOICE AT my door, just as the church clock was striking eight o'clock, and hurried downstairs at once, though I was wearing only one shoe. 'Mr Blackbeard!'

'Good morning, Mrs Rodd.' He had not shaved; that stiff face had a hoar-frost of white bristles. 'I'm just come from Oxford, ma'am.'

'From Oxford?' I stopped thinking of my sore feet, and my every sense sharpened. 'But of course – the limekiln! You found something!'

'Indeed we did, and very interesting, too.' He raised his eyebrows at me briefly. 'I'm still making sense of it.'

'Come inside, Inspector; I don't expect you to tell me on the doorstep!' I sensed the importance of what he had to say; he was a veritable boulder in his inscrutability. 'You must have been travelling through the night; have you had breakfast?'

He had been in my house on several occasions and was quite at his ease beside my kitchen fire. Mrs Bentley, who had the highest respect for him, made a pot of strong tea and a handsome breakfast of bacon and bread-and-butter.

'When I passed you the message about the limekiln,' I said, 'I did not think you would investigate in person.'

'You'd call it "instinct",' said Blackbeard. 'I call it a smell. I went myself because it didn't smell right. And also because certain high-up gents are starting to complain that the police are being too slow. They're putting the screws on my superiors, as you might say.' There was a pause while he chomped deliberately at a rasher of bacon. 'Ever since that second murder, you see, there's been more public noise about Barton and Mrs Somers, and more people are talking about how they should not go to trial.'

'I have observed as much, and I'm most profoundly thankful for it.'

'Did you find that treasure, then?' asked Mrs Bentley.

Blackbeard stared at her for a full half-minute, still steadily chewing. 'No.'

'Well – what, then?'

He gave her a twitch of a smile. 'That was fine bacon, Mrs Bentley. Thank you kindly and I only wish I had a tale of treasure to bring you in return. Upon the day in question, I went to that old kiln, accompanied by two policemen and two hired labourers with pickaxes. Under all that ivy and whatnot was the stone shell of the kiln with part of the roof collapsed. There was a sort of seam in the stones, Mrs Rodd; that's the only way I can describe it: someone had broken them apart and then tried to cover it up. And not long ago, neither. So I told the men to break it open again. And off they went with the pickaxes. It was not a quick job, ma'am.'

'I should think not!'

'And it was not an easy job. But we went at it with a will, until we had hacked out a good heap of the stones. Whereupon one of my men gets down on all fours and sticks his head through the hole. He calls out that there's some sort of chamber or cellar – and then back he scrambles, quick as the wind and white as a sheet. "There's a corpse inside," he says, "and its grinning skull was inches from my face!"'

'Sir Christopher Warrender!' I cried out, my heart hammering. 'I knew it! Has there been a formal identification?'

'Not as such,' said Blackbeard. 'I flashed a lantern in there before the body was moved, and a strange sight it was, I can tell you. If you ladies will pardon me, he had bits of flesh still on him, on account of the atmosphere he'd been kept in, and a blue swallowtail coat that looked good as new.'

'The gossips and storytellers were right all along,' I said (shuddering slightly at the thought of that poor withered thing in its blue coat). 'This is justice as it operates in the countryside – people do not forget things, and they are not impatient, knowing full well that the truth will work its way out eventually, like a splinter!'

Blackbeard sighed and shifted his chair closer to the fire. 'I'd like a word with my wife at this moment. I should've listened to her, Mrs Rodd, for she always turned out to be right about things in the end. And she always wanted me to investigate the death of Sir Christopher.'

'Perhaps Mrs Blackbeard's theories were sounder than you thought,' I said. 'Who was her preferred murderer?'

'Well now,' said Blackbeard. 'I couldn't give you any names, ma'am, after such a time. But she reckoned it was one of the local blackguards.'

He fell into a meaningful silence, watching me closely, whilst my entire world turned a somersault.

'Mrs Goodly gave us a list of local blackguards,' I said (my voice sounding oddly calm and distant in my own ears). 'But only one of them is still alive.'

'Dan Smith,' said Blackbeard.

'Yes—'

'I'd like a word with Mr Daniel Arden,' said Blackbeard. 'And that is another reason for my presuming to call so early, ma'am. I'm hoping you can tell me where to find him.'

I apologize to the reader for my density, and must admit that I did not see it because I did not wish to see it.

But it all fitted together, as neat as the drawers in my mother's satinwood bureau.

Dan Smith arrived in Plymouth quite alone.

Alone, because he had killed Warrender and hidden his body in the old kiln.

This was the great crime that Mr Arden confessed to Jacob Welland, upon that bare hillside in Desolacion – the greatest of them all.

This was the reason he had made his entire life one act of atonement. And this was the reason he had agonized over the morality of his getting married.

Hannah Laurie was the key to it all, as I have said before. She was in Mr Arden's sights when he returned to Binstock – for she was the last Warrender, and he wanted to make amends to the rightful descendants of the man he had murdered. When he found that she had died and her twin sons were orphans, he saw it as a clear sign of the Almighty's innate rationality.

'He ain't at the hotel,' Mr Blackbeard said. 'They haven't seen a hair of him since yesterday morning. He ain't at Binstock. I was hoping you might know his whereabouts, ma'am – for it's my belief that Mr Joshua Welland came across that corpse, and knew who done it – so Arden put a bullet in him, to shut him up.'

I was on the point of exclaiming that this was nonsense, and Mr Arden would never risk such a wild and desperate act, when the words died on my lips.

'Joshua did all that hiding away in hedges and ditches,' said Blackbeard, 'on account of dodging Arden.'

'Oh, dear heaven!' I cried out. 'Now I see why he was so eager to assist me in my search! No wonder Joshua did not dare to trust me! Oh, I have been so gullible, so smugly blinded by goodness knows how much prejudice and snobbery!'

'You're not to blame yourself, ma'am,' said Mrs Bentley staunchly. 'He had me fooled!'

'I'm not crowing, neither,' said Blackbeard. 'I wasted too much time betting on love for my motive, and it would have done no harm for me to listen to you, when you reckoned it was fear of being found out.'

'That's handsome of you, Inspector.' I could not help being touched by this rough admission (which I knew I would never hear again). 'I know of one more place Mr Arden might be, and if you allow me a few minutes to struggle into my least penitential shoes, we will go there at once.'

Forty-one

ALL I WILL SAY of my surprise and my mortification is that it is extremely hard to revise one's opinion of a person; to be compelled to see them exposed as someone else entirely. I had liked and respected Daniel Arden, I had felt the burning sincerity of his desire to do good. But if the inspector was right, this same humane, compassionate Daniel Arden was a ruthless killer.

Tough old bird that I am, it all made me feel quite ill, and I was only distantly aware of the carriage stopping. Blackbeard jumped out into the street and returned a short time later with a thick earthenware cup of hot coffee, which he handed to me with a bow.

'It's off the stall, Mrs Rodd, which ain't exactly genteel. But I thought you could do with bucking up.'

'Oh, how very kind of you, Inspector!' The sweet, scalding brew was precisely what I needed. 'Where are we?'

'Charing Cross, ma'am; we'll do the rest of the journey by boat, if you have no objection.'

'I should like nothing better,' I assured him. 'And the river breezes might help to clear my poor head!'

'It'll take a hurricane to clear mine,' said Blackbeard. 'I'm making all sorts of new connections now, and Arden's in every one of them.'

The coffee was hot and heartening and made me strong enough to face up to the new intelligence. 'I believe he did probably murder Sir Christopher, but I'm not sure about Joshua Welland—'

'There's plenty of murders,' he cut in, 'but only the one murderer, ma'am.'

'Oh—' For once, I was lost for words and could only gape at Blackbeard foolishly.

'Do you know if the old lady keeps any men about the house?'

'I saw a rather elderly manservant at the station – but you can't possibly – Mr Arden would never—'

'Come along now, Mrs Rodd!' The inspector was rather amused, I thought, by my feeble expressions of horror. 'The trouble with you and me, ma'am, is that we both hate being wrong. I wanted to hang the curate – you wanted to hang pretty much anybody else. But that is all over now and we are both confounded. If we find Arden at the house, he will leave it in fetters; I've more than enough evidence to arrest him. And I'll take a couple of men, in case he turns vicious.'

'That won't be necessary,' I said. 'He would never do anything to upset Miss Yates.'

'Hmm,' said Blackbeard. 'The question is, how much does the young lady know?'

'In my opinion, very little; I don't think he could bear her to know the whole truth.' I handed him my empty cup. 'I beg you, Mr Blackbeard – please try not to frighten her!' My faculties were now sharp enough to think of poor Minna Yates, and the fact that we were about to break her heart.

We travelled the few miles to Putney in a small police steamer, which cut the journey time considerably. I sat on

a locker on the deck, out of the worst of the wind, and if I
had not been so sick at heart, I would have enjoyed the
chilly autumn sunlight that glanced off the water, and
the noise and bustle of all the other boats around us on the
river. It is always more pleasant to travel along the Thames
in the westerly direction, for the warehouses and coal-
barges quickly fall away and turn into pretty suburbs; when
we stopped at a wooden jetty near to Putney, the water was
cleaner than in the city and there were ducks in the reeds.

Two policemen accompanied us to Minerva Cottage.

'I'll post 'em at the end of the road,' said Blackbeard,
'in case anyone sees us coming and tries to skedaddle,
ma'am.'

I remember our short journey as having a dreamlike
quality; we passed prosperous-looking villas, sitting
serenely in their fine gardens, as if we were fifty miles from
the centre of London instead of five. Miss Emma
Critchley's house was the only building in a short turning
off the principal thoroughfare – and when we took the
turning, I saw at once that something was wrong.

All the windows of Minerva Cottage had the shutters
or curtains drawn; there was a piece of black crêpe tied to
the door-knocker.

'Hallo,' said Blackbeard. 'Someone's gone and died!'

'It must be Miss Critchley – but this is most unexpected!'
I absolutely ran to the front door of the neat little red-
brick villa.

Blackbeard followed at a more deliberate pace and
grunted out a couple of directions to the policemen.

A red-eyed young maidservant opened the door to us; I
began to explain that I was a friend of Miss Yates and her
face crumpled into tears. She did not need to say anything
more, but led us, weeping, to a room at the back of the
house.

The picture is printed upon my memory and I see it now – a small, ladylike drawing room, with the curtains left open to fill it with light. Some items of furniture had been pushed aside to accommodate an open coffin set upon wooden trestles. I wept to see poor Minna Yates, frozen into her last sleep, with white roses placed around her head and another in her folded hands.

Charles Yates knelt on the floor beside his sister, sobbing fit to make the heart bleed for him. He did not look up at me. His right hand was clumsily bandaged.

'You are Mrs Rodd.' The other person in the room was Miss Critchley, a stooping yet vigorous old woman, dressed head to foot in swathes of black crêpe, with a cumbersome necklace of Whitby jet and matching earrings (I hasten to add that this was no vanity on her part, but simply the mourning fashion of an earlier generation). Though she dabbed at her eyes, she was more collected than her nephew, and stood to shake my hand. 'I knew you would come calling, for I read your letter.'

'Yes – she wrote to me – poor girl!' I did my best to be calm and collected, but the shock had hit me like a bullet and I could not help breaking down in tears. 'I beg your pardon – but please, if you can bear it – please tell me—'

Miss Critchley, after a sharp glance at her sobbing nephew (she took no notice at all of Blackbeard), grabbed my sleeve and tugged me across the room to the window.

'It happened all of a sudden, yesterday evening; I left her resting in the easy chair, and when I came in – it was getting dark, Mrs Rodd, the lamps were not lit, the fire had gone out – at first I thought she was asleep, for she looked so peaceful!'

'Had she been feeling unwell?'

'No – the dear girl was merry as anything, singing as she went about her work – the doctor said it was her heart and she felt no pain.'

'Peaceful?' In the midst of my sorrow, I was profoundly glad that she had not suffered.

'Yes, Mrs Rodd.' Miss Critchley wiped her eyes. 'She passed into Heaven between one breath and the next!'

'And even as she lay here, he claimed that she'd been happy – because of him!' Mr Yates cried out passionately. 'I would not let him think he had taken her away from me!'

'What did you do to your hand, then, sir?' asked Mr Blackbeard.

The distraught young man broke into a fresh outburst of weeping; Miss Critchley wiped her eyes and gestured to the inspector to join us at the window.

'I sent for Charley at once, poor dear boy!' she murmured. 'Unfortunately, when he arrived he found—'

'That damned man was here!' snapped Mr Yates. 'He has no place near Minna – so I told him to get out!'

'My dear boy!' The old lady's eyes filled with tears and her voice dropped to a whisper. 'I shouldn't have let Mr Arden in to see her – but he was so stricken with sorrow that I couldn't turn him away. I had seen for myself that she loved him.'

'Miss Yates was of too candid a nature to conceal her feelings,' I whispered back. 'I saw it too.'

'I'm sorry to intrude, I'm sure,' said Blackbeard, not whispering in the slightest. 'And, believe me, I would not in the normal way of things. But I'm very anxious to find Daniel Arden, and must ask you, Mr Yates, when the man left this house, and where he was going.'

I thought his tone too harsh, but it had a bracing effect upon the poor young man. His sobs stopped, he stood up proudly to face Blackbeard.

'I arrived here at eight o'clock this morning. Arden was here, and he left perhaps ten minutes later. The fact is, I – I chased him out.' He seemed amazed to hear these words coming out of his own meek mouth. 'And I struck him.'

'Is that what hurt your hand, sir?' asked Blackbeard.

'No – that was when Arden slammed the carriage door in my face and my hand was in the way. I don't think it's broken. I'm afraid I don't know where he was going.' Mr Yates pulled his handkerchief from his pocket with his good hand and forlornly blew his nose. 'I'm awfully sorry, Aunt Emma; it was unforgivable of me to lose my temper.'

'Never mind, my dear,' said Miss Critchley. 'You were not to blame.'

'Thank you, sir,' said Blackbeard, flicking a glance at me, which meant that we were about to depart.

I respectfully took my leave of Miss Critchley and Charles Yates, and said a short prayer to myself over Minna's coffin; I remember that her still face was half-smiling and at its loveliest, all radiant with the light of another world.

And it occurred to me then that the Almighty had been merciful, for he had taken Minna when she was still happy, before she had to hear the truth about the man she loved.

Forty-two

'I'M STUMPED, THAT'S WHAT,' said Blackbeard, once we were walking briskly away down the lane. 'He might be anywhere by now. He might have left the country.'

'I'm sure he intends to leave the country eventually,' I said. 'I do not think, however, that he would do so without at least seeing the twins.'

'So you reckon he's on his way to Binstock?'

'Yes.'

'Will he take 'em along, do you think?'

'He would have to be desperate to take the boys with him, for they would make him too conspicuous.' I blew my nose resolutely, putting my own 'sorrowing' aside. 'But I'm sure he'll risk a good deal to see them one more time.'

'Hmm,' said Blackbeard. 'I daresay you're right; I might put another couple of men on, to watch out for him.'

'But not in uniform – or you will scare him off.'

'Arden ain't a man to scare easy,' said Blackbeard. 'He's as black a villain as I've ever had to deal with.'

I was still struggling to accept the emerging truth about Mr Arden's character and it must have showed, for Blackbeard halted on the path and turned to face me, very stern.

'You're not to go a-chasing him by yourself, Mrs Rodd – just in case you had any such foolish notion.'

I could not reply at once, for of course I had already started to entertain this notion. 'He is not a savage, Inspector.'

'You've only met him in drawing rooms, ma'am. He's dangerous, and he'll be more so, now that he has nothing left to lose – like a cornered rat.'

'But he is such a rational being! All his actions are driven by his warped idea of reason. And he has no reason to harm me.'

'That's as maybe, ma'am,' said Blackbeard. 'But you'll oblige me if you keep away from him.'

'Very well, Inspector.'

He touched his hat gravely and resumed walking back to the boat, barely speaking another word until we disembarked in the middle of town. I did not take it personally; the brow of thunder and obsidian silence meant simply that deep thought was taking place inside the Blackbeard brain.

I returned to Well Walk in the police carriage, giddy with hunger, fatigue and disillusion.

'Dearie me, you look like you've been dragged through a hedge backwards!' was Mrs Bentley's exclamation when she saw my wind-tossed appearance. 'This came for you, ma'am; I didn't catch sight of who left it.'

It was a single, folded page and I recognized the hand-writing at once.

Dear Mrs Rodd, please see to it that Jack and Ferdy are well cared for. Whatever money I can keep hold of is administered by Mr Angus Grant of Mason Court, Gray's Inn Rd. I know that I can trust you to be kind. Daniel Arden.

The following morning brought a prettily worded note from Mrs Welland, to the effect that her husband was better and wished to speak to me. I don't think I have ever anticipated a meeting so keenly.

I found his sickroom at Stoppard's quite transformed since the last time I had seen it; Mrs Welland knelt upon the carpet playing with two King Charles spaniels, and jumped up to greet me, wreathed in smiles.

My wandering scholar was awake, propped against a bank of pillows. 'Mrs Rodd, this is momentous.' He held out his good arm to shake hands, still weak and pale yet greatly restored. 'You have been tangled up in my affairs for ages. Now we are face to face at last.'

'He wants to apologize, for leading you such a dance,' said Mrs Welland, smiling. 'Don't you, my dear?'

'That won't be necessary,' I said. 'You had good reason to avoid me; I'm mortified now to think of how much I tattled to Mr Arden. I told him about the papers you had left with Silas Jennings – and he then ransacked the poor man's rooms!'

'You trusted him,' said Joshua. 'So did I, at first. He let me rove undisturbed about his land. He encouraged me to borrow his books and even hinted that he would assist me if I wanted to go back to my college.'

'He was bringing up your sons,' I said, 'and knew he was in your debt.'

'I was never tempted to accept his help,' said Joshua. 'I no longer wanted to belong to that world. And after Hannah died, I got it into my head that Heaven was punishing me. I was quite out of my mind.'

'That you were, my darling,' murmured his wife, leaning over to stroke his cheek with a tenderness that made her face very pretty and sweet. 'Fairly howling at the moon!'

'Your brother told me about Hannah,' I said. 'The girl you both loved.'

341

'We were promised to each other,' said Joshua. 'Jacob knew it, but chose to take no notice and marry the unfortunate girl himself.'

'But you did not leave your college in order to join her in the woods,' I said, 'for you were living there already.'

'With the gipsies!' Mrs Welland said, with a soft laugh.

'It's not an edifying tale.' Joshua reddened a little. 'You know that I was poor and in debt. I had a sore heart and an empty stomach, and a certain girl from the gipsy camp took pity on me.'

'Took a fancy to you, more like,' said his wife merrily.

'She was older than I,' said Joshua.

'And bigger!'

'Stop it!' he said, laughing. 'Let me get it out, and then you may tease me as much as you like. At first, Mrs Rodd, I divided my time between the camp and the college.'

'That was when you told Mr Jennings you were seeing sermons in stones.'

'Yes – just like dear old Jennings to remember that!' said Joshua. 'I left college for good when Hannah ran away from my brother. We had kept in contact behind his back, and he never once suspected. And we hid ourselves away because we knew that Jacob was after us – truly, it seemed that everybody was after us! The men from the gipsy camp only left off hounding me when their sister took up with some other unlucky fellow. I see now that I might have been a little "touched", but there were good reasons behind my mania for secrecy.'

'When did you fall foul of Arden?'

'A year or so before my brother sent you searching for me, Mrs Rodd,' said Joshua, 'Arden caught me hacking my way into the old limekiln in Freshley Woods. I had a notion that there might be space inside it for one of my shelters.'

342

'He had them all over,' said his wife fondly, 'and in places you wouldn't credit!'

'Unluckily for Arden, however,' Joshua went on, 'I came across a withered corpse in a blue coat. I scrambled out of the ghastly chamber. There's a dead body, I told him; we must tell the police. To which Arden replied: we will not tell the police. But why? I asked. And he said it again: we will not tell the police. He took a step towards me and my every instinct shrieked danger – I suddenly saw how easy it would be for him to kill me, and hide my corpse beside the other. I yelled out: you did this! You're a murderer! He lashed out at me, but I was too quick for him; I knew those woods even better than he did and ran off like a squirrel. The rest you know; I did not dare to tell a soul what I had seen; I took it into my head that the man had the whole world in his pocket, and hid myself away.' Joshua added, 'It wasn't because of my brother; I had long forgiven him.'

'I'm very glad that you and Jacob were reconciled at last,' I said. 'You helped him to a peaceful death.'

'I wanted to stay with him, God knows, but the boy was with him – his son.'

'You will be pleased with your nephew, if you have not yet met him; Mr Carlos is a fine young man.'

Joshua was very tired now and Mrs Hurley intervened, to say firmly that he must rest. Mrs Welland left the room with me, to escort me to the street.

'I must thank you, Mrs Rodd, for never in my life have I seen him so happy.'

'My dear Mrs Welland, I only wish I could take the credit for it! I have bungled and stumbled my way through this business, until I'm quite ashamed of myself.'

'You have done more than you think,' she said softly. 'Who knows what might have happened, if you had not defended your friends? Two blameless people could've been hanged, and we would still be living in fear of our lives.'

'I missed a thousand things that were right under my nose! I'm only grateful that I did not make it worse.'

We were halfway down a staircase when Mrs Welland suddenly stopped and turned to face me. 'But Arden must be found – have they got him yet?'

'Not so far as I know; we must trust Mr Blackbeard to track him down.'

'I won't feel safe till then,' said Mrs Welland earnestly. 'Until that man is hanged!'

Forty-three

THE MESSAGE THAT CAME for me, early in the afternoon on the following day, was not news from Blackbeard, as I had hoped, but a joyous scrawl from Fred.

My dearest old L, come to Highgate forthwith. F.

Rachel's arms were about me the moment I stepped into the hall of my brother's house. 'Thanks be to heaven – we are free!'

And so it was, for no less a being than the Home Secretary had quietly released Rachel and Mr Barton that very morning. They were both dazed and pale and keeping a shy distance between them. Rachel had removed the awful widow's cap; I was concerned to see how thin she was in her plain black gown.

Mr Barton shook my hand. 'I cannot thank you enough, Mrs Rodd; I dread to think – if you had not believed us from the first—'

My brother, in stark contrast to these solemn, black-clad figures, was jubilant in a crimson waistcoat and in the process of opening a bottle of champagne at his desk. 'Letty, my dear! Isn't this wonderful?'

'Amen to that,' I said. 'But Fred, such extravagance—'

'Pish!' said Fred happily. 'Fanny's taken the little ones to her mother's, so we're free to enjoy ourselves. And it's all going on the bill. What about you, Flint?'

'I don't like the stuff,' said Mr Flint. 'Thank you.' He was back at his post before the fire, with one foot planted upon the tiles in the grate, scowling and showing no sign of the appropriate rejoicing.

'Mr Flint.' My dear Tishy sat at the tea-table in her mother's place, rather perilously close to the young man. 'Will you have some tea?'

'Oh—' He blinked for a few seconds, as if drawing her into focus, and I was glad to see that he softened. 'Thank you, Miss Laetitia.'

'You are too close to the fire; I'm afraid you will be hurt again.'

'Bless me, yes,' said Fred. 'A hot coal jumped out the other day, and burned a great hole in his sock!'

Mr Flint looked down at his foot for a moment, as if surprised to see such a thing at the end of his leg, and then withdrew it, with a fleeting smile at my coltish sixteen-year-old niece. I wondered what ailed the man, as I so often did with Mr Flint, and suspected that the presence of Rachel and Barton made him uneasy; he could not bring himself to pardon the 'sinners' quite yet.

'Would no one like champagne, or am I doomed to drink the whole bottle myself?' My brother, who had never been troubled by the strictest of moral scruples, refused to be deflated. 'Oho, just wait until this all comes out!'

'Is there any more news of Arden?' I asked.

'Not yet, but my obliging friend at Scotland Yard tells me Blackbeard has posted his men at all the docks and ports and principal roads, and I bet you a pound he gets his man before this day is over—' There was a knock at the door. 'Come!'

346

'Beg your pardon, Mr Tyson.' It was Mrs Gibson, my brother's indefatigable and irreplaceable housekeeper; she held a dirty scrap of paper between two fingers. 'A boy brought this to the back door for Mrs Rodd.'

She gave it to me and my pulse leapt, for I knew the hand.

I am ready. Come to the same place on HH. Bring Flint.

'I don't know why he has asked for me,' said Mr Flint. 'I respectfully suggest, however, that at such a solemn moment, poised to give himself up, this man might want someone he knows to have a high sense of Christian morality. And without wishing to speak badly of your brother—'

'Oh, feel free to speak as badly of him as you like! I know he can be disgracefully light-minded sometimes.'

'Indeed.'

'You must take my word he doesn't mean it, Mr Flint; he never can resist teasing those who do not like being teased.' (If I hadn't grown up being teased by Fred, I would now be an even greater old fusspot.) 'This is the path, and if he's there we will soon see him.'

The weather was cold, grey and autumnal; though it was relatively early, we did not have much time before sunset. The few people about on Hampstead Heath were all in a hurry, heads bent against the damp gusts that stirred the bare branches and scattered the dead leaves.

Mr Arden was waiting for us upon the fallen tree, a black, still figure, doubled over with his face buried in his hands. He heard our approach, twitched nervously, then proudly rose to his feet.

'Mrs Rodd, Mr Flint.'

I was shocked; never had I seen a man so shattered by sorrow. His spry figure was bent, his face was scored and haggard, and all at once he was old.

'I am ready.' The words had a biblical ring to them. 'It is finished.'

'I know that Minna Yates has died,' I said softly. 'And I am very sorry.'

'There's nothing left for me now, except to make my peace with the Almighty. Mr Flint, I'm obliged to you for coming; I knew that Mrs Rodd would be prevented from meeting me alone. And I'd like you to defend me.'

'I can't prevent you being hanged,' said Mr Flint. 'I don't wish to prevent it!'

'Ah, but that is precisely why I need you.' There was, for a moment, a spark of the old humour in Mr Arden's manner. 'You do not fear the truth, and I am not looking for mercy. At the very last, I must shrink from nothing – I must tell everything, for when I'm hanged, I know that I will find myself before the greatest of judges.'

'You have killed, and killed again,' snapped Mr Flint. 'You must have known there could be no possible justification!'

'Mr Arden—' I sat myself down beside him on the tree trunk. 'I'm sure you will be glad to hear that Joshua Welland is out of danger.'

'I am glad,' he said softly. 'That is one less burden upon my conscience. I did not enjoy terrorizing him; I was still convinced that I was doing the Lord's work. I knew that if my crimes were exposed, countless other people would suffer for it, and all that I had built would be destroyed.'

Mr Flint took a step closer to him. 'Did you honestly believe Heaven would condone cold-blooded murder?'

'Yes, I think I did,' Mr Arden said mildly, as if speaking of someone else. 'Though when I took my reckless shot at Welland, I was operating from base instinct instead of cold reason. I could not allow him to wreck the happiness I thought I had been granted by Heaven. It seemed so near – almost in my grasp.'

'But then Miss Yates was snatched from your wicked grasp,' said Mr Flint, who loomed over Arden, arms folded and face scowling. 'And you suddenly saw the Almighty's true opinion of you.'

I felt this was unnecessarily harsh. Mr Arden, however, appeared to approve of his accuser's manner. 'I could no longer avoid looking at my true reflection – the scales fell from my eyes—'

'When you had your great experience in Desolacion,' I suggested, 'you took it as a sign that you were forgiven for the murder of Warrender.'

'That's about the size of it – appallingly presumptuous as it looks now. But the man I killed was a wicked man, and I decided he was no great loss to the world. I felt that Heaven had allowed me to take his place – to be the man he ought to have been.'

'No more theology, if you please,' said Mr Flint shortly. 'Just facts; who was your accomplice?'

'All the responsibility was mine.'

'You were practically a child; don't tell me you bricked him up on your own!'

'Goodly!' I cried out, as the connection became clear to me. 'Thomas Goodly!'

'Yes,' said Mr Arden. 'That drunken idiot was my chosen accomplice. He did not steal from me. I gave him those coins as his "cut", for his silence. And he had nothing to do with the murder; in fact, he was terrified out of his remaining wits.'

'And how did you—'

'How did I do it, Mr Flint? I picked up a great rock and smashed his skull open. I had very good reason to hate that man, and before my conversion I felt no shame for killing him.' He made this statement with a calmness that chilled my blood. 'I even felt that I had Heaven's approval, if not its blessing.'

'It was not your place to make such judgements,' said Mr Flint. 'Your arrogance is extraordinary.'

'I see that now,' said Mr Arden. 'At the time I did not. I killed Warrender and stole his tainted gold. I then left the country – for ever, as far as I was concerned. But I was haunted by the memory of that dead body in the kiln. I worried that it would be found and linked to me. When I returned as a wealthy man, and saw an advertisement for the auction of Binstock, I took it as yet another sign.'

'According to Joshua Welland,' I said, 'another man died to preserve your secret.'

He took the prompting easily. 'Yes, Mrs Rodd – I might have known you would sniff out the action that most troubled me – the man Woods. It was one thing to rid the world of a blackguard, but quite another to kill an innocent young man. I had employed him to help me secure the stones upon the old kiln, and some of them fell away to reveal my guilty secret. My work was at a critical stage – exposure would have brought ruin to so many – the man had to die. As you know, I took good care of his widow and children. Unfortunately, that was not the end of it.'

'You murdered Arthur Somers,' I said wretchedly. 'And all because of Goodly's deathbed confession!'

Mr Arden's voice hardened. 'I was certain Goodly had babbled to him about the murder. Nobody remembered me as Dan Smith; even so, it was a risk I simply did not dare to take, though I had a personal respect for Somers.'

'Good God, man,' said Flint, 'your soul is surely damned to hell!'

'That may be so,' said Mr Arden. 'All I have left now is honesty. The facts will come out and I will be hanged; so be it. Heaven will judge me; I have an eternity of repentance before me.'

'You did not kill Arthur on an impulse,' I said, seeing more clearly with every passing moment. 'You planned the whole thing very carefully.'

'My plan was to question him about Goodly, to test how much he knew; I carried the poison as a last resort. I had already observed the illicit feelings between Mrs Somers and Henry Barton; they were really perfectly placed to take all the suspicion.'

'So you decided to do the Lord's work by allowing two innocent people to be hanged!' Mr Flint cut in, with scalding sarcasm.

'Let me give you chapter and verse,' said Arden steadily. 'Rightly or wrongly, I felt that they were grievous sinners and could therefore be sacrificed with impunity. Upon the day of his death I followed Somers when he left Hardinsett – that was the true date of the encounter I told you of, Mrs Rodd.'

'You discovered him sleeping at the old kiln,' I said.

'Yes – I had been looking for such a chance for some time. I did not ask outright if he knew of my crime – but he gave certain signs that he did and it was clear to me that he would have to be removed. I quickly found my opportunity to lace his lemonade, for I had already decided this would be the best way to do it.'

'Arthur would never have betrayed you!' I took a breath, to keep the anger out of my voice. 'What excuses did you make to yourself this time?'

His quick black eyes darted up to meet mine (to this day I shiver to recall how changed was their expression – cold, hard, pitiless). 'That it is sometimes necessary to sacrifice the few for the sake of the many.'

'Fogle – you killed him, too,' said Mr Flint. 'What had he ever done to you?'

'He heard Somers's confession,' said Mr Arden. 'Once again, I could not take the risk. We had a fascinating discussion about the sacrament of confession, during which he hinted that Somers had told him everything he knew. I returned to the house in the small hours to see him off.'

'You inspired Mr Fogle's last sermon,' I said, 'which I now understand more fully.'

'How many more were you planning to "see off"?' demanded Mr Flint.

'Welland would have been the end of it.'

The scales had fallen from my eyes at last and I did not believe him. 'Did you intend to tell Miss Yates?'

'No – she only loved the man she thought I was, and could not have endured it.'

'That's four murders, plus one attempted,' said Mr Flint. 'I can't make any sort of case for your defence – Socrates himself couldn't do it!'

'I don't wish to be defended, Mr Flint,' said Arden, his customary mildness restored. 'I want you to paint me as black as you like. Let us give the other side an easy time.'

'But – you actually want your own counsel to beg the jury to hang you?'

'Once the facts are before them, they will have no choice.'

'Mr Arden, we are baffled,' I said (seeing that Mr Flint looked as if he was about to explode). 'Please explain your reasoning.'

'People must know of the circumstances that moulded me,' said Mr Arden. 'They must be brought to understand that I could only escape from my poverty by committing terrible crimes – that a life of virtue, as preached from the pulpits, would have brought me little more than a virtuous death. And that poverty is the darkest, most hopeless of all prisons.'

'Many people are poor,' I returned, 'without regarding their poverty as an excuse for murder!'

'No, Mrs Rodd – not an excuse!' He turned to me with a shadow of the old eagerness. 'I want people to see this world we have made, in which the wicked flourish and the good get nothing! I should not have been left to grow up in hedges and ditches, like a wild animal! It is your favourite quotation again – "every door is barred with gold, and opens but to golden keys", and I say: throw that door wide open!'

'Good heavens, Mr Arden, you are advocating revolution!'

'Again, you misunderstand me; I abhor violence and mistrust politicians. My guide in everything is my Bible.'

'What about *Rights of Man*?'

'You said yourself, Mrs Rodd, that nothing in that book is incompatible with the Holy Scriptures.'

I was on the point of retorting that we had never had any such discussion, and then remembered my conversation with Minna Yates on the train – such a short time ago! – and for a moment could not speak. Mr Arden's flash of energy died away; he sighed and stared through the lace of bare branches at the darkening sky.

'Very well,' said Mr Flint, after a long spell of silence. 'If that's what you want, I'll do it – though God knows, it'll be the strangest defence in history.'

'Thank you,' said Mr Arden.

'Truth, Mrs Rodd!' said Mr Flint, seeing that I was startled by such an abrupt change of mind. 'This is why I took up the law in the first place – because God is truth, and truth is God!'

I did not understand – surely there was only one way to be hanged? – but we were interrupted by the sounds of footsteps and voices along the path. Mr Blackbeard was marching towards us, accompanied by two policeman with lanterns.

Mr Arden stood up, utterly calm, and politely held out his arms to be chained. 'Mrs Rodd, I should like to see that sermon of Fogle's, if you are able to send it to me; I am sure you know the address.'

He bowed to me before being led away down the path and disappearing into the darkness.

Forty-four

RACHEL AND MR BARTON were married by special licence the following morning, in a private ceremony at St Michael's Church in Highgate. I was a witness, and it was a solemn experience, for I could not help recalling Rachel's first wedding to poor Arthur. This time the bride was all in black and wept silently throughout. I was glad to observe, however, the couple's love for one another, that no amount of sorrow could break or hide, and I had a fancy that Arthur blessed them from the next world.

My brother refused to be solemn, and when the new-made Mr and Mrs Barton returned to his house he welcomed them with more champagne and what he called 'a good stab' at a wedding breakfast. Rachel tried to protest that it was 'unsuitable', but Fred would have none of it, loudly declaring, 'This is a celebration, not a funeral!'

He chivvied us all into smiles, if not uproarious jollity, and afterwards Mr Barton played football in the garden with two of my nephews.

'He's a lively fellow,' Fred said privately to me, watching through the window. 'And he'll provide Gloomy Miss Garnett with so many babies that she won't have any more time for gloom.'

'I hope so!' I murmured.

I cannot resist adding now that my brother's rather crudely worded prophecy came true; just over a year later,

I agreed to stand godmother to Rachel's firstborn, Arthur (and oh, how radiant she was with her new baby in her arms!). Three more babies arrived in quick succession. I have visited them many times over the years since the scandal, and rejoiced in the happiness of their home. Mr Barton kept his holy orders, and though they could not return to Hardinsett, Rachel used her fortune to pay for the new church there as a memorial to her first husband. After a few years, when the fuss had died down, Mr Barton was given a living in Somerset, a few miles outside Taunton.

I am running ahead of myself, however.

The trial of Daniel Arden was a sensation that swept away all other sensations. There were street-ballads, there were plays, there was even a popular Murderer's Polka. The enormity of his crimes, coupled with his equally enormous repentance, made some people treat him almost as a hero. When the judge put on the black cap and gave out the sentence, there were groans in the public gallery.

Mr Flint's performance in court was very much admired (he begged the jury to pray for the guilty man with an eloquence that reduced one of them to tears). On the day before the hanging, he summoned me to Newgate, because Arden had expressed a wish to 'take his leave' of me.

It was very strange to see Daniel Arden in a cell for the condemned, sitting at the small table with his Bible open before him, and all his accustomed elegance intact.

'Mrs Rodd.' He rose to shake my hand. 'Thank you for coming.'

'I wish with all my heart that we did not have to meet in this place, Mr Arden,' I said. 'Is there any service I can do for you?'

'No – I have everything I need. And it is oddly peaceful to feel that all is finished and resolved. Metaphorically speaking, my bags are packed for my last journey.'

He presented me with the single chair and sat himself down upon the bunk. The cell was large enough to accommodate a warder, who left the door open and retreated to the corridor outside.

'I brought you Mr Fogle's last sermon,' I said, and took the pages from my bag.

'I shall read it with interest, knowing that I was his inspiration.'

'Did you make a full confession to him?'

'I did, though not in any formal sense. On the day of Fogle's death—' Mr Arden paused, and then added, 'I mean, of course, the day that I killed him, for let us call things by their right names – we met in the village and Fogle cordially invited me into his study, to continue the discussion we had started out in the street. He seemed to sense the black state of my conscience, yet he did not judge me. I'm sorry to say that I decided to tell him everything only after I had made the decision to get rid of him.'

'What – truly everything – even Arthur?'

'Yes, Mrs Rodd, and it was a very interesting experience,' Mr Arden said mildly. 'It was the first time, in fact, that I had ever spoken the truth about my sins to anyone – apart from Jacob Welland. And I had accumulated a few more since then.'

'How did Mr Fogle respond?'

'He said he pitied me for the burden I had been carrying; the great weight of guilt that had crushed my soul. His compassion moved me almost to tears, for my secrets had been a millstone around my neck, and there was a glorious sense of release when I gave them up. I told him of my atonement, my vow to improve the world around me. But he would have none of it, and he gently rebuked me for assuming that I was doing God's work, when I was playing fast and loose with the laws of the universe.'

'I understand the sermon better now,' I said. 'But – when you told him everything, he must surely have known he was in danger himself – you could hardly have made it plainer! Wasn't he afraid of you?'

'If he was, he didn't show it,' said Mr Arden, very grave. 'When I took my leave of him, Fogle seized my hand and said, "It is not too late; you can still save your soul." And then he said, "I shall pray for you – in this world and the next." I understood at that moment why some believe the man was a saint. Unfortunately, my respect for Fogle did not stop me killing him. It comforts me a little to know that he had time to prepare his soul. He was a brave man.'

'You are very calm, Mr Arden.'

'I have no reason not to be calm. I can change nothing. Tomorrow morning I go to the gallows.'

I could not help being moved by the dignity he maintained, with such horror looming before him. 'I shall pray for you,' I said shakily.

'Thank you, Mrs Rodd.'

'Are you sure there's nothing I can do for you?'

'My affairs are in very good order,' said Mr Arden. 'Binstock is well secured for my boys.'

'I wish that you could see your boys,' I said. 'How far are they aware of what has happened?'

'They will know that I am dead; perhaps they will know more when they are older.'

'Do you know where they are to live?'

'Joshua Welland has claimed them, quite rightfully, as his sons. He has written to assure me that they will continue to live at Binstock, which is their inheritance. I'm quite satisfied that they will be well loved and well cared for.' For a moment there was a dreadful sorrow in his face and his voice. 'It's a great comfort to know that they will not suffer for my crimes.'

'You may be sure of that,' I said. 'His wife is a good, kind young woman.'

'Welland has promised to take good care of my people at Binstock. It was God's mercy that I did not succeed in killing him; I believe that I am now as ready as I'll ever be to take my punishment.'

'I beg your pardon, Mrs Rodd.' Mr Flint stepped into the open doorway. 'I must ask you to leave; there's quite a line of people waiting to see Arden.'

'And my time is somewhat limited,' said Mr Arden wryly. 'I can't ask them to come back tomorrow.'

We both rose; he took my hand and I could not speak.

'Don't be afraid for me,' said Mr Arden, smiling. 'As I said to you once before, when the truth is properly revealed it is always beautiful.'

He was hanged at eight o'clock the next morning, at Newgate, with a great crowd waiting outside.

Mr Flint stayed with him until the very last, for the two men had struck up a friendship during the trial. 'He didn't tremble, he didn't flinch,' he told me afterwards. 'He was calm and courteous as ever – a model of courage, even as he stood with a sack over his head and the noose around his neck!'

In his will, Mr Arden left his gold watch to Patrick Flint. To me he left a handsomely bound edition of *Rights of Man* (a touch of 'gallows humour' here), and he also sent a very generous sum of money to Cousin Wilfred at the Mission in Plymouth.

'And would you believe it,' said Mr Blackbeard, who dropped in at Well Walk especially to tell us, 'he left a whacking great donation to the Police Widows and Orphans – I don't think I ever chased a better villain!'

The light has begun to fade, and I am too old and generally decrepit to write by just one small lamp. Never mind; I have set down my story, and will give these pages to my dearest niece Tishy – now grown into a wife and mother, and still my pride and joy.

'I had better read it first, Aunty,' she told me the other day, 'before my fearsome husband picks it to pieces and argues over every detail!'

This made me smile, for her fearsome husband is none other than Patrick Flint. He married the dear girl upon her nineteenth birthday (my brother nearly drowned us all in champagne), and he has lately become a judge – with clean cuffs and a full quotient of sleeve-buttons. I hear him above me in the schoolroom at this moment, playing a rowdy game with his children.

My life in this house is never quiet, and Tishy marvels that I don't mind it, but the noise of happy children is the music of Heaven. And these days I can sleep through anything.

Afterword

THIS NOVEL IS SET in 1851, two years before Matthew Arnold published 'The Scholar Gipsy'. Arnold was – like my character Joshua Welland – inspired by the story of the poor Oxford scholar in Joseph Glanvill's *The Vanity of Dogmatizing* (1661), and his beautiful poem is a great sigh of nostalgia for a simpler age. His scholar is immortal because he lives according to the ancient rhythms of the passing seasons, outside the pressures of the modern world.

The character of Daniel Arden was inspired by Edward Bulwer-Lytton's novel, *Eugene Aram* (1832), in which he recast the real-life murderer Aram as a kind of romantic hero who killed in order to get himself the education he craved. If he killed someone 'worthless', and then used his knowledge to do good, did he deserve to be hanged? Yes, obviously – but the novel is interesting for its awareness of a seemingly intractable inequality, where 'every door is barred with gold, and opens but to golden keys', as Alfred Tennyson wrote in his 1835 poem, 'Locksley Hall'.

Mrs Bentley is based upon a real woman, wife of the Hampstead postman, who let lodgings to John Keats. She really did live in Well Walk with a noisy swarm of red-headed boys, and I have always liked her for her kindness to the poet and his two brothers. She deserves to be more than a footnote.

The goings-on at Swinford are entirely fictional, but inspired by John Henry Newman's 'monastic' community at Littlemore, just outside Oxford.

Endless thanks are owed to my parents, Basil and Betty Saunders, who gave me the best possible upbringing for a writer by stuffing their house with books, books, books and allowing me to spend untold hours reading them all beside the gas fire.

And many thanks to everyone who has helped me with this book – Caradoc King, Alexandra Pringle, Alison Hennessey, Marcus Berkmann, Amanda Craig – and my beloved family, Bill, Charlotte, Louisa, Etta, Ewan, Ed, Tom, George, Elsa, Claudia and Max.

Note on the Author

KATE SAUNDERS is an author and journalist. She has worked for *The Times, Sunday Times, Sunday Express, Daily Telegraph* and *Cosmopolitan* amongst others, and has contributed to BBC Radio 4's *Woman's Hour* and *Start the Week*. She has written numerous books for adults and children, including the bestselling *Night Shall Overtake Us*, and her follow on to E Nesbit's *Five Children and It* stories, *Five Children on the Western Front*, which won the Costa Children's Book Award in 2014. *The Secrets of Wishtide*, the first book in the 'Laetitia Rodd Mysteries', was published by Bloomsbury in 2016. She lives in London.

Note on the Type

The text of this book is set in Baskerville, a typeface named after John Baskerville of Birmingham (1706–1775). The original punches cut by him still survive. His widow sold them to Beaumarchais, from where they passed through several French foundries to Deberney & Peignot in Paris, before finding their way to Cambridge University Press.

Baskerville was the first of the 'transitional romans' between the softer and rounder calligraphic Old Face and the 'Modern' sharp-tooled Bodoni. It does not look very different to the Old Faces, but the thick and thin strokes are more crisply defined and the serifs on lower-case letters are closer to the horizontal with the stress nearer the vertical. The R in some sizes has the eighteenth-century curled tail, the lower case w has no middle serif and the lower case g has an open tail and a curled ear.